Kellan Publishing books by
Ken Brigham

Death in Printers Alley
a Shane Hadley Mystery

Death in Printers Alley

a Shane Hadley Mystery

By Ken Brigham

Kellan Publishing

c-4

Copyright © Ken Brigham
Front cover by Myles Maillie
Back cover by Myles Maillie
First Kellan Publishing: April 2015
www.kellanpublishing.com

Death in Printers Alley
a Shane Hadley Mystery

By Ken Brigham

Dedication and Acknowledgements

This book is dedicated to Mark Manner, polymath and legal mind extraordinaire; probably the smartest man I know. His gracious attempts to help me understand the legal stuff integral to the book were more than I had any reason to expect. If there are errors in that area, they are mine; Mark could only do so much. The cover drawings and text were done by Nashville artist and longtime friend, Myles Maillie. Richard Stecenko of Interactive Computer Services in Winnipeg engineered the design and production of the cover and did some major spiffing up of the text.

Your cheatin' heart, will tell on you.
–Hank Williams

1

The still familiar *pop pop pop pop...pop* of gunshots drew Shane Hadley like a magnet toward the sound. He struggled for a moment with the brake on his wheelchair, forgetting that he had locked it, and then sped as fast as he could spin the wheels down the long corridor toward the front of the apartment, shoved open the French doors, and wheeled himself onto the second floor balcony that hung out over Printers Alley.

Leaning over the balcony rail Shane caught a brief glimpse of the back of someone running from the alley toward Union Street, away from the red brick building with the flashing neon *Bonz's Booze and Music* sign. He thought he recognized something about the person but he wasn't sure. There was something vaguely familiar about the person's gait, the way his right foot pigeon-toed inward. It wasn't a limp really, but an odd movement that made his stride just slightly asymmetrical, a rhythmic little list to starboard with each step that seemed oddly familiar to Shane.

Then he noticed Bonz Bagley's lanky body sprawled awkwardly beside the chair in front of his club. Bonz often sat there for long hours holding Pecan Pie, his pet miniature poodle, and chatting with the passersby.

Bonz's body lay prone with his head turned to one side. His face was a bloody mess. Blood matted the sparse strands of hair plastered spider-like against his pale smooth skull. A pool of blood expanded around his head and rivulets of the dark liquid were beginning to form, gravity sucking Bonz's lifeblood away down the alley that had been the center of his life for longer than most people could remember; Printers Alley was no stranger to blood. And Pecan

Pie.

The dog lay as lifeless as her master, her white coat almost completely blood red. The bronze glints of five pinpoint reflections of the morning sun caught Shane's eye—spent cartridges, he thought. If so it wasn't a very careful killer.

Shane reached for his cell phone and was about to dial 911 when he heard the sirens and saw the flashing blue lights of three squad cars entering the alley from the Church Street end. He dropped the phone back into his shirt pocket.

It was early Sunday morning and the alley was deserted. It was always quiet on Sunday mornings. But Bonz Bagley appeared at his usual spot early every day, including Sunday when he just sat there alone in the morning silence. The clubs wouldn't be open for several hours yet. That's when the crowds would filter in. Had they already started to arrive they would have scattered at the sound of gunfire.

Interesting how people react to the sound of gunfire. Cops, even ex-cops with useless legs, are drawn to the sound. Normal people run as fast as they can the other way.

The guys in blue descended on the scene, abandoning their squad cars, engines running, lights flashing. Shane might have recognized a couple of them from when he was an active member of the force. It had been several years since Shane was part of that scene. He would only know the older guys and the older guys would rarely pull this kind of duty. This part of the job was pretty much a young man's game.

One of the cops knelt and felt for a pulse in Bonz's neck, smearing his hands with the congealing blood coating the old man's head and neck. The cop just shook his head and stood up again. Bonz was dead.

One of the younger cops ran into the club and then down the alley looking in all directions hoping, Shane guessed, to catch the killer on the spot. The older guys knew how unlikely that was and didn't bother. They had learned to conserve their energy for more urgent situations.

The men in blue stood for a few minutes staring down at the dead man and his dog, sizing up the situation. They all knew Bonz. The cops knew pretty much everybody who had any regular connection with the alley. Shane overheard the officers' conversation.

"Who the hell would want to kill Bonz?"

"Yeah, who is right. And the dog? Why kill the dog? Sadistic bastard."

"Maybe a robbery?" one of the younger cops said. "Everybody around here knows that Bonz always had a wad of bills on him."

"But Pecan Pie don't carry no wad. Besides, everybody around here knows that Bonz would give you money if you asked him. Give you the shirt off his back, he would."

"Not many folks would want that shirt," one said.

Years earlier, Bonz had been a regular on a popular TV show that was a parody of the Nashville country music subculture. He was mostly an extra but sometimes was featured playing the bones which is how he acquired the nickname (pronounced *bones*; the odd spelling and the underlined o were the brainchildren of a long forgotten publicist for the TV show) that everyone still knew him by.

On the show Bonz wore a ridiculous get up, old bib overalls and a garish red, white and blue shirt decorated with sequins in a stylized pattern of an American flag. That was years ago, but he still wore the getup, the colors fading and the cuffs fraying, when he presided over his disintegrating Printers Alley night spot. The shirt wasn't likely to appeal to the kind of person who would do a thing like this. The well-known wad of bills might be another matter.

"We better get the crime scene guys out here before we move him," the cop in a rumpled business suit, obviously the detective assigned to the scene, said. He took the phone from his belt and punched in the numbers.

"Zack," the older detective called to one of the young

guys, "round up anybody you can find in the alley and ask them if they saw anything."

The younger cop nodded and started off down the alley with the exaggerated swagger that this new generation of cops seemed to feel was a requisite part of the image. Shane wasn't impressed. He never thought much of the tough guy image that some cops seemed to get off on. He thought it got in the way of the job.

Hardy Seltzer looked up toward the balcony. He recognized Shane from the old days. Seltzer was on the force when Shane's career came to a sudden and what was generally considered a tragic end. They hadn't actually worked together and didn't know each other well.

"Shane Hadley," Seltzer called up to him, "how the hell are you?"

Shane recognized the voice and then remembered Seltzer's face.

"I'm OK, Hardy," he answered. "Looks like you've got a spot of work to do there."

"Looks that way," Seltzer responded. "Did you see anything?"

"I didn't see it happen, but when I heard the shots I came out here. Please join me and I'll tell you what I saw. I fear it may be of little help."

12

"Sure," Seltzer said. He turned and spoke to one of his colleagues, "Stay here until the crime scene guys arrive."

"I'll release the door and the elevator for you. Just punch floor two," Shane called down.

The flat where Shane and KiKi had lived since moving from Oxford, England to Nashville over a decade earlier occupied a floor in a rehabilitated warehouse. The other floors were lawyers' offices, except for the sixth floor penthouse which belonged to Rory Holcomb.

Holcomb had bought up several Printers Alley properties some years earlier. He leased most of the properties to clubs and other small businesses (including an incongruous sushi bar at the Church Street end of the alley), but renovated this one into units that he sold as condos. Except for the penthouse; he kept that as his in town *pied-a-terre* where he periodically entertained the many political and music industry acquaintances he had cultivated over a long and interesting career as a real estate entrepreneur and raconteur.

How Holcomb, a country boy from Greenbrier, wound up in his current position was a matter of some speculation among the locals. The truth was that a childhood friend of his who had risen to become governor of the state hired Rory as a driver and then convinced him to take advantage of inside knowledge of impending state projects that would require buying up large tracts of otherwise worthless land in west Tennessee.

Rory borrowed the money and bought the land dirt cheap, resold it to the state at an exorbitantly high price and used the proceeds to buy up properties in the city. In the course of achieving his remarkable financial success, he had made a lot of friends as well as some enemies. The enemies were pretty much neutralized by Rory's knowledge of where their skeletons were buried.

There were a lot of skeletons.

Access to the building from the alley was via a secured door controlled by the occupants from inside. The elevator opened directly into the living room of Shane and KiKi's apartment and access to their floor required a key release in the elevator. Shane rolled back into the living room, released the front door and unlocked the elevator.

Shane kept thinking about the man he saw running from the alley. At least he thought it was a man. He couldn't make out much about the person except the way he ran.

Shane couldn't get that out of his mind. Something resonated that he couldn't put his finger on. He wasn't sure whether he should mention that to Hardy Seltzer. Shane couldn't remember ever fingering a criminal based on the way he ran. He smiled.

Detective Seltzer approached the door with some trepidation. He had never visited Shane Hadley in his home and didn't really want to. He preferred not to think of Hadley at all, not as a living person. He preferred the myths that pieced together the jigsaw puzzle memory of the detective when he was active, before the accident. There were many myths.

Seltzer thought of tales about Hadley's uncanny ability to construct a story from subtle and often overlooked clues. The old guys called him Sherlock Shane, the nickname coined by a local newspaper reporter, when they regaled their new colleagues with those memories. Seltzer didn't want whatever the current reality of Shane Hadley was to spoil the myth.

"Why Bonz?" Seltzer asked.

They sat in the living room facing each other. It was difficult for Seltzer to look directly at the paraplegic former detective. Hadley was still a strikingly handsome man. The waves of his expensively styled dark hair rested just slightly over his ears and the edge of his shirt collar. And those legendary pale blue, almost gray, eyes that seemed to bore into one's soul. But it was hard for Seltzer to reconcile the man with flaccid legs in the wheelchair with the Shane Hadley of the department's cherished legend.

"It's really sad," Shane responded. "Bonz was pretty much a shell of his younger self but he had a good heart. The alley was his territory. He knew all the characters. He seemed happy to be one of them, just sitting out there every day and gradually fading away. I doubt he ever contemplated the possibility of a violent death."

"Probably not," Seltzer commented, "probably not. So tell me what you know about what happened."

"Well, I was in the back of the house, watching the Third Avenue barristers and their clients come and go. Our back window looks out on Third Avenue where the better class of lawyers does business with the better class of criminals."

"Your place spans the whole block?" Seltzer seemed surprised.

"Yes, yes," Hadley responded, "I think of it as a bridge that connects the perpetrators in the alley with the barristers on that stretch of Third Avenue who'll wind up defending the erring alley denizens who can afford their price. I spend most of my time patrolling the bridge. I have a lot of time."

He paused for a minute. Seltzer squirmed. He didn't want to know how Hadley spent his time these days. Didn't want to have that stuck in his mind. Sherlock Shane was the memory he preferred.

"At any rate," Shane continued, "I was back

there when I heard the gunshots. There were five shots, four in rapid succession and then a short pause before a fifth. As soon as I heard them I rushed up here to the front as fast as I could and went out onto the balcony. By then the scene was quiet. That odd stony silence that descends suddenly in the wake of gunfire."

"Yeah," Seltzer said, "I know."

"I saw someone running from the alley toward Union. He, or I should say the person, I couldn't be sure of anything specific. I couldn't swear to even gender or race. I only had a quick glimpse as the person's back disappeared around the corner. I couldn't tell if he had a gun. I only saw poor Bonz and his dog after that. I was about to call 911 when you and your men arrived."

"Nothing at all about the person?"

"He wasn't very big. But he was wearing a hooded shirt, dark blue, that covered his head so I don't know hair color, no details. I can't think of anything else," Shane answered, not sure why he chose not to mention the odd way the person ran.

"You know the alley pretty well, I gather," Seltzer continued. "Any idea who might want Bonz dead?"

"If it wasn't a robbery, I can't imagine a reason for it. Or anyone who would do it. But I'm an alley observer, not a participator. There may be activities that aren't obvious from my vantage point. I do wonder why they killed the dog. If it was a robbery gone wrong, you'd think the perpetrator would want to get away as fast as possible. Why would he risk attracting even more attention by killing the dog?"

"Yeah. That is strange if it was just Bonz's money they were after." The detective thought about that for a minute and then continued, "Bonz's bar hasn't done much business in years. How'd he stay open? Any hint of drugs or something like that?"

"No, I don't think so. I seriously doubt that Bonz was into that scene. He was old school. Did he have any money on him? Could this just have been a random robbery?"

"That seems to be the most likely thing, like you said, except for the dog. And maybe the shots to the head, not the usual target for a challenged robber. Looks like there were several shots, all to the head. We waited for the crime scene boys to check his pockets."

Seltzer was anxious to go. He wasn't comfortable in the presence of a former cop reduced to a shadow of who he had been by a stray bullet taken in the line of duty. It could happen to anybody.

"Thanks Shane for telling me what you saw," he said. "If anything else comes to mind, give me a call. I better get down there and finish up the immediate chores."

Seltzer got up and reached down to shake Shane Hadley's hand; he noticed how thin and cold it was.

"You're welcome, Hardy. Good luck with solving this one. If I think of anything else or hear anything, I'll let you know."

The officer left and Shane rolled himself back onto the balcony. An ambulance had arrived and the crime scene guys were going about their business. The ambulance attendants were loading Bonz's body into their vehicle, moving slowly and chatting with the cops. There was no hurry. Bonz's time in his small world was over. Hardy Seltzer joined the group and exchanged some words Shane couldn't hear.

Seltzer looked up at the balcony and called to Shane, "Wasn't a robbery. Or if it was it was aborted. Big wad of hundreds in his pocket."

"Thanks," Shane called down and wheeled back inside.

He went to the bar and retrieved his prized leather case from a shelf. He placed the case carefully on the bar, opened it and lifted one of the cut crystal sherry glasses from its bed of crimson satin. The set of six Oxford sherry glasses was a treasure from his days at that venerable university.

Those two years had headed Shane in a different direction than anyone would have predicted for him — molded the man and plotted his course. He returned to Nashville with the hint of an accent and a habit of using words and how they were assembled that an English intellectual might have recognized as faintly Oxfordian. And a demeanor to match.

When he was on the force, the more generous of his fellow policemen thought him idiosyncratic; the less generous ones thought him arrogant, pretentious and self-centered. There was some truth to both opinions. He didn't identify with the other cops. He was different. But he had been one hell of a detective. No one could deny that.

Shane polished the glass with a bar towel. He took down a bottle from a shelf. The intricately etched label on the bottle read, "Sherry, Lincoln College, Oxford". KiKi had somehow managed to get the special sherry from his Oxford College *alma mater* shipped to them in Nashville. He had no idea how she accomplished that. But he wasn't surprised.

KiKi was a very resourceful woman. The sherry was mainly for him. KiKi rarely drank alcohol. Her explanation was that she was too fond of the human brain's normal functions to impair them with drugs of any kind, including ethanol. She didn't mean that as criticism of people who did drink. It's just that, if she had a vice, it wasn't alcohol.

Shane thought KiKi would be home by now. But you could never be certain when she would return from these Sunday morning meetings of what had

18

been dubbed the *Brain Trust*— Sunday school, she called it. When that group of neuroscientists got deep into discussions of their research, they often lost track of time.

Shane was glad she hadn't arrived in the middle of the Bonz business. KiKi was frightened by violence and to witness it first hand on her doorstep would have been more than unsettling. Just hearing about it would be bad enough.

The noise from the alley, the cacophony of violent crime and its aftermath, had died down. Lonnie's was opening up. Shane could hear the wail of a bottom tier country singer blaring a slightly off color song from the loudspeaker, something about Viagra sung to the tune of Elvira, a hit for some country quartet a few years back.

Wail was the right description. There was always some good country music in the honkytonks on Lower Broad; they were venues for the up and comers. But if that was ever true of the alley, it hadn't been for several years. The up and comers had long since ceded the alley to the hapless has-beens and the no talent wannabees. Shane had become oddly fond of the sound. The Printers Alley Serenade, he called it. In his more somber moments, he identified with the plaintive wail of the hapless has-beens.

Shane refilled his glass and sat staring at the flashing neon reflections in the window. He thought again about how the fleeing murderer ran, the funny asymmetry of his gait. There was something definitely familiar about that. But for the life of him he couldn't remember what.

And multiple shots to the head? Odd, almost like a gangland execution. But it didn't look like a professional job. Any half-way expert killer would have at least picked up the spent cartridges. It didn't make sense. Whatever petty crime went on in the alley wouldn't interest the big time criminals. If there was organized crime in the city it would be centered elsewhere, maybe Music Row or the more creative parts of the city to the north.

And why kill the dog?

2

When Katya Karpov turned off Church Street into the alley, she sensed something was wrong. For one thing it was deserted, unusual for a Sunday evening after the clubs opened. Lonnie's loudspeaker was blasting into the empty space — *Viagra, Viagra/My heart's on fire/for Viagra.* The same phrase over and over like a stuck record. The tangle of neon spanning the narrow alley was in full bloom.

But there were no people. And Bonz wasn't sitting on his habitual perch outside his bar. Something wasn't right. She punched the garage door opener and eased the white Porsche into the narrow space under the balcony.

Dr. Karpov's arrival in the alley always attracted attention. She was oblivious to the attention. She was used to being noticed but it didn't matter to her. That's just how things were. Part of life.

She always kept the car top open except when it rained because she liked the feel of the open car. She and Shane had the only garage that opened directly off the alley and the sight of this gorgeous blonde with big designer sunglasses in a fancy car breezing into the alley, waves of blonde hair wafting in the wind, and disappearing under the balcony triggered the imaginations of the gaggle of strangers who came from everywhere to Nashville looking for the glamorous TV and fan magazine brand of the country music scene. They wouldn't find that in the alley.

Katya's late afternoon arrivals were about all the glamour that was to be seen there. It would take a seriously active imagination to turn that brief tableau into any generalization about the city. Who knew what stories the strangers imagined? But whatever their fantasies, it was unlikely that they were as interesting as the reality.

"What's up in the alley?" Katya asked Shane.

Before he could answer, she bent over and kissed him full and soft on the mouth. Among her considerable assemblage of physical assets, Shane had always thought that KiKi's mouth ranked near the top. The feel and taste of her full lips still excited him. It wasn't the same as before the accident, but the thrill wasn't gone. He couldn't imagine that it would ever be.

Shane said, "It's been a pretty exciting day around here, KiKi my love."

Shane was the only person in the world who called her KiKi, a phonetic play on her initials. Shane had come up with it shortly after they met. She liked the familiarity, intimacy, of how he used the nickname. She often smiled when he called her that.

Shane reached an arm up around her waist and pulled her as close as he could.

"Where's Bonz?" she said.

"Somebody killed Bonz," he answered, sounding like his old matter-of-fact police officer self. "Just apparently came into the alley and shot him and ran away. Killed his dog too."

"Damn!" Katya blurted. "Damn! Who on God's earth would do such a thing?"

Shane knew that KiKi was fond of Bonz. He was too. The old guy had been a fixture in the alley for as long as anyone could remember. In earlier days, his club had been a launching pad for future country stars.

Bonz had befriended a long list of Nashville luminaries when their stars were just starting to rise. All that had been a long time ago. But even in his dotage, Bonz was still a sympathetic figure. All the alley regulars were fond of him. He was part of the place. A fixture.

Katya was fond of Bonz personally, like

everybody else, but she also had a professional interest in him. He had been part of the initial clinical trial of Cy's new Alzheimer's drug. Bonz had been their poster child, at least at first. Katya had begun to suspect that his striking initial response to the drug had taken a bad turn. She mentioned that one time to Cy and he pooh-poohed it.

"We know he got a good response," Cy had said. "We have the proof!"

Katya knew the proof well. There were the computerized tests of brain function. And also the blood protein measurements. Cy put a lot of stock in those. He was completely convinced that the protein that was discovered in his laboratory was a perfect biomarker for Alzheimer's. Katya thought that might be true but her conviction didn't reach the evangelical depth of Cy's.

Bonz was scheduled to see Katya the next day for the physical exam that would conclude his participation in the drug study. She had also scheduled him for some follow up cognitive testing without telling Cy.

Now she would never know whether her suspicion that his condition was worsening was justified. Never have any objective evidence. While the tragedy of Bonz's murder was a graver concern than Katya's suspicion about his response to Cy's drug, some hard evidence supporting that suspicion would have been more important than she knew at the time.

"Have you talked to Bonz much recently?" Katya asked.

"Not really," Shane answered. "I wave at him, say cheerio. That's about all. Why?"

"I try to strike up a conversation with him every now and then when I come home," she said, "but lately it seemed to me that he wasn't quite his old self."

"His old self was pretty hard to get a handle on. Has been for a while now. Not sure how you'd know if he was taking further leave of his senses."

"But he got a lot better there for a while, didn't he?"

"Maybe. Difficult to tell from where I sit."

"Yeah," she said, "yeah. But we did the follow up testing after he started on Cy's drug and the results were pretty convincing."

Shane had only a vague understanding of what Katya did professionally. She had told him about the phase I-II clinical trials of the drug and that Bonz was a subject, but he hadn't been very curious about the details.

He really couldn't say that he noticed any effect on the old man's behavior. Still sat out there holding the dog and striking up conversations with the passersby. Whether those conversations made any more sense than they ever had, Shane had no idea.

"I'd scheduled him to come in for some more tests," Katya mused. "I really wanted to document his current condition."

"His current condition is pretty clearly documented," Shane responded.

"Yeah. Sad," she said.

Hardy Seltzer sat in his office reviewing the Bonz Bagley case in his mind. His office in the old Municipal Police Building just off the northeast side of the courthouse square was one of the smaller ones. The air conditioning was erratic. The thermostat was located some place outside his office that he had been unable to find so that he usually left the window open to get at least a little air circulating in the room.

The summer evening was hot and he sat jacketless, tie loosened with his feet propped on the desk staring out the window at the court house across the square and trying his best to imagine that a cool breeze was wafting through the window.

But his imagination wasn't that good. His brain circuits seemed to be hard wired to reality. Katya Karpov would have classified him as a left brain person.

They had scoured the entire area around Printers Alley immediately after the crime scene was secured and the routine procedures were underway. For some reason, Seltzer was fixed on conversations with two teenage boys who had been hanging out on the corner of Fourth and Union that Sunday morning. According to Shane Hadley, the person he saw running from the alley right after the shooting, the poorly described person in the dark blue hoodie, had run to Union and turned left toward Fourth. It was only half a block to the corner.

The two young men said they had been standing there for some time, so they must have been there when the fleeing suspect passed. But they swore that they hadn't seen him. No one running or appearing to be in a hurry. Certainly no one in a hoodie. Not in the heat. They would have noticed that.

Then Hardy's men had found a dark blue hoodie in a garbage can just at the corner of the alley and Union. So this guy had shed the hoodie and presumably walked casually up Union trying, apparently with surprising success, not to attract attention. But the two potential witnesses hadn't seen him. They couldn't remember a single man passing by where they stood. Puzzling.

The guy just disappeared into thin air. Seltzer hated being confronted with a physical impossibility. He liked his possibilities tethered firmly to realities that he could understand.

He stood up and paced about the small room. He wanted a cigarette but stifled the urge. He was trying to quit again but it got harder every time he tried. He thought quitting should get easier with practice but it didn't. He'd had a lot of practice.

He thought of Shane Hadley. The real Shane Hadley not the Sherlock Shane of myth. Seltzer thought how hard it must be to be suddenly incapacitated like that. Especially hard for a cop. Inactivity was the bane of a cop's existence. Stakeouts. Everybody hated stakeouts. The long hours of inactivity. But to be permanently immobilized all of a sudden by a stray bullet finding a home in a critical area of one's spine?

And Hardy Seltzer was painfully aware of the fact that the potential of sharing Shane Hadley's fate was lurking out there in every cop's future. Including his own. He didn't like those thoughts. But they were unavoidable and probably necessary. Once a cop quit thinking about the possibility of catching a bullet, stray or otherwise, the possibility of sharing Shane Hadley's fate increased. The worst thing a cop could do was to stop paying attention.

Then there was the other curious thing about the Bonz Printers Alley case. The gun. Or at least what could be told about the gun from the spent cartridges found near the body and the single slug recovered from the dog, no doubt identical to those that the coroner would retrieve from Bonz's body later.

According to the ballistics person pulling weekend duty, a quick run through the ATF's National Integrated Ballistic Information Network (usually referred to by the acronym NIBIN) indicated that the bullets were .38 Rimless Smokeless, no longer available except on the collector's market. Of course they had no gun, but the most likely model was also a collector's item, a Colt Hammer model 1903. That was a best guess of course.

The only bullets in the NIBIN database were from committed crimes. The only bullet similar to this one in NIBIN was from a murder committed in Boston by Nicola Sacco in the twenties.

According to what Hardy could find on the Internet, the Sacco-Vanzetti case was notorious at the time and the unusual bullets tying Sacco to the murder had been the most convincing evidence. It would be interesting if the same ballistics solved this case, an ironic contribution of Nicola Sacco's legacy to the discipline of criminal justice.

Seltzer thought about that. The perp couldn't have been a regular criminal type or if so he was an especially arrogant one. Seltzer learned from the Internet that this kind of gun could run several thousand dollars. There was even a limited edition version on sale for over a hundred grand. No regular street criminal would have such a weapon.

And why use a gun like that even if you had one? Using such an unusual weapon should make the cops' job easier. Any half way savvy street crook would know that. But, on the other hand, what would a rich gun collector be doing in the alley and why would he want to murder Bonz Bagley at all, much less with a weapon that would surely be easy enough to trace? It made no sense. But it did fit with the wad of hundreds left in Bonz's pocket. Whoever did it didn't need the money.

Seltzer started packing up his stuff to go. It was nearly midnight. It had been a long day. He closed the office window and slipped on his jacket even though he had sweated through his shirt. Force of habit.

"Sunday midnight and I'm just now heading home," he muttered to himself, "helluva job."

As he found his way through the lower level of

the parking garage to the aging black Crown Victoria assigned to him by the department, Seltzer thought again of Shane Hadley, how cold his hand felt and how helpless he looked. Seltzer thought if, God forbid, he took a bullet to his spine he would be inclined to eat his gun. He couldn't imagine living like that.

But Hardy Seltzer lived alone. He didn't live with Katya Karpov.

3

Cyrus Demetrio Bartalak paced the floor of his office waiting for Katya Karpov to arrive for their regular Monday morning meeting. He was anxious about the meeting, more anxious than he thought he should be. He'd read about the murder in Printers Alley in the morning *Tennessean* and, although he didn't understand why, he knew that Katya lived there with that paralyzed policeman.

There were a lot of things about Katya that Cy didn't understand. Why live downtown in that seedy alley? And what was the attraction of the paralyzed ex-cop? Cy had met him socially a couple of times and just didn't get the attraction. Not for Katya. My God, she could have practically any man she chose. A real man with two good legs and all his other parts in good working order was what she needed.

Cy had moved from the oppressive confines of the little office off his suite of laboratories to the posh office with the polished brass, "Chairman, Department of Psychiatry", plaque on the door when he was elevated to that role. He was especially proud of the office. He looked around the room, admiring the antique Persian rug and his hand-picked original art that decorated the walls.

This was the kind of office he was destined for, he thought. Trappings worthy of his talents. Spartan offices, typical of the academic hair shirt mentality, were fine for most of the faculty. But not for Cy Bartalak.

In the interest of at least giving lip service to any appearance of conflict of interest, Cy had made sure that there was appropriate oversight of the studies of his drug, but he personally kept close tabs on the study's progress. He knew that the aging proprietor of a downtown bar was one of the subjects who had an especially gratifying response. Beth had told him that. He made the connection when he read the newspaper story and realized that he wasn't the only person who would make that connection.

That worried him. The viability of the biotech startup company that Cy had launched, leveraging the department's investment, depended on the drug. And the viability of the drug depended on those studies. He had already put out some feelers to a group of west coast venture capitalists and anything that troubled the waters could queer any possible deal. Several million dollars might be riding on that.

Cy remembered that Katya had voiced some doubt about the effects of the drug, especially in the now dead subject. At least there wouldn't be any more follow up tests on that subject. And the data they had on him were solid. But Cy feared Katya would keep prying into the data. He wasn't sure why she would want to do that but he knew her well enough to suspect that she would.

The study was essentially done. The conclusions were solid. Let it be. Cy had learned early in his career that you never ask questions if you don't want to know the answers. But Katya Karpov was cast from a very different mold than Cyrus Bartalak. Her curiosity was not confined to what was likely to serve her own ends. She really wanted to know the truth. Cy respected Katya's brilliance but he thought her hopelessly naive. He thought that perceptions *were* truth. And he was a master manipulator of perceptions. Otherwise he wouldn't be where he was.

As Katya made her way from the parking deck to Bartalak's office, she thought about Bonz Bagley and the drug trial. And about Beth Bartalak, Cy's wife. Katya didn't like Beth and the feeling was entirely mutual.

Beth was a biostatistician who had worked in

Cy's lab in Houston before she became his second wife. The details of that transition in her status were never discussed. Apparently there was some unpleasantness involved. It happened before Cy moved his operation from Houston to the medical center in Nashville. They came as a package and Beth managed the data from the tests performed as part of the drug trial.

Since Cy's elevation to a major administrative role, Beth's power and authority in the laboratory had increased. She had essentially taken over and she ruled the lab with an iron hand. She believed that she owned the data, regardless of their sources or who else was involved in collecting them.

Beth was especially difficult with Katya. Katya wasn't sure why although she suspected that it had something to do with how plain women commonly reacted to her. Katya thought that her physical attributes were often a mixed blessing, too important to members of both sexes ... usually for different reasons.

Katya had always thought that Cy and Beth were an odd couple. Cy seemed to be an olio of samplings from multiple ethnic gene pools, as his name suggested. He was a world traveler, comfortable moving in the circles of the moneyed classes.

Beth was pretty much straight uncomplicated Texas tough. One would guess that this plain woman was a product of a much more homogenous source of genes and much simpler life experiences than her husband. But Beth was pathologically devoted to Cy. She virtually worshipped him. He could do no wrong. She may have also disliked Katya because Katya had no problem disagreeing with Cy.

No doubt Beth thought it presumptuous to dare to disagree with the great and infallible object of her adoration. Bullshit! Katya thought. Cy Bartalak wasn't half the man even a paraplegic Shane was. A woman like Beth could never understand that. But then Katya could care less what Beth Bartalak understood.

The standing meeting on Monday mornings was with the three of them; Cy, Katya and Beth. The main topic of the meeting in recent months had been the drug. Cy's interest in the drug, and therefore Beth's, bordered on obsession. They didn't talk much about the data anymore. As far as Cy was concerned there was no need to talk about the data. He was all about logistics. How to secure the financing of the startup that would get the drug into a phase III trial and how to move as quickly as possible to FDA approval. That's when the really big money would come.

Katya entered Cy's office without knocking and was surprised to find him alone, staring out his office window. He was profiled against the light of the window. His flat sloped forehead, massive blunt ended nose and protruding chin seen in profile made Katya acutely aware of what an ugly man Cy Bartalak was. He was half a head shorter than she was with a prominent stomach bulging over his pants. Lately he had grown a scraggly mustache and goatee which did nothing to improve his looks.

"Is Beth coming?" Katya asked, intruding on Cy's reverie.

"No," he answered without looking at her, "she won't be here today."

That was very unusual, but Katya was relieved not to have to deal with the woman. That task often got the week off to a bad start. The previous day's events had already headed things in a bad direction and the last thing Katya needed that morning was a confrontation with Beth Bartalak. She didn't ask for an explanation and Cy didn't offer one.

Cy turned from the window, walked over to his desk and sank into the overstuffed leather chair, resting an elbow on the desk and cradling his substantial chin in the palm of his meaty left hand. Katya sat opposite him in the uncomfortable straight chair that he reserved for visitors.

"Katya," he said, "we're making progress toward a deal on the drug."

"That's nice," she answered distractedly. After a pause she said, "Did you see that Bonz Bagley was murdered? You know Bonz, from the alley? One of the subjects in the drug study?"

"Yeah," he answered.

He got up from his chair, walked to the window and again presented his grotesque profile to Katya.

"That's too bad," he said, "too bad. Wasn't he one of the subjects that got an especially robust response to the drug?"

"That's right," she answered.

She was annoyed at Cy's apparent lack of any personal feeling about the murder. But she wasn't surprised. Personal feeling for his fellow humans was not Cy's long suit.

"I'd like to review Bagley's data," she said.

"Why is that?" he snapped.

"I think I mentioned to you a while back that I thought he was deteriorating. I'd actually scheduled him for some follow up tests."

"Beth told me that," Cy answered, "but I don't see why. The study is almost over. The data are solid. We just need to move this thing forward as fast as we can. We don't need any more data right now. That'll come in time with the phase III studies."

"OK," Katya said, "but I'd still like to look at Bonz's data. Can you have Beth give me access to them?"

"I don't think that's necessary."

"It is necessary," she responded. "She has all of the data from the drug study firewalled in her computer or sequestered somewhere, and she is the only one who can access it. She refuses to let me see the data."

"Well, of course," Cy answered. "The integrity of those data is critical if we're to use them with the FDA. We can't have those documents out there for just anybody to see."

"I don't think you would describe me as just anybody," Katya said, the tone of her voice decidedly indignant. "After all, I collected most of the specimens and managed the trial."

"I know, I know," he answered, "I'll talk to Beth about it. The two of you really should try to get along better, you know?"

"Thanks," was all Katya could bring herself to say while keeping a civil tone.

She didn't think that attempting to get along with Beth Bartalak was a useful way for her to spend time and energy. Beth was Cy's problem.

Shane Hadley had retrieved his worn copy of *The Complete Sherlock Holmes* and was searching through the index looking for *The Adventure of the Devil's Foot*. It was one of the stories recounted by Dr. Watson, as he recalled. It was the *devil's foot* in the title that surfaced in his mind as he contemplated the gait of Bonz Bagley's fleeing murderer.

Shane had the vague recollection of the title of the story but also a feeling that the story actually had nothing to do with a real foot. But, unable to remember for sure what the story was about, he felt compelled to look it up.

Shane had wheeled himself out onto the balcony facing Printers Alley. Sunshine filtered through the iron latticework of the balcony supports etching their

34

filigree patterns onto the brick wall. A soft breeze ruffled his hair. He looked up and down the alley, almost empty at this time of morning.

Shane had been fascinated with Sherlock Holmes since his teen years. His parents desperately wanted him to follow in the footsteps of his successful physician father but Shane was seduced by the intellectual challenge of crime solving before they could head him in a proper direction.

Arthur Conan Doyle, a physician of another sort, got to Shane first. His parents never recovered from that disappointment. They thought that Shane had wasted his considerable gifts on a lifetime effort to realize an adolescent fantasy.

Shane's parents didn't understand any of his life choices. The University of the South at Sewanee instead of Princeton. Then wasting the Rhodes scholarship by choosing advanced study in English instead of something in the hard sciences or medicine. What good did he think an advanced degree in English would do him? And coming back from Oxford with a phony accent and with his Sherlock Holmes obsession even stronger. Taking a job with the Metro Police? This would have been ludicrous if it weren't their son. And the Russian woman. At least she was a real doctor, but still, she wasn't the sort of person they had expected for a daughter-in-law. The seedy lifestyle. And, of course, the accident, if that's what it was. So many things about Shane saddened and disappointed his parents.

As Shane suspected, the devil's foot of the Holmes story had nothing to do with a real foot. *Pedix diaboli* was an African plant, source of a peculiar poison that presented the great detective with an especially challenging case of multiple murders. Nothing to do with a real human foot that turned slightly inward creating the vaguely familiar slightly lopsided gait that he couldn't get out of his mind. In spite of that he couldn't help thinking of Bonz Bagley's murder as his *Pedix Diaboli Case*.

Case. He hadn't really thought about being involved in a *case* in several years. But this one came to him. He didn't seek it out. And he was intrigued by the possibility of getting involved in a real case again. He felt a nascent stirring of the old juices.

Looking for connections, even tenuous ones, between cases that interested Shane and the fictional experiences of Sherlock Holmes was a habit. The hunt was an excuse to resurrect the old leather bound volume that he had bought at Blackwell's in Oxford during his student days as a Rhodes Scholar at Lincoln College. And an excuse to recall the freedom and excitement of those days.

It was probably the immersion in the real history surrounding Conan Doyle's creation as well as the fiction that was the basis for his master's thesis in English that sealed Shane's fate. He had forever perceived the line separating reality and fantasy as a fairly porous barrier so that reconciling his Sherlock Holmes obsession with a career spent attempting to understand the real motives and actions of violent people wasn't that difficult.

He hadn't considered the personal risk. Since suffering the results of that miscalculation it seemed to Shane that the line between reality and fantasy had faded even more. He needed fantasy to thrive in his new world, suddenly shrunken by his immobility. His real world was small but his imaginary one was boundless.

Shane was contemplating whether to phone the detective, Hardy Seltzer, to tell him about the odd gait of the man he'd seen fleeing the alley when he heard the phone ring. He wheeled himself inside and answered it.

"Hadley here," he said.

He pronounced *here* as the two-syllabled Oxfordian *he-ah*, a lingering influence of those seminal years.

"Shane," Hardy Seltzer's raspy monotone was unmistakable, "how are you?"

"I'm fine, Hardy," Shane answered. "I was just thinking of calling you."

"Really?" Seltzer responded. "Do you have some thoughts about the Bonz case?"

"Probably nothing important," Shane said. "There's a small detail that I omitted when we talked earlier."

"Yes?"

"It has to do with the way the person I saw leaving the alley ran; his gait. There was something odd about it. It was his right foot that appeared to toe inward so that he favored it a bit listing ever so slightly to starboard with each step. Subtle. And I'm not even sure why I noticed it except that there was something familiar about it. Probably not important but I thought that I should mention it."

Seltzer was reminded of Shane's legendary fondness of nautical terms. He smiled to himself.

"Familiar?" Seltzer queried. "Did you associate that with someone specific?"

"Not really. It's quite vague at the moment. But I keep trying to sort it out. If I come up with anything I'll let you know," Shane answered. "What were you calling about?"

Seltzer was reluctant to dismiss this new information considering the source, but for the life of him he didn't see how it could be much help. He jotted the information down in the small note pad that he used for keeping track of things. He had the habit of starting a fresh note pad with each new case and this one was just beginning to accumulate a few pages of his jottings.

"I just wanted to run something by you," Seltzer answered. "It's about the weapon in the Bonz Bagley case."

"You have a weapon?"

"Not really, but we have an interesting description of it."

"From the cartridge shells and the slugs? The NIBIN?"

Shane pronounced the acronym as though it was a word, *nibin*, a sure sign of an insider.

"That's right," Seltzer was reminded again of Shane's history, wondering if he was sensing something of the old Sherlock Shane.

Seltzer continued, "From the shells collected at the site and a single slug recovered from the dog it looks like a very unusual weapon. A collector's item. And very expensive. What do you make of that?"

"There should be some registries, shouldn't there? If it's rare enough you may even be able to get names and locations of the owners," Shane's wheels were turning now; you could sense that. "But strange isn't it? Why would a collector of expensive guns want to kill Bonz? And even if he did, why use such a unique weapon? Hardy, can you give me the details about the weapon? I may be able to help with some of the leg work. I am quite familiar with computers now."

Leg work, Seltzer thought. An unfortunate choice of metaphor. But Shane seemed to use it unselfconsciously.

"Sure," Seltzer responded, "any help you can give us would be appreciated."

So, the old juices had been stirred, Seltzer thought. This could prove to be a particularly interesting case for more reasons than one. He hadn't worked directly with Shane Hadley but knew the myths well. This could prove very interesting. He told Shane everything he knew about the weapon, agreed to stay in touch and rang off.

Shane hung up the phone and wheeled himself back out onto the deck. The afternoon sun splayed building shadows across the cobblestones that had paved the alley since its days as the epicenter of Nashville's Gentleman's Quarter where the well-heeled from the affluent west and south parts of town ventured for the kinds of entertainments that were not found at The Club.

Shane had grown up with those people. He was more than familiar with the façade, the open secrets they fed on. It was that pretense that he had needed to escape. Although his Anglophilia was a kind of affectation, at least it was transparent.

Some remnants of Printers Alley's checkered past were still there. The Brass Rail, now a strip club, had been The Brass Rail Stables where, in an earlier era, you could get a drink when it wasn't yet legal and most anything else you wanted. No doubt there was still some of that marginal commerce going on down there. But the cache of those early days was gone.

Shane looked across at Bonz's club, now locked down and obviously abandoned. The vacant chair sat in its usual place, an icon that conjured the memory of its former occupant. One could imagine Bonz's spindly frame suddenly materializing there from the dark beyond, his precious Pecan Pie perched impudently on his lap.

Shane had often thought that all murder was pointless. Nothing was resolved by such an act regardless of the motive. In this case the murder seemed especially pointless. He could not imagine a motive and even if there was one, Bonz was such an innocent and benign victim. Killed by a well off gun collector? Truly strange. But, of course, it was always the inexplicable crimes that were the most intriguing.

He sat on the balcony for a while as the sunlight disappeared. He remembered that other small world across the pond, the heady enclave of mossy elegance and brainy sophistication where he had fallen in love with all things English ... and with KiKi. He remembered his life before the accident and relished for a moment the memory of past pleasures. He felt too the nascent thrill of the hunt, the challenge of explaining the apparently inexplicable.

It was that challenge that had seduced him all those years earlier, the adrenalin surge that had always come with the realization that a *game is afoot*. He had the distinct feeling that there was a game afoot and that for the first time in a while he might be a player.

4

Beth Bartalak drove to The Club on Monday morning. She went directly to the gym and started her usual long run on the treadmill. She didn't explain to Cy why she chose to take the day off. She just said that she didn't feel well and he didn't inquire further. She had told him the truth. She didn't feel well.

Although she rarely mentioned the fact, Beth had been a track star when she was in college at TCU and she still kept in shape by running regularly. She preferred running out of doors but the heat and humidity in midsummer in the city often drove her to the air conditioned comfort of The Club's gym and to the treadmill. She tuned the treadmill mounted personal TV to CNN as she ran.

The murder of the Nashville semi-celebrity Bonz Bagley in Printers Alley had made the national news and CNN was doing a brief segment about it that included some file footage of a younger version of Bagley playing the bones on the old TV show.

Beth knew that Bonz Bagley was one of the subjects in the study of Cy's drug. She also knew that his data were especially important to Cy. It was an anecdote of course, but an impressive one. Cy said that the money guys were more impressed with a good individual story than with tables of boring statistics. The anecdote was safe now. No chance that the true story would see the light of day. Beth had made sure of that.

Beth didn't want to see the news story. She switched channels. Her legs were starting to feel heavy although she had covered only a couple of miles and wasn't running very fast. She stopped the treadmill and went to the sauna.

She felt nervous and the penetrating heat from the sauna seemed to calm her. The sweat washing down her body felt good. She lay back and closed her eyes trying to let the heat also purge her mind.

Beth was surprised at the intensity of her reaction. Killing living things was not a new experience for her. She grew up hunting with her father. She had killed all sorts of animals. She didn't see why killing a human should be that different. Especially a human approaching the end of his days anyway.

It wasn't very difficult to decide to do it. It had to be done and she was the only one who knew that. It wasn't very hard to actually do it either. There was something particularly satisfying about using a weapon carefully selected from the collection that her father had left her to accomplish something tangible. It brought life to the collection, gave it meaning beyond the aesthetics that motivated her father.

She had never understood the aesthetics of firearms. There were a lot of things about her father that she didn't understand. The guns were nice looking but she thought they had to do something useful to be fully appreciated. And Beth learned from her father the value of taking matters in her own hands. "You make your own bed," he often told her. If he were still alive maybe he would finally be proud of her.

Looking at herself in the mirror as she dressed after showering, Beth felt that her history as an athlete and the continuing attention she paid to her body served her well. She was still trim and firm at forty. Cy was still interested in her body at least occasionally and that was enough for her. She would die if Cy lost interest in her. She couldn't live without him. She had to make certain that he stayed interested and would do whatever it took to make sure of that. She desperately needed Cy to need her. She must be indispensable to him.

Her addiction to physical exercise wasn't really a sacrifice. She enjoyed the process as well as the outcome. But she was prepared to make real sacrifices too. She would do whatever she had to. She had proven that.

Shane's physical therapist came to his Printers Alley flat on Monday mornings. Although Shane was making some progress toward being able to walk, the progress was incredibly slow and the sessions with the therapist were physically and psychologically painful.

In his wheelchair, Shane could relax and sometimes almost forget about his paralysis. He had become quite skillful at maneuvering the chair, had adapted to the challenges that his injury forced on him. But attempting to use his legs was humiliating. He was still embarrassed by the awkwardness even with the sympathetic and professional therapist.

He frequently thought of giving up on recovering any function of his legs, firing the therapist and resigning himself to his fate. But KiKi wouldn't hear of it. She insisted that he had to keep at it. You could never tell. There might yet be some gratifying results. So Shane kept at it. KiKi was the expert. But Monday mornings were not the highlight of his week.

"How much do you know about gait, Mike?" Shane asked.

Mike Borden's head was shaved slick and his lean body reeked of virility. He moved with the easy grace of the professional athlete that he had been. Over time, he and Shane had developed a comfortable relationship, comfortable but with a healthy professional space between them.

"Shane," Borden answered, "I think you should

be concentrating on walking at all at this point. We can worry about how you walk after you've mastered the basics."

Borden slipped a muscular arm around Shane and helped him up. Shane emitted an involuntary grunt as the searing pain shot down his right leg. He gripped the arms of the walker and tried to steady himself in the now unfamiliar erect position.

"That's not it, Mike," Shane said, taking a deep breath and suppressing a grimace with difficulty. "For reasons that you don't need to worry about, I was interested in a pigeon-toed gait. What causes that?"

"I'm not sure. I think it happens in childhood, maybe congenital, I'm not sure," Borden answered.

Shane thought that he would get on the computer for some serious Googling on the topic as soon as he could get through the ordeal of trying to coax his reluctant lower extremities to do their job. He was regaining some strength in his legs recently, but the process was excruciatingly slow and Shane was not by nature a patient man. Learning patience may have been the heaviest burden of his incapacity.

After resting a while from the ordeal with the therapist and polishing off a couple glasses of sherry, Shane fired up his laptop and Googled, "pigeon toed gait in adults". Over 4 million hits. As he scanned through the first fifty or so titles, several caught his eye.

The gait is far and away more common in women than men. It seems that some athletes think that running that way actually makes them faster. Babe Ruth was given as an example, although Shane didn't think the beefy Babe was a very good example of athletic speed.

Some track stars have deliberately altered their natural gait to a toes inward style without, apparently, any real reason to think that it helps.

Then, there was a string of blogs claiming that a knock-off imitation of a popular brand of women's boots could cause a pigeon toed gait.

And, finally, the fascinating claim under, *Bruce Charlton's Miscellany*, that a pigeon-toed gait had recently become, "endemic among intelligent young women," with no apparent explanation for the phenomenon.

All fascinating trivia but Shane couldn't readily connect any of it to the diminutive person in the dark blue hoodie who shot Bonz Bagley and triggered Shane's interest in the topic.

He switched off the computer, wheeled over to the bar, refilled his Oxford sherry glass and rolled out onto the deck. The guys in the Blues Bar just opposite the deck were apparently testing their sound system, checking things out for when they would open up later. The loudspeakers aimed directly at Shane blared Koko Taylor's earthy raunch. He liked blues, especially the Chicago variety, better than country. And Koko was a favorite. The volume was a little high, but good hard driving blues — *Everything's gonna be alright, yeah.*

He pondered what information he had about Bonz's killer, sorting through the pieces in his mind and trying to assemble them into a picture. Small person of unknown gender, race and physical characteristics. Probably a wealthy collector of rare guns. Most likely handy with such rare firearms (many collectors were), but not an experienced killer of human beings. Except for the fact that the shots were to the head, this had no signs of a contract job, quite the contrary.

And now, add the pigeon-toed gait information. Either an athlete, a wearer of Ugg knockoff boots, or an intelligent young woman. Or all of those. The knockoff boots didn't make sense. Why would a rich person buy imitation boots? So throw out the information about the boots. But what he was left with was still puzzling.

Shane had learned from painful experience that there had to be a motive and a criminal to fit the crime. What possible motive could a wealthy, intelligent young woman athlete and rare gun collector have had for killing Bonz Bagley in broad daylight in the middle of Printers Alley on a sunny summer Sunday morning in front of God and everybody?

He was also puzzled by the nagging feeling that there was something familiar about the person he had seen fleeing the scene. But, for the life of him, he couldn't think of anyone he knew who fit this concocted description. Maybe he was off base. But the possibility that the killer was female seemed real. Remembering what he had seen, Shane thought the person could well have been a woman. The size was right. And, on reflection, maybe there was something feminine about how the person ran.

He should discuss this with Hardy Seltzer. Maybe by now Hardy had some more information that would help make sense of it.

Shane rang Hardy's office and the detective answered, "Seltzer," an answer that seemed ironically appropriate to the dyspeptic tone of his voice.

"Cheerio, Hardy," Shane said. "Have I caught you at a bad time?"

"Oh, Shane," Hardy answered, surprised at the call. "It seems like anytime is a bad time lately. But what's up?"

"I've been doing some spadework that may be relevant to the Bonz Bagley murder case. Do you have anything new?"

"A bit," Hardy replied, "and the autopsy is this afternoon. That may tell us something. I'm not very optimistic though. Tell you what. Let's meet and compare notes this afternoon after I've got at least the preliminary results from the autopsy."

Seltzer had decided to include Shane Hadley in the investigation without asking permission from the front office brass. Because they were seriously shorthanded, Hardy had been assigned the case by himself for the time being and he didn't see how using Shane could hurt.

Seltzer was also intrigued by the prospect of seeing firsthand how Sherlock Shane would go about trying to solve the crime. God knows, Hardy needed all the help he could get with this one. It wasn't going to be easy and what with the publicity, there would be a lot of pressure to get it solved as fast as possible.

"That's super," Shane replied.

"I'll come by your place in the alley around four if that's OK?"

"Jolly good," Shane said, "I'll watch for you."

The morgue and the coroner's office were in the basement of the aging and largely deserted city hospital, a red brick anachronism perched atop a hill overlooking the Cumberland River that snaked along the eastern edge of downtown. Hardy Seltzer maneuvered his black unmarked Crown Victoria down Lower Broad past the honky-tonks and souvenir shops and turned right on First Avenue away from the giant replica of the iconic Les Paul model Gibson guitar that fronted the Hard Rock Café on its Broadway side.

He wound along the river's edge for a block or two and then hung left and climbed the steep hill. The entrance to the hospital grounds was at the crest of the hill through a sagging pair of rusting wrought iron gates that had never, in Hardy's memory, been closed and so were both ugly and useless.

The hospital complex was a cluster of decaying buildings scattered over several acres. The only activities there since the inpatients were moved to the historically black medical college in the north part of the city several years earlier, were an outpatient AIDS clinic and the morgue. There were periodic plans to renovate the buildings, convert them into shops and condos. The hilltop site overlooking the river was attractive. But that hadn't happened for whatever reason.

Seltzer virtually always attended the autopsies of the victims of murders that he was charged with investigating. He felt obligated to do that, but he hated doing it. He was overtaken by a sense of foreboding as he drove the few blocks from the police station to the morgue.

And the hospital grounds had the eerie feeling of a cemetery, largely abandoned by the living, left to the morbid necessities of dealing with the dying and the dead.

By the time he arrived at the door to the autopsy suite, swiped his access card and entered the haunting cold silence that dwelt there, he was, as usual on such occasions, depressed.

"Ah, if it's not the Maestro of Murder, the good detective Al K. Seltzer," welcomed Dr. Jensen, the rotund coroner with the shock of white hair, fake Irish accent and disquietingly morbid sense of humor. "Good to see you Al K., feeling fizzy are you?"

Hardy had long ago tired of jokes about his name and the fact that Jensen seemed incapable of refraining from such feeble attempts at humor even when Hardy was obviously displeased, did not make for a particularly amiable relationship between the two men. Hardy just wanted to get this morbid

48

business over with.

"You started on Bonz yet?" Hardy asked.

"Your timing is impeccable, detective," Jensen replied. "I am just about to grant what remains of the unfortunate Mr. Bagley the benefit of my skills. Please, if you would don a gown and mask, you may observe."

Hardy went to the small dressing room, put on a green surgical gown over his clothes, tied on a mask and returned to the autopsy table where Bonz's pale corpse lay naked, except for a green drape that covered his head. Cold and dead.

Only a few days ago he was sitting in front of his club, the poodle wriggling about in his lap, chatting with the alley passersby. Hardy was often struck with how suddenly death struck. In the space of a few seconds, the exotic bullets of an unknown murderer propelled Bonz Bagley from the sunny confines of his small piece of the living world into the darkness of whatever there was on the other side.

At least it was sudden. If there was anything Hardy feared it was a protracted death. He wasn't afraid of dying, only of doing it too slowly.

The buzz of the bone saw ripping through Bonz's ribs jarred Hardy from his reverie. Jensen had flayed back the skin and subcutaneous tissue over the chest exposing the muscles and ribs and after a careful inspection of the area, sawed through the ribs on each side and lifted off the thoracic shield — sternum anchoring the protruding rib stumps.

It was like removing the carapace of a clam. The insides of Bonz's thorax were strikingly pale and dry. The heart lay flaccid, silently reclined against what remained of the left side of the chest wall. Fine black spidery patterns covered the gray-pink surfaces of the deflated lungs.

Jensen dictated his observations into a recorder

microphone suspended over the table as he went about his grisly work. Once Jensen started an autopsy he was totally engrossed in what he was doing. He was very fast at it and Hardy was glad of that. Jensen rummaged about in the chest cavity, taking samples here and there and dropping the pieces of tissue into the formalin-filled vials proffered by his young assistant, while maintaining a running monologue into the recorder.

Hardy listened to Jensen's dictation to see if he could pick up anything of note, but there weren't any real surprises. Jensen stopped the recorder with a foot switch and turned to Hardy.

"Nothing much here," he said. "The real action will be in his head, or what there is left of it."

He touched the foot switch again to restart the machine and resumed the rhythmic monotone with which he described the unremarkable findings in an old man's abdominal cavity. Jensen took about an hour and a half to finish everything but the brain. Removing the brain was always left to last and Hardy stayed to the bitter end.

It was not as though Hardy had never witnessed the havoc wreaked on a human face by a handgun at close range, and he had seen the results in this case earlier at the crime scene, but the sight of what had been Bonz Bagley's face still shocked him.

The coroner whisked away the drape that had covered the face during the rest of the autopsy with a flourish revealing the horrific site. In place of what should have been a left eye, there was a gaping hole. The right cheek area was also distorted by an entrance wound, giving the face an eerie lopsided asymmetry — intact cheekbone but no eye on the left and a glazed staring dilated eye on the right with a glob of mangled flesh beneath it where the cheekbone should have been.

Two additional entrance wounds were evenly spaced on either side of the midline of the forehead. While Bonz's intact face had been nothing to brag about, the killer had distorted his features into something grotesque and inhuman by the apparently careful placement of the four fatal gunshots.

"Jesus Christ," Hardy blurted.

Jensen was dictating in careful detail the description of the facial wounds into the suspended microphone. Interrupted by Hardy's exclamation, he touched the foot pedal switching off the recorder.

"Pretty gross, huh, detective?" Jensen said. "Four shots directly into his face. Inside will be a bloody mess."

"Yeah," Hardy replied, "yeah. Why four? Looks like one would have done the job. Why would the killer hang around in broad daylight long enough to fire four times and also increase the likelihood of being discovered by making all that unnecessary noise?"

"Well," Jansen responded, "of course figuring out such things is why you detectives get paid the big bucks, but in my experience this kind of overkill suggests vengeance of some sort. Somebody driven to a desperate act by pent up rage, settling a long festering score. Or a betrayed lover which in Mr. Bagley's case doesn't seem very likely."

Jensen switched the recorder back on and finished describing the gross appearance of the head. With a scalpel, he cut a deep line that circumscribed the top of the head, traversing the occiput and aiming just below the two entry wounds in the forehead. Having retraced the scalpel's path to make sure the incision had penetrated to the bone throughout its course, Jensen lay the scalpel aside, cranked up the Stryker saw and cut through the bone along the path of the incision creating a detachable piece of bone that

Jensen could not help but think of as a skull cap. He lifted up the cap of skull to reveal a gelatinous mass of dark magenta clotted blood and macerated brain. Jensen switched off the recorder again.

"Bloody mess," he said. "We'll be lucky if we can tell anything about the brain."

He reactivated the recorder and began describing the gory cranial contents. He suctioned away as much of the blood clot as he could and reached into the cavity, a hand on either side of what tissue he could grasp.

He elevated the brain, severed the spinal cord just below the medulla and lifted what appeared to be a shapeless mass, depositing it on the stainless steel table. He returned to the empty cranial cavity and felt around. After a few minutes, Jensen retrieved four slugs and held them up for Hardy to see.

Again stopping the recorder, he said to Hardy, "Since there were no exit wounds, the slugs had to be in the cranium. The fact that they entered and just rattled around in there is why they did so much damage to the brain tissue. I'll formalin fix what's left of the brain, but not sure how much of the structure is still intact. Maybe the brainstem and cerebellum. Not sure. At any rate, the brain will have to sit in the fixative for a couple of days before we'll be able to tell what's left. At least ballistics can identify the slugs."

There was no real reason for Seltzer to be there the whole time. He didn't know why, but he felt obligated. That was an especially strong feeling in this case. Bonz had been a presence in the life of the city where Hardy had been born and raised. And he loved the city, warts and all.

Granted, his chosen profession exposed him to the warts more than to the city's more pleasant features, but it was his city. Bonz had been a part of the city's reality and whoever killed him had done

52

violence to the place as well as to Printers Alley's honorary mayor.

Hardy stopped for a drink at a seedy beer joint a block or so toward town from the old hospital. He knew the barmaid there although he hadn't seen her in a while. In his distant and innocent past, he had known her quite well. They had been classmates at North High School.

Hardy still remembered Marge Bland as a cheerleader and senior prom queen who was married for a while to the jock who had been captain of the football team. Early success had taken a turn downhill in the last few years, but Marge had handled her declining fortunes pretty well.

It had been a while since he'd visited the bar at the Dew Drop Inn and chatted with Marge, and he felt a strong need for the familiar face of a living breathing person. And for a drink.

"Hi Hardy," Marge Bland greeted him as he took a seat at the far end of the bar, away from the couple of guys in work clothes downing their third beer and talking too loudly. "I haven't seen you in a while."

"It's been busy, Marge," Hardy answered, "too damn busy."

"You involved in the Bonz murder case?" she asked. "That's all anybody around here talks about. Sad thing. Really sad. Who'd do a thing like that?"

"Yeah," Hardy said and after a long pause. "Can you pull me a Sam Adams?"

Marge laughed. "Bud or Bud Lite, hon, that's all we've got and you know it," she said. "You must've been drinking at some upmarket place lately. Need to spend more time among us real folks."

Hardy didn't answer, just stared off into nowhere. He was still thinking about Bonz, his swift exit from the land of the living. Hardy felt a knot of anger taking root deep in his belly. Violence, especially senseless violence, always angered and confused him. He needed reasons for what people did, explanations. Maybe Shane Hadley would come up with one in this case. Hardy sure hoped so.

Marge Bland leaned over the bar toward Hardy and said, "You're somewhere else, Hardy," looking directly into his eyes, "like to talk about it?"

5

Katya Karpov was not having a good day. She didn't have clinic on Mondays. She spent those days in the lab. They were usually good days once the morning meeting with the Bartalaks was over. Katya really loved the lab. She was thrilled by the process of discovery that went on there, genuinely thrilled to be a part of that. But this day she had trouble concentrating on the work at hand.

She kept thinking about Bonz Bagley's tragic murder and about his experience with Cy's drug. The more Katya thought about it, the more convinced she became that something was wrong. She really must review those data.

Since Beth Bartalak wasn't in the lab, Katya decided to see if she could get into Beth's computer where she thought the data must be sequestered. It was a long shot since Katya didn't know the password, but she went to Beth's cubicle and turned on the machine.

After only a brief pause, the screen lit up with the usual array of icons indicating that she was into Beth's protected area. Otherwise, she would have been prompted to log in and that would have required a password. Apparently Beth had left the machine without logging off.

But Katya still didn't know where the data from the drug studies was located. She stared at the icons. She clicked on "documents" and read through the titles of the folders that appeared on the screen. There was a long list of folders and none of the titles sounded like they contained the data from the clinical studies with the drug. She would have to open them one-by-one and review the contents to find what she was looking for.

"What the fuck are you doing, Katya?" Cy yelled,

leaning over her and peering at the screen.

The sudden interruption startled Katya. Absorbed with what she was doing, she didn't hear Cy enter the room and walk up behind her. He never came to the lab anymore. Katya was the only one there on that Monday and she had no reason to expect any interruptions.

"What are you doing?" Cy repeated. "Don't you know that breaking into a computer is a felony? Katya, this is serious."

"I didn't break into this computer," Katya answered, trying hard to sound composed. "I just opened it. I guess Beth left without logging off."

"I don't give a tinker's damn whether Beth logged off or not. You have breached laboratory ethics, Katya. That is not like you. What were you thinking?"

"Cy," Katya replied, sounding quite composed now, "I need to review those data on the clinical studies with your drug. Beth has refused to give me access. I had no alternative but to try to find them for myself."

"No alternative? No alternative?" Cy yelled. "How about following ethical and standard procedures for accessing laboratory data? How about that approach? I told you I would speak with Beth about this. What in the living hell is so urgent about it?"

Katya didn't respond and Cy stood up heaving a deep sigh.

"Turn off the damn computer, Katya," he said. "Turn it off and do not ever do anything like this again. If I wish you to have access to data I will make them available to you. Otherwise, they're off limits! Do you understand that?"

Katya closed the computer without logging off. She stood up to face Cy. She drew herself up to her full height, towering over the little man.

She looked down directly into Cy's face and said, measuring her words, "Cy, I am going to review those data, with or without the approval of either you or your difficult wife."

There was a long pause as the tension arced between them. A purple flush crept across Cy's face and the arteries bulged from his temples pulsing violently. He struggled to react to Katya's blatant challenge to his authority, but all he could muster was a staccato string of uninterpretable guttural rasps from deep in his throat. He turned on his heel and left the room, slamming the door behind him.

Katya sighed and stood there for a moment. She went to the door and locked it. She returned to Beth Bartalak's cubicle and settled into the chair. She turned on the computer, clicked on "documents" and started again scanning the titles to the folders.

By late afternoon Beth Bartalak was feeling somewhat better. She returned home from The Club and relaxed a while by the pool, soaking up the sun. She made herself a gin and tonic, and then another one. After a while she decided that she would go into work for a couple of hours.

Beth went into the house to get dressed and on the way to the bedroom stopped by her private study and stared for a while at the glass case where the gun collection that she had inherited from her father was displayed.

The 1903 Colt hammer model was the centerpiece of the collection. It had been her father's favorite, his most prized possession. She had deliberately chosen it for the deed that she honestly believed her father would have understood, maybe even admired. After using it, she had cleaned the gun carefully and placed it back in the case.

It seemed to her that it shone more brightly than ever. It was no longer an innocent object to be admired only for its beauty, but a real functioning firearm, christened with real blood. Beth smiled and thought about her father again. She really wished that he was still alive. She hoped that he would have been proud of her at last.

Beth dressed and drove to the medical center. In the parking deck she noticed that Katya's Karpov's white Porsche was in its usual spot. Damn pretentious car, Beth thought, tasteless glam like its owner. There were more important things than looking glamorous. Damn that pretentious bitch!

It was precisely four PM when Shane Hadley greeted Hardy Seltzer from the Printers Alley deck where Shane sat basking in the afternoon sun, awaiting the detective's arrival.

"Hi-ho, Hardy, my man," Shane said. "Come on up."

"Afternoon, Shane," Seltzer answered. "Lower the drawbridge and I'll join you."

Shane rolled inside and released the door and the elevator, chuckling to himself at the detective's metaphor.

"Join me in a sherry?" Shane asked, gesturing his guest to a seat in the living room. "It's a special sherry from my old Oxford college. Decent wine."

"I'm not much on sherry, Shane," Hadley responded, aware that he had no idea what sherry tasted like. "Got any beer?"

"Dreadful drink," Shane mumbled to himself. "Afraid not, Hardy. Sure you won't try some sherry?"

"I'll pass," Seltzer answered, thinking about how little he had in common with Shane Hadley.

Shane wheeled over near to where Seltzer sat.

"So, any surprises at the post mortem?" Shane asked.

"Not really," Hardy answered, "but the coroner did recover four slugs from inside the skull. The guys are running them through NIBIN. I'm sure they're identical to the one we retrieved from the dog, but we'll see. I'm still baffled. Why four shots directly into his head? One well-placed head shot is all you need to do the job. And the shots were well-placed, that's for sure."

"That is troubling," Shane mused. "The killer clearly wasn't taking any chances on the old boy surviving."

"Jensen thinks it looks like a vengeance job, settling an old score. That makes some sense to me."

"Could be, could be," Shane said. Then he continued, "Good work. What else have you got?"

"Nothing concrete," Seltzer said. "I keep hitting a wall, having trouble making sense out of what little we have."

"Tell me what you have."

"So there were two kids hanging out at Fourth and Union when the murderer was running away. From what you told me, the perp should have passed by them. You said he went to the end of the alley and turned left up Union. Fourth is just a half block up the street."

"Right, that's what I saw. Didn't the kids see anyone?"

"Nope," Hardy replied, "that's the problem. They were standing there when he must have passed them, but they swear they didn't see anybody. We found the blue hoodie in the trash at the end of the alley, so he'd shed that, but the kids didn't see a single man go past. And they sounded convincing. This guy seems to have just disappeared into thin air."

"Not a single *man*?" Shane said. "What if it the murderer wasn't a man?"

"You mean it might have been a woman?" Hardy's surprise showed.

"That is the most likely alternative," Shane said.

It wasn't that Seltzer thought that women were incapable of murder. He had plenty of experience that contradicted such an idea. But women usually killed someone they knew, crimes of passion, spite or vengeance. And unless there was a story in the Bonz case that no one seemed to know about, this looked like random violence. Women rarely do random violence. The requisite ingredient for random violence is testosterone.

"Maybe, Hardy," Shane answered. "Let me tell you what I've discovered about the funny gait I mentioned earlier."

"I'm all ears."

"It looked to me that the fleeing murderer ran with the right foot turning inward, what's known as a pigeon-toe gait."

"I remember you said that," Hardy interjected. "I even wrote it down but couldn't think how it told us anything."

"I also puzzled over that," Shane said, "but it stuck in my mind and so I did some computer searches and found out some potentially interesting facts. One fact is that pigeon-toe is much more common in adult women than in adult men. Then when I thought more about it, I thought that the person I saw running could have been a woman — right size and maybe even a hint of femininity in how the person ran."

"OK," Seltzer said, "so might have been a woman. Anything else?"

"Three other things," Shane said. "One of them is that apparently a particular knock-off version of a popular woman's boot can cause pigeon-toe."

"That doesn't make any sense," the detective answered. "Why would somebody who could afford a multi-thousand dollar gun buy knock-off boots?"

"Exactly my thinking, Hardy."

The two men smiled at each other.

"What else?"

"Athletes, especially track athletes, sometimes deliberately develop a pigeon-toe style of running. There is a myth that it makes one run faster," Shane replied.

"Hmmm," Seltzer murmured.

"And," Shane added, "this is the oddest tidbit, apparently pigeon-toe has recently become inexplicably prevalent in intelligent young women. No explanation that I could find. Just an observation."

Seltzer got up and walked over by the fireplace, resting an arm on the mantelpiece and rubbing his chin. Shane said nothing. He was giving the detective time to digest the information.

"So," Hardy finally said, turning toward Shane, "are you telling me that the murderer was a rich intelligent young gun collecting woman athlete? I'm not sure, Shane. Isn't that a little far-fetched? Do you know something else that you're not telling me?"

"It does sound a trifle far-fetched, Hardy. I'll grant you that," Shane replied, "but perhaps there is something that neither of us knows ... yet."

"Yet?"

"We'll know sooner or later, Hardy, my man," Shane said, "whether we're chasing a wild goose or getting closer to the killer. Truth may be elusive, but sooner or later it reveals itself. Have you dug through Bonz's life, any connections that might help? Anything there that sounds interesting?"

"Yes, Shane," Hardy sounded a bit impatient, "of course we've scoured his life private and public. He didn't seem to have any secrets. The life of Bonz Bagley appears to have been pretty much an open book, at least in recent decades. Nothing there that looked like a clue." Then he added almost as an aside, "Bonz had been losing his mental faculties of late. He was taking some kind of medication for that."

Shane was reminded that Bonz was part of a drug trial that Katya was working on.

"I knew something about that," Shane said. "Katya said that he was part of a drug trial of some sort being done at the university. I don't know any details. Do you think there could be a connection between his participation in the drug trial and his murder?"

"I don't see how," Hardy answered.

Shane didn't either but he thought that he would ask KiKi more about it when he got the chance. Difficult to see how there was any connection. But Shane knew well that the absence of an obvious connection between facts, especially in the early phases of an investigation, did not rule out the possibility that facts were connected.

"Shane," Seltzer said, "how much are you willing to help with this? So far I'm pretty much by myself with the investigation. If you and I could work together, you know, stay in touch, meet regularly to review progress, that sort of thing, that would be a great help."

"What does the front office brass think about that?" Shane asked.

"Don't know, Shane," Hardy replied. "Haven't asked them."

"And, I would strongly advise you to continue that course. I doubt that they'd be enamored of such an arrangement. But count me in, my man, count me in for as much as I can do. I won't be much good when the physical action starts, which it may. Although I never developed a taste for it, brute force often rears its ugly head as a case nears its climax. But I'll do what I can in the meantime."

Seltzer sensed a new energy in Hadley's voice.

"That's great," Hardy replied. "How about if we stay in touch by phone if anything develops and meet every couple of days, or whenever it seems important, to review things. I'm happy to meet here if that works."

"Thanks, Hardy," Shane said, smiling broadly, "that would be great. But I warn you that I may turn you into a sherry drinker if you're not careful."

"Not likely," Seltzer said. "It's just not in my genes."

Hardy Seltzer left Printer's Alley thinking that he and Shane Hadley were about as different as two men who shared an interest in crime could possibly be. But Hardy was looking forward to their collaboration. He could learn a lot for one thing. For another thing, he was becoming rather fond of the arrogant paraplegic ex-cop.

As Hardy walked back toward the courthouse square and the police headquarters, he took off his jacket and threw it over his shoulder. He walked down Church Street toward Second Avenue and turned left up the hill toward the square. As he turned he looked off down Second the other way where the warehouses that served the river traffic in earlier years had been converted to restaurants, bars, apartments.

The Wildhorse Saloon was down there, the Hard Rock Café, and everything else from an Irish pub to a sushi bar. People wandered along the street. Hardy stood for a minute, absorbing the scene. He really did love this city.

Shane refreshed his sherry and went out on the porch where the late afternoon sun reflected from the bar fronts. He pondered again the conversation with Hardy Seltzer, the discussion of the case, but also the pact they had agreed on. He was excited to be active again, or as active as his condition permitted.

The somewhat conspiratorial nature of the pact — don't tell the brass — enhanced the thrill. It had been a while since Shane had broken any rules. He worried a little that this might get Hardy in trouble. But Hardy was his own man. He could take care of himself. Breaking a few rules might do Hardy Seltzer some good.

Shane also reflected on the fact that Bonz had been involved in the drug trial that KiKi had mentioned. He would have to ask her about that.

Neither of them was aware that they were in adjacent elevators moving in opposite directions, passing like ships in the night — Katya descending toward the parking deck and Beth ascending toward the fifth floor laboratory.

Katya had spent several fruitless hours going through the folders in Beth's computer. After scanning about half of the folders, Katya concluded that the data she was looking for wasn't there. That made sense. Unlikely that Beth would be that careless with the data. Especially if, as Katya was coming to suspect, there was something to hide. Beth probably had stored the material on a portable hard drive, likely backed up on more than one that she had secured someplace.

Katya's initial excitement about accessing Beth's computer had gradually subsided. She left the laboratory disappointed and still angry from the exchange with Cy. They had had disagreements in the past, but Cy generally knew better than to yell at her. Katya Karpov was not the sort of woman who would tolerate being yelled at. Cy should have known that.

Beth Bartalak unlocked the laboratory door and switched on the lights. She went to her cubicle and sat down. The seat felt warm, as though someone had been sitting there recently although no one was in the lab. Her computer also felt warm and lit up immediately when she switched it on.

Someone had been at her desk and on her computer. And it hadn't been very long. If she wasn't mistaken, she also got a faint whiff of perfume. Not just any perfume, but the very distinct scent that hovered like a cloud about that pretentious bitch, Katya Karpov.

6

Shane Hadley's mind was unencumbered by Victorian notions about the behavior of women and the taboos that such notions imposed on the creator of the fictional character that so interested him. So, although he knew that most murderers were men, Shane had no difficulty thinking of Bonz's murderer as a woman. He would go where the facts led. Any preconceptions about how the investigation should go were, as had always been his practice, put aside.

Shane did rely on his gut feelings, intuitions, on occasion, but he had a general conviction that when dealing with crime involving human beings, absolutely anything was possible and to rule out a possibility based on prevailing conceptions of how people should behave was foolish. People shouldn't kill other people at all, regardless of gender, social class or anything else. Since murder was outside the social norm, one's attempt at logical explanations must be tempered. An explanation had to be found, but the logic might not be obvious to one whose mind was not inclined to violence.

That was especially true in a case, like this one, where there was no apparent pattern to the assembled facts that made any sense. If things didn't make sense, then maybe a critical piece of information was missing. There was a dead person, the death obviously the result of actions of another person. There was an explanation for the route, however tortuous, that connected those two facts and if the available dots couldn't be made to connect those facts, that just meant that there were either missing dots or that divining the connections between them required thinking in a different way.

Shane was sitting in the living room, staring at nothing, lost in those thoughts, when he heard the rumble of the garage door that heralded KiKi's return home from her academic ivory tower.

"Pour me a drink, Shane," KiKi said as she exited the elevator and dropped her Gucci briefcase by the bar.

Whoa, Shane thought. This is serious. KiKi did not drink alcohol as a rule and the rare request for a drink, the tension in her voice and her body language declared that this was trouble of unusual proportions.

"And good evening to you as well," Shane said, a feeble attempt at levity.

"Sorry, Shane," KiKi responded. "It's just that it's been a bad day."

She walked over to where he sat and kissed him lightly on the lips. It was an uncharacteristically perfunctory gesture that disappointed Shane when he thought of how she usually kissed him when she arrived home of an evening. He always looked forward to that.

Since the accident, Shane was sensitive to any hint that KiKi's feelings for him might be cooling. They had discussed that and she had done all she could to reassure him, but there was still a latent fear that things could change between them. Even that remote possibility could shake Shane to the depths of his soul. Life without KiKi was beyond his ability to imagine. Shane refused to allow his imagination to enter that inviolable territory. He simply would not go there.

"What would you like, KiKi?" Shane asked.

"Scotch. Do we have any of that peaty Islay single malt, what is it?"

"Lagavulin?"

"Probably," KiKi answered. "Pour me a generous one and let's sit on the deck and bury this day in the sordid sounds of the alley's nocturnal fantasies."

Shane thought the remark oddly cynical, unlike

KiKi. She was anything but a cynic.

It was after dark in the real world, but a brilliant glare illuminated the alley, decorating the teeming flock of jostling alley partiers with splotches of neon-vibrant color like a work of abstract art. The alley itself was an abstraction. If it was once connected to the reality of the city, that was no longer true. The place was now more a relic, a curio, like the Ernest Tubb bobble head dolls for sale in the Lower Broad record shop that still bore the name of the long dead Texas Troubadour. It was the abstraction, the unreality of the place, that mesmerized Shane. He had more than enough reality to deal with.

They sat for a while on the porch sipping Scotch and watching the milling crowd, vaguely aware of the music—country, blues, and from somewhere something that sounded like it might be rap. The mixture of competing sounds was more interesting as a cultural phenomenon than as an esthetic experience. Maybe that was true of everything about the alley.

And the music was loud, too loud for the two of them to talk. Shane looked at KiKi— her strong face, devastating cheekbones, full lips—changing colors chameleon-like in the flashing neon. She appeared to be deep in thought.

"Would you like to tell me about it?" Shane asked.

They had moved inside and sat in the living room. KiKi had not spoken. She sat rolling the glass of Scotch between her hands, sipping at it occasionally, and staring vacantly into the too large space that separated them.

"I'm not sure what to tell you," she answered. "I'm not even sure what to tell myself."

"Why don't you have a go at it?"

She hesitated awhile, staring at the brown liquid in the glass. She drank the last of the Scotch and sat the glass on the coffee table.

Turning to Shane, she said, "I had a run-in with Cy today."

"What's so unusual about that?" Shane answered.

He was well aware that she had frequent disagreements with Cy Bartalak which didn't usually seem to cause her a lot of concern.

"This one was unusual. Beth wasn't there and I was at her computer when he came into the lab. He blew a gasket! Is that right? Blew a gasket?"

"Yes," Shane answered. "And what were you doing at Beth's computer?" he continued, honestly wondering why his wife whose integrity surpassed that of anyone he had ever known would enter another person's computer without permission.

"Well, Shane, to explain that I would have to tell you a much longer and more complicated story that is still incomplete and fuzzy in my mind. I am not prepared to share that yet with anyone, even you. We can talk about it when things are clearer. I'm sure things will be clearer at some point."

Shane wasn't happy with that answer, but he didn't pursue it. He didn't need information. He needed KiKi's trust. He liked to believe that they had no secrets from each other. What was there that was so private that she wouldn't share it with him? He wanted to press her, but sensed that given her emotional state it wasn't a good time to do that.

"Would you like more Scotch?" Shane asked.

When Cy Bartalak arrived home, punched the button in the car's ceiling panel that opened the iron gates, and wound the black Mercedes sedan up the long serpentine driveway, parking in the brick-paved expanse that fronted the main entrance to their Italianate mansion on Jackson Boulevard, his wife was sitting in her private study nursing a gin and tonic and thinking back over the events of the past two days.

The earlier nervousness had subsided and now she was going over things in her mind. The data were secure, insulated from scrutiny; even Cy didn't know where they were or how to access them. And Beth was pretty sure that her clean-up of the data had been sufficiently thorough and opaque that they could withstand the kind of scrutiny that the FDA submission would require. She was a magician with data.

Beth was feeling pretty good about what she had done. No one, not even Cy, needed to know the details. She had covered his back. She stood, walked to the French doors and stood there, looking out at the perfectly manicured English garden, thinking.

The only potential problem was that arrogant bitch, Katya Karpov. Cy really needed to get rid of her. Why not just fire her and solve a potential problem before it matured into something insoluble?

But when Beth had approached that subject with Cy, he had cut her off. He wouldn't discuss it. He even accused Beth of trying to tell him how to do his job which was ridiculous. His accusation caused Beth considerable pain but she didn't let on to Cy. He had enough things to deal with. He didn't need any worries about her.

"Beth," Cy called as he entered the front door and dropped his worn briefcase in the foyer, "Beth. Fix me a drink, will you?"

He loosened his tie and sat in his favorite chair by the fireplace in the large den. Beth kept a big arrangement of cut flowers in the fireplace in the summer, and the vase of blood red gladiolas annoyed him. He hated gladiolas, thought them garish and intrusively vertical. He must tell Beth that.

He looked at the wall of empty bookshelves. He kept intending to hire someone to populate the shelves with books that would be appropriate for the elegant house and would duly impress important guests. But he hadn't gotten around to it, so the shelves were still empty.

"Beth," he called again, "can you fix me a drink, please?"

She heard him the first time and had immediately started toward the den, but Cyrus Bartalak was not a patient man.

"Hi, Cy," she said, brightly, as she entered the room.

She walked to the bar, iced a martini glass and located the Plymouth gin that he favored for his nightly drink.

"How was your day?" she said, trying to sound bright and cheery.

She could never tell what mood he would be in at the end of a day and so always opened the conversation carefully. She wanted his arrival at the house he was so proud of to be pleasant, a highlight of his day.

"Don't ask," he said. "Can you hurry up with that drink please?"

Not an afternoon for small talk, obviously. Beth finished the drink and took it to him. She bent to kiss his cheek and bumped his glass as he was raising it to his mouth sloshing some of the gin onto his shirtfront.

"Damn, Beth," he said.

He sat the glass on the side table, stood up and started brushing at his shirt.

"Look what you've done. Damn!" he said.

"I'm sorry, Cy," Beth responded, "I'm sorry, let me get you a napkin."

She headed back over to the bar, retrieved a napkin, and started to dab at the wet spot on his shirt, but he grabbed the napkin from her.

"Let me do it," he said, "You've done enough already."

"I am sorry, Cy, I really am. I was just trying to kiss you."

"Well, you see where that got us," he said.

He sat back down, picked up his drink and took a long swallow of the cold gin.

Glaring at his wife, Cy asked, "Can you bring me the papers? Think you can manage that?"

"Of course, I'm sorry. I should have brought them in earlier," Beth responded.

She left the room briefly and returned handing him the two daily papers that he always read. He opened the *Tennessean* and perused the headline that he had seen earlier.

"Did you see this?" he asked Beth. "That old geezer in Printer's Alley went and got himself killed. He was in the drug study, wasn't he? One of the good responders as I recall?"

"Yes," she answered, "I saw that. He was the best responder to your drug. But we have all the data on him. Fortunately he didn't get killed until after he had essentially finished the study."

"We're damn lucky he didn't, you're right about that," he said.

Cy leafed through the local paper, and then picked up the *Wall Street Journal* and started reading it in earnest. Beth sat opposite him. Neither of them spoke for a long time while he caught up on the day's business news.

Beth sat quietly and just watched her husband as he read, occasionally sipping from his drink. He paid her no attention, but she was used to that when he was engrossed in the newspapers.

Cy's mood seemed to be softening some when he finally put down the paper and polished off the last of his martini.

"You do have all the data from the drug study secured, Beth," he said, more a statement than a question.

"Of course," she answered. "The data are absolutely secure, no one can get to them except me."

"In your lab computer?"

"Well, duplicates of the complete data set are on two portable hard drives that are locked away in separate places. There may be some of the original data still on my lab computer, but nothing that anyone could make sense of I don't think. Why do you ask?"

"Just wondering."

"It's funny you should ask, because when I went in this afternoon, I could have sworn that someone had been into my lab computer. And, you can guess who I immediately thought of."

"Of course," he sighed. "You and Katya obviously have a real problem with each other. You should try to get over that. I've told her the same thing. Conflict like that in the lab is not good for our work."

"I think our differences are irreconcilable, Cy. I really do. Now that the study is about over, do you really need her anymore?"

"Beth, we've talked about this before. Katya Karpov is the brightest and most productive member of my faculty. This drug study is only part of her value to the department and to me. She is really an outstanding scientist and physician. How many times do I have to tell you that? The answer to this conflict is for the two of you to figure out how to coexist without compromising the work."

"I just don't think she has enough respect for

you. That's my problem with her."

"That's probably true. If she weren't so good that would be harder to tolerate."

"Well, I'm just afraid she may undermine you if she gets a chance."

"I don't think she would do that deliberately, Beth," Cy said, "but we should make damn sure she doesn't get the chance anyway. Damn sure."

"You know I'll do everything I can to prevent that, Cy. You know that."

"Good old Beth," he replied, "I can always count on you."

The earlier unpleasantness seemed unimportant now. Just that small expression of Cy's confidence in her was enough for Beth. She smiled at him and he returned the smile.

He was actually thinking that it was good that he could count on Beth, alright, dependability had its value. But she was no match for Katya Karpov.

Beth was beginning to wonder if some of her husband's fascination with Katya was related to her non-scientific assets. Beth really needed Katya Karpov out of their lives.

When Hardy Seltzer dropped back by the Dew Drop Inn after finishing up at headquarters, it was almost ten o'clock, but Marge Bland was still tending bar. About half the barstools were occupied, mostly working stiffs smoothing off the rough edges of another hard day.

There were a couple of women of the sort Hardy knew well, hard drinking types who had racked up a lot of obvious mileage running in place as fast as they could; rode hard and put up wet as the saying went. Probably not prostitutes in the strict sense, but available for the price of a drink or two. But, hell, didn't everybody have a price?

"Hardy," Marge greeted him, mopping the space on the bar in front of him with a cloth that had an apparent history Hardy didn't want to know about, "twice in one day after all this time. To what do we owe the pleasure, detective Seltzer?"

"Hi, Marge," Hardy said. "Can you give me a Bud?"

Seltzer didn't answer her question because he didn't know the answer. He wasn't sure why he had come back there other than for a drink and a familiar face. It wasn't really a conscious decision. He had thought about Marge Bland for the first time in a while that evening as he sat in his stifling office going over what facts he had about Bonz's murder for the umpteenth time.

He kept pondering the possibility that the murderer was a woman; that troubled him. He just couldn't come up with a motive for one thing. And then there was the weapon. Women rarely killed with handguns. And a fancy rare collector's gun? Four shots point blank to the face? If this killer was a woman, she was some piece of work, that was for sure.

After a while Seltzer's mind wandered and he remembered Marge asking earlier if he wanted to talk about it, whatever *it* was. Sounded like an invitation but to what he wasn't sure and wasn't even sure if he wanted an invitation from Marge Bland.

But he was there. He had fought his way through the late night Lower Broad snarl of cruising teens and drunk jaywalking tourists, braved the blaring cacophony of dueling loudspeakers blasting a dissonant mix of contrasting aspirations for the future of country music into the limited space of Lower Broadway's wet night air.

At First Avenue, he had intended to turn left and head up the hill and over the Woodland Street Bridge to the emptiness of his simple flat in the east part of town, but found himself turning the other way and winding up the hill to the bar where he now sat nursing a flat beer and looking into the dark eyes of his old high school classmate, unsure of what he saw there and unsure of what he was looking for.

7
BONZ KILLED BY WEALTHY GUN COLLECTOR?

The headline screamed from the front page of Tuesday morning's *Tennessean*. The story that followed recounted how the slugs recovered from Bonz's dog had been run through NINIB to obtain a preliminary description of the expensive and rare gun that must have been the murder weapon. There were speculations about how the dots might be connected.

The latter part of the story was pure fantasy, but the facts were accurate and there in surprising detail. The possibility that the killer was female was not mentioned. The byline was Harvey Green's.

Shane had awakened alone, picked up KiKi's note from the bedside table and read it, "Shane, had to go in early and didn't want to disturb you. Shouldn't be late. Love, KK."

He was disappointed that she left without waking him. He struggled into the wheelchair parked next to the bed, rolled up to the kitchen near the front of the flat, made some coffee and opened the paper that Katya had retrieved and left on the kitchen table. Surprised by the headline and the story, he phoned Hardy Seltzer.

"Not good, Hardy my man, not a good idea to get the press onto this so early," Shane said.

Shane had called Hardy at his home number immediately after reading the story. Although he thought that Hardy would surely know better than to leak this information to the press at this point, Shane wondered whether he had overestimated the detective.

"Wasn't me, Shane. If it wasn't you I don't know where the leak was," Seltzer answered.

When Seltzer first saw the headline he was furious. The only *Tennessean* reporter, maybe the only reporter on earth, that Hardy trusted was Harvey Green. Green had left a couple of messages on Hardy's home answering machine trolling for information about the murder, but Hardy didn't return the calls. Hardy wasn't even sure how Green knew he was on the case but then the reporter no doubt had other contacts in the department.

"It certainly wasn't me," Shane answered. "I doubt that anyone would come to me looking for news anyway. Who even knows that I'm helping you with the investigation?"

"You tell me, Shane," Hardy said. "I haven't told anybody."

"Neither have I. It's probably good to keep it that way."

"Yeah."

After a pause, Shane asked, "Who in your shop knows about the gun?"

"The ballistics person who was covering Sunday for sure. The info's also in my report so the big brass should have known. That's assuming they read the report and they might have since this thing is bound to attract a lot of attention."

Everybody in the department knew that the chief and his cronies didn't pay much attention to the daily reports from the detectives in the field unless it was a high profile case, something that might get the chief some air time or ink in the local press.

"That's for sure," Shane answered. "The chief wouldn't miss a chance like this if I remember him correctly."

"You do."

"Could he be the leak?"

"Doubt it. If he wanted the info out, he'd want credit. Probably do a high profile press conference or something like that."

"Yeah," Shane responded, "this has all the

earmarks of some intrepid reporter with an inside contact."

"That bothers me. The story byline was Harvey Green's. I know him and he's the only one at the paper that I trust not to take potshots at the force. I've been a source on occasion, but not this time. He's tried to contact me but I've avoided him."

"Must have another inside source. What about the ballistics guy?"

"Gal, actually," Hardy answered. "I don't know her very well. She's pretty new, that's why she had to cover on the weekend. Low person on the totem pole gets that gig."

"Among other gigs," Shane said.

"Right. Anyway, I don't know her well enough to guess what she'd do. I'll confront her and see how she reacts."

"That's a good idea. I really do think that we should guard any information about the case very closely. If the murderer is a rich and influential local, broadcasting information that points that way prematurely might precipitate events that would complicate the situation even further. Having some high roller leaning on the department brass and the politicos won't do much for the cause of truth and justice."

Hardy was tempted to add *and the American Way* but restrained himself. He was getting more comfortable with Shane but was still guarded his words.

Hardy said, "Agree. I'll talk to the ballistics gal."

Neither of them wanted to end the conversation but neither had anything else to say at the moment.

After a long lull in the conversation, Hardy said, "This thing about it being a woman still bothers me, Shane. I just don't see it."

"It seems to me that based on what little we have,

the possibility can't be ignored."

"It's putting a lot of confidence in how the person ran. Pardon me, Shane, but that seems like making a big deal out of a really small observation."

"That is true, Hardy, my man, that is true. But it's such small observations that sometimes answer big questions. We'll see. We'll see."

Seltzer really did think that Shane was pushing in the wrong direction. Maybe the legendary detective's powers had waned during the years of disuse. It was interesting to see how he went about it, but Seltzer was starting to worry about the investigation getting off track. He knew how to develop a case. There was a standard approach that usually worked.

Maybe he was getting too enamored of who Shane had been, mixing that up with the different person he was now. But then, Shane Hadley had always been unorthodox, not one for paying overmuch attention to the rules. That intrigued Hardy alright, but he needed to keep focused on the job at hand. And he had a lot of respect for rules. Hardy Seltzer liked order.

That's what Hardy was thinking as he drove the familiar route from his East Nashville flat down Woodland Street, across the bridge to the square, around the court house with its twin marble fountains still illuminated in the morning dusk and into the covered parking garage under the police headquarters. He was also thinking about Marge Bland.

Katya Karpov arrived early at the lab on Tuesday morning. She hadn't slept well. After lying awake for an hour staring at the ceiling and listening to Shane's steady breathing, sensing the rhythmic rise and fall of his chest beside her, she got up, showered, had a cup of coffee and left for work. She left a note on the bedside table for the soundly sleeping Shane.

That was unusual. Shane almost always maneuvered himself out of bed while Katya was getting ready for work and wheeled up to the kitchen where they shared morning coffee before she left. They both enjoyed the morning time together. But that morning, her thoughts were elsewhere.

Katya was the first to arrive at the lab. She was still troubled by what seemed to her a discrepancy between Bonz Bagley's apparent recent clinical condition and the data. She had decided to go over the stuff in Beth Bartalak's computer in more detail if she could get at it again.

Katya went directly to Beth's computer and opened it up. Good, Beth had again left the machine without logging off. Not like Beth to be that careless, but good. Katya navigated to the folders that she thought seemed most likely to contain the data from the drug studies and e-mailed the folders to her personal address as attachments. She then went to the sent messages and deleted the ones sent to her address. She shut off the machine and went to her small office beside the lab. She closed the door and fired up her computer. She spent several hours there.

Beth Bartalak went to work late. She made breakfast for Cy and sat quietly with him while he ate. They didn't retrieve the morning papers since he was in a hurry to leave. It was not an unusual morning for them.

After Cy left, Beth took her time getting ready. There was no need to hurry. The feeling of satisfaction at an essential job decisively done lingered with her from the previous day. She had a leisurely shower, brushed her teeth, took her morning complement of supplements, and applied her makeup. On her way out the door, she picked up the newspapers from the porch and tossed them into the entrance hall. She didn't notice the headline.

Beth felt good as she drove down Jackson Boulevard and turned right on Belle Meade. She drove slowly, taking time to admire the columned estates of the old moneyed folk that fronted the venerable boulevard. In recent years you could buy your way into this life if you had enough money, even if it was new (Cy had done that), but that hadn't always been true. And there was still a clutch of the multigenerational moneyed who controlled

The Club and the subtleties of access to other amenities that defined the two distinct social classes of the city's rich. Time had brought some change that was accepted if not welcomed, but the line between the *vieux riche* and the *nouveau riche* was still there and carefully maintained.

Beth made her way down to West End Avenue, turned right and drove on north to the medical center that sprawled across several acres at the southern edge of downtown next to the university. She could not keep herself from looking for Katya's white Porsche when she drove into the parking deck even though the site of the car always riled her.

It was there, in its usual place. In spite of Cy's defense of that woman, Beth still harbored the hope that one day before too long that parking space would be empty. Cy had to understand eventually that Katya Karpov's departure from their group was inevitable. He just had to understand that.

When Beth entered the lab, she noted that the door was unlocked and the lights were on but no one else was there. Then she saw that Katya's office door was closed and light was visible in the crack beneath it. The bitch was in there. God only knew what she was up to.

Beth had decided to delete everything related to the study of Cy's drug from her personal computer in the lab. There was no need to keep it there anymore and since it seemed clear that Katya was determined to do everything she could to get at the data there was every reason to make doubly sure that it was secured in a place where it could not possibly be discovered.

When she opened the computer, Beth realized that she had left it the previous afternoon without logging off and was disappointed in herself. She often forgot to log off lately. She really must be more careful about that.

She navigated to the C drive and started the task of highlighting and deleting each of the folders that contained any of the data from the drug study. This would be a load off her mind. She could assure Cy that everything was secure. That ought to satisfy him if he had any doubts.

On the other side of the door that separated her office from the lab where Beth Bartalak sat, Katya pored over one particular folder that she had retrieved from Beth's computer. The folder tab read IIa-1 and it contained what were apparently raw data from cognitive tests and serum protein analyses from one of the subjects in the study of Cy's drug.

After carefully studying the data, it was clear to Katya that this subject either got the placebo or didn't respond favorably to the drug. What troubled Katya was that both the computerized tests of cognitive function and the protein studies indicated that this subject had initially improved and then deteriorated considerably during the final months of the study. The file had not been updated after the code was broken so that there was no way to tell whether subject IIa-1 had drawn the lot that assigned him to the treatment group or to the control group.

But Katya was troubled because she could not recall any of the subjects in either group who had been shown to get this much worse according to Beth's summaries of the data. Since this file included measurements from six month follow up studies and only one subject in the study had completed the six month observation period, these data had to be from the first subject entered into the study. That subject was Bonz Bagley. But Katya wanted to establish that with absolutely no room for doubt.

Katya noted that the subject was male. She took out a note pad and pen from the desk drawer and began to write down everything in the file that might identify this subject — age, gender, height, weight and of course the study number which could be linked to the subject's actual identity if one had access to the identification code which was held by the research pharmacist. That's who was responsible for dispensing either drug or placebo for each subject, the choice of agent determined from a list of random numbers. No one else involved in the study had access to the code until the study was ended.

Beth was the keeper of the data. Only the data that had been analyzed by Beth were reviewed by Katya or anyone else as far as Katya knew, including Cy. Up to now, Beth alone had been privy to the complete set of raw data. Beth had assumed the task of analyzing the data and insisted on presenting only the fully analyzed results to the group. Cy had supported that. This folder appeared to contain original information ... raw data.

###

"So, Detective Seltzer," the chief of the Metropolitan Police Force reared back in his leather chair, tilted his head back and peered at Hardy through the narrow slits of a rectangular reading glasses perched precariously near the tip of his nose, "been hobnobbing with your buddy at the paper again, I see."

A copy of the paper with the troubling headline lay on the chief's desk.

"It wasn't me, chief," Hardy answered. "Swear to it. Green tried to contact me but I've avoided him."

No need to play games with the chief about his acquaintance with the reporter. That relationship had served the chief and the department well over the years, avoiding some potential embarrassments. Harvey Green could be counted on to do his homework and write honest well-informed stories.

"So where did Green get his information?"

What bothered the chief was that the morning headline was the first he had heard of this. As was his usual practice, he had not read Seltzer's report until after he saw the newspaper story. The chief didn't have time to read all of those often useless reports usually written more to create the impression that the author was working harder than he actually was than to report anything relevant.

"Don't know," Hardy answered. "It could have been the person on weekend ballistics. I'm looking into that."

Hardy dealt with the chief and his other superiors by telling the truth but not too much of it.

The chief got up from his chair, tossed his reading glasses on the desk and started pacing about the room. To follow him, Hardy had to rotate back and forth in his chair as though he were watching a sporting event of some kind.

Hardy noticed that the boss was putting on more

weight and walked with a hitch like he had a bad knee. He was showing his age more than Hardy had noticed before. The chief's hair had become almost completely white and there were deep furrows in his brow and at the corners of his mouth.

"Hardy," the chief stopped just in front of where the detective sat and looked him in the eye, "I know you are good at what you do and I'm not worried about trusting you with this case. But there's likely to be an unhealthy interest on the part of the media and one of my jobs is to control that. So be sure you keep me fully informed. I don't want to learn anything I didn't already know about this case from the evening news or the morning paper. The last thing I need is to be blindsided by a reporter who knows more than I do about it. That's the last thing any of us needs."

"Yes sir," Hardy answered.

"So, we're agreed on that. What else have you got?"

"You know about the gun," Hardy answered, trying to decide whether to tell the chief about the possibility that the murderer was a woman. "The news story was pretty accurate about that. So, the gun was the property of a collector with a lot of dough to spend on his hobby."

"Yeah, I got that, although it doesn't make much sense. A gun like that could be a dead giveaway. More likely the gun was stolen, don't you think?"

"I'm working that angle as well."

"What else?"

"Well there is a remote possibility that the perp was female."

There, Hardy had said it.

"Female? Very unlikely, Hardy. What raises that possibility?"

"Well, chief, the only reliable witness just saw the perp running away from the scene and, while he didn't get a good enough look to identify the person, he thought there was something feminine about the way the perp ran."

"Pretty flimsy, Hardy. You know as well as I do that this is not the kind of crime that women do, that is unless there's something in Bonz's private life you haven't found out."

"Nope," Hardy replied, "Bonz's private life, at least in recent years, was pretty boring. Nothing at all there that we can find."

"Maybe you better go over all that again," the chief said.

"Of course, of course. We'll turn over all the rocks we can find."

"Good, good," the chief said, obviously ending the conversation, "and be sure to keep me informed. Like I said, I don't want any more surprises here."

Back in his office, Hardy rehashed the conversation with the chief. Maybe Hardy should have told his boss about Shane Hadley's involvement. The reason he hadn't was that he feared that the chief would nix the idea. Even though Hardy had his doubts about the direction Shane was taking things, Hardy still wanted to keep up that interaction. He thought he might learn something. And, too, he was enjoying getting to know Shane Hadley.

Shane could not rid himself of the notion that he had seen the person running away from Bonz's lifeless body before. He even felt that he may have seen the same person running through the alley. Especially early in the mornings when he occasionally sat on the balcony contemplating how he might amuse himself through another long day without Katya, he watched the occasional jogger passing by below.

Maybe that was it. Maybe the murderer was a downtown morning jogger with an unusual gait that stuck in his subconscious, one of those insignificant observations that just stuck somewhere in a remote cranny of his brain, unattached to his consciousness because there was nothing there for it to attach to.

He wheeled himself out onto the deck. Long afternoon shadows stretched down the narrow street, dark swaths slashed across the streaks of sunlight leaking through the narrow slits of space that separated the surrounding buildings. Shane stared down at the alley, rummaging through his brain trying desperately to locate that elusive specific bit of memory.

8

Shane sat in the living room staring at the screen of his laptop and was not aware of the sound of the garage door as Katya arrived home. He had been sitting there for a while, pondering what he could not help thinking of as the *Pedix diaboli* case and searching for anything he could find about collectors of rare guns in the city and its environs, specifically anything about the rare gun that seemed the best fit for the spent cartridges and slugs retrieved in the investigation of Bonz Bagley's murder. He had had little success. Most of the collectors of such guns seemed to be concentrated in Texas. Big surprise.

On her way home, Katya had stopped at Provence, an elegant little boutique deli in Hillsboro Village, and picked up some take out for dinner along with a selection of cheeses and a baguette. She dropped her briefcase by the bar, deposited the food in the kitchen and came back to stand beside Shane, caressing his shoulder. He looked up at her and she kissed him warmly.

"What are you looking for?" she asked.

"I'm looking for the owner of a very rare antique gun."

"Don't tell me you're working."

"Sort of."

"Is this about Bonz's murder?"

"It is. I've gotten sort of unofficially involved. Helping out one of my old colleagues. I'm beginning to enjoy it."

"Well I hope to hell you find out who did it. It really disturbs me to think that anyone would do such a thing."

"Afraid our species is capable of all kinds of inexplicable acts of violence, my dear," Shane answered.

Shane turned off the computer and laid it on the coffee table. Katya sat in the chair that faced him.

They looked at each other for a long time before Katya spoke.

"I need your help, Shane," she said.

Shane didn't like the sound of it. Of course he wanted to help KiKi in any way he could, but there was an undertone of what sounded like desperation in her voice. Shane had never known KiKi to be desperate about anything. Well, almost anything.

"Of course, KiKi," Shane responded, reaching for her hand, "of course."

Katya got up and walked through the French doors that separated the living room from the library. Shane followed her and she closed the doors, shutting out the sounds from the alley. She picked up the remote for the CD player and the elegant strains of a Mozart sonata filled the room. Katya sat in a chair beside Shane and neither of them spoke for a while.

"Did you know," she said, "that listening to beautiful music does something to your brain to make it work better? It's called the Mozart effect."

"It actually does something to your brain? How is that?"

"Not really too surprising. You feel something and your brain is where feelings happen. So there must be some biology there."

"I suppose so. You should know. It just seems so mystical somehow. Not like the world where you operate."

"You're wrong about that. That is exactly the world where I operate, demystifying apparent mysteries. That's what research is about."

"Sounds a lot like detective work."

"It is, actually. Or I imagine it is. But your kind of detective work is what I need help with."

"Can't imagine it, but tell me about it," Shane said.

Katya repeated her suspicion that B<u>o</u>nz had been deteriorating in the couple of months before his death. She added that she had come to suspect that Beth Bartalak was hiding something about the data from the patients in the study of Cy's drug.

"What makes you think that?" Shane asked. "I know you don't like her, but do you really think she is intellectually dishonest? That she would manipulate data? Isn't that taking a big risk? Wouldn't somebody be sure to discover it?"

"I think she is capable of almost anything if she thought it would please Cy. She is pathologically devoted to the man for reasons that aren't clear, at least not to me. I'd guess something to do with her relationship with her father if I wanted to be analytical. But I don't know anything about that and don't really care to. What I care a lot about is the integrity of what we are doing."

"So you're suspicious. Do you have any evidence?"

Katya hesitated. She wasn't anxious to tell Shane that she had basically stolen data from Beth's computer. Although she wasn't proud of how she got the information, she was convinced that her action was justified by the potential importance of what she found. But she also knew how much Shane admired her dogged honesty. She loved him for that.

"I think so," she said.

"So tell me what you have."

"I will, but you won't be pleased with how I came by it, Shane."

"You stole it from Beth Bartalak's computer, no doubt."

"Stole is a little harsh."

"Let's don't go there for now. Tell me what you

have."

"I have some raw data on one of the subjects in the study of Cy's drug that doesn't fit with the data that Beth has been presenting to us," Katya said, some nervousness creeping into her voice.

"Bonz's data?"

"I don't know for sure, but that is almost certainly the case. The material is coded. The subjects name is not there. But it sure sounds like it's him. And the tests for whoever this was show rather marked deterioration of mental function in the last few months of follow up."

"Maybe it wasn't Bonz, but someone who got the placebo," Shane said.

Shane was only vaguely familiar with how these drug tests were done, but he knew that some people got the drug and some people got a look alike pill without the active ingredient.

"I thought of that, but none of the data that Beth has presented showed a pattern like this, regardless of which group they were in. I think Beth was deliberately altering these data in her analysis. That's what I think."

"Can't you just confront her?"

"I don't think I want to do that until I know more than I do now. Cy would blow a gasket if I accused Beth of scientific misconduct and he would be tarred with that brush as well. It would not be a pretty sight."

"Any way you can link these data to Bonz directly? Isn't there a key to the ID code somewhere?"

"Yes, of course."

"But you can't get access to it, I suppose."

"Right."

Shane rested his chin in a palm and thought for a while. He was contemplating the challenge of figuring this out, but also troubled some by KiKi's apparent compromise of her principles by basically stealing the data. Not hard to rationalize given her determined honesty about her work, but there was a paradox. Shane had certainly used some questionable methods to gather critical evidence in the distant past. But it was unlike KiKi not to put all her cards on the table.

"Well," Shane finally said, "I'm not sure what to say. If you can't insist on getting the identity of the person whose data is in this mysterious file, you're sort of stuck. No way you can get the ID key without raising suspicions? An excuse of some sort?"

"Probably not and anyway I wouldn't be comfortable with such deception, Shane. Surely you know that."

Shane thought he knew that, but then she had stolen information from someone's computer which didn't seem that different. Deception is deception.

"Hmm," Shane mused, "so help me parse this, KiKi. Theft of supposedly secure information is OK but a small ruse to obtain the key to interpreting the purloined info is not permitted? I fear I fail to see much of a distinction between the two."

"Maybe I should just come clean with Cy. Tell him what I have and what I suspect."

"Sounds like what I would expect you to do. Not what I'd do, but then we approach problem solving in somewhat differently. I've always presumed that that is because the nature of the problems we deal with is different. But this one sounds more like solving a crime than probing the secrets of the mind."

"But isn't that how you solve a crime? Probe the secrets of the criminal mind?"

"Not really. I don't understand the criminal mind. I think most crime is not a rational activity. Motive is another matter. Of course we need to establish motive. That's why Bonz's murder is so baffling. There has to be a motive and we can't come up with one."

"Well," Katya answered, "the motive for Beth Bartalak altering Bonz's data isn't hard to figure out if my suspicion that he wasn't doing well is right."

Shane said, "One usually establishes that there was a crime before looking for a motive, rather than the other way around. I find a motive in search of a crime a bit unusual."

Katya responded sharply, "If this file I found is from Bonz Bagley's studies, then there has certainly been what amounts to a crime in my book."

"Is it really that important?" Shane asked. "Are the results in one subject that important? Isn't it the data from the whole group in the study that matter?"

"Well, yes and no," Katya answered. "Anecdotal results that are dramatic can have inordinate influence on how things are perceived. And Cy clearly uses Bonz's response as ammunition with potential investors in his company. Cy says that those people are impressed with individual responses more than statistics."

Katya stood and paced about the room, obviously troubled by the ethical dilemma she had been drawn into. She had not hesitated to retrieve the data from Beth Bartalak's computer because, if Katya's suspicions were right, the truth had to come to light somehow. Beth obviously wasn't going to reveal it voluntarily and Cy seemed reluctant to go there.

Katya felt, even on reflection, that she had no choice. As with her research, she went where the hypothesis and the opportunities led her. True, she detested Beth, but this was not about personalities or vendettas.

Shane wheeled himself out to the bar in the living room, poured a full glass of sherry and returned to the library. The impeccable integrity that he so admired in KiKi would not be an asset in solving a crime. With a criminal investigation, Shane had always felt that the ends justified the means. But means were very important to KiKi. In her profession, methods and results were inextricably connected. One could not compromise either without damaging the whole process of discovery.

"KiKi, my love," Shane said, "I noticed that you brought provisions. I suggest that we avail ourselves of the fruits of Provence and put this discussion to rest for a bit."

"An excellent suggestion," Katya replied.

###

Beth Bartalak arrived at their Jackson Boulevard mansion early in the afternoon. She picked up the morning papers from the foyer and put them in the den beside the chair where Cy liked to sit for his afternoon drink. As she placed them on the side table, the front page headline in the *Tennessean* leapt out at her. She read the article.

The description of the presumed murder weapon concerned her. It was an uncannily accurate description of the gun her father had left her. Although she couldn't imagine how they would ever connect her with the murder, she thought that she should take precautions. She would have to do something about the gun.

She went into her study and stood for a while studying the six guns in the display case. She couldn't imagine disposing of any of the precious gifts from her beloved father. But perhaps she shouldn't leave that gun at the center of the display in such a conspicuous place. She opened the case and picked up the gun. She caressed it, relishing the texture of the smooth cold steel.

She put the gun in a drawer of her desk and rearranged the others to obscure the vacancy it left in the display. She would decide later where to put the special gun, somewhere where it could not be discovered. In the remote possibility that some potential connection of Bonz Bagley's murder with her gun collection was made, she could say it was stolen, or that such a gun was not part of her collection.

It should be easy enough to fabricate an explanation. The authorities would not be anxious to implicate Cy Bartalak's wife in such a nefarious act. He was too important. And if it came to that, Cy would protect her. Surely he would do that. He would have to. After all, she had done it for him.

Beth wasn't sure how much her husband knew about her gun collection. For the most part they occupied separate spaces in their sprawling mansion. Cy had designed it that way. Beth wasn't sure if he had ever been in her private study. They shared some common spaces — the den, the breakfast room, the dining room on those occasions when they had guests. But they had separate studies and separate bedrooms and dressing areas. Cy visited her bedroom on occasion when the notion struck him, but their other separate spaces were their own.

But Beth decided that she would keep Cy from seeing the newspaper story. There was an outside chance that he would recall that she had the rare gun collection and she didn't want to have to lie to him.

She went back to the den, retrieved the copy of the morning paper and put it in the kitchen garbage compactor. If he asked, she would just tell him that they didn't get the paper today.

9

Harold Whitsett Jensen, III, MD (Harry to his few intimates) wasn't an expert neuropathologist, but he relished cutting brains.

There was something sensual and intimate about it. The feel of the razor sharp knife slipping smoothly through the fixed mass of fat and nerve that had been the control center of the person whose remains he had carefully dissected, bits of it parsed out to be examined under the microscope's revealing eye, still thrilled him even after having done it more times than he could count.

The brain cutting was the *coup de grace*, the climactic conclusion of the autopsy. But brains couldn't be sliced fresh. Fresh brains were mush. It took a few days in formalin to give them the semi-solid consistency that Jensen relished feeling yield to the knife's razor edge.

But Jensen had not looked forward to delving into what was left of the brain of Bonz Bagley. It would be a messy job and Jensen put it off as long as he could. So it was three days after his desecration of the other parts of Bagley's body when Dr. Jensen fished the mass of brain tissue from the container of fixative and plopped it on the stainless steel table.

The upper parts of the brain, the cerebrum, were grossly distorted with large areas of hemorrhage and almost complete loss of the normal architecture. The usual elegant procedure of sliding the gleaming knife blade through the organ at two centimeter intervals creating a lovely symmetrical array of ovoid slices wouldn't be possible. But Jensen did the best he could to cut the mass into slices so that he could see if there was anything that could be learned from examining the gross specimen.

Jensen adjusted the overhead light so that it

shone directly on the slices of tissue and scrutinized them. He was no expert, but there was something very strange there. The cerebral hemispheres were so distorted that he couldn't say much about them. It did appear that the ventricles were enlarged, not surprisingly given the person's age. Just the process of aging takes its toll on that organ; the tissue gradually shrinks so that the ventricles, the hollow spaces in the center, enlarge.

But there was something about the region at the base of the right hemisphere where the structures were reasonably intact. There were holes barely large enough to see with the naked eye within the substance of the tissue, holes where there should have been solid tissue. This was not a result of acute trauma. Jensen had never seen anything like it before and he had seen the insides of a lot of brains of all kinds of people.

He snipped small pieces from several areas and put them in vials of fixative for later microscopic examination. But he couldn't stop looking at the gross specimen and searching through his memory for something similar that he might have seen in the past. He couldn't come up with anything that he had seen or read about that was anything like what he was seeing in the brain of Bonz Bagley. Jensen was fascinated.

He left the brain slices on the table and went into his small office beside the autopsy room. He took a pipe from the rack on his desk and fondled it for a minute, admiring the bearded face of the figure carved intricately into the meerschaum bowl. He zipped open a leather pouch and filled the pipe with the pungent latakia tobacco that he favored. He lit the pipe with the desktop lighter, aiming the flame carefully so as not to char the meerschaum. He drew a few puffs, relishing the sharp aroma, and pondered the strange anatomy of Bonz Bagley's brain.

It took several rings of the telephone on his desk to rouse Jensen from his thoughts.

"This is Dr. Jensen." He spoke distractedly into the mouthpiece.

"Dr. Jensen," Hardy Seltzer replied, deliberately avoiding addressing the pathologist as Harry; Seltzer was not an intimate of Jensen's and did not care to be, "do you have any more information from the Bagley autopsy?"

"Ah, detective Seltzer," Jensen replied, "so good to hear from you."

Seltzer was too familiar with the pathologist's penchant for idle chatter before engaging in a substantive conversation. Maybe it was an occupational trait of pathologists who spent most of their time in the lonely company of human remains that were indifferent to their clever banter. Jensen was the only pathologist that Hardy Seltzer had any contact with but he thought that such a morbid profession probably attracted weirdoes.

"Sure," Hardy replied, "but do you have any information for me?"

"Interesting that you should call just now," Jensen said. "I was just this moment slicing up Mr. Bagley's brain. It is the most enjoyable part of the procedure you know."

"Sure," Hardy answered, "but do you have any information?"

"Well, not information, detective," Jensen said, "but some observations."

"And?"

"Well, I'm going to need to consult with experts at the university, but there are some changes in the brain that I find strange."

"Strange?"

"Strange. Unlike anything with which I am

familiar, detective."

"When will you have something more definitive?"

Hardy was losing patience with the pathologist and it showed.

"One cannot rush these things, detective," Jensen replied. "I will need to contact the local experts at the university and have them review the findings with me. And we'll need to review the microscopic sections. Be patient Detective Seltzer. When I have something definitive, I will let you know."

Seltzer ended the call on his cell phone without responding. He was dealing with the Dickerson Road traffic while trying to see the street numbers. This was not very familiar territory for him. He couldn't remember the last time he had driven this far out northeast of downtown. But, Shane Hadley's Internet searches had come up with the address of a rare gun dealer (there were very few in the area and Shane thought this one was especially interesting for reasons that he did not disclose) that was out here someplace and the two of them agreed that Hardy ought to pay the place a visit.

He scanned the facades of pawn shops, down-market retail stores and a variety of shabby looking ethnic restaurants that may serve the best food in the city for all he knew. He'd have to give some of them a try. Maybe Marge Bland would be up to venturing out here; she had been an adventurous soul as he remembered. Marge kept haunting his mind lately for some reason that escaped him. She was a pleasant if uninvited guest there. Did there have to be a reason?

He located the place he was looking for in a strip mall sandwiched between a check cashing service and a drab looking storefront that proclaimed itself to be a Bolivian restaurant. The sign read just *Rare Guns*.

Hardy parked and approached the small shop

with blacked out windows and a steel door that was painted an incongruous bright red. A bell that sounded oddly like that of a children's ice cream vendor tinkled as he entered the empty shop.

The walls of the place were bare except for some posters for old war movies — actors he didn't recognize, their faces contorted into angry expressions, brandishing vicious looking firearms. A glass display case with several conspicuous padlocks was in the center of the room. Hardy walked to the case and looked at the array of handguns the makes of which he didn't recognize.

No Glocks or Colts, at least not of sufficiently recent vintage to be familiar. Hardy took the picture of the old Colt Hammer model that he had printed out from the Internet from his pocket and unfolded it. He looked for anything resembling the gun in the display case, his gaze moving between the picture and the case, but nothing caught his eye.

"Can I help you?"

The man was probably in his forties, maybe a decade older than that. He wore army desert fatigues and tan combat boots. He was tall and thin, apparently fit. His head was shaved and a long scar traversed most of the right side of his face. His clipped pronunciation of the words said that he wasn't a local. The words came in staccato bursts, like gunfire, said without inflexion.

"Yes," Hardy answered, "I'm looking for a special gun. A vintage Colt hammer model from the early nineteen hundreds," he spread the picture of the gun on top of the display case. "Do you have anything like that?"

The man studied the picture for a few seconds without speaking.

"You a cop?" the three words were shot rapid-fire directly at Hardy's face — bang, bang, bang.

Hardy flipped open his badge and showed it to the man. "Yep."

"So, I read the papers, mister." Again the staccato fusillade of words. "You're on the B<u>o</u>nz case." A statement not a question.

"Yep."

Hardy was being deliberately tough with the guy, reacting to his less than gracious welcome.

"I don't have any guns like that."

"Sold any?"

"The people who buy guns from me aren't generally anxious to have the police informed of their purchases." The man's tone was softening some.

"I am less concerned about the anxieties of your customers than I am about who murdered B<u>o</u>nz Bagley, Mister ... I didn't catch your name."

"Bando, Harvey Bando," he answered, not extending his hand or giving any other sign of amiability.

Hardy said, "So, Mr. Bando, unless you want to attract more attention to your little enterprise than I suspect you and your clientele would find comfortable, why don't you tell me who you sold this gun to."

Hardy could do the tough cop dance when he thought it necessary but it wasn't his favorite part of the job.

"OK," Bando said, obviously losing the pissing match that he'd invited, "it was Jody Dakota. I'll double check the records, but I'm sure that it was him. I don't generally handle guns that rare. Several years ago, when he was still performing, Jody Dakota came with a specific request for that gun and I had to locate it and get it for him. Found a Texas dealer who had one. Jody paid a handsome price for it. Biggest sale I ever made by a long shot."

Some years earlier, Jody Dakota had been a big

deal in the country music business — Grand Ole Opry, platinum records, big concerts, international tours, the whole deal. Hardy recognized the name from somewhere in a remote recess of his memory, but hadn't heard anything of him in several years.

He assumed that the career of Jody Dakota (or whatever his real name was), like that of countless other music business has-beens, had descended from its peak into that special place in Oblivion where those who revel for a spell in the bright lights and outsize paychecks that enable the illusion inevitably go to reminisce and nurse their wounded egos.

"Would that be the old country singer?" Hardy asked.

"Yep." A single word shot straight to Hardy's gut.

The last thing Hardy Seltzer wanted to do was get involved with the byzantine and often sordid world of country music. Those were not his kind of people; that was not his world. And there would be publicity. Too much publicity. The public and the media would sympathize with the denizens of the world that fed the coffers of the city whose name was synonymous with that genre of the performing arts. It would be a losing proposition for the cops.

On the other hand, this could be progress toward identifying Bonz's murderer. He was heavily involved in the music subculture in the past, probably around the time that Jody Dakota's star was rising. There could be a connection. Hardy's job was to find the killer and he'd do whatever was necessary to get the job done.

As he drove from the parking lot heading back toward downtown, Detective Seltzer took out his cell phone and rang Shane Hadley's number.

103

Beth Bartalak decided to go for a run. She had come home from work early. She was spending less and less time at work recently, going in late and coming home early. She wasn't sure why. It just seemed the right thing to do. She wasn't sure why there seemed to be a lot of changes in her behavior lately. But that didn't concern her. She was not in the habit of analyzing her behavior, just went with the flow ... whatever. Beth Bartalak was not an introspective sort of person.

It was a sunny but unseasonably cool afternoon. The hilly trail through Percy Warner Park would be a good workout for Beth and she anticipated the thrill that always came over her with strenuous physical exercise. She dressed in her brief running shorts and a short tee shirt, admiring her muscular legs and her flat belly in the mirror as she exited the Bartalak manse, trotted down the long winding driveway to Jackson Boulevard and jogged down to Belle Meade, turned left and headed for the entrance to the park.

There was a soft afternoon breeze and the trail was shaded by the dense growth of hardwood trees that covered the park's rolling hills. There were no other runners this early on a weekday afternoon. Beth lost herself in the rhythm of her footfalls on the paved path. Dappled spots of afternoon sunlight filtered through the leafy canopy.

She thought about her dead father. Not the relic of a man wandering about the netherworld of lost cognition where he had been at the end. She detested those memories and repressed them as much as possible. She preferred to remember the robust small town Texas defense lawyer who had made his name by skillfully navigating the nuances of the legal system to spare a long list of shady characters the consequences of their nefarious deeds.

He loved beating the system. How many times

had she heard him say that a man's primary responsibility was to himself, the law be damned. Laws were the starting point for negotiations, not immutable rules. You did what you had to do to protect your interests and dealt with any complications after the fact. He had mastered the art of dealing with the complications and had parlayed those skills into a comfortable living for many years.

Beth still sometimes regretted that she hadn't followed her father's example and gone into law. But her father didn't think she had the stomach for it. Law was a man's world, he said. She still felt keenly her father's obvious disappointment in the fact that his only child was a girl. She had tried to be what he wanted.

He taught her about guns. Even got her a rifle and spent some time training her how to use it. Taught her to hunt a long list of animal species, the enjoyment of stalking a prey and the satisfaction of a clean kill. But she couldn't overcome the disadvantage of her gender in his eyes. She couldn't be a man.

That part of the running trail in the park was up a steep hill and Beth felt the burning in her thighs as she picked up her pace. The conversations with Rory Holcomb seemed a long time ago now.

She felt a sense of satisfaction, accomplishment, that bordered on exhilaration, as she reflected on how she had managed to deal with the Bonz problem. Although Cy probably didn't fully appreciate its magnitude, Holcomb said it was a potential problem of major proportions. He had bet a fair amount of money on this deal and Cy's reputation with the local investment community was at stake too. She had mulled the plan over in her head for a while before actually carrying it out. It was a meticulously conceived plan; she was a detail kind of person.

Beth had a habit of running early in the morning,

before Cy awakened. Unbeknownst to her husband, she had started driving into downtown for her early morning run, making sure that her route included the short stretch of Printers Alley. She ran there every day for over a week, confirming that the alley was completely deserted on Sunday mornings.

Cy slept in on Sundays and Beth's Sunday run was later than on weekdays. Not only was the alley deserted then, but also Bonz Bagley habitually appeared in that spot in front of his club early on Sundays, before anyone else was around. He would nod to her as she jogged by. She decided the risk was minimal.

And there was the gun. Beth's father collected rare guns and admired them, but his guns were not just for display. He often said that there was no sense in having a gun if you couldn't shoot it, so he only bought guns for which he could get ammunition. Beth inherited her father's collection of bullets for each of the rare guns and using one of those prized possessions felt to her like a tribute to the man whose affection she had been unable to win while he was alive.

She located a shooting gallery south of town and went there a couple of times, making sure that her chosen weapon was in good working order. Feeling the heft of the rare weapon in her hands and the shock of its discharge thrilled her. It brought back memories of the few times when her father had complemented her; she had become an excellent shot under his tutelage and he took some pride in that at least.

Then, too, there was the thrill of the kill. She hadn't really expected that, hadn't thought about it. But there was the startled look in the old man's eyes as she aimed the gun carefully at his face and pumped four rapid fire shots into his brain abruptly cutting short the old man's protest. And the explosion of his eyeball as his face morphed into a hideous shapeless mass and he crumpled forward from his chair sprawling headlong into the alley.

She hadn't anticipated the adrenalin rush. The anamnestic thrill of the kill that she had experienced many times hunting game with her father. *The thrill of the kill.* Her father's words. Beth understood them better than she ever had.

Her only regret was killing the dog. But after she shot Bonz, the dog went into such a barking frenzy that Beth had to shut it up. It was easy. A single shot aimed just at the base of the animal's neck. And it was necessary, like disposing of Bonz, eliminating whatever information lived in that old man's brain. But the feeling was different.

The key to success, Beth thought, was managing appearances, perceptions. How many times had she heard Cy say that perceptions were more important than reality; more than that, *perceptions are reality*, he often said. It shouldn't surprise anyone who knew anything about that seedy alley that someone sitting out there when no one was around was vulnerable. And there were surely some enemies lurking in the dark recesses of Bonz Bagley's past.

The entertainment business attracted some shady characters and Bonz must have encountered some of them. All kinds of potential criminals probably hung around the alley, foraging along the fringes of the music scene. The last thing anyone would imagine was that the wife of a prominent university psychiatrist entrepreneur and important community personage would kill an aging and addled has-been Printers Alley club operator in broad daylight on a Sunday morning. Why? Impossible!

Beth was into the hilliest section of the Warner Park trail. She felt her thighs tightening and was breathing a little heavier. It felt uncommonly good.

She thought about her nemesis Katya Karpov. According to Cy, Katya was pressing pretty aggressively for access to the raw data from the clinical trial of the drug. No way was the bitch going to get at those data.

The Printers Alley-Katya Karpov association crept into Beth's mind. She thought that perhaps she should resume her observations of the habits of the alley denizens. There might be other situations where such knowledge would be useful.

Beth felt good. She smiled.

"Hadley here (*hee-aah*)," Shane answered the ringing phone.

He sat in the living room, nursing a glass of sherry. His worn copy of *The Complete Sherlock Holmes* lay across his lap. It was opened to page 954, *The Adventure of the Devil's Foot*. That story, at least the title, kept intruding on his consciousness. He had retrieved the book with the idea of rereading the story, but didn't get past the first page before becoming again preoccupied with the Bonz Bagley case. That vision of the person fleeing down the alley, the odd gait. There was something familiar about the person that he still couldn't bring to mind.

"Shane," Hardy Seltzer replied, "can we get together? I have some new information about Bonz's murder that could be important."

"Oh, Hardy, my man," Shane said, "I was just thinking about the case. Of course. Can you come by my flat?"

"I'm just on my way back downtown from a visit with that gun dealer we talked about. I have to run by the office. How about if I meet you there in a couple of hours?"

"Jolly good, Hardy, jolly good."

Hardy chuckled to himself. Jolly good indeed, he thought.

10

Medical discoveries that have the potential to benefit people are often made in university laboratories. But the only way discoveries can actually get to the clinic is to commercialize them. In Cyrus Bartalak's words, borrowing a favorite term from the venture capitalists, "*monetizing* university research is critical to the future of academic medicine."

Cy could make an articulate and convincing case even to his most skeptical university colleagues, that it was no longer possible to rely entirely on philanthropy and federal grants to support the academic enterprise. And university laboratory discoveries had dollar value in the marketplace. Unless that value could be realized, even the most promising new drug would never get from the laboratory to the clinic where misery and pain could be relieved and sick people could be cured.

The costs of operating an academic enterprise were always increasing and money from commercializing discoveries was, more than ever, an important source that must be tapped. Even the federal government knew that. Institutions were required to do everything they could to move discoveries financed by government grants into the world of commerce. Years earlier, with the Bayh-Dole act, congress wrote that expectation into law.

Cy Bartalak felt that he had mastered the process of moving laboratory discoveries into the clinic and his efforts with this new Alzheimer's drug were a textbook example. Do the laboratory work. Patent the discovery and any processes, reagents or procedures that could be remotely considered proprietary. Set up a company to handle further development of the drug. Then, for the initial studies in people, leverage university, philanthropy and grant resources by attracting a few million dollars from high net worth individuals (*angels* in venture jargon) who get a stake in the startup company.

Ideally, these were local people who had the wherewithal to take financial risks, and the stomach for it. If you could get through phase I-II clinical studies and they looked promising, you had the ammunition to go for venture capital, the big investors mostly on the west coast, and begin the phase III studies, the real test of safety and effectiveness — and the ticket to the big money. The new company could then be taken public and either partnered with or sold to big pharma who would bear the exorbitant costs of finishing the phase III studies and, if the results were positive, completing the arduous process of getting final FDA approval and marketing the drug.

There was big money to be made from the startup even if the drug never came to market and if it did even bigger rewards from royalties and escalating value of the startup company. Professor Bartalak had made considerable amounts of money this way for himself and the institution where he had worked previously. It was familiar territory.

Although initial small investors may have been angels to a startup company, that was not necessarily an appropriate description of the other aspects of their lives and activities. Their ticket to angelhood was that they had money, were susceptible to the promise of big returns on an investment and were willing to take risks. There need be no ethical or moral litmus tests. At least Bartalak didn't think so. At heart, angels were gamblers. He was also a gambler and nobody expected gamblers to be squeaky clean.

When he took on his new role at the university, Bartalak set about to identify potential angels in the city. After extensive research, he identified three promising candidates: Mitchell Rook, a highly successful lawyer who had parlayed his inside knowledge of several business ventures and his annual seven figure salary into a considerable fortune and was always on the lookout for new opportunities (he was also an alumnus of the university, a neighbor of Cy and Beth in Belle Meade and a fellow member of the country club there); Wilmington (Will) Hadley, a long time physician to the blue stocking set, who in his retirement had taken to fairly aggressive investing with a lot of success (also a university alumnus and a member of the University Governing Board; Bartalak thought the university connections could work to his advantage); and Rory Holcomb, a real estate magnate with extensive local connections in politics and in the music business whose less than spotless history was fodder for gossip among the city's well-heeled, but he clearly had plenty of cash and wasn't very careful about what he did with it.

Bartalak had long ago observed that men (it was always men) who made a lot of money thought that made them smart, which in his experience, was anything but true. He thought most of those people had more dollars than sense. They were easy prey for his brilliant and articulate presentations of the earning potential of a new biomedical discovery.

He knew where their buttons were and how to push them (he was, after all, a psychiatrist). That, coupled with his history of previous financial success and the imprimatur of the prestigious university, made his start-up company, *Renaptix, Inc.,* exclusive licensee of the rights to the new Alzheimer's drug, an easy sell.

After a whirlwind courtship — much wining and dining, several Sunday afternoons in the university's skybox at the football stadium just across the river, countless tumblers of George Dickel bourbon and branch water consumed — the courtship was consummated at a carefully choreographed private dinner at the Bartalak Belle Meade manse.

Cy had a favorite caterer that he used for special occasions like this. Beth was there of course, but was relegated to her familiar place at the periphery of the action. She wore the red dress that Cy selected for her. The dress was backless, cut low enough in the front to reveal (with the aid of an uplifting undergarment) some cleavage, and short enough to display an only slightly immodest amount of her muscular tanned legs.

Beth knew that she was not a beautiful woman, but she had a good body that she was proud of. She was entirely comfortable with her body and didn't mind at all appearing as a decoration. She wasn't very good at conversing with Cy's business-related friends and was perfectly happy to display enough of herself to minimize the need for making clever conversation.

Mitchell Rook was a dapper high rolling lawyer with a quick tongue who was clearly not impressed with the Bartalaks' carefully constructed trappings of wealth and success. Those were just the basics for doing business in this city. Will Hadley was a stereotypical country club type — aging elegantly, insincerely solicitous. After greeting them when they arrived, Beth barely spoke to either of them.

Rory Holcomb was different. Flashy sharkskin suit, gray ostrich cowboy boots, bolo tie neatly anchored by a turquoise and silver medallion. Beth knew the uniform. She grew up doing everything she could to impress such a man without much success. Holcomb's outfit could easily have been selected from her father's extensive wardrobe. That was a while back, but fashion didn't change for these men. Why should it?

The others didn't seem to be paying much

attention to Holcomb and he sought Beth out at the fringe of the group as they had a pre-dinner drink and made small talk. It felt to Beth like they connected, like old friends. It was a relief to Beth that there was someone important to her husband with whom she felt comfortable.

The attraction wasn't sexual it seemed to her, for either of them. Just a feeling that they had something in common. Rory Holcomb looked out of place in this group and Beth felt the same way. Maybe that was the connection.

Dinner was served in the large dining room. The size of the polished cherry table could be modified by choosing the number of leaves to insert, and Cy had supervised the arrangement so that two people could be seated on each side and he could preside at the head of the table. Beth was seated beside Holcomb on one side with the other two guests opposite them. The table was sized to make the occasion intimate without being crowded.

Dinner was served by three white coated waiters who were moonlighting from The Club. On that evening two of the waiters were elderly black men and the other one was a younger Hispanic. The ethnicity of the waiters varied at these business dinners depending on Bartalak's reading of the probable biases of the guests. He thought that the guests that evening were likely to be sufficiently steeped in the city's southern history to appreciate, like most patrons of the club, his choice of waiters.

Nothing substantive was discussed during the meal and, after finishing the main course and polishing off the last of several bottles of wine that had been selected by the caterer and were roundly complemented by the guests, Cy suggested that they have dessert, coffee and brandy in his study.

Brandy and coffee were arranged on a side table

and the guests were invited to serve themselves. Once comfortably seated with their libations in the several oxblood leather chairs that had been carefully arranged so that the host was at the focal point of the group, the waiters appeared and passed trays of an assortment of finger-food desserts.

Bartalak had met with each of the three on several occasions over the previous couple of months and they all had a pretty good idea what he was trying to sell them, but there had been no formal presentation before this evening.

There was an expectant lull in the conversation as Cy instructed Beth to hand out the slick brochure with *Renaptix, Inc.* printed in large blue italic letters on the tan cover (the well-known university colors were blue and tan). When the brochures were distributed and the three guests had had a chance to leaf through them, Bartalak began his spiel. He relished these presentations.

Cy began by repeating what was basically his stump speech: commercializing laboratory discovery was essential to getting new drugs to the people who need them; initial investments in promising new discoveries were what made it possible to start the process; big returns on those initial investments were essentially guaranteed if the initial clinical studies were as good as the preclinical data, etc. He then used the tables and graphs in the brochure to go through the basic theory of how the drug worked and the promising preclinical data from animal studies.

He moved on to the business model for *Renaptix, Inc.* emphasizing the amount of investment already made in the drug by the university and from federal research grants, documenting the patent status, outlining the funds needed to do the initial clinical studies, and projecting the earning potential for the initial investors. When he finished the presentations, he invited the men to refresh their brandy and then he would be happy to answer any questions.

Beth had been sitting quietly beside her husband, her crossed legs prominently displayed, as he spoke. She got up, walked to the side table where she poured generous amounts of brandy into the proffered glasses of the three *high net worth individuals*, as Cy referred to people like this. She made eye contact with Rory Holcomb but they didn't speak. When everyone was reseated, there were questions.

"How solid is the IP, Cy?" Mitchell Rook asked.

Cy noticed that Rook had drunk very little over the evening and had barely freshened his untouched glass of brandy during the break. Rook was clearly the brightest of the three and the only one who worried Bartalak. He wasn't so much worried about whether Rook would invest in the start-up. If not, there would be someone else.

It was something about the lawyer that Cy couldn't quite put his finger on. Maybe Rook was too smart. Maybe that was the problem. And Cy was always suspicious of high rollers who didn't drink.

"Rock solid, Mitchell," Cy responded. "A composition of matter patent for the drug has issued. As you know that's the strongest possible protection of intellectual property. We still have pending patents on some processes for synthesizing the drug but even if they don't issue, we're in good shape IP wise."

Will Hadley, well into his cups at this point, raised his hand like a college student before asking, "What about safety? Any doubt about that?"

"None at all, Will," Bartalak responded. "We're almost finished with the tox studies that are required for the IND and they look great so far."

"Excuse me, Cy," Rory Holcomb drew up his long legs, leaned forward in his chair and rested his elbows on his knees, "but, what the hell is *tox* and

116

what the hell is an *IND*? If you want me to put any money in this you're going to have to talk in plain English."

Bartalak sighed, smiled and looked directly at Rory, "Sorry Rory," he said, "tox is short for toxicology; studies that determine whether there are any negative effects of the drug. And before you can do any studies of a new drug in people, you have to get FDA, uh that's the Food and Drug Administration, approval and that requires submitting an Investigational New Drug or IND application that describes all of the animal results and includes extensive studies of toxicity in several animal species. We're in the process of compiling the IND and we've had several discussions with the FDA people. I don't see any problem with getting the application approved."

"Another thing," Rory said, apparently satisfied with Bartalak's explanation of the IND, "I dug up this picture on the Internet, a diagram of a big funnel that shows ten thousand potential drugs entering the big part of the funnel and only one coming out the other end as something that can go to market. One in ten thousand looks like pretty long odds to me. I'm as up for a good gamble as anybody, but not with odds like that. Just as well buy lottery tickets."

"You're right about that, Rory." A broad and confident smile broke across Cy's face. "But those are data compiled from the entire drug development experience. That's not where we are with this drug. We're way down the funnel because the university and the federal government have put in the money to do all of the work needed before going into humans. Federal grants get reviewed by the smartest folks in the country and the university doesn't throw money at things that don't have a good chance of working.

"If you remember your funnel figure you'll recall

117

that after successful preclinical studies, the odds go down to one in five. Meaning that one of every five drugs that get into human trials come out as approvable and marketable and, I hasten to add, profitable products. Since the work on this drug has been reviewed and supported by a lot of smart people, I think our odds are a lot better than that. I'm not saying there's no risk, but considering the potential payoff, they aren't unreasonable. Add the fact that we can make a lot of money by selling to big pharma before the phase III studies are finished and even if the drug never sees the light of the marketplace day it starts to look like a pretty sweet deal, don't you think?"

The three men looked at each other, sipped at their drinks and thumbed absently through the brochures without speaking for a while. Bartalak sat quietly, letting the facts sink in. Beth sat at his side, legs crossed, hands folded demurely in her lap.

"Uh, Cy," Will finally spoke up, "who's going to do the human trials?"

"We are," Cy answered. "We have plenty of patients for the phase I-II trials and my team is expert at this sort of thing. I'll head the team. My lovely wife, Beth, here," he placed an arm across Beth's shoulders, "is our data expert. You may not have suspected it, but this beautiful lady holds a PhD in biostatistics and is a magician with data. She is amazing."

Beth smiled broadly and blushed. Cy often complemented her in groups like this but never when they were alone. She wished it was the other way around, but took what she could get.

"And I have a brilliant neurologist to handle the logistics of the clinical studies. She couldn't be here this evening," in fact she had not been invited, "but trust me, she is the best possible person for these kinds of studies. We've got a crack team."

Even though Cy hadn't used her name, it took a considerable amount of effort on Beth's part to suppress a grimace at the reference to Katya Karpov.

After sitting quietly for a while, Rook asked, "Can you direct the studies? Isn't there a conflict of interest problem? I assume you stand to profit from the success of the drug, don't you?"

"You don't need to worry about that Mitchell," Cy answered. "I can handle any appearance of COI with the university. We may need an oversight committee to review things occasionally, but I can work that out. I've done this before, you know."

"So I've heard," Rook mumbled to himself.

After a brief pause, Bartalak said, "Well, it's getting late and if you don't have any more questions, maybe we should call it an evening."

Cy was pretty sure that his timing was right. Timing was critical is closing a deal like this. He was expert at staging the performance. He knew the script by heart. He had been there before. The questions had been good, they were obviously interested. You didn't want to push too fast. They were sold, but they didn't know it yet. They needed time to digest the matter and to convince themselves that they had thoroughly critiqued the opportunity. But he had sold them. He was sure of it.

Cy continued, "I really appreciate you guys coming tonight and I hope you are as excited about this as I and my colleagues at the university are," again deliberately invoking the prestige of the university, "and, you know, it's not about the money when you get down to it. It's a chance to do something for people who are victims of a devastating brain disease." He stared off into the distance for a few seconds, as though contemplating the good of mankind, then turned back and looked directly into the eyes of each one of his three guests.

Cy continued, in his most sincere tone, "It would be a pleasure to work with you to make that happen."

His summation completed, they all stood and Cy and Beth saw them out, shaking hands and bidding them goodnight. Beth's eyes met Rory's again as he exited the front door, but they didn't speak. Several months would pass before the two of them would connect again.

After the door was closed and the three men were walking to their cars, Mitchell Rook said to no one in particular, "Cyrus Bartalak may be the ugliest man I have ever seen."

The others nodded.

Rory Holcomb asked, "Where did he come up with that strange name for the company, Renap, something or other?"

Dr. Hadley answered, "I asked him about that. He said it was a play on the words regeneration and synapse."

"That doesn't help me," Holcomb responded.

"Synapse, that's where the impulses get transmitted in the brain," Hadley explained.

"If you say so," Holcomb sighed.

Mitchell Rook wondered whether, if the drug worked, Rory Holcomb might stand to benefit personally from it.

Over the next week, Bartalak met with each of his three angels individually and they each agreed to invest a million dollars. *Renaptix, Inc.* became a reality and the phase I-II studies of Cy's drug, designated RX-01, were launched.

11

"So, Hardy, my man, what have you discovered?"

The day was warm and the alley was quiet so Shane suggested that he and Hardy sit on the balcony. Although an overhanging awning shaded the space where they sat, the sun was bright and reflected harshly from the surrounding buildings. Shane had poured himself a glass of sherry and offered to pour Hardy one which he refused.

Shane was determined to introduce his colleague to some of the finer things and Hardy Seltzer was equally committed to avoiding any pretense of being someone whom he clearly was not. He was enjoying Shane, was amused by his idiosyncrasies, but Hardy wasn't into idiosyncrasies personally. He was who he was and wasn't about to pretend otherwise.

"Couple of things," Hardy responded.

Shane interrupted, "What was it about the autopsy? You were a trifle obtuse on the phone."

"Not obtuse," Hardy said, "I told you everything that the coroner told me. He thought there was something unusual about the brain, but said he'd have to wait for the microscopic examinations and would probably need to consult with the experts at the university before he could say anything conclusive."

"Any idea when he would decide to do his job?" Shane sounded impatient; although he was working on it, patience did not come naturally to him.

"Said he'd let me know. Jensen is an odd duck. Hard to read."

"Pathologists tend toward oddity, I suspect," Shane answered. "Their usual audience isn't particularly sensitive to quirks of personality. But, then, I suspect most of us are potential odd ducks, as you say, if we weren't so concerned about what others think of us."

Well it was true that Shane Hadley was a bit of an odd duck, Hardy thought, and maybe the comment was meant to disparage Hardy's stolid persona but he wasn't going to worry about that.

Hardy said, "Let me tell you about the gun."

"Yes, yes," Shane said. "Please do."

Shane stared pensively into the warm space that blanketed the alley in the afternoon sun. His eyes were drawn to the spot where Bonz Bagley's body lay that Sunday morning. And he envisioned again the slight figure running away from the scene listing ever so slightly to starboard with each step.

"I visited the dealer you identified. After a little persuasion, he admitted selling a gun like the one we're trying to find. Although it was several years ago, he remembered the sale because it was the rarest and most expensive gun he had ever sold. And also because he sold it to Jody Dakota, the country music star."

"As in Little Jody Dakota, the Opry performer of a bygone era?"

Hardy was surprised that Shane knew enough about country music history to know who Jody Dakota was.

"That's right," Hardy answered. "I did a brief computer search and you're right. His stage name was Little Jody Dakota and he was sort of a novelty act but very popular back in the day."

"Yes, yes," Hardy said, "Back before the genre's gentrification."

"An interesting way to put it, gentrification."

It was not a word that Hardy would have thought of using to describe how the music had evolved over the years. In fact it was probably not a word he would have used for any reason.

"Perhaps that's not the right word to describe it," Shane said, then continued. "Has Little Jody ever had difficulties with the law?"

"I did have a look at the police records and apparently he's been in a skirmish or two. He was a drinker and sometimes a brawler."

"Hmm," Shane responded, "the 'little man' syndrome?"

"Something like that. There was one episode when one of his band members accused him of attempted murder, but nothing came of it. Looked like an overreaction to a bar fight."

"Interesting, though."

"Yes."

"Does the wee one still live in the city?" Shane asked.

"I checked that as well," Hardy responded. "Apparently he has a farm out in Hickman County."

"That's strange," Hardy responded. "So he has fled the entertainers' ghettos and hid out in the boondocks?"

"Looks that way. No log McMansion on the lake. No Williamson County horse farm. Hickman County is not anybody's notion of the high life."

"No glitterati there, I suspect," Shane said, "but interesting. You'll need to venture into the boondocks it appears."

"Yep. On my agenda."

"Did you learn any additional provenance for the gun? Where did the dealer procure it for example?"

Hardy didn't know exactly what provenance meant and was relieved that Shane clarified his question.

"Not much," Hardy answered. "He said he got it from a dealer in Houston who specializes in very rare firearms."

"Did you get the name of this Houston dealer?"

"Yes," Hardy said, "wrote it down."

He took his pad from a shirt pocket and thumbed through it.

"Here it is," he said, "*Jergensen's Rare Guns*. I got a phone number and an address from the Internet. They have a pretty fancy web site."

"Why don't you give those to me and I'll follow up with the Houston folks while you pursue wee Jody in the hinterlands."

"Good plan."

Hardy smiled. While he didn't relish the thought of probing at the soft underbelly of the music scene, he was starting to think that he was making progress with the case. It was possible that the pieces were starting to fit together. He liked that. He especially liked the idea that there might be a solution that made sense.

Shane, too, thought that this was a lead that bore investigating. He recalled the Holmesian dictum that one arrived at the right answer by first eliminating all of the wrong ones. But when he remembered the fleeing person who must have been the culprit, the unusual gait and what he had learned from his Internet search, he still harbored the possibility that the person they were looking for was a woman.

It was not rare for a subtlety to trump the obvious as a story unfolded. Shane was forever suspicious of the obvious, the trail too cleanly made. In this *Adventure of The Devil's Foot* revisited, time would tell.

Katya was enjoying the fact that Beth Bartalak came to work less often, and when she did come in worked shorter days than had been her habit. But it was unusual behavior for Beth and Katya wondered about it. Maybe Beth had less to do as the studies of Cy's drug wound down.

The phase I-II studies were designed for only a six month follow up. Bonz Bagley was the first subject enrolled in the study and had completed the last follow up lab studies before his untimely death that had precluded Katya's final clinical exam that would have completed the study protocol.

It was those six month follow-up lab studies of Bagley's that concerned Katya. If the information she had lifted from Beth's computer was indeed from Bagley, almost certainly the case, Beth had some serious explaining to do. But identifying a study subject and linking the person's identity unequivocally to the data wasn't easy.

When people volunteer to participate in the study of an experimental drug, they are guaranteed anonymity. There is a committee that reviews all such studies called the Institutional Review Board (known by its initials, IRB) and they must OK an agreement that includes an explanation of the potential benefits and hazards as well as the guarantee that no data will be linked to the subject's personal identity. The agreement must be signed by the participating subject and an investigator responsible for the study.

Of course the scientists doing the study know who the subjects are, but there is supposed to be a firewall that separates the data from personal information. A master key exists that links study numbers with identities, but that is isolated from the investigators who are actually doing the study. It is usually the data analyst, a biostatistician not directly involved in subject interactions, who is responsible for maintaining the firewall. For this study, that person was Beth Bartalak.

It was in another Monday meeting with Cy that Katya broached the subject. Beth hadn't been at these meetings recently which gave Katya the opportunity to raise the issue with her boss.

They met as usual in Cy's opulent office, he enfolded in the maw of his big leather desk chair and she perched on the uncomfortable straight chair opposite him. She was fine with that. Cy's intended purpose of the seating arrangement had no effect on Katya. While she respected the fact that he was her boss, she felt that she was his equal in every other way. Who sat where when they met was irrelevant.

"Is Beth OK?" Katya approached the subject carefully; she did wonder if there was something wrong with Beth other than her excessive devotion to her husband and her obnoxious personality.

"Why do you ask?" Cy leaned forward with his elbows resting on the desk and looked into Katya's face.

"Just wondering. She's in the lab a lot less than usual. I just wondered if something was wrong."

"I don't think so, although she has seemed a bit distracted recently," Cy said.

Maybe Beth had been acting a little strange but he hadn't thought much about it.

Although he was a psychiatrist, Bartalak studiously avoided trying to analyze the behavior of people he was close to. He thought that such a subjective business was hazardous because one couldn't isolate the analytical process from the myriad other factors that influenced how one perceives another person. Beth was Beth as far as he was concerned. He felt no need to understand her beyond that.

"Cy," Katya said, "we really need to talk about the clinical data from this drug study."

She had decided to take this on head first and see where it went. Katya was used to putting all the cards on the table with nothing up her sleeve and felt most comfortable doing business that way. It was a style very different from how Cy went about things which, in his opinion, gave him the upper hand in most circumstances. He heaved a deep sigh, stood up and walked to the window.

"Katya, Katya," he said, "why can't you drop this? The study is essentially done. The data are analyzed. We know the outcome and we're ready to move forward with the drug. Why are you so determined to cause trouble? Let it be, for Christ's sake."

Katya sat without responding as Cy returned to the chair behind his desk. Neither of them spoke for a few minutes and the tension was clear. Finally Katya spoke.

"Cy," she said, looking directly at him, "if there isn't some explanation for the data I retrieved from Beth's computer, there's going to be really big trouble. Whether I'm the one who stirs it up or you leave it to the FDA auditors won't matter in the long run. In fact, if what I suspect is true, you'd be better off discovering it internally and doing something proactive."

Bartalak realized that he was going to have to hear Katya out although he had no intention of doing anything *proactive* that would queer the deal on this drug. There were always glitches in the process of getting a drug through the early phase testing. It would all get sorted out with the phase III studies and by then he and the early investors could have cashed in their chips if things started looking doubtful.

He'd done it before. He knew how to handle this process. Katya was hopelessly naive about how the real world works. He would hear her out and make whatever promises that were necessary to pacify her. But he was on a roll with this drug and nothing was going to stop that. He knew exactly what he was doing.

"OK, Katya," Cy said, "tell me exactly what's troubling you."

Katya cleared her throat and thought for a moment about exactly how to say what she had to say as accurately and dispassionately as possible. She believed that she had credible evidence that at least some of the data from the study had been misrepresented in the analytical summaries that Bartalak had seen and used to hype the drug to current and potential investors.

But this was not a time for histrionics. If there were some explanation she just wanted it clearly stated so that everyone involved understood. If there wasn't, there would be hell to pay no matter when it was discovered or who discovered it.

"I was able to download some of the files of raw data from a couple of subjects in the drug study," Katya started.

"You had no business doing that," Cy interrupted. "I told you to stay away from Beth's computer and you deliberately disobeyed me."

"That's true, Cy," Katya responded, "but hear me out. You may even agree before this is over that the ends justified the means."

"Rarely true, Katya, my dear. Rarely true."

Ignoring him, Katya continued, "At least one of the files I have indicates a severe deterioration in cognitive function and a marked increase in the brain biomarker protein at the six month follow up. From the dates, I think this must have been subject number one which we all know was Bonz Bagley. That would fit with my observations of him and he is the only subject to have undergone the six month follow up tests. While he completed the laboratory tests a week or so before he died, he was killed the day before I would have seen him for the final clinical exam. But,

I've seen no data like his lab tests in any of the summaries that we've reviewed."

There. She had said it.

"So, let's get some things straight here, Katya," Cy said, folding his hands and resting them on the desk in front of him. "You've been after Beth ever since we moved here, haven't you? Are you now telling me that she has fudged the data? I find that impossible to believe and your antagonism toward her makes the accusation even more dubious. Beth has worked with me on drug studies in the past. She knows exactly what she's doing. She knows how to deal with data. She's the data expert, Katya, you're not. And an accusation like this is not going to do anything positive for your career, you know. You're a brilliant neurologist with a bright future and something like this could derail things. You might find it difficult to recover from that."

The threat was thinly veiled. She hadn't expected it, at least not until Cy had looked into matters and had some credible way to defend Beth. His response showed little concern about whether or not what she had told him was true. He seemed only interested in defending his drug, his wife and the process that got them where they were.

It was hard for Katya to believe that a scientist, and Cy was a widely respected medical scientist, was more concerned about appearances than truth. But Cy Bartalak appeared incapable of telling the difference.

"So," Katya responded after enduring Bartalak's diatribe and giving him a chance to settle down a little, "what are you going to do?"

He stood again, and assumed his familiar position profiled against the office window. Katya was again impressed at what an ugly man he was. He seemed to her at that moment even uglier than usual.

"Katya," he said, still looking out the window,

"you have stated your suspicions and I appreciate that. You were of course obligated to make me aware of your concerns."

He walked back to the desk and sat down resuming his folded hands pose and looking directly into Katya's eyes.

"I will follow up on this information in the way I deem appropriate. You will turn over all of the data files that you have to me and forget about them. You are not to mention this to anyone else. You have done your duty and I will do mine. You'll just have to trust me on that."

"What are you going to do?" Katya repeated.

"My job," Cy answered, "and I suggest you do yours."

He was right, of course. Katya knew that as well as he did. But the problem for her was that she didn't trust him to do what she believed needed to be done. Talk about a conflict of interest! He was married to the person who'd done the cheating! There was a viper in his bosom that could very well prove fatal whether or not he was willing to believe it.

Katya wasn't happy with the outcome of this conversation but she wasn't sure what to do about it. She could, of course, lodge a formal charge of scientific misconduct against Beth. But that would trigger an investigation by the university. Those were never pretty sights. A charge against the wife and major collaborator of a department chairman with a national reputation who brought in God knows how much money to the institution would require some pretty incontrovertible evidence to stick.

Regardless of the outcome, Katya wouldn't emerge unscathed. She could very well be a victim of the process no matter how things turned out.

Well, for the time being, she would play by Cy's rules. She would wait to see what he did. She would give him the data files after first making copies for herself.

12

Hardy was tempted to take the back roads west from town out toward Hickman County where his information indicated former Grand Ole Opry star Little Jody Dakota was living out his waning years.

Those roads wound through the low hills that rimmed the city. They wandered through the remnants of villages that had once thrived in a small farm economy and now were wasting away — store fronts abandoned, gas stations left with rusting hand crank pumps that once fueled the internal combustion engines powering the machines that tilled the brown dirt and moved its tillers about the countryside. No longer.

But Hardy had no connection with that past life. He was a city boy and he didn't care to be reminded of his state's decaying rural history. He was vaguely aware of that history but it didn't really concern him.

He maneuvered the big car up the ramp onto the interstate and headed west.

Hardy had called Jody Dakota's home before heading out and the woman who answered the call gave him directions, an interstate exit number and the instructions for navigating the maze of two lane roads leading to the locked gate behind which the former country music star had retreated from the world that promptly forgot him when it ceased to be amused by his antics.

Hardy pulled his standard issue black Crown Vic up to the gate, got out of the car and looked about.

Sunlight filtering through the dense green leafy pall that shrouded the area scattered big white circles of light across the grassy expanse beyond the gate. Hardy was struck with the penetrating silence of the place. He couldn't imagine living so far away from human activity. What would you do out here? Who would there be to talk to? Why in the world would an entertainer choose to hide away in such a remote place, so far removed from the babble and clatter of public life?

Hardy recalled the few summers when he was sent away to an uncle's North Carolina tobacco farm to work where the profound silence kept him awake nights. They weren't pleasant memories. He didn't get the appeal of the rural life. For one thing it was hard work. Granted the part of the city where he grew up had its flaws. It wasn't an elegant upbringing, but it was real. At least that's how Hardy remembered it. He didn't understand the pull of naked land. Connecting with people was what made life worth living. Without those connections what's the point?

On the way out of town, Hardy had stopped off at a Handy Pantry to pick up a cup of coffee for the trip and had yielded to the siren call of a pack of Camels that lay in wait behind the cashier. He had done pretty well with his latest effort to kick the habit over the past week, but the flesh was weak that afternoon.

He took the pack of cigarettes from his jacket pocket, carefully peeled away half of the foil top and tapped the pack against his hand to summon one of the little beauties. He put it to his lips, flicked the red disposable lighter with *Handy Pantry* lettered in white on the side and lit up.

He rested a foot on the car bumper and drew the lovely warm smoke deep into his lungs, holding it there for a few seconds and then slowly exhaling. This would be his last pack, he thought to himself. He meant it this time.

While he smoked, Hardy pondered the case. He was having some second thoughts about involving Shane Hadley. While it made the process more interesting, Hardy feared that Shane was headed in the wrong direction. If the motive was buried in Bonz's long history, then Jody Dakota was a much more likely culprit than Shane's hypothetical young affluent athletic woman, whoever she turned out to be. And Jody's historical penchant for violence, Bagley's at least peripheral connections with the music world, and the fact that the two of them were of a similar vintage, certainly raised the possibility of a motive.

The woman Hardy had spoken to on the phone told him to call when he was at the gate and someone would open it for him. He dropped the cigarette butt, ground it into the dirt with the heel of his comfortable policeman's shoe, pulled his cell phone from an inside jacket pocket and punched in the number.

After a couple of rings, there was a loud buzz, a click and a long low hum as the gate drifted slowly open. He closed the phone, got into the car and wended his way along the rutted dirt track up the short hill to the home of Little Jody Dakota and presumably the youngish sounding woman to whom Hardy had spoken on the phone.

It was an unpretentious house, a one-story bungalow probably dating from the fifties when the style was popular. The house was brick with dark green shutters flanking the windows. The front door opened from a small concrete stoop shaded by a sloping roof. The door was painted an incongruous shade of robin's egg blue that contrasted with the red brick façade and the surrounding greenery.

As he approached the house, Hardy wondered whether he should have brought another officer with him. If this guy really was a murderer, Hardy might be taking more risk than he intended. He had the feeling that a person could disappear out here and nobody would be the wiser.

But the woman on the phone had been amiable

enough, gave him the directions and invited him to, "come on out," said, "Jody'd be glad to talk with you." And now Hardy was past the point of no return. He knew that he was pushing the envelope.

The Metro police had no jurisdiction outside of Davidson County. That's why Hardy came alone. It would have been unwise to involve anyone else. In fact he hadn't told anyone about this little foray into the hinterlands. He was breaking some rules and was entirely on his own. He knew that.

As he got out of the car and walked toward the door, Hardy patted his chest, feeling for the familiar contour of the 40 caliber Glock model 22 in his shoulder holster. It felt solid under his searching hand. He was OK. He had brought a reliable friend who had served him well and wasn't limited by territorial boundaries. He didn't have many friends like that.

To reach the front door, Hardy had to skirt the considerable bulk of an aging *Mary Kay* pink Cadillac parked directly in front of the entrance to the house.

Just as he had a fist poised to knock on the door, it opened suddenly, jerked wide open by a young woman wearing cowboy boots and a red checkered gingham dress, the full skirt billowing up around her tan thighs in the breeze rushing through the opened door.

On closer inspection, the woman was probably not that young, or if so, she had logged more miles than years. Her hair was dyed blonde and needed attention; the dark roots were beginning to show. Although her face was smooth and tan, the skin had that too taut appearance that reeks of plastic surgery or botox or whatever was the current method of choice was for smoothing over the ravages of age and sun and cigarette smoke.

She smiled at Hardy, exposing a perfect set of

abnormally white and unnaturally straight teeth. But it was a nice friendly smile. Hardy relaxed some.

"Good afternoon, sir," Miss Teeth greeted Hardy. "You must be the detective that called. Is that right?"

"Yes'm," Hardy answered, removing his wallet from his coat pocket and flipping it open to expose the badge. "My name is Hardy Seltzer. I'd like to talk to Mr. Dakota if I may."

"Sure, honey," she said, "I'm Bunny Waller," extending her hand with a little curtsy, "and you don't need to be so proper, you know. Just call him Jody. We're just plain country folk, you know."

Hardy shook her hand. It was small and smooth. And very cold. Maybe Bunny Waller was plain country folk as she claimed, but Hardy seriously doubted that most plain country folk had benefitted from the services of plastic surgeons and orthodontists. No matter. He wasn't interested in Bunny Waller, whoever she was. Unless she had something to do with the subject at hand, her only function was to get him connected with Jody Dakota.

"OK, Bunny," Hardy said, trying without complete success to suppress a smile. "Can you let Jody know I'm here?"

"Sure," she said, "but he may be down back at the shooting range, I'm not sure. Come on in and I'll find him."

"Shooting range?" Hardy said.

"Yep," Bunny replied, "Jody loves guns. Always has, long as I've known him. He set up a shooting range down in the back. He practices there with those guns a lot." She gestured toward an upholstered leather sofa. "Come on in and sit down here on the couch, Hardy. Can I get you something to drink?"

"No, thanks," he replied.

He was imagining Little Jody Dakota practicing his marksmanship at his private and very remote

Hickman County shooting range.

"Suit yourself, hon," she said.

As Bunny Waller walked the length of the long living room toward the back of the house, the unmistakable sounds of gunfire echoed in the distance. Hardy was distracted by the sound so that the slightly odd way Bunny walked barely registered somewhere in deep recesses of his brain. He wasn't interested in Bunny Waller, whoever she was.

After Bunny was gone from the room, Hardy got up from the sofa and wandered around. The space was long and narrow running the width of the house. At the far end of the room, Hardy encountered a display case that contained several handguns.

He took the picture of the Colt Hammer model that he had printed out from the Internet from his jacket pocket and smoothed it out on top of the case. He eyed each of the six guns in the case, his eyes moving back and forth between each gun and the picture. One of the guns in the case at the edge of the arrangement looked to him exactly like the one in the picture.

"You into guns, sonny?"

Hardy's muscles tensed at the sound of the voice from behind him. Concentrating on the gun comparisons, he hadn't heard the two people enter the room. He picked up the picture of the gun, refolded it and returned it to his coat pocket as he turned to face Bunny Waller and a strikingly small leathery-faced man probably in his seventies wearing a very large white Stetson hat.

Jody Dakota was short and also slightly built. The moniker *Little Jody Dakota* seemed especially appropriate. The small man moved easily though, the quick, sharp movements of a wary animal on the lookout. His dark eyes darted about, not fixing on anything in particular.

Bunny's eyes were fixed on Jody, following his every move with more interest, it appeared, than affection. Maybe Bunny deserved more attention than Hardy had thought on their first meeting. He noticed now a certain grace in her manner. And he just now noticed that Bunny Waller had very large breasts, unnaturally large for her petite frame, perfectly symmetrical mounds created, no doubt, by the same skilled professional who had ironed away the wrinkles in her face.

Hardy didn't immediately respond to Jody's question and the small man strode toward him extending a hand.

"I'm Jody Dakota," he said. "Just call me Jody. And who are you?"

Hardy shook Jody's hand briefly, feeling the surprisingly firm grip of the small hand.

"As I told Miss Waller," Hardy replied, "… er … Bunny," he corrected himself, still not entirely comfortable with the invited familiarity, "my name is Hardy Seltzer. I'm a detective with the Metropolitan Nashville Police Department."

Once again he brandished his wallet and flipped it open to reveal the badge. Jody bent forward, eyeing the badge carefully, scratching his chin as though he were registering the exact details of each word and image.

After what seemed an inordinate amount of time scrutinizing the badge, he straightened back up and looked at Hardy.

"Well, detective Hardy," Jody said, emphasizing the given name to make it clear that the familiarity was deliberate, "what in the world brings you way out here? You're a city cop. Thought surely we'd escaped the attention of the city's finest this far out from town."

Hardy thought the word *escaped* seemed odd, but

maybe he was influenced too much by his suspicion and by his need to solve this riddle as soon as possible. Hardy wasn't comfortable with the situation. He was out of his element in more ways than one and anxious to get down to the business at hand. All this affected bonhomie was not to his liking.

"I'm ...," Hardy started to speak but Jody interrupted.

"What brings you here, detective Hardy?" Jody said. "Can't imagine why you'd come way out here unless you had a good reason. Sit down, sit down," he said, motioning toward the sofa where Hardy had sat earlier. "Can Bunny get you something to drink?"

Hardy didn't sit down but both Jody and Bunny did. Jody removed his hat to reveal a largely bald head, tan and shiny, rimmed by a fringe of gray. Because of the size of the hat, it wasn't clear until he removed it that Jody had a very large head, out of proportion to his small body. Hardy thought of the cartoons of Humpty Dumpty that appear in children's' books and wondered whether Jody too was headed for a great fall that would shatter this carefully crafted illusion of bucolic bliss. Hardy couldn't help but hope that that was true.

"No thanks," Hardy replied. "She offered earlier. I would just like to ask you a few questions if that's alright."

"Questions about what?" Jody said.

"Well, I'm investigating the Printers Alley murder of Bonz Bagley," Hardy said, "And "

"That stingy bastard!" Jody interrupted. "I saw it in the paper. Couldn't help but laugh when I read it. Somebody should have killed the bastard a long time ago. Id've done it myself if I'd had the balls. Pardon my language, honey." He turned to Bunny and patted her bare knee.

Bunny crossed her arms beneath her very large

breasts and smiled as though the subject of male genitalia was neither unfamiliar nor offensive to her.

Shocked at Jody's outburst, Hardy responded, "That's an interesting reaction, Jody. Most people I've talked with seem to have been fond of Mr. Bagley."

"Well, you just ain't talkin to the right folks," Jody said. "For every person Bonz helped there are a dozen he did a heap o' harm to. I happen to be one that survived it, but a lot didn't."

"When was the last time you saw Mr. Bagley?" Hardy asked.

"You mean saw him or talked with him?"

"Well, either one."

"Oh, I've seen him when I go downtown which is pretty rare lately. That is, seen him sitting out there in the alley acting like a big shot. He never was a big shot. He was barely a shot at all, hangin' on the coattails of some folks with talent and livin' off their leavings."

"But when was the last time?"

"Bunny and me went into town a week or so ago. On a Sunday. I was meetin' with a guy who wants to write a book about the business and he's interviewin' a bunch of us old-timers. He might've even talked to Bonz. Wouldn't doubt it. We didn't see Bonz when we was there though, didn't even go near the alley. We was meetin' with this guy at the fancy hotel out by the university and we just met, and then came back home. I don't like the city anymore. It ain't the same as it was and ain't better for it. Come to think of it, we was probably in town the same day Bonz got himself killed. Wouldn't that be funny?"

"What time did you go into town on that Sunday?" Hardy asked.

Bunny answered, "Early. We went in early so Jody could have pancakes for breakfast."

"I love them pancakes," Jody said. "There's a

place out on Hillsboro Road makes the best flapjacks I ever ate. Big fluffy things. They mak'em with buckwheat flour and they get some country butter from somebody local, and red clover honey? Makes my mouth water just thinkin' about'em."

Jody chuckled but Hardy wasn't laughing. Bunny and Jody began to sense the growing tension in the room.

No one spoke for a few minutes.

Hardy was letting the potential significance of the developing information sink in for both him and the other two. On the one hand, if these were the guilty parties, it would be very unlikely that they would so readily provide both a motive and an opportunity for the crime. On the other hand, maybe these two were cleverer than they wanted to appear. Volunteering this information could be a strategy for hiding their guilt. Hardy had seen criminals use that approach before. It worked sometimes.

Presently, Bunny spoke, "Whoa, now detective," she said, "you're not thinking we had something to do with this?"

Hardy put on his game face, looked directly in her eyes and responded, "If I didn't think that was a possibility I wouldn't be here."

"That's ridiculous," Jody said, standing up and pacing about, thumping the white Stetson against his thigh, "totally ridiculous. I made peace with all that old stuff a long time ago. Hell, you can ask anybody about that. Like I said, if I'd had the balls I might have done it a long time ago, but I'm too old to get riled up about that history now. And too content. Ain't that right, Bunny?"

Hardy didn't think that Jody Dakota looked like a contented man. Too restless. And his hard, dark eyes darted about, the wary look of a man who might well be hiding something.

Jody walked over and sat down next to Bunny again. He patted her bare knee. She smiled as contented a smile as she could muster. Whatever it was that attracted Bunny to this man and this remote life style, Hardy doubted that it was contentment. He very much doubted that.

Sitting there together, they did not look like the contented happy couple they were attempting to portray. Hardy was developing more of an interest in the woman. If there was something hidden there it probably involved them both.

"Let's talk about guns," Hardy said, ignoring their comments. "Mr. Bagley was shot with a very unusual gun and I was noticing before you came in that there are some very unusual guns in the display case over there," he said, pointing toward the far end of the room.

"I like guns," Jody replied. "So does Bunny. I used to collect some unusual ones back when I had the money for it. Them's the ones in the case there. They're show pieces. We don't shoot them. Too damn expensive. And where on God's earth would you find ammunition for them? Wouldn't be easy. We shoot newer guns at my shootin' range out back. Bunny here's a really good shot." He looked at Bunny who smiled again.

"I see," Hardy said. "The gun that killed Bonz was a really rare one. A Colt hammer model 1903 made in the early nineteen hundreds. Sound familiar?"

"Sure. That was in the paper. I've got one of those. Got a dealer to locate it for me a while back. Found it in Texas as I remember. Mine is a beauty, a really rare one, gold plated, engraved too."

Hardy had been impressed with the gleaming gold gun when he first saw it. Especially impressed with how much it resembled the gold plated "All

American" 1903 hammer model Colt pistol in the picture from the Internet. According to the Internet piece, it was an extremely rare collector's item.

Jody continued, "Cost me better than ten grand when I bought it. Came with an official certificate, too. It's there in the display case. But it didn't kill Bonz or anyone else, at least not since I've had it. Bunny keeps those guns cleaned up good, but none of 'em's been fired in ten or fifteen years."

"Then you won't mind if I take it in for ballistics testing."

Hardy knew that he was on thin ice here. If Jody would voluntarily surrender the gun for testing, ballistics ought to be able to determine for certain whether it was the weapon that fired the slugs recovered from Bagley's body. If so, there could be a pretty airtight case—motive, opportunity and the murder weapon.

But, Hardy couldn't force Jody to surrender the gun. To do that he would have to go through the county sheriff. And God only knew who that was. Probably some good old boy who had doled out enough Jack Daniels on election day to corral the necessary votes. And Jody Dakota was probably the most famous resident of Hickman County. It wouldn't be surprising if he was bosom buddies with the sheriff.

Jody got up and paced back and forth in front of the sofa, staring at the floor and rubbing his chin, thinking.

"What good's that going to do me?" Jody mumbled.

Hardy responded, "Well, if the tests show that your gun wasn't the murder weapon, you'd be free and clear, don't you see?"

"I'm not sure about that," Jody said, sitting down again by Bunny and massaging her knee. "That's a very expensive firearm, detective Hardy. I'm not sure I'm willing to trust you with it. And what if the test, I think you called it bombastics or somethin', makes a mistake? I mean, I know for sure that my gun didn't kill Bonz. I don't care what your test shows. I know that for a fact. Hell, we don't even have any bullets for it. Except for when Bunny takes them out for cleanin', those guns have sat in that display case for fifteen years. Just sat there lookin' pretty and doin' nothin'."

"Then," Hardy answered, "I don't see the problem. Since you know it wasn't your gun, let us prove that and we'll all be happy."

Bunny broke in, "Hell, Jody," she said, "let him take the damn thing. We don't need this hassling from the cops and he's obviously going to keep at it unless we do what he wants. Detective," she continued, turning her attention to Hardy, "how long will it take to do the test?"

"Yeah," Jody said, "how long? And where are you goin' to get any bullets for it? I don't think they make'em anymore."

"I don't know for sure, but it shouldn't take long. The ballistics guys have their sources. They can get the bullets."

Only after a lengthy discussion of the matter did Jody and Bunny agree to let Hardy take the gun. Hardy watched as Bunny walked the length of the room to the display case, retrieved a key from a drawer in an adjacent cabinet, unlocked the case and carefully removed the weapon. She placed it in a purple velvet bag also retrieved from the adjacent cabinet and brought it to Hardy placing it gently in his hand. Hardy wrote out a detailed receipt for them and handed them the receipt and one of his business cards.

"OK," Hardy said, "my contact information is on the card. If you have any questions feel free to call. As soon as we have the results, I'll get in touch. In the meantime, you should stay close in case we need to talk again."

"We sure as hell ain't goin' anywhere, not as long as you've got my gun. Just get this thin' over with and done," Jody said.

Hardy was troubled as he drove back into the city, the velvet sheathed golden gun resting on the seat beside him. He desperately wanted to wrap up this case and he wanted to believe that he was close. But, either Jody Dakota was unaware of the power of ballistics testing or this gun was probably not the weapon that killed Bonz Bagley. Otherwise, why did they let him take it?

Or were these two yokels a lot cleverer than they wanted him to believe? Little Jody Dakota was a performer, after all, or had been. Hardy had often thought that people didn't *become* performers, they were born that way. It was something in the blood that didn't go away with age or loss of fame. How else do you explain the has-beens and no-talents who kept at it when there was no longer any hope for money or fame? How do you even explain the continued existence of places like Printers Alley? Must be a compulsion.

Were Little Jody Dakota and his friend Bunny doing that dance for Hardy's sake? Still shaking it for the paying customers.

13

There were six floors of six thousand square feet each in the building where Shane and KiKi lived. Each floor had a separate owner so that there were six owners and, therefore, six representatives on the building's condo association board.

The board met quarterly as specified in its bylaws. They met in the third floor conference room of one of the lawyer owners, a location Shane thought of on those occasions as the *belly of the beast*, a facetious tribute to the six-six-six symbolism. In fact there were usually no more than five people at the meetings; Rory Holcomb rarely showed up.

Shane represented the second floor since he was always there and KiKi was usually at work when the meetings took place. He didn't relish venturing up to the next floor and into the belly of the beast; not because he harbored any superstitions about the symbol, but because there was rarely anything of substance that transpired at the meetings and he wasn't particularly fond of the other owners. In truth, having explored Dr. Conan Doyle's eerie spiritualism as part of his research at Oxford, Shane was somewhat amused by the six-six-six symbolism.

It was late afternoon when Shane rolled his wheelchair off the elevator on the third floor and was confronted by Rory Holcomb sitting just outside the belly of the beast waiting for the others to arrive for the meeting. This was to be one of the rare meetings when the third six would roll up—the spiritual jackpot.

Shane and Rory nodded to each other as the rotund figure of the third floor lawyer emerged from his office and invited them to join him in the conference room.

"The others should be here shortly," the lawyer

said. Speaking to Rory, he continued, "What do you make of Bonz's murder, Rory? Not good PR for the alley."

"Probably right," Rory responded, "probably right. Although more adventurous folks might think it adds some cache to the place. The alley could use a little polishing of its cache, don't you think?"

Shane interjected, "Who do you think could have done it, Rory? You're more knowledgeable about this place and its history than anyone else I know of."

"True, true, Shane," Rory responded. "I've been around here a while. I'll tell you what. I have no idea who did it but if I was a betting man, I'd put some serious money on Jody Dakota."

Shane was shocked and a few seconds passed before he responded, "Jody Dakota? You mean Little Jody Dakota, the old country music personality? Why in the world do you think it he might have done it?"

"Yeah," Rory said, "that's right. Little Jody Dakota. He'd be high on the list in my book although I have no idea why he would have waited so long."

"What's the story, Rory?" Shane asked, smiling at the unintended rhyme.

"OK, yeah, there is always a story isn't there. The story goes back, oh must be close to forty years now, when they were planning that old TV show that made fun of the country music folks. Jody Dakota was all set to be the star. The show was going to be silly and Little Jody Dakota was a novelty act, silliness was squarely in Jody's sweet spot. And he was looking for his big break.

"This would have been his ticket to the big time — national exposure, fame, maybe even fortune. At least that's what Jody thought. And apparently they were all ready to do the deal when the producers of the show had a sudden change of heart. They dropped Jody like a hot potato and signed up a singer and a guitar player to preside over *Kuntry Kuzzins* and its ridiculous bunch of characters, including Bonz. Turned out to be a good decision, most folks think. The show was a real hit on TV for a couple of years."

The lawyer had propped his feet up on the table and was listening intently to Rory's monologue; he asked "So how does that explain fingering Jody Dakota as Bonz's killer?"

"Well," Rory said, "I don't know whether it's true, but Jody thought that Bonz was responsible for nixing the deal for him. Jody said that Bonz told the producers that he was an unreliable and sometimes violent drunk who couldn't be trusted. Now, fact is, that was pretty much true in those days, but I don't know if Bonz was responsible for nixing Jody's deal. Jody sure thought so, though. I personally heard Jody threaten to kill Bonz back then. More than once. But I figured he was just blowing off, especially since he didn't actually do it. Well, maybe that sore's been festering all these years and he finally got up the gumption to go through with it."

Shane registered the information, storing it with the accumulation of confusing data in the *Devil's Foot* file in his brain. But he just couldn't believe the case would be so easily solved. Shane had rarely seen a murder that easily solved unless there were eye witnesses or the perpetrator was caught in the act. Crime solving wasn't such a simple undertaking in the vast majority of cases. Had the process been simple, it wouldn't have interested him. And in this case there were too many unanswered questions.

Shane couldn't ignore this new information and he would have to share it with Hardy Seltzer. But he feared it would only reinforce Hardy's bias, close his mind to any alternative. The mind must always remain receptive to new information until the case comes to an absolute and incontrovertible conclusion.

And this case was a long way from an incontrovertible conclusion.

There were too many examples of overly anxious prosecutors, hell-bent on getting a conviction, who ignored or even concealed evidence that didn't fit their developing story. Shane didn't like lawyers very much. He had frequently clashed with the prosecutors when he was on the force. In his experience, once the lawyers thought they had a coherent story that they could sell to a jury, they closed their minds, and the sooner they could get to that point the happier they were.

Shane thought that Hardy Seltzer was too good a detective to buy in to that approach, but he didn't know for sure. And in Shane's opinion, Hardy was already too focused on Jody Dakota. Granted, that lead had to be followed up, but there might yet be other possibilities that would emerge. Do everything possible to rule out Jody Dakota as the killer and see who was left.

Shane still thought that who would be left was likely to be a woman with an odd running gait.

When Hardy Seltzer arrived back at the station, it was almost five o'clock. He was anxious to get the gun to ballistics before Peter Harvey left for the day. Harvey was the man he wanted to do the work with this gun. He was the senior guy in ballistics and exactly the man for this job. Hardy wanted to be sure that the job didn't get shuttled off to one of the newer people and so decided to deliver it personally to Harvey.

Hardy parked the car in the garage, picked up the velvet cloaked rare golden gun and made his way to the elevator. He punched the button marked SB, instructing the car to descend to the sub-basement, the lowest level of the building, deep under the city's court house square. That was where Harvey and his minions plied their craft.

Peter Harvey was approaching seventy now and had been in ballistics for over forty years. There wasn't much about guns, especially hand guns, that he didn't know. Although he was uniformly addressed with great deference to his face as Mr. Harvey, a practice that he encouraged, he was known on other occasions as either Pistol Pete or Peter Gun (sans the redundant n of the old TV detective). But in person he was Mr. Harvey, the Metropolitan Police Department's senior ballistics expert who had earned the respect of everyone in the department from the chief on down. Harvey accepted that respect with the confidence of a man satisfied that he was the best there was at what he did.

"Good afternoon, Mr. Harvey," Hardy said as he entered the windowless room.

Harvey was sitting at one of the several workbenches that filled the large room. He was hunched over a piece of equipment that looked like two large microscopes fused together creating a mechanical equivalent of Siamese twins. Harvey was a small, pale, balding man whose neck and head appeared to be permanently angled forward, perhaps a result of the countless hours he had spent hunched over the various pieces of equipment that were his stock in trade, staring at small pieces of metal and pondering their encoded messages.

Without looking up, Harvey answered, "Greetings, Detective Seltzer."

Neither of them spoke for a few minutes as Harvey continued his intense concentration on whatever he was looking at under his Siamese twin microscopes. Hardy and everyone else who had any dealings with the ballistics expert knew better than to interrupt him when he was at work. In fact, Harvey concentrated so intensely on the task at hand that it was difficult to interrupt him even if you tried.

Hardy didn't try. He stood patiently by the doorway, caressing the velvet clad rare pistol and waited for Harvey's invitation to continue the conversation. Hardy didn't mind waiting for things that were worth waiting for.

Finally Harvey looked up from the microscope and said, "What can I do for you, detective?"

"Well, Mr. Harvey," Hardy replied, "I may have here the murder weapon in the Bonz Bagley case. And I'm hoping that you can tell me if that's true."

"If you have it, there's a good chance," Harvey said. "Let's see what you've got."

Harvey got up from his seat at the work bench and Hardy walked over and handed him the gun. Harvey took it out of the velvet pouch and held it, eyeing it from all angles as he moved it about in his hand. He held it up pointing toward the ceiling, removed the clip, eyed it and then snapped it back in place.

Finally, Harvey said, "Could be, detective, could be. It's indeed a Colt Hammer model 1903, and a special edition ,too. That fits with the slugs we got from the body."

"Can you be definitive, Mr. Harvey?"

"Have to do ballistics to be sure."

"Any problem with that?"

"Well," Harvey said, "the only problem I can think of is the ammunition. This gun uses a very unusual kind of cartridge that is no longer manufactured. They're probably available on the collector's market."

"Is that a problem?"

"Yes and no," Harvey replied. "Assuming I can

get permission to spend the money I'm sure I can get a few rounds which should be sufficient for the tests. But it may take a while."

"How long?" Hardy asked.

"Probably a few days. I doubt there'll be a hold up on authorizing the expense since the case is so high profile. Then I'll have to locate a vendor and get the stuff sent here. I can have it done next-day delivery. And once I get the ammo, I'll give the test priority."

"That's great," Hardy said. "That's great."

"Here," said Harvey, "we'll need to do the paperwork to sign the gun in. You'll have to vouch for it."

Harvey went to his desk near the wall, opened a drawer and took out several forms. He laid them at a work station and motioned to Hardy who sat down and started doing the paperwork. He was familiar with paperwork.

It was paperwork that caused Shane Hadley to ponder the significance of *Jergensen's Rare Guns'* sale of another Colt Hammer Model 1903.

The rare gun dealer kept meticulous paper records of its sales and when Shane called to inquire about this specific gun, it took John Jergensen Jr., the current proprietor of the shop, only a few minutes search through his files to identify those sales. The dealer's records indicated that they had sold only two of the rare pistol. One was to the Nashville dealer. The other was to a small town Texas lawyer with whom they had done business on previous occasions.

The two sales were within a couple of days of each other several years earlier. It was John Jergensen Sr. who had made the sales. Jergensen Sr. had died five years ago when his son took over the business.

While Jergensen Jr. had no personal recollection of the transactions, he was confident of the accuracy of the records. His father was a compulsive record keeper, a trait which his son was proud to perpetuate.

Shane was of course gratified by the confirmation of the history of the gun that wound up in the possession of Little Jody Dakota, but that was just confirmation, nothing new. For some reason that he could not readily explain, Shane was even more interested in the small town lawyer who apparently owned the gun's identical twin. Shane's experience told him that no information was irrelevant until proven so by thorough investigation. And it was the seemingly spurious information that most intrigued him.

He recalled a quote from an Oxford science professor that went something like, "results that tell you what you already know are confirming, but unexpected results are the seeds discovery."

Shane feared that Hardy Seltzer was so fixed on Jody Dakota as the killer that Hardy would ignore information that didn't support his suspicions. But, Shane Hadley did not ignore information.

Shane wheeled himself over to the bar, refilled his glass of Lincoln College Sherry, picked up his laptop and rolled out onto the deck. A dark angry cloud hid the sun and the alley took on an especially seedy appearance in the afternoon gloom. The gray pall that settled over the alley on afternoons like this depressed Shane. The last thing he needed was to allow into his head the encroaching darkness that could threaten to breach the wall he had built to contain the black internal cloud lurking at the edge of his mind. He had done everything he could to keep that cloud at bay but it was still there. He gathered up his sherry and computer and wheeled himself back inside.

Shane fired up the computer and clicked on the browser icon. He typed in, *Archibald Stewart Reid Greensward Texas* and hit search. The top match was almost perfect and routed him to a newspaper site, *The Greensward Weekly,* and an obituary for an Archibald Reid from a few years back.

It read in part: *Archibald Stewart Reid, prominent local citizen and noted criminal defense lawyer, died of complications of Alzheimer's disease at the Greensward Home for the Infirm. His health had deteriorated over the past several years. He is survived by his only child, Elizabeth Anne Reid, of Houston.*

There were some brief comments about his law career but not much more. Shane thought how readily a few years of dementia could obscure whatever went before that in the public memory.

He paged back to the search screen and typed in *Elizabeth Anne Reid Houston Texas.* There were several hundred hits with the surname spelled either Reed or Reid and with the middle name with or without the terminal *e.*

He had no idea what he was looking for but started scanning through the entries. Nothing he saw attracted his attention and he quickly lost interest. As he closed the laptop he was startled by a crash of thunder and the dull thud of heavy raindrops pounding on the metal roof that covered the balcony outside.

The dark clouds shadowing the alley before the rain came threatened to depress Shane but a full blown thunderstorm excited him. He loved to sit on the balcony under cover of the metal roof and relish the sensations, the rhythmic staccato thrum of heavy raindrops pounding the tin roof and the ozone laced smell of fresh rain.

He wheeled out onto the deck and forgetting for a while about dead men, strange guns, country music

154

has-beens and small town Texas lawyers, he settled back and enjoyed Mother Nature's grand performance. He sat there, entranced by the storm until the rain died down and he heard the throaty moan of KiKi's Porsche entering the alley from Church Street.

He wheeled back into the living room and waited for KiKi. There was the familiar low rumble of the garage door, the sound of the closing car door, the mechanical rustle of the elevator. She emerged from the elevator into their living room, walked to Shane and kissed him the warm soft kiss that daily fed his addiction to this brilliant and beautiful woman.

"I love you, KiKi," Shane said.

"How much?" she asked, flashing her electric smile.

Shane answered, "A lot."

14

The protocol for the clinical study of the experimental Alzheimer's drug, RX-01, required that each test subject have a full battery of tests before being assigned randomly to receive either a placebo or the drug. The tests were then repeated at monthly intervals for three months and a final test battery done at six months, the conclusion of the study.

The placebo and drug pills appeared identical and were coded by the research pharmacy so that no one directly involved in the study knew which pill a given subject was receiving. The code was kept securely by the research pharmacist and would not be broken until the study was completed or stopped for one of any number of reasons that would dictate that the study be concluded. Likewise, the test results were known only to the biostatistician who would not know which medication the subjects had received until the code was broken.

That is how clinical trials of new drugs were supposed to work.

However, when Beth Bartalak analyzed the data from the first three months of the first study subject, she was positive that he must have received the active drug. There were such dramatic improvements in the tests of cognitive function it was impossible to believe that this was a placebo effect. And there were also marked decreases in the blood protein that Cy believed was an accurate indicator of disease activity. The changes were so large, that they could not be due to random fluctuations in the course of Alzheimer's; the course never fluctuated that much in a positive direction ... never.

When Beth told her husband about the results, he was as excited as she was. He was so excited that he arranged a lunch meeting with his three angel investors and reported the results to them. Beth had also been present at the luncheon although she and Cy arrived separately; she drove into town from their home in Belle Meade and he came directly from his office at the university.

Cy had arranged the lunch in a private room at the Capitol Grille, an elegant restaurant that he favored on the lower level of The Hermitage, a venerable downtown hotel. The hotel had been restored a few years back to the grandeur that had attracted Andrew Jackson and other historical notables as clients in another time. While Cy was not a student of Tennessee political history, he chose the venue for this meeting after carefully considering what might impress his guests.

Cy arrived early and looked over the room. They had set up the screen and a laptop computer was positioned beside his place at the head of the table, as he'd requested. He fired up the computer, took the flash drive from his pocket and clicked it into the USB port. He had made only a couple of PowerPoint slides and flashed them onto the screen to be sure things worked correctly. They did and he switched off the computer. He was happy with the arrangements.

Mitchell Rook, Rory Holcomb and Will Hadley arrived together and Beth was only a few minutes behind them. Cy hurried through the obligatory greetings, anxious to get everybody seated so that he could share the exciting information about the first test subject.

Of course he knew that early results on a single subject without knowing for sure whether the subject was taking placebo or drug were nowhere near conclusive. But he also knew from experience that guys like these investors were inordinately impressed by dramatic anecdotes presented with enthusiasm and he had a doozy for them.

"Gentlemen ..." Cy tinkled a spoon against his glass to quiet the conversations. "...and lady, I should add," he said, gesturing toward Beth. "I have some very good news for you. The clinical trials of RX-01 are on track and looking good so far.

"But the reason I asked you here today was to tell you the results from the first three months of the study in the first subject. I must preface this by making sure that you know that this is very preliminary yet and it is data from a single subject. Also, the placebo-drug code will not be broken until after all of the subjects have completed the protocol so, technically, we don't really know for sure whether this first subject was getting drug or placebo. However, with those caveats "

"Damn!" Rory Holcomb boomed, "with all those conditions I don't see how you can be so excited. I don't see how you can make anything out of whatever information you've got, no matter what it is."

He looked around the table. The others nodded tentatively but didn't say anything. What appeared to be a wry smile crossed Mitchell Rook's face. Cy noticed that, but a wry smile was Mitchell Rook's default expression so that Cy wasn't sure whether Rook was reacting to the conversation or not. Cy had thought for a while that he should keep a closer eye on the dapper lawyer.

"You know, Rory," Cy responded, "ordinarily I'd agree with you, but these results are truly extraordinary, like nothing I've ever seen. And I've been dealing with Alzheimer's patients for almost twenty years now. Bear with me for a few minutes, Rory. You may find yourself sharing some of my excitement."

Cy switched on the laptop and Beth, on cue, got up from her chair and dimmed the lights in the room. The multicolored slide was titled *Cognitive Function*

Over 3 Months in a Single Patient With Moderately Severe Alzheimer's Disease. The figure was a line graph that ascended dramatically from its starting point, forming an essentially straight line connecting the dots at baseline with the progressively higher dots at one, two and three months.

Cy didn't speak for several seconds, just stood apparently mesmerized, staring at the graph. The others also stared at the graph, although they appeared less rapt than their host.

Finally, Cy said, "You will pardon me gentlemen if I seem to get emotional about this, but understand, these results are unique. Such dramatic improvements in brain function just don't happen in this disease. Not only am I certain that this subject was taking RX-01, but I am tempted to believe that the drug may not only stabilize the disease as we thought from the animal studies. Gentlemen, RX-01 could be a cure for Alzheimer's disease. I don't need to spell out what that means for human suffering and, of course, for the market value of the drug."

He advanced to the next slide. It was a similar graph except the changes it showed were in the concentrations of a blood protein that Cy maintained was a biochemical marker of Alzheimer's disease activity. This line plummeted from the baseline value through months one and two to near zero at month three.

Cy said, "These biomarker results are entirely consistent with the improvements in cognitive function. This fortunate gentleman may be the first person in human history to be cured of this dreadful disease."

He switched off the computer. Beth got up from her chair and raised the lights again. The melodramatic presentation quieted the group for a few minutes.

At last, Will Hadley said, "Well, Cy, this is indeed exciting. But aren't you overdoing it a bit? Shouldn't we wait for some more results before getting so overheated? I mean, this subject still has three more months in the study and his final six month data will be critical. Not to mention results from the other subjects."

"Of course, you're entirely correct, Will. I apologize if I've gotten carried away about this. But it is just that I have never seen anything like it before. And the possibility of a cure, I mean a cure! Well if I'm overreacting, please indulge me a bit. Time will tell."

"So, Cy," Mitchell Rook said, "when will you move on this, start trolling for big pharma interest? Waiting for more results is a risk. If what you've shown us isn't supported by the additional studies, the value of our investment may be at its peak right now."

"Damn straight," Rory Holcomb interjected, "damn straight, Cy. What do you plan to do? How can we realize something out of this, something real and green?"

"Well," Bartalak responded, "here is what I suggest. If this subject's six month data continue to show such dramatic improvements, I'll take the data to the DSMB "

Rory interrupted, "What in hell is the DSMB?"

Cy answered, "Sorry, Rory. That's the Data Safety Monitoring Board. It's a group of experts who have to approve any move like this. They can be a pain, but they're necessary."

"If you say so," Rory grumbled.

Bartalak continued, "I'll see whether the board will agree to breaking the code for this subject and whether they might be inclined to start thinking about stopping the study early because of the strikingly beneficial effects. That would depend on results from other subjects as well, but if we could do that we'd be sitting pretty with big pharma negotiations."

"So," Rory said, "this guy's six month results will decide the thing?"

"Yes," Cy answered, "well, those and the results from the other subjects. Those will be coming along over the next few months as well."

"A whole lot riding on this guy's six month tests," Rory mused aloud, scanning the faces of the others.

Rory's gaze paused at Beth as their eyes met for a moment.

Three months later when Beth first saw the results of the final studies on subject number one, that lunch meeting was still clear in her mind. Although she had shared Cy's excitement at the time, she thought he went overboard in the presentation. She didn't question that, of course. Cy would not have liked having his judgment questioned and Beth did not do things that she knew would displease her husband. But Beth was very uncomfortable with that lunch meeting.

As a result of that meeting she had been anxious to see the six month results from the first subject. When she first saw the data she was shocked and confused about what course she should take. Because of the way the study was structured, Beth was the only person who had access to the data and could connect it with a specific study subject.

The six month studies on subject number one showing marked deterioration in cognitive function and a marked increase in the blood protein that indicated disease activity were her private knowledge. She agonized about what to do with that knowledge.

Beth pondered her dilemma as she ran through Warner Park early in the afternoon. Dark clouds hovered overhead and a warm, soft rain clattered gently through the leafy canopy. Birds tittered among themselves oblivious to the lone figure intruding on their private space.

Beth liked running in the rain. She relished the feeling of solitude that the rain lent to the experience. And the cleansing sensation of fresh water falling from the heavens washing over her. The exertion and the cleansing rain purged her body and cleared her mind.

As she ran, she remembered something her father often said about rules. "Rules," he'd said, "are arbitrary. They are not boundaries, but just the place where you begin negotiations." Beth liked that idea. And even Cy had said many times that smart people create their own reality. "Perception is reality," was a favored mantra of his.

It would not be difficult for Beth to create a favorable perception of how subject number one had responded to the drug. She had exclusive control of the data. She could just replicate the three month data with enough modifications to make it credible and present those as the results from the final six month studies. Cy need not know about her little ruse.

He wouldn't question the data. What was it he said, "Don't ask questions if you don't want to know the answers"? He wouldn't question results that confirmed his expectations. And he trusted her. She was sure of that. Trusted her to see that his expectations were realized. She wouldn't disappoint him.

But if subject number one really was deteriorating as badly as the tests indicated, that was likely to be discovered. That bitch Katya Karpov was responsible for the final clinical examination and for following the subjects after conclusion of the formal study. She would surely recognize the situation. If this really was a delayed toxic effect of the drug on the brain, it would be impossible to hide forever.

Of course it was only necessary to maintain the perception long enough to cash in on the investment. Whatever happened after that was immaterial. But if Cy was to cash in, he would have to know the real situation before anyone else did. And Beth knew that Cy needed plausible deniability. She could manage that.

As she loped down the hill toward the park gate, a brilliant flash of lightning illuminated the park's green expanse and a crash of thunder ushered in a sudden torrential downpour. She picked up her pace, sprinting face-on into the driving rain down the boulevard to their home and collapsing breathless in her wet clothes in the foyer. As she sat there, her breath coming in short gasps, she decided what she had to do. It was subject number one's brain that was the problem.

Beth still sat on the foyer floor, pondering her next move when the ringing phone interrupted her thoughts. She was tempted to ignore the phone, but after several rings decided to answer it.

"Bartalak residence," she said.

"Beth," a vaguely familiar voice responded, "This is Rory Holcomb. How are you?"

Beth assumed that Holcomb must want to speak with Cy for some reason; she said, "Oh, hi Rory. I'm fine, thanks. But Cy isn't here just now."

"Actually I wanted to talk to you, Beth."

"Me?"

"Does that surprise you?"

"Yes, it does, Rory. What did you want to talk

about?"

"Well, Beth," Rory answered, "it's been about three months since that lunch meeting where Cy was so worked up about the results from the first subject in the drug study. I was wondering whether the follow up studies were done yet. And I figured that you were the person who would be most likely to have that information. Thought it might be best to get the info directly. Your husband can get a little heavy with the sales pitch. And it seems there's a lot riding on those results. What can you tell me?"

Beth didn't respond immediately. Damn, she thought. She wasn't going to tell Rory or anyone else anything about those results. Probably not even Cy. She was going to take care of that situation herself.

Finally, Beth said, "Well, the lab studies were done, Rory, but we are still analyzing the data, and the final clinical exam hasn't been done, so there's not much to tell yet. I'm certain Cy will inform all the stake holders as soon as we're sure of the results."

"Not even a hint? How much analysis do you need to do? Aren't the measurements pretty straightforward? Either the guy is still getting better or he's not. Which is it?"

There seemed to be urgency in Holcomb's voice. That troubled Beth. Did he suspect something? She didn't see how that was possible. No way could Holcomb know that Bonz Bagley had been that first subject. And even if he did, he couldn't have suspected how bad the test results were.

Holcomb did know Printers Alley; owned most of it, was the rumor. So she guessed that he might have some connection with Bagley. Maybe he had seen some change in the old man's behavior or something. Damn!

"It's just not that straightforward, Rory," she finally responded. "I'm certain that Cy will fill you in just as soon as we have the answers you're looking for."

"Well, he damn sure better fill me in, Beth." He paused for a moment and then added, "You're not hiding something are you? That wouldn't be very smart, you know."

"Of course not, Rory," Beth answered, "of course not. You'll get the information. Cy will fill you in at the right time."

"See that he does, Beth," Rory said and hung up.

If Beth had harbored any doubts about what she had to do, that conversation with Rory Holcomb laid them to rest. She would go about the task with all the meticulous care that she devoted to any task that she took on.

She would do what had to be done.

15

Dom Petrillo walked the six blocks down Broadway from the United States Attorney's office to the Batman Building. The US attorney's office was housed in a nondescript building near Broadway and Eighth Avenue. The building was named for Estes Kefauver, the former Tennessee senator and one time vice presidential candidate who was remembered by most people for the trademark coonskin cap that he wore when campaigning.

That fact amused Petrillo. He wondered if there was another federal building in the country named for someone with so pedestrian a public memory. Of course he knew that the answer to that question was *yes.* There were probably several.

When he exited the front of the building, he always looked to his left toward the grand old post office building transformed complements of the prodigious monetary rewards of for-profit medicine into the Frist museum. And across the corner sat the pale gray stone façade of what was still Hume Fogg High School, alma mater of Dinah Shore. "See the USA in your Chevrolet," he hummed to himself.

Petrillo looked up at the twin spires of the Batman Building as he made his way from Broadway up to Commerce Street toward what had become in the few years since its construction an iconic feature of the Nashville skyline. The thirty-three story skyscraper was built in 1994 with what was then South Central Bell as the anchor tenant. It became officially the AT&T building when the Baby Bells re-coalesced into the original megabusiness that determined how most Americans communicated with each other.

Whether the deliberate creation of an architect with a sense of humor or the result of a design accident, the building's silhouette — twin spires joined by a black arced roof — was strikingly similar to the familiar Batman logo. So the building was known from the time of its completion as the Batman Building regardless of what company name adorned its facade.

Petrillo was amused by the building as he was amused by much about this oddly idiosyncratic town. It was a town, not really a city. Petrillo grew up in Brooklyn and still missed the excitement of life in The City, in his view the only city worthy of that designation that Americans had managed to build.

His assignment to the federal prosecutor's office in Nashville was not his choice. He was sent there. But he had been delighted to discover on arriving that his old friend, Mitchell Rook, the smartest person it had ever been Petrillo's privilege to know, had established himself as one of the city's foremost business lawyers. Rook had done a brief stint in the Washington federal attorney's office about the same time that Petrillo was resigning himself to a career as an indentured servant of the federal government. They had become quite good friends for a while before Rook decided to return to his hometown, enter private practice and enjoy the monetary benefits of attending to the interests of the high rollers, forsaking the much less lucrative business of finding ways to lock up bad guys. Rook and Petrillo reconnected in Nashville.

That still seemed an unlikely locale for their reunion to Petrillo. Maybe serendipity. Their reunion had certainly turned out to be fortuitous.

Petrillo entered the soaring atrium of the building at 333 Commerce Street, aware of the click of his shoe heels on the terrazzo floor as he walked to the bank of express elevators that bypassed the first twelve floors. He waited with a growing clot of faceless people for what seemed like five minutes before a car arrived that was going up.

He edged his way into the elevator, elbowing aside an overweight man with red braces and a red bowtie showing beneath his unbuttoned pinstriped suit jacket; a lawyer, no doubt. Petrillo leaned over and punched the button to floor fifteen, retreating to the rear of the car as the Batman Building express sped skyward.

The offices of Rook, Lipchitz and Associates, LLC occupied floors fourteen and fifteen. The main reception area was on the fourteenth floor, but Rook's office was on fifteen and Petrillo chose to bypass Caroline, the lovely receptionist with an incongruous British accent who greeted the firm's clients on fourteen, and go directly to his old friend's office on the floor above.

During the ascent, Petrillo recalled the sequence of events that brought him there. The attorney general had called from Washington directly to the head of the US attorney's office in Nashville with the request. Warren Hedgepath, senior senator from Texas, had contacted the attorney general. It seems that a close friend of the senator had been a major investor in a startup company that a well-reputed academic psychiatrist, Cyrus Bartalak, had founded in Houston when he was on the faculty at a university there.

The company was founded to develop a new antipsychotic drug that Bartalak had discovered. Based on very promising preliminary clinical data, Bartalak had struck a deal with a major pharmaceutical company to continue developing the drug. When Bartalak moved from his position in Texas to Nashville, he had sold his interest in the startup company to Hedgepath's friend, claiming that since the company was a subsidiary of the university in Texas with which Bartalak was no longer affiliated, it would not be proper for him to maintain an interest in the company.

The drug looked so promising at the time that Bartalak sold his interest at a premium. However, since Bartalak's departure, further clinical studies of the drug didn't go so well, a fact that sent the value of the startup company precipitously southward.

The senator's friend strongly suspected that Bartalak knew something that he didn't reveal in the transaction and he was livid. "The guy is a crook," were his words to the senator. Hedgepath had total confidence in his friend and if this Bartalak guy was a crook, the attorney general ought to nail him!

Senator Hedgepath was a very powerful man who had recently taken on what he saw as corruption in academe as a *cause celebre*. He and his sizeable staff were ferreting out every detail of industry-academic relationships, scrutinizing among other things the finances of allegedly underpaid professors who seemed to live too well.

His people busied themselves chasing the sources of the money that supported the incongruous affluence of those few members of the tightly knit academic medical community who apparently considered themselves protected by an impervious shroud of presumed academic integrity and therefore immune to the scrutiny of headline seeking politicians.

"Bullshit," Hedgepath said. He had used the power of his office to demand detailed information from universities in a number of cases, information that raised serious questions about the time honored mantle of presumed academic integrity. Bartalak was a big fish. If they could nail him it would "bode very well for the stature of the Department of Justice" in the senator's words.

So when his boss chose to drop this hot potato in Petrillo's lap, he was delighted. He had instigated a quiet investigation of the professor, taking care not to tip his hand. While he hadn't uncovered anything specific, he had found that some of Bartalak's colleagues were not complementary.

Off the record, some even strongly suspected that Bartalak was less than completely honest. And he did live very well, way better than his university salary could explain. When Petrillo found out that Bartalak was founding another startup to develop yet another of his drug discoveries, Petrillo proposed the sting operation to his superior.

They agreed that Petrillo's friend, the highly respected local business attorney Mitchell Rook, would be an excellent front for the operation. They needed somebody with local credibility, obvious money and connections to play that role. If Rook would play ball, they would risk a million of the federal government's dollars to go after Bartalak. Given the origin of the request, they were certain that the attorney general would go along.

They knew it was a risk. They had nothing concrete to support the suspicion of the professor. But, if it worked, it would be an enormous coup for the Nashville office and for both Petrillo and his superior. Rook was fascinated by the proposal and readily agreed. This was likely to be much more interesting than the boring minutiae of business law that was his usual daily fare.

So far, so good. Rook had managed to get himself identified by Bartalak as one of his three angel investors. Rook seemed to have Bartalak's confidence although it was difficult for the lawyer to keep up the façade of camaraderie with the professor whom Rook found less than stimulating company.

"How can a man that ugly, arrogant and self-absorbed demand such respect from academic colleagues who are supposedly intelligent and perceptive people?" Rook once asked Petrillo. Petrillo did not have a ready answer.

The elevator stopped at the fourteenth floor and disgorged several of its occupants. The red braces guy got off and Petrillo wondered if he was the Lipchitz of Rook and Lipchitz. If so, he was an interesting contrast to his svelte and quietly stylish partner. Maybe the odd partnership of brains and panache was a deliberate gesture aimed at broadening the appeal of the firm to the spectrum of personalities that made up the Nashville business community. Mitchell Rook was one clever guy.

Petrillo got off the elevator at fifteen and walked directly down the long corridor that terminated at the entrance to the corner office suite. When the secretary announced Petrillo's arrival, Rook emerged from his office immediately and greeted his old friend.

"Good to see you, Dom," Rook said, extending his hand. "Do come in and catch me up on the nefarious doings of our federal government's legal eagles."

They shook hands and Rook held the door for Petrillo, ushering him into the most unusual habitat for a business attorney that Petrillo had ever seen. Every time he entered his friend's office Petrillo had to stand for a few minutes to take in the scene, get himself oriented.

There were none of the usual trappings. No dark cherry bookcases filled with law books bound in antique leather. No deep chocolate Corinthian leather easy chairs. Rook had worked with a local artist and craftsman with a growing national reputation, to design the furniture and populate the walls with original art. The artist had designed and built the custom metal and wood desk and several of his abstract two and three dimensional art pieces complemented the controlled edginess of the space that was so uncannily like the personality of its occupant.

The chairs were glistening aluminum, imported from Spain. An antique Criterion Dynamax SCT telescope perched atop a heavy duty cinema tripod perused the horizon from the southeast facing window.

The view from the floor to ceiling windows was a panorama of the city's past, present and future: the venerable Ryman Auditorium, mother church of country music; the Schermerhorn Performing Arts Center, where the symphony that its eponymic maestro had conducted for many years regularly attracted the musically sophisticated crowd into the city center from their mansions south of town; the new convention center that the mayor promised would elevate the city into the top ranks, building on its history and expanding its appeal; a bank building symbolizing the growing financial industry that was bringing in new money much of which was no longer tied to the music business.

From this vantage point, Nashville looked like a town perched on the brink of cityhood. Petrillo, as always, was impressed by the site, but he thought that the view from the street level where he usually worked gave a distinctly less generous impression of the place.

"Do sit down, Dom," Mitchell said. "Can I make you an espresso?"

Rook was addicted to espresso and had installed a very elegant copper machine in his office to feed his addiction. He went to the machine and began his ritual of creating a cup of the brew that always amused Petrillo. He thought that, in addition to his brilliance, Mitchell was perhaps the most organized and purposeful person he had ever known. Mitchell Rook did not do anything by accident. All his moves were carefully planned.

"None for me thanks," Petrillo replied.

Rook brought the *demitasse* of fresh coffee to his desk and sat down. Petrillo sat in one of the shiny metal chairs opposite him.

"So," Mitchell said, "tell me where we are with this little ruse. Any news from your guys in Houston?"

The feds in Houston were still trying to find something criminal in Bartalak's dealings there.

"Nothing solid," Dom Said. "The attorney responsible for the investigation there is absolutely convinced that Bartalak acted illegally, but he can't prove anything yet. He's still digging."

"Yeah," Mitchell replied, sipping at his coffee, "securities fraud is a hard rap to nail down alright, especially when dealing with a privately held company. A 10b-5 violation ought to cover that situation, but that's devilishly hard to prove. Which brings us to the topic at hand. What's going on with Bartalak's new venture in which you are so heavily invested?"

They smiled at each other.

Rook said, "Yes, I suppose I am heavily invested in a way, although your investment is substantially greater than mine. You have more to lose."

"And maybe more to gain."

"Maybe, yes. As strange as it may sound, though, I'm not in this to make you look good. It's that guys like this Bartalak character are what give business a bad name. If he's a crook, and all my instincts tell me that he is, I want to see him get what he deserves. These guys shouldn't be allowed to get away with cheating. Business can be an honorable undertaking that makes money the old-fashioned way. You don't have to cheat." He paused to sip the last of his espresso and continued. "So there's my little sermon,

Dom. Not like you haven't heard it before."

"Right, Mitchell," Dom replied, "may even have preached it myself. But, back to the subject. What makes you think our good doctor is not dealing from the top of the deck?"

"Hubris," Rook replied. "He's just too damned slick. Too sure of himself. And the preliminary data he showed us is too good. As we both know, things that seem too good to be true usually are."

"Tell me more, Mitchell. Is there some follow up information after that presentation of the results from the single subject that had Bartalak so excited?"

"Not yet. Not yet, but soon. I'm sure he'll schedule another lunch meeting with the investors to reveal all of the up to date information. Bartalak likes those lunch meetings where he can perform before a captive audience. The final evaluations of that first subject should be available now and it will be interesting to know what they showed. Bartalak thinks that those data may be all he needs to clinch a deal with one of the big VCs or maybe even big pharma. I'm guessing that he'll tell us that his initial enthusiasm is confirmed. I strongly suspect that crow and humble pie are dishes with which Cy Bartalak is determinedly unfamiliar. No matter what the facts are, he'll spin them to his advantage. I just don't trust this guy."

"But we need something concrete before we spring the trap. Any way to get past Bartalak's interpretations of the data, get a look at the raw numbers?"

"Yeah, that is a problem. It seems that his wife, the biostatistician, is the keeper of the data. And she is one scary woman. Again, hard to put a finger on it, but something about her is scary. I don't trust her either although maybe I just figure that one, both literally and figuratively, in bed with the good doctor has to be in on whatever game he's playing. She is a strange one though."

"How's that?

"Just something about her. She is virtually nonverbal in these meetings. Sits there deliberately exposing her tan and very lovely legs and either staring into space or looking adoringly at her husband. I'll lay you odds that something is not right with her. She's not going to do anything to upset her precious husband's plans, whatever they are. That's for sure."

Petrillo pondered the situation for a moment before responding.

"What about other scientists involved in the study of the drug? There must be more than the two of them," Petrillo mused.

"Well, it's apparently a small group. He did mention a neurologist, a woman, who is part of the team."

"Hmm," Petrillo responded, "any way to get to her? Can you find out who she is, something more about her?"

Rook thought for a few minutes, gazing out at the city skyline.

"Well," he said, "I have a friend at the university who might be able to help. I'll ask around and see what I can find out."

"Good. That's somewhere to start looking at least. But do be careful. We don't want to spook the guy before we have something more solid than we have now. So far I've tried to find out what I can but I've kept a lot of distance especially from his operation at the university. Maybe it's time to close that distance a bit. What do you think?"

Rook responded, "Probably." He paused for a moment and then said, "This guy is smart, Dom. I'll give him that. And he carries a lot of clout. This won't be easy. If he's hiding something, it will be hidden in a well-fortified place. These university people go to considerable lengths to protect their own. Almost as bad as the church."

Petrillo was Catholic and Rook knew that but he occasionally betrayed his contempt for organized religion in spite of himself. Petrillo didn't respond.

After Petrillo left, Rook placed a phone call to an old undergraduate classmate. Rook was an undergraduate physics major at the university before deciding to change direction and heading off to Yale Law School. His best friend during undergraduate days, Sydney Shelling, had gone on to med school and was now a pathologist on the medical school faculty.

Rook thought that Shelling might be able to shed some light on the workings of Cy Bartalak's operation without raising any undue suspicion. The call went unanswered and rolled over to voice mail.

At the sound of the tone, Rook said, "Syd, this is Mitchell Rook. Hope all goes well in the hallowed halls of academe. Just wanted to ask about one of your colleagues. Nothing important. Could you give me a call when you get a chance?"

16

On the eleventh phone call, Shane Hadley thought that he hit pay dirt.

It was a Monday afternoon. Shane's physical therapy session that morning had gone especially well. He was gaining more strength in his legs, could even take a few steps with the aid of a walker and a very strong assistant. And the pain was a lot less. He was feeling pretty encouraged as he settled back in his wheelchair, ushered his therapist to the elevator and bid him goodbye.

Then Shane poured himself a glass of sherry and thought about the Bagley case. He focused on the gun. Perhaps the killer had felt the need to assure herself that the antique gun actually worked before doing the deed. If she lived in the city she would probably have gone to a shooting range for some practice rounds. Since those places were generally run by gun freaks, it seemed likely that a person with such an unusual gun would be remembered.

Shane fired up his laptop and hunted for shooting ranges in the area. To his surprise, he found only eleven. One of the sites listed each of them with addresses and telephone numbers. He started at the top of the list and struck out until on call number eleven he connected with a character named Clem Horsely, proprietor of the Williamson County Shooters Club which was near Brentwood, just south of the city.

"Oh yeah," Horsely responded to Shane's query, describing the gun, "yeah, I remember that gun. Must not be another one like it anywhere around here. A real beauty. Never actually saw one before but I recognized it from the pictures in a collector's magazine. And the one she had was gold plated too, special edition of some sort. Really rare."

Shane said, "She?"

"Yep," Horsely answered, "a woman showed up a couple of times with that gun. I thought at the time that it didn't look like a woman's gun. But, hell, you can't tell nowadays. And she was a hell of a marksman too. Why are you so interested?"

"Well," Shane answered, "you may have read in the paper that it was a gun like this that was used to murder Bonz Bagley down in Printers Alley recently."

"Really?" Horsely sounded surprised. "I didn't know that. Must have been in the *Tennessean*. Never read that rag. Gave up TV news a while back too. There just wasn't ever any news that I was interested in hearing about. Bunch of people killing each other. What's new about that?"

"Can you tell me more about the woman with the gun?"

"Sure. Nice looking. Average size. Probably around forty. Well-preserved, though. Looked pretty fit, like maybe a runner or maybe did aerobics or Zumba or whatever they call it nowadays. Nice tan. Dressed well. Had money I'd guess since you'd need money to get a gun like that. Didn't say much, just signed in and went about her business. I tried to get her to tell me about the gun, but she wasn't a talker. I didn't press her. None of my business. We get all kinds in here from time to time. None of my business who they are or what they're up to."

"Anything else that you can remember about the woman?"

"Not really. I have her name in the log. Want me to look it up? Are you a cop, by the way?"

"Sort of," Shane stretched the truth a bit. "Interested party you might say. If you could look up the woman's name and anything else you have on her, I'd appreciate it."

"Sure, just a minute."

Shane heard the clunk of the phone being laid down and then some rustling sounds.

"Got it," Horsely said. "I've only got the name. I make everybody sign in the log even when they pay cash like she did. So name is all I've got. No address or anything like that."

Shane was getting impatient.

"So, Mr. Horsely, the name?"

"Got it right here. Says Elizabeth Reid, that's R E I D, *ei* instead of *ee*."

"Thank you very much, Mr. Horsely," Shane said. "You've been a great help."

As soon as he had hung up the phone, Shane Googled Elizabeth Anne Reid Nashville. There were seven hits, one Elizabeth Ann (no terminal e), one Elizabeth A and three with no middle name or initial. The other two had the middle initials D and M respectively. The only two who were under sixty years old were Elizabeth Ann, age 35 and Elizabeth A, age 42. He was unable to find an address or other contact information for either of them, but was sure that Hardy Seltzer would be able to do that. That is assuming Shane could get Hardy interested enough to go to the trouble.

Of course, Shane would have to tell Hardy about his conversation with Rory Holcomb, but Shane feared that it would focus the detective's efforts too narrowly on Jody Dakota. Shane thought now that there was another potential suspect that needed the attention and resources of the legitimate police department and hoped that he could convince Hardy of that. But it wasn't a sure thing. From what he could tell, Hardy Seltzer was a pretty linear thinker, and Shane's experience had taught him that many routes to solving a murder were anything but straight lines.

When the intercom buzzed, Shane confirmed that it was Hardy and released the door. After hearing the elevator door open on the floor below, signaling that the detective was aboard, Shane pressed the call button so that the car would stop at the second floor flat.

"Greetings detective," Shane said, as Seltzer entered the living room. "Punctual as always, I see. Do join me here in the living room. Dare I offer you a sherry?"

It was early afternoon, and the meeting had been arranged the previous evening. Although excitement was never an exuberant emotion for Hardy, he was as excited as nearing the solution to a crime was capable of causing him to be. He was anxious to fill Shane in on the Jody Dakota story. He expected Shane to share his excitement.

"Dare whatever you like, Shane, but I'm not there yet."

"In time, my friend," Shane responded, "in time."

Shane wheeled to the bar and refilled his glass.

"So," Shane said, maneuvering back to position himself opposite the detective, "what have you been up to? Any news from the hinterlands?"

"I really think, Shane," Hardy began, "that we are close to cracking this case."

"Cracking the Bonz case," Shane mused. "If punnery were not such a base form of humor I would be tempted, but go on."

Seltzer told Shane the details of his visit to Jody Dakota: Dakota's old grudge with Bagley; the gun; the fact that Jody had been in town on the Sunday of the murder.

"And I took Dakota's gun to Pistol Pete to get ballistics testing," Hardy concluded. "We have motive, opportunity and with a little luck the murder weapon. That seems like a pretty airtight case doesn't it? Then there's the four shots to the head, overkill that reeks of a smoldering vendetta. It all fits. Makes a story."

"It makes a story, alright. I should add that Rory Holcomb, my neighbor who has been involved in the music business as well as a lot of other things over the years, corroborates your information about Dakota's grudge against Bagley. Holcomb even says he heard Dakota threaten to kill Bonz forty odd years ago. But you have to admit that forty years is a long time to hold a grudge. The ballistics on Dakota's gun will be critical."

He paused for a minute, and then continued, "So the indomitable Mr. Harvey is still around, haunting his netherworld beneath the police station? Interesting. Pistol Pete will handle it alright. He's a competent chap. Is the DA involved yet?"

"Only peripherally so far, but the chief has arranged a meeting of the three of us tomorrow to bring the DA up to date and get his opinion about whether to bring Dakota in and formally charge him. We're that close."

Shane thought for a minute then wheeled himself up toward the front of the room that looked out over the alley.

Staring out the window with his back to Hardy, Shane said, "What interests you in this kind of work, Hardy? Why do you choose to spend your life foraging among the darker doings of our citizens?"

Seltzer wasn't sure how to answer. There was a back story to his life that had influenced his choice of careers. But he wasn't yet ready to share that story with Shane Hadley. Maybe never would be.

"I'm not sure," Hardy responded. "Maybe I like the logic involved in solving a crime. Life, what people do, ought to make sense, don't you think? How about you? Why did you get into this business?"

"Certainly not because I thought it made sense,"

Shane answered, wheeling back into the center of the room to face Hardy. "In fact, it is the parts that don't make sense that most interest me. And I think murder never makes sense in any realistic way."

"Well, maybe," Seltzer answered, not sure where Shane was going with this and therefore choosing to remain noncommittal.

"In fact," Shane continued, "when the story is too easily put together, I am very suspicious that something is being overlooked. I think of that as the *rule of the other gun.*"

"What do you mean?" Hardy said.

"It's not the gun you see that should concern you, but the other one. And there is always another one. Forget that at your peril. I am living proof of the consequences."

Hardy was beginning to realize that this conversation was really about the Bagley case.

"And," Shane continued, "the other gun may be real or literal, an unappreciated piece of information for example that is the critical clue to the real solution rather than the apparent one. Do you understand what I am getting at, Hardy?"

"Do you have some more information about the Bagley case, Shane? If so, please just tell me what it is."

Seltzer was way past ready for Shane to stop the philosophizing and cut to the chase. He would hear Shane out, but Hardy was very close to being completely convinced that he had solved the case. Very close. And nothing would make the chief happier than getting this thing solved and passed on to the DA.

"There is another gun."

"Would this be a real gun or a figurative one?" Hardy answered.

"Perhaps both," Shane responded. "You see, I

182

talked with the rare gun dealer in Houston. It turns out that they keep very good records and could easily document that several years ago they sold a rare Colt handgun like the one owned by Mr. Dakota which you believe dealt the unfortunate Mr. Bagley the mortal blow to the Nashville dealer. However, about the same time they sold an identical gun to someone else."

"So," Hardy said, "they're a rare gun dealer. Why does the other gun interest you?"

"I suppose because it is there. The rule of the other gun tells me to ignore this bit of information at my peril. And, I tracked it to a deceased lawyer in a small Texas town who apparently willed his collection of rare handguns to his only child, a daughter, Elizabeth Anne Reid who lived in Houston at the time of her father's death."

"Where are you going with this, Shane?"

"Hear me out, please," Shane replied. "Surmising that the killer might have felt the need to test the antique gun prior to using it in the crime, I also contacted shooting ranges in the Nashville area. What I discovered was that a woman visited one of the facilities twice, bringing with her a handgun like the one we seek. The establishment's proprietor, an interesting chap incidentally, gave me a description of the woman. And her name. Her name is, pay attention, Hardy, the rule of the other gun you know. Her name is Elizabeth Reid, *ei* like the Texas lawyer, not *ee*. Through Google, may God bless the sagacious Google, I found two Elizabeth Reid's in Nashville who generally fit the description. Although neither name is a perfect fit with the Texas lawyer's daughter, they are certainly close enough to pursue."

"So, Shane, what do you propose we do with this information? Seems to me we put it on the back burner until we get the ballistics on Jody Dakota's version of the gun from Pistol Pete. If that gives us an unequivocal identification of that gun as the murder weapon, then the case is closed as far as I'm concerned no matter who else has a gun like it and visits shooting galleries to fire it."

"We would be wasting time to do that."

"I think we'd be wasting even more time and energy by any other course," Hardy answered.

"Think what you wish, my man," Shane responded. "If Mr. Harvey tells us without reservation that Dakota's gun killed Bagley, then I will believe it. But, I am quite certain that that will not be the case. Quite certain.

"Can you humor me a bit, and do two things. First, contact any law enforcement connections you have in Houston and ask them to get a copy of the lawyer's will. That document should establish whether an antique gun like the apparent murder weapon was among the possessions that his daughter inherited. It will be necessary for someone to go in person to the office of the probate court in the county where Greensward, Texas is located and copy the document. I am not familiar with the geography of Texas but the office should not be difficult to locate.

"The will has been filed and so is public information, but it's not possible to get it online. I tried that. Second, see if you can find out addresses, contact information, and anything else you can learn about the two Elizabeth Reids in Nashville. It would be especially interesting if one of them moved here from Houston at some point, don't you think?"

Hardy was annoyed at Shane for attempting to open a completely new line of investigation when the case against Jody Dakota seemed so clear cut. This rule of the other gun sounded like a license to chase wild geese in this case. And Seltzer had to present the findings in the case to the DA and the chief tomorrow.

What would he do about this new information of Shane Hadley's? They didn't even know Shane was helping with the case and the chief would be none too happy to discover that, Hardy suspected.

"OK, Shane," Hardy responded, "I'll follow up on this on one condition."

"Which is?"

"Which is that if the ballistics implicate Dakota's gun as the murder weapon, we drop this line of inquiry and turn it all over to the DA."

"Dropping a line of inquiry prematurely is not an approach that I have found fruitful in the past, my man. But, you have the advantage here so I will agree to your proposal."

After giving Hardy Seltzer his notes on the conversation with Rory Holcomb and writing down the names of the two Elizabeth Reids and the Texas lawyer, Shane showed the detective out.

Shane wheeled himself back to the rear of the flat and settled in at the windows overlooking Third Avenue to check out the action at the lawyers' offices lining that street. He often did that without looking for anything in particular.

Shane was intrigued by that part of the legal system, the part of the process where the maneuverings of the manipulators were set in motion. Shane did think of lawyers as manipulators. He once asked a prominent defense attorney how he could bring himself to defend a client who was obviously guilty. Shane was not satisfied with the attorney's answer that guilt was decided at trial, not before. Innocence was presumed until a jury of one's peers decided otherwise.

A defense lawyer's job was to use every tactic that the law allowed to assure that the jury did not reach that conclusion regardless of, even in spite of, the facts in the case. Shane understood the concept of presumed innocence and the defendant's right to competent legal counsel. But he still thought that the guilt should be dictated by the facts whether or not a jury of one's peers could be convinced to conclude otherwise.

People of all sorts were entering and leaving the law offices. Men in dark suits and red power ties. Gaudily dressed women their blond tresses troubled by the afternoon breeze. A couple with two small children in tow. People whose life stories had somehow led them to seek the services of these manipulators of the law.

As he sat there musing and sipping at his glass of sherry, a particular couple caught his eye. A small man wearing a white suit with a bolo tie and a large Stetson hat accompanied by a blond woman in a short denim skirt with conspicuously large breasts. They were entering through a glass door on which was emblazoned in large gilt letters, *X Coniglio, Esq., Attorney*, the name and profession of the notorious mouthpiece of the country music stars. Shane studied the man entering the office for a moment before his identity surfaced from some remote corner of Shane's memory.

So Little Jody Dakota was feeling the need to get himself lawyered up. Interesting. Wonder who his lady is. And wonder how she runs?

Shane was unaware of KiKi's presence behind him until he felt her warm strong hands massaging his shoulders. He leaned back and looked up at her. She kissed him, the warm soft kiss that was his sustenance. He wheeled around to face her.

"You're home early," he said.

She pulled up a chair and sat close in front of him, reaching for his hand.

"Shane," she said, "I may have committed professional suicide today."

186

He massaged her hand.

"Professional suicide?" he said. "Surely not, my love."

"Quite likely," she answered. "I would never have thought that possible either, but I may have done it."

"What did you do?"

"I told Cy that I suspected that Beth had altered the data from the drug study. And, this may be the suicidal act, I gave him copies of the material I took from Beth's computer that convinced me that she had done it. I thought about it a lot and I decided that I had no choice."

"How did he respond?"

"Basically told me to mind my own business. That he'd take care of it."

"So?"

"He won't do anything about it. I'm sure of that."

"And if he doesn't?"

"I'll have to lodge a formal complaint of scientific misconduct."

"That makes sense to me."

"You don't understand, Shane," KiKi looked directly in his eyes. "Cy is a powerful person at the university. He'll ruin me if he can. And he probably can."

Shane drew her hand to his mouth and kissed it.

"KiKi," he said, "I have to believe that the bad guys don't win in the long run. I spent much of my life trying to make sure of that."

"I hope to God that you're right, my love. But the academic community doesn't always play by the rules that you're familiar with. We have our own norms of behavior that can be heavily influenced by the aura of success. Cy lives within the glow of that aura. Compared to him, I'm a small fish."

"But surely the rules of academe aren't oblivious

to right and wrong. There is something basic in human nature that must transcend professional stature. The bad guys can't win in the long run."

"Perhaps. But I'm more concerned right now about the short run," she said.

"Well, you're right about that. Short runs can be a problem," Shane said, then. "You did keep copies of the documents?"

"Of course."

17

Hardy Seltzer's command performance was to happen in the office of the District Attorney. The Office of the District Attorney, twentieth judicial district, was located in suite 500, Washington Square, 222 Second Avenue, just at the south fringe of the courthouse square. The building was once the home of Washington Manufacturing Company, producer of DeeCee brand work clothes long favored by the blue collar set. When the abandoned building was overtaken by the tsunami of gentrification that transformed that part of downtown, Washington was retained in the building's name as a gesture to its history.

Seltzer walked across the square from his office in the Police Department Building. He could vaguely remember when the square was fronted by a row of mom and pop establishments where politicians hung out and did the city's business over beers and cheap cigars. The seedy little Gerst House restaurant and bar had been a favorite of the politicos before it moved across the river into a kitschy chaletesque establishment aimed at luring the tourists from the freeway for bratwurst, sauerkraut, wiener schnitzel and a pitcher of beer.

Places like that were long departed from the square, their modest buildings razed years ago to make room for lawyers, accountants, and various other functionaries who fed on the largesse of the city's taxpayers. They worked from a sterile array of low brick offices that squatted there, hunkered down on the meager remains of the place's fecund history.

As he approached the building and looked at the polished brass Washington Square sign, Seltzer thought that Nashville was rapidly becoming a city of gestures. The heart of the real city that he knew and loved was still beating in there somewhere but an expanding canopy of gestures threatened to choke out the oxygen that kept the real place alive.

Seltzer was ambivalent about this meeting for several reasons. On one hand, he was anxious to get the matter dealt with and turned over to the DA and thought that he had a pretty good case. But a couple of things about it still troubled him. There was the mysterious disappearance of the killer after running from the alley. Those two kids hanging out at Fourth and Union should have seen him and Hardy was convinced that they told the truth when they said they hadn't seen a single man passing that way. People don't just vanish into thin air. That didn't make sense.

Then, he couldn't dismiss the fact that Sherlock Shane was trying to steer the investigation in a completely different direction. True, Shane hadn't been an active investigator for a while, but it was difficult to dismiss his theory out of hand. Hardy didn't think Shane's theory made sense and Hardy was inclined to dismiss things that didn't make sense. He'd get a copy of the will. He'd run down the two Reid women as best he could. But he thought all that was a waste of time and he desperately hoped that the ballistics on Jody Dakota's gun would nail the case once and for all. A lot was riding on the ballistics.

Hardy also didn't relish appearing before this particular audience. It was unusual for the Chief of Police and the DA and his crew to arrange such a meeting. The chief and the DA were hardly on good terms. The long smoldering hostilities between the two were no secret. And in such a high profile case, they would be vying for credit once a solution was in sight. The meeting could take a nasty turn and if it did Hardy was likely to be caught in the crossfire.

When Hardy was ushered into the DA's private conference room on the back side of the building overlooking the river, the four others were already there. The chief, the DA and two assistant DAs whom Hardy only vaguely recognized sat on one side of the rectangular table with a vacant chair on the opposite side obviously meant for him. Hardy didn't like the looks of the arrangement. He was outnumbered and outgunned.

"Do sit down, detective," The DA gestured to the vacant chair without getting up.

Hardy thought that the chief looked especially tired. There were dark pouches under his eyes; he leaned forward with his elbows on the table and his chin resting in his cupped hands. The DA was the DA, a persona that he worked hard at. Hardy thought that the DA had watched too many Law and Order reruns and labored too conspicuously at an imitation of his old friend Fred Thompson.

"I'm sure you are aware, Detective Seltzer," the DA continued, "of how important it is that we get this Bagley case solved. Both the chief and my office are under some pressure and we're depending on you to get this thing sewed up as fast as possible."

"Yes sir," Seltzer replied, fiddling nervously with his hands and scanning the faces of the opposition.

"So, tell us what you've got," the DA continued. "I mean convince me that you have a case that we can prosecute."

Hardy thought the choice of words was interesting. Not, convince them that he had identified the killer, but that he had a prosecutable case. They weren't necessarily the same thing.

Hardy recounted the details of his investigation that implicated Jody Dakota as Bonz Bagley's killer; there was motive, opportunity and possibly the murder weapon. The group listened quietly as he recounted the evidence.

When Seltzer finished his recitation of the facts,

the DA asked, "Eye witnesses? The alley is a public place. The murder took place in broad daylight. Surely somebody must have witnessed the crime."

"It was early on a Sunday, sir," Hardy responded. "Not much happening down there that time of day on a Sunday."

Hardy thought for a few minutes about what to tell them about Shane's observation.

After a short pause, Hardy added, "There were no actual eyewitnesses that we could identify. However, one resident of the alley alleges to have seen the killer running away just after the murder. He couldn't provide any clear description since the apparent killer was wearing a hoodie and the witness only saw him from the rear and at a distance."

"A resident of the alley? Who in hell was it? Not many folks actually live there. Who the hell would want to?" the DA responded.

"The name of the resident in question is Shane Hadley," Hardy said.

The group went silent.

Finally, the DA said, "Goddam. Sherlock Shane come back to haunt me after all these years. Thought surely I wouldn't have to deal with that sonofabitch anymore." He turned to the chief and continued, "Why didn't you tell me this, chief?"

Seltzer had told the chief of the witness but had not told him who it was. He realized now that his attempt to keep Shane's involvement in the case from the chief was a mistake. But they still didn't need to know that Shane Hadley was involved in any way beyond revealing what he had seen.

"Apparently," the chief responded, "detective Seltzer did not believe the identity of this witness was of sufficient importance to reveal his identity to me before this moment."

The chief was pissed.

Hardy said, "That's correct. I don't think the fact that the witness was a former police detective matters. He is a private citizen like anyone else. In fact, his observations may be even more reliable than is often the case for witnesses of a crime."

"Well," the DA continued, "maybe. But just be damned sure you don't let Sherlock Shane get any notions about doing anything beyond telling us what he saw. That doesn't sound like much help anyway to me. That sonofabitch is nothing but trouble. Never could leave well enough alone. He screwed up the prosecution's case more than once when he was on the force."

The chief said, "But regardless of that, the question we're here to answer is whether we have enough to bring in Jody Dakota. The case looks pretty strong. What do you think?"

The DA thought for a minute and then said, "Ballistics. We wait for the ballistics. If Pete Harvey tells us Dakota's gun did it we bring in Dakota and go to trial as fast as possible. If Pistol Pete says it's definitely not the gun, we forget Dakota and look elsewhere," turning to speak to Seltzer he continued. "Is there an elsewhere to look, detective?"

"Not at the moment, sir," Hardy answered, "but we're continuing the investigation and will continue it until we identify the killer."

That was all that Seltzer was prepared to tell them about Shane Hadley's theory. If he said more, he feared that he would be forced to betray its source which obviously would not sit well with this august audience.

"A prosecutable case, detective," the DA said, slamming his fist on the table. "Just bring me a goddam prosecutable case."

###

Cy and Beth Bartalak were huddled in Cy's office at the university going over the drug study results for a final time before the lunch meeting with the *Renaptix* investors. Beth had presented the data the previous morning at their regular meeting with Katya Karpov, but Cy wanted to review everything one last time before his presentation. He was ready to move ahead with his efforts to nail down commitments from the additional investors or industry partnerships or both that would be necessary to take the next major step in developing the drug. Cy was convinced that they had the ammunition to accomplish that and was excited about the possibilities.

The first three-month follow up studies had been completed on four subjects with moderate to severe Alzheimer's disease. As with subject number one, two of the subjects showed marked improvements in cognitive function and in the biochemical tests; two showed no real change. And, the *coup de grace* was that the six month studies from subject number one indicated that his early marked improvement was sustained.

The code was still not broken, but Cy was convinced that the subjects who had improved must be the ones taking the active drug and that the ones who were unchanged must have received placebo. He was pondering whether to go to the DSMB with the data and suggest that they break the code and move on to design the phase three studies.

Phase three studies are expensive but with such promising preliminary data, there should be plenty of VCs and major pharmaceutical companies who would be anxious to take the risk given the exorbitant rewards that would come if those studies confirmed Cy's suspicion that he had discovered the first effective treatment for the five million Americans who suffered from this devastating disease. The angels should be pleased. The value of their investment would skyrocket. *Renaptix, Inc.* was poised for entry into the heady world of the big time drug business.

After going over all of the information and reviewing the few PowerPoint slides that Cy had made, he said, "Beth, Katya came to see me yesterday afternoon. She keeps harping on her suspicion that there is something funny about the data on subject number one. I'm getting a little worried about her."

"Like I said earlier, Cy," Beth responded, "that woman has to go. Everybody knows she doesn't like me. She's likely to do anything she can to discredit me. But I'm surprised that she came to you about it."

"Well, I am her chairman."

"Yes, but she's aware that you have other loyalties," Beth said. "I doubt that she thinks that you would conspire against your own wife."

"She's not that stupid."

Beth replied, "She's certainly not stupid, but for some reason that I don't understand, she seems to have this desperate need to do me in. She surely knows that you won't let that happen."

Cy opened the drawer to his desk and withdrew a folder, placed it on his desk and slid it across to Beth.

"Katya gave me this file," he said. "I haven't looked at it, but she claims that it contains information that raises questions about the results of some of the drug studies. Can you have a look at it and let me know if there's anything there that should concern me?"

"Where did this supposed incriminating information come from?"

"She allegedly retrieved it from your computer in the lab," Cy said.

"Isn't that illegal?" Beth said. "Isn't the fact that she admits to breaking into my computer grounds for getting rid of her once and for all? She is nothing but trouble, Cy."

"Well, maybe," he responded, "maybe. But have a look at the file and if there's anything in it that I need to know, tell me."

"If not?"

"If not, then I suggest that you destroy the material."

"I can do that," Beth said. "But the data will still be in her computer. And she probably made hard copies for herself as well, don't you think? If this is something she has contrived to get at me, she surely wouldn't have given her only copy to you."

"That's very likely," Cy answered, "but it will be of no use to her."

"No use? Suppose she goes over your head with this. Like I said, she seems desperate."

"She won't do that," Cy said with his familiar air of confidence. "That would be professional suicide and, if my knowledge of the human psyche tells me anything, it is that Katya Karpov is not suicidal."

Beth responded, "Too bad."

Beth was troubled by this turn of events. It had been careless of her to leave her computer open when she wasn't there. And she should have destroyed all of the raw data that didn't fit with her official records much earlier than she did. She shouldn't have left it on her computer at all. That was not like her. Beth was ordinarily a meticulous person. It was attention to detail that made her good at her job. And it was her brilliance as a biostatistician that first attracted Cy's attention when she was just another member of his lab group in Houston.

It was Beth's meticulous planning that lured Cy away from his wife of many years, a carefully conceived and boldly executed plan that brought them to this point. This was no time to get careless.

Cy did wonder what was in the file that Katya Karpov had given him, but decided that it was not in his best interest to read it. *Never ask questions to answers to which you don't want to know* was a dictum that he lived by; it had served him well. He had the information he needed and was prepared to act on it.

Cy sensed that Beth was concerned, maybe even troubled, when he gave her the file. And as he thought about it, there had been some changes in Beth's behavior recently. She was spending less time at work. She had always been an avid runner, but what had been a harmless habit seemed lately more like an addiction. If she had left her computer accessible to Katya, that was careless and the Beth he knew was not a careless person.

What he liked about his wife was that she was loyal, careful and dependable, there when he needed her and not in his way when he didn't. She didn't require a lot of care and feeding and he liked that. Care and feeding of other people were not activities that Cy relished and he didn't do them very well without a compelling ulterior motive. He had plenty to do without having to worry about Beth. He hadn't taken her on as a professional project. He had married her, for God's sake. But, maybe he should start paying more attention. He could tell if there was something wrong with his wife ... if he paid attention.

18

Lawrence Walker, the chairman of the university psychiatry department before Cyrus Bartalak ascended to that role, had been Katya Karpov's mentor for several years. He saw her as a rising star. He even thought that she might succeed him as chairman in a few years although naming a neurologist to that role in a department of psychiatry would be a distinctly unusual move. But Walker thought that such a bold appointment was justified by Katya's brilliance and her integrity, an increasingly rare characteristic of the new generation of overly ambitious opportunists who seemed to be gaining control of universities. Walker was a gentleman of the old school.

Walker had recruited Bartalak and his drug development group from Houston at the urging of the dean. Bartalak was wildly successful at attracting federal grant money. He brought several million dollars in grants to the university when he came and had competed successfully for several additional millions after the move. Walker didn't suspect that what actually attracted Bartalak, what sealed the deal, was the promise from the dean that he would be Walker's successor.

When movement in that direction was too slow to suit Bartalak, he approached the dean and threatened to explore the numerous offers he regularly received from other institutions unless the dean made good on his promise. The result was that the elegant and distinguished psychiatrist, Lawrence Walker, was eased into early retirement. A faculty committee working at lightning speed with a headhunter firm handpicked by the dean concluded *after an extensive national search* that Cyrus Bartalak was the perfect candidate, a conclusion that the majority of the cynically inclined medical faculty believed to have been patently foregone. Bartalak was appointed to the chair, an event announced in an elaborate press release and celebrated by an extravagant reception hosted by the dean in the main dining room at the University Club.

On his first day in his new role, Bartalak gave notice to virtually every member of the department that he would be replacing them with people of his own choosing. He cleaned house. Except for Dr. Karpov. That surprised both Katya and most of the other faculty since she had been a special favorite of the previous chairman.

However, she was also the only real rising star that Bartalak inherited, so it made sense as an academic move. It was one of the few things that Bartalak did that gained him some grudging admiration from his colleagues in the other departments. Some suspected that keeping Katya was a condition imposed by the dean for Bartalak's promotion. But no one, including Katya, knew for sure if that was true.

Katya agreed to stay on in spite of her better judgment and it came with a price. Bartalak made it clear that she was to do his bidding and he gave her considerably less freedom to pursue her own research interests than was true earlier. That and the necessity to work in the same laboratory with the chairman's wife whom Katya disliked and didn't trust made her job considerably less pleasant and less interesting under Bartalak's leadership than she had hoped it would be.

Katya often thought that she should have looked for employment elsewhere and she might still do that. She was certain that if she put out the word that she was in the market, there would be opportunities. But she liked her life style in Nashville with Shane and didn't relish the thought of uprooting them. She had tried to make the best of the situation. That effort, she was coming to realize, was probably futile.

Those were Katya's thoughts as she took the stairs down a flight from her office on the fifth floor and approached the door to the pathology laboratory. She didn't have an appointment with Sydney Shelling, but the neuropathologist was always available to her when she needed to talk. Syd was the nearest thing to a confidante that she had at work. They had been colleagues for several years and Shelling was a respected member of the medical faculty. He was the one person she most trusted to be honest, genuinely concerned and discreet. She valued his advice even when she chose not to follow it. Had she followed his earlier advice when her department chairmanship changed, she would be elsewhere now and no doubt better off.

"Hi, Syd," Katya said.

He sat at a workbench in his habitual pose, hunched over a microscope peering intently at the greatly magnified details of a very small piece of a human brain.

"Oh, hi Katya," he answered, turning to face her. "Come in and have a seat."

"Looks like you're busy, Syd," Katya said. "I can come back later if you like."

Syd was always busy and she knew that, but she also knew that he was rarely too busy to interrupt what he was doing to talk with her.

"I was just puzzling over this slide," Syd responded. "Never saw anything like it before. I've seen a lot of hippocampi in my time, but never one like this."

"Really?" she said. "What is it?"

"The coroner sent over some sections from the brain of a poor guy who got himself shot in the head,"

Shelling answered, "multiple shots directly into the brain. Most of the cerebral hemispheres were essentially mush, but the hippocampus on the left side was still intact. And these sections through the hippocampus are particularly interesting.

"Here," he continued, "let me put this on the teaching scope and I'll show you what I mean."

He removed the slide from his scope, moved to the other side of the bench and inserted the slide under a microscope with a single stage but with multiple binocular viewing ports. The scope was used as a teaching device so that several students could view the same section as the instructor as he described it for them. Katya took a seat at one of the viewing ports.

"What I find strange are these vacuoles," he said using the pointer that could be moved around to identify the area he was describing. "And here ..." He moved the pointer again, "... some of the cells have these inclusions that aren't typical of anything that I can think of. They aren't at all like viral inclusions. Maybe more like toxic granules of some sort."

Katya knew a lot about normal brain anatomy, but she wasn't an expert pathologist. She accepted Syd's opinion at face value.

"Did the guy have Alzheimer's?" she asked. "That might explain abnormalities in the hippocampus. But this doesn't really look like that does it? So what do you think it is?"

"There are some Alzheimer's like changes, but like you say, these vacuoles and inclusions are different. My best guess at this point is that it's some kind of toxic reaction. Maybe something the person was exposed to, some environmental toxin. Or a strange reaction to a drug. I'll need to get more details from the coroner about the possibilities."

"Was this a recent case?" Katya asked.

"Yes, pretty recent. A murder case that's apparently still being investigated."

Katya thought. A recent murder case. Multiple shots to the head.

"Does the victim have a name?" she asked.

"I'm sure he must, Katya," Syd answered, "but the coroner just gave me the number he had assigned to the case. Like I said, I'll need to get more information. I just got the sections this morning."

Damn! Katya thought. What if this is what's left of Bonz Bagley's brain? Drug toxicity? Damn! It would fit with her suspicions about the clinical and biochemical tests. Cy's drug could be killing people. If this were true, her options were suddenly diminished.

She considered revealing the identity of subject number one in the drug study to the pathologist, but knew she was not authorized to do that. If this was the brain of that subject, everyone would know soon.

"You look surprised, Katya, anything wrong?"

"Can we talk?" Katya replied.

"Sure," Shelling responded, rising from his chair; sensing that his might be something serious, he continued, "Shall we go into my office?"

Shelling's office was adjacent to the laboratory. His standard issue office furniture was unremarkable. The faux wood top of the black steel desk was piled high with charts, journals and books. The computer screen on the credenza behind the desk was virtually obliterated by yellow sticky notes. Syd removed a stack of journals from a chair and motioned her to sit. He sat down behind the desk.

"You'd think the magic wand of the computer age would make all this paper disappear," Syd said, "but it just seems to get worse."

"Going paperless takes a lot of paper," Katya replied.

"Yeah," he said, "like wires and wireless. The

computer age is full of oxymorons."

"Isn't all of life?"

"That, too. That, too," Syd repeated, then said. "So what's troubling that brilliant mind of yours, Katya Karpov?"

Katya confided the entire story. She included the evidence of Beth Bartalak's scientific misconduct that she had purloined from Beth's computer and the fact that she had revealed her suspicions and the evidence to Bartalak. She asked if Shelling thought she should lodge a formal complaint with the dean or whether he thought there was some other course that was wiser.

"Wiser?" he mused. "Well, I'm not sure about that. This is a difficult dilemma. It's no secret that you and Beth Bartalak don't get along. And Cy doesn't appreciate having anything about his operation questioned. We're all painfully aware of that. He's also a creature of the dean. It could look like you're just out to get at Beth rather than being concerned about the integrity of the science."

"But I do have some evidence to support the suspicion."

"But you obtained it illegally. Not such a good idea, Katya. It would've been better to lodge the formal complaint and let the investigating committee retrieve the data from Beth's computer. Unauthorized access to a colleague's computer is not a violation that is likely to be overlooked."

"I was trying to be fair," Katya protested. "I know that my attitude toward Beth is common knowledge. I thought that I needed something concrete before going as far as a formal accusation."

"I understand your motive, I really do," Shelling said, "but I'm not sure I agree with your actions. Anyway, that's done. The question is, what next? And this may be the really big problem. If you make the charge formally, Cy Bartalak and likely the dean will do everything within their power to make you the victim. There is a lot more invested in Cy and the reputation of the institution than there is in you. As ugly as it sounds, Katya, you are expendable. I don't have to tell you what powerful academics can do to the careers of those beneath them in the pecking order. Cy is not a nice man. He will ruin you if he can."

"And he probably can," Katya sighed, then continued. "But what if it's true?"

"That's the problem," Shelling said. "The fact that you believe it's true really gives you no alternative. If Cy doesn't do anything about it, you'll have to lodge a formal complaint through the proper channels. But, Katya, I desperately fear the consequences for you."

"I never thought that I would make a very good martyr," Katya said.

"Unfortunately martyrs don't usually volunteer for the job. They're more often cast into the role by circumstances."

"If I'd taken your earlier advice, the circumstances would be different."

"That's probably true," Syd responded, "but if this drug study would still have been done. And if you're right about it, a lot of innocent people could have been victims of a misanthrope masquerading as a saint."

"So, will they burn me at the stake?" Katya smiled.

"Only metaphorically," Shelling responded, "but you'll feel the heat."

Hardy Seltzer reflected on his meeting with the chief of police following the interesting session with the DA. Hardy was making his way across the square from his office toward Printers Alley to meet with Shane Hadley. They had a lot to catch up on. Hardy believed that the investigation was rapidly moving toward a close and he was pleased about that. He would be interested in Shane's response to how things were developing, whether he would keep pushing for more details about the Texas lawyer and the Reid women, whoever they were. That line of investigation had met a dead end and he hoped that Shane's vaunted powers of observation and reasoning would lead him back to what seemed to Hardy the obvious conclusion.

The chief was obviously pissed in the meeting with the DA when Hardy revealed that Shane was the witness who had seen the killer running from the alley. Hardy had steeled himself for a thorough tongue lashing when he answered the call summoning him to the chief's office. But the chief surprised him.

The chief was not upset by the fact that Shane was involved in the case, only annoyed that Hardy hadn't told him earlier. In fact, the chief even hinted that the investigation might benefit from Shane Hadley's thoughts about the situation. The chief suggested that Hardy might give Hadley some more of the details and get his thoughts about how the story might play out.

"Shane Hadley has his faults," the chief had said, "but I remember him as the best damn detective this police department has ever had," he said, thumping the desk with his fist, then hastily adding with his characteristic tact, "present company excepted, of course."

When Hardy said that this wouldn't be likely to please the DA, the chief emitted a long stream of obscenities expressing his opinion of the chief prosecutor in greater detail than Hardy felt was necessary. But the chief had made his point. Hardy didn't tell him that Shane was already involved and was doing everything he could to take the investigation in another direction. There would be time enough for that if it became necessary.

When he arrived at the Union Street entrance to the alley, Hardy paused and looked up toward Fourth Avenue. The killer had apparently ditched the hoodie just as he exited the alley and, according to Shane, turned up toward Fourth. It was only a short half block to where the two teenagers had been loitering. But they didn't see him. Could it be that Hardy had asked them the wrong question? Could Shane's obsession with the gender of the killer be right? Did the two boys see a woman passing that way but not a man and so answered Hardy's question honestly but without adding any additional information?

He should have taken contact information from the two boys, but didn't since they hadn't appeared to see anything relevant. If he had done that he could question them again, but it was too late for that now and likely would have been useless anyway. It was Hardy's impression that the two boys were not fond of cops and so weren't likely to volunteer anything that would make his job easier. Hardy still could not believe that this crime was committed by a woman. And the case against Jody Dakota seemed so logical. All the elements were there. Well, the ballistics should answer the question. Pistol Pete ought to have those results in the next day or so.

The alley noise was just cranking up as Hardy walked up toward Shane's building. Hardy could only think of it as noise. There was a good music of all sorts in the city, but not much of it filtered down to the alley. The place still had a seedy sort of appeal, but what passed for music there wasn't a major asset if the point was to attract the music lovers. Then again, maybe that wasn't the point of the alley at all.

The *Bonz's Booze and Music* sign that had hung on the front of the club near the Union Street end of the alley for as long as Hardy could remember had been replaced by a sign announcing SPACE AVAILABLE in large letters and in smaller letters, *Call Rory Holcomb* followed by a phone number.

A few people wandered along, occasionally shading their eyes and peering into the clubs' storefronts. It seemed to Hardy Seltzer that Bonz's murder may have dealt a mortal blow to the whole alley enterprise. He feared that he was witnessing its death throes and that saddened him.

"Hi-ho, my man," Shane called to Hardy from the balcony where Shane seemed to spend the majority of his time observing the locals from a reasonably safe distance. "Won't you join me?"

Hardy waited for the "… for a sherry," that usually completed the greeting, but it didn't come. Maybe Shane had given up his efforts to alter Hardy's drinking habits.

"Here," Shane continued, "I'll lower the drawbridge so you can come up."

Shane had found the metaphor that Hardy had used earlier amusing.

Shane disappeared through the French doors into the flat. Hardy waited for the buzz indicating release of the door. He entered the small foyer and boarded the elevator, waiting for Shane to call the car to the second floor.

"So," Shane said after they were seated in the living room and Shane had refilled his glass at the bar, "what new developments have you managed to uncover, my man? What about the killer? Have you identified her yet?"

Shane smiled broadly. Hardy was mildly amused

by the gentle ribbing. And the fact that he also smiled was more a response to the infectious good humor that Shane seemed to radiate than to what was said. Hardy marveled at that. If their situations were reversed, Hardy seriously doubted that his sense of humor, such as it was, would have survived.

"Are you questioning the manhood of Little Jody Dakota?" Hardy answered, deadpan.

Shane chuckled, "Perhaps. But I am certainly not questioning your tenacity. When Hardy Seltzer gets an idea in his head, there is no stopping him. Ah, well," Shane sipped at his sherry, "tenacity has its place. We'll get to your Jody Dakota story, but first, have you made any progress on the will and the Reid women?"

"I had one of my assistants follow up. Pretty much of a dead end I'm afraid."

"How so?"

"Well we did manage to get the state police to agree to track down the will of the long dead Archibald Stewart Reid of Greensward, Texas. They'll FAX us a copy when they have it. I seriously doubt that the chore is likely to be high on their list of priorities, though, so I'm not sure when we'll get it."

"Well, that's something. And the Reid women?"

"Total dead end there. Elizabeth Ann Reid was killed in a car crash out on I-75 three months ago. That was obviously well before the Bagley murder and she was a Nashville native as well. Never lived in Texas."

"And the other one, Elizabeth A.?"

"Her full name is Elizabeth Abramowitz Reid. She is married to an engineer, Sam Reid, and her maiden name is Abramowitz. She is a native of New York if that matters. So she can't be the Texas lawyer's daughter that you seem so interested in."

"Bloody hell," Shane exclaimed. "I would have sworn that I was onto something there. Bloody hell."

Hardy smiled. "Can we talk about Jody Dakota now?" he asked.

"Sure, sure," Shane answered, waving a hand at Hardy and staring up toward the front window. "Bloody hell," he repeated.

"Ahem," Hardy cleared his throat and then continued. "The meeting with the chief and the DA was interesting. Incidentally, is there some bad blood between you and the DA? When I mentioned you as the witness who had seen the fleeing killer, he exploded into a less than complementary tirade about his dealings with you in the past."

"Oh," Shane replied, waving a dismissive hand, "the DA was an idiot when I knew him and most likely still is. In my experience idiocy is not a condition that tends to improve with age."

Hardy continued, "The upshot of the meeting was that the case against Dakota seemed strong but that he wouldn't be arrested until we have the results of the ballistics tests on his gun."

"That's a fortunate outcome, Hardy," Shane answered, "fortunate for both your department and for Little Jody; for the DA as well although the DA is of no concern to me. He will still be an idiot regardless of the outcome of this case."

"Don't you think the ballistics will answer the question?" Hardy queried.

"I suspect they may, detective," Shane said, draining the last of his sherry and eyeing, not too discreetly, the half full bottle sitting on the bar. "Yes, I suspect that the ballistics may answer the question of Little Jody Dakota's guilt or innocence. However, I also strongly suspect that the answer will not please any of the officials involved in this case. Including you, my man." He wheeled over and clapped Hardy on the shoulder as he slid past the detective on his way to the bottle of sherry.

Hardy called after him, "Why are you so sure about that, Shane?"

"Think, my man," Shane said, refilling his glass, and turning toward his guest. "If you were Jody Dakota there is no way that you would voluntarily surrender the gun for testing unless you knew for a fact that it was not the murder weapon. Mr. Dakota may not be the brightest candle on the cake, but unless he's brain dead, he wouldn't have done that."

Of course Hardy had thought the same thing and was surprised that Dakota had let him take the gun. But he was counting on his impression that the old country music star may well not have enough functioning brain cells to alert him to the risk he was taking. The guy might not know anything about ballistics. But still, why take any risk if he did it?

"Well, Shane," Hardy said, "he may not be brain dead but my impression was that he's not all that far from it. Maybe he just made a mistake. Maybe he's really stupid."

"Perhaps," Shane responded, "perhaps. We shall see." He paused and raised his glass to Hardy. "Cheers," he said, taking a generous swallow of the wine, "cheers, Hardy my man."

19

The neuropathologist, Sydney Shelling, placed two phone calls. It was late in the afternoon, but he was pretty sure that both of the parties he wanted to reach would still be at work.

As he searched for the telephone number of the coroner's office, Shelling thought about the differences between medicine and law. While both dealt with conundrums they used different methods to solve them. There was, for example, the different attitude toward the relationship between means and ends, whether the former justified the latter. In medical science results were neither more accurate nor more reliable than the methods used to obtain them. He doubted that the same held in matters of law. It seemed to him that lawyers usually formed a conclusion and then set about to construct a story to support it *post hoc* rather than letting the facts lead them to the answer.

Maybe the better analogy was between his science and the work done by the police detectives who did the investigating before the lawyers got involved. Still, the differences in the means and ends thing probably was also true of the detectives — anything to nail the bad guys. He thought that Katya Karpov might have something interesting to say on the subject since her husband had been a police detective before his tragic accident. Shelling would have to ask her about that.

"Dr. Jensen," the coroner answered.

Shelling had called the number of the direct line to the coroner's private office and the answering voice conjured up the coroner's persona in Shelling's mind. Shelling knew that many people, even some of his colleagues, thought that pathology attracted strange personalities, but he didn't believe that. Of course there were some weird ducks in pathology, but the same was true of surgery and medicine, even pediatrics, for Christ's sake. Because Jensen was fuel for the weird pathologist stereotype, Shelling wasn't particularly fond of him. Shelling avoided Jensen's attempts at familiarity by keeping the coroner at arm's length.

"Yes, Dr. Jensen," Shelling responded. "This is Sydney Shelling. I was reviewing those brain sections you sent over earlier today and wondered if you could give me more information about the unfortunate victim."

"Hold on, laddie," the coroner replied, using the affected term that he knew annoyed Shelling. "Let me get my copy of his medical chart. I'm not sure if you knew, but the victim's name is Herman Bagley, better known as Bonz, the old guy who hung out in Printer's Alley and got himself shot recently."

Shelling didn't know that of course. He had read some of the newspaper accounts of the murder and seen the news stories on TV, but didn't really make the connection. It seemed obvious in retrospect.

Shelling could hear Jensen rustling some papers while continuing the conversation.

"So, have you found something interesting Syd?" Jensen said.

"Actually I have found something interesting, but I don't know what it means. There are some changes in the hippocampal region that look definitely abnormal to me but not typical of anything that I know of. Some vacuolization in the neurons and some strange cellular inclusions. My best guess is that it's some kind of unusual toxic reaction. Is there anything in his history to suggest environmental exposures, ingestion of chemicals, anything at all to indicate exposure to a toxin?"

"I have his record here," Jensen replied. "I don't

212

recall anything in particular from when I reviewed it earlier. Let me see. I do seem to recall something unusual now that you mention it."

Jensen could hear the coroner rifling through the chart.

"Yes, yes," Jensen said, "here it is. He had been followed for several years at the university medical center for his Alzheimer's disease which seemed to be progressing. But, here is the note. The chart was flagged because he was involved in some experimental study. Looks like it was some kind of study being done in your department of psychiatry."

"That's interesting," Shelling answered. "Does it say what kind of a study?"

"Not really. As you know these notes are only meant to give the information that might be important to the patient's regular medical care. It appears that it's an early phase study of an experimental drug. The note instructs anyone caring for the patient to contact a research coordinator and gives her name and phone number."

"Does it say who the PI is on the study?" Shelling asked.

"Looks like the Principal Investigator is your university's rock star, Cyrus Bartalak."

Jensen knew that Bartalak was one of the medical center's stars. He was often in the news. His recruitment from Houston made the local news a few years earlier. And there was a big to do in the local media when Bartalak was made chair of the department of psychiatry. Frequent university press releases announced yet another of the psychiatrist's professional accomplishments.

Bartalak was an academic star and the PR people milked him for all the favorable publicity they could get for the medical center. And it was obvious to even a casual observer that Cyrus Bartalak did not shun the

213

glare of the media spotlight.

Shelling was quiet for a few moments, contemplating this new information and wondering if there was some connection with the topic of his earlier conversation with Katya Karpov.

"Thanks, Dr. Jensen," Shelling finally responded, "this is a great help. I'll dictate a formal report on my examination of the sections you sent and get it to you."

"And your conclusion?"

"I'm going to have to be a bit noncommittal I'm afraid. It will probably be something like atypical findings suggestive of a toxic reaction to a chemical agent."

"Obviously not related to the cause of death," Jensen mused.

"Well, Dr. Jensen," Shelling responded, "I should think you will have no difficulty making an unequivocal statement about the cause of death."

"That's true, laddie," Jensen responded to Shelling's obvious sarcasm. "Nice thing about gunshots to the head. Makes my job easy."

"Perhaps not as easy as you think in this case," Shelling answered.

Sydney Shelling was still pondering the troubling information from the coroner when he placed the second call.

A soft feminine voice with a distinctly British accent answered the call, "Rook and Lipchitz, how may I help you?"

"Yes," Shelling said, "this is Dr. Shelling at the university. I'm returning a call from Mitchell Rook."

"Certainly, sir," the soft voice with the incongruous accent responded. "Let me connect you to his office."

Shelling remembered his old college classmate as not only one of the smartest people he had known but also as a stickler for details. Shelling imagined that Rook had deliberately chosen the receptionist for the quality of her voice and for the accent that projected an elegant image of the firm to the caller. First impressions and all that.

After three rings another pleasant female voice answered, "Mitchell Rook's office."

"This is Sydney Shelling," he responded. "I'm returning Mitchell Rook's call."

"One moment please," she said. "Let me see if he's in."

No doubt her script was designed to give Rook cover if he didn't want to take the call.

"Syd," Rook answered, "thanks for returning my call. How have you been?"

They didn't speak often, but when they did there was the pleasant anamnestic response typical of longstanding friendships. Although they had not been close recently, they had a lot of mutual respect and affection that had persisted over the years since they were undergraduate classmates.

"I'm fine, Mitchell, "Shelling responded, "and you? Still thriving in world of the big dogs?"

"Running as fast as I can," Rook answered.

"So what did you call about, Mitchell? Your message sounded like you wanted some information."

"Yes, yes," Rook said, "I'm working with a startup company out of the university and doing some due diligence. Thought you might be able to help me out."

"Sure," Shelling replied, "I'll do what I can. Shoot."

"This company is developing a new drug for Alzheimer's disease," Rook said. "The chair of your department of psychiatry, a Dr. Bartalak, is the company's founder and apparently inventor of the drug."

Rook paused for a moment to see if Shelling would respond. When he didn't, Rook continued.

"I wanted to get some more information about his team. I know that Bartalak's wife, Beth, a biostatistician, is working on this project. Is there anyone else involved that you know of?"

There was another pregnant pause before Shelling responded, "Why are you asking me, Mitchell? If you're representing the company, you must know who the principals are."

"Yes, of course, Syd," Rook answered. "But I thought you might have some inside scoop that would give me a better idea of who I'm dealing with. Just between you and me, I have some doubts about this Bartalak fellow. I'm not sure he's always dealing from the top of the deck."

Yet another pause. Shelling trusted his old friend, but the guy was a lawyer after all so Shelling felt that he should be careful about what he said. He had a lot of information but really didn't know what it all meant, and certainly didn't want to say anything that would be a breach of confidence or that would reflect negatively on the university. He also knew that if he was responsible for calling Cy Bartalak's integrity into question there would almost certainly be serious personal repercussions.

Shelling was an honest man who did his job conscientiously and well. He was perfectly happy to leave the larger issues, no matter how important they were, to the very well-paid administrators whose job was to manage the complexities of a large institution with a lot of moving parts.

Rook continued, "Bartalak mentioned a neurologist, a woman who's apparently involved in the clinical studies."

"Sure," Shelling said, "that's Katya Karpov. She's brilliant."

"Interesting. Bartalak also spoke of the neurologist's brilliance, but for some reason never told me her name. Interesting."

"Not terribly surprising," Shelling answered. "He might choose to keep her distanced from his business dealings. There seems to be some tension between the two of them."

"Tension?" Rook answered.

Shelling was not prepared to say anything more about that. He had planted the seed and he had not told Rook anything that wasn't common knowledge among the faculty. If his old friend was as curious and creative as Shelling suspected, planting the seed would suffice.

"Yes. I'm not sure what all the reasons are, but that's my impression."

"What about Bartalak?"

"Big academic star," Shelling said, "favorite of the dean. He brings in buckets of money to the institution. Highly thought of in the larger psychiatric community."

"Does he lie and cheat?"

"Not that I know of," Shelling responded, smiling to himself at his friend's candor.

That was true. He had serous suspicions but he didn't have any proof and didn't really want to go there.

Mitchell Rook was getting the message. He knew Syd Shelling pretty well and Rook's skills at extracting information from people included an ability to read between the lines of a conversation. He was getting the message. Cy Bartalak was a crook and this Karpov woman might be the key to establishing that fact.

"Thanks Syd," Rook said. "You've been a great help. I really do appreciate it. Let's do lunch sometime."

"Great idea," Shelling responded. "Give me a

217

ring when you have some free time."

"Will do."

The universally broken promise of old friends who had grown apart.

After ending the call, Mitchell Rook brought up the university web site on his computer and clicked on medical faculty. That section of the web site gave short bios and some personal information on members of the faculty along with head shots of most of them. Katya Karpov, MD was a gorgeous blond neurologist with haunting green eyes who was an associate professor of psychiatry. Her specialty was chronic diseases of the brain. Although the site gave little personal information about the faculty, there were email addresses for most of them.

Rook clicked on Katya Karpov's email address and typed:

Dr. Karpov;

My name is Mitchell Rook and I am a business attorney in the city. I am doing some work with a startup company and have reason to believe that you may have information that would help me with the necessary due diligence. I would like to talk with you at your convenience. This inquiry should be kept in strictest confidence at this time and any information you might provide would also be strictly confidential. Please either respond to this email or phone me to arrange a time and place for us to meet.

Thank you in advance.

Mitchell

Mitchell Rook, Esq
Rook, Lipchitz, and Associates LLC
333 Commerce Street, Nashville
Tel: 615-434-6262

Rook would discuss this with Dom Petrillo before actually meeting with Dr. Karpov, assuming she responded. But at least the initial contact had been made, hopefully with enough care that Dr. Karpov would keep the request confidential.

"I had an interesting conversation with Syd Shelling, today," Katya said.

She had delayed starting this conversation with Shane until they were comfortably ensconced at their favorite table overlooking the river at the back of their favorite restaurant. The restaurant, *Mere Bulle*, was in one of the elegantly restored warehouse buildings that fronted the block of Second Avenue between Church Street and Broadway.

The rear of the building was on First Avenue that ran along the Cumberland River. The tables by the windows at the back of the room had a nice view of the river toward the east. The restaurant was allegedly named by the owners in honor of a favorite grandmother who was inordinately fond of the bubbly well into her ninth decade.

For a long time after his injury, Shane had been reluctant to go out to dinner or for any other reason if he could avoid it. But lately he had become more accustomed to the complicated logistics and was also less self-conscious in public. It was no longer rare for the beautiful blond neurologist to be seen wheeling the handsome paraplegic former detective along Second Avenue. And their favorite table at their favorite restaurant was always made available to them.

"Tell me about it KiKi, my love," Shane responded.

Shane knew that Syd Shelling was one of a vanishingly few members of the medical faculty whom Katya respected and whose advice she valued. Shane remembered meeting him at the only departmental event hosted by the Bartalaks that Katya had ever convinced him to attend. He recalled the elaborate picnic on the back lawn of the Bartalaks' Jackson Boulevard manse. There was a big tent set up near the tennis courts.

Katya introduced Shane to the pathologist and he and Shane had a brief and amiable conversation accompanied by the thump thump of tennis balls colliding with Beth Bartalak's impressive forehand ground stroke. He remembered watching Beth demolish one of the junior faculty, sprinting about the court and relentlessly pounding shot after shot beyond the reach of the hapless assistant professor who was probably at least ten years her junior. Shane had known scenes like that as a youth but they were not fond memories.

Shane sipped occasionally at a glass of chardonnay. Katya, as was her habit on such occasions, drank San Pellegrino, her wine glass frequently replenished from the large green bottle nestled in an ice bucket on a stand beside the table. She would finish the bottle before the evening was over. Katya believed that careful attention to adequate hydration was largely responsible for the quality of her skin and hair that had changed little since she was a teenager. She drank a lot of water.

"I wanted his advice about this thing with Beth Bartalak," Katya continued. "I really don't like the woman and thought I needed an objective professional opinion about what more I should do if anything."

"Makes good sense," Shane responded. "And?"

Katya took a long swallow of the cold water.

"Well," she said, "apart from disapproving of my getting the data from Beth's computer, he pretty much agreed with me that I don't really have a choice at this point. However, Syd also feared the consequences for

220

me professionally. He said something like, 'Cy may ruin you if he can and the dean is likely to take his side'. He pointed out what I already knew, that I'm much more expendable than Cy Bartalak. But he basically thought that I had to lodge a formal complaint even though all hell would probably break loose if I did."

"Hmm," Shane responded. "So, KiKi my love, are you going to do it?"

"This is really hard, Shane," she said. "The consequences for me will also be consequences for you, for us."

Shane reached across the table, took her hand and looked into the lovely green eyes that always took away his breath. He felt how deeply he loved this woman who had made his life worthwhile at a time when without her he would probably have thrown in the towel.

"KiKi," he said, "I can't imagine any consequences that would change how I feel about you. Surely you know that."

She looked away from him toward the river view and was quiet for a few minutes. When she turned back toward him her eyes were wet.

"There was something else, Shane," she said, "an odd coincidence that probably makes my decision final. Syd was looking at some brain sections sent to him by the coroner. Although he didn't identify the person, I am virtually certain that they were from Bonz Bagley's autopsy."

"Hardy Seltzer told me that the coroner was going to have a university pathologist review Bonz's autopsy specimens, so that's possible," Shane said. "What did Syd say about them?"

"Well," she replied, "he's not sure, but he thinks the brain sections show evidence of what is very likely to be toxic effects of a chemical, possibly a drug."

"And Bonz was a subject in the study of Cy's drug," Shane replied. "You told me that earlier."

"That's right. And I'm sure that the data I got from Beth's computer, the evidence that she is cheating, were the results from Bonz's six month follow up studies."

"Are you telling me that you think this drug is toxic? What about Bonz's earlier studies? Or studies from the other subjects?"

"Bonz was subject number one and is the only one so far who'd been on the drug for six months," Katya answered. "His first three months results showed marked improvement. And some of the other subjects are also showing early improvement. I don't have any reason to doubt the accuracy of those earlier results. If I'm putting this together correctly, the drug works in the short run but when taken for as long as six months it may cause severe damage to the brain."

"So the evidence for that is only from Bonz's autopsy and since he's dead there is no way to find out anything more about how the drug affected him."

"That's right. And the fact that the shots to his head demolished most of his brain means that we don't even know how extensive the effects were in him. Who knows what havoc that drug is capable of wreaking?"

"How sure can you be that this was an effect of the drug?"

"Not certain," Katya answered, "but coupled with the functional and biochemical studies, the real six month data that I got from Beth's computer certainly looks that way. You're the detective. Convince me that there's another explanation. I wished to God that was true."

"I wish I could think of another explanation, KiKi, my love," he answered, "but if there is one it's not obvious to me."

Shane drank a swallow of the wine and rotated the glass between his hands for a moment, then continued, "Drug works in the short run but kills in the long run. The short run/long run problem we talked about earlier. The drug is one of the bad guys."

"You're still working with that detective Seltzer on this?" Katya asked.

"Unofficially, yes."

"Will you have access to the coroner's final report on Bonz's autopsy? All I have is the conversation with Syd and that's at least technically confidential. In fact, he probably shouldn't have shown me the slides, probably wouldn't have if he had any idea that there was a connection with anything I was doing."

"I'm sure Hardy Seltzer will get a copy of the report as part of his investigation. He may give me a copy if I ask him for it. Should I do that?"

"Yes," Katya replied, "this is going to be a dogfight and I'll need all the ammunition I can get."

"Done, my love," Shane replied.

Shane thought that if he were ever forced into a dogfight, the last dog he would want to confront would be KiKi when she knew she was on the side of what was right. He smiled at her. She rose from her seat, walked around the table and stood beside him, placing her hand on his shoulder.

She said, "I love you Shane."

He looked up at her and she kissed him the familiar soft warm kiss that once saved his life. She stood by him for a moment, gazing out the window with her hand still resting on his shoulder.

Katya returned to her chair, flashed her electric smile, picked up a menu and said, "Let's order dinner. I'm starving."

20

The mayor's call to the chief of police followed close on the heels of Rory Holcomb's call to the mayor. Rory had the mayor's ear not because of any particular affection for him on the mayor's part, but because the mayor occupied that high office largely as a consequence of Rory's generous support of his election campaign. But Rory Holcomb's largesse was never bestowed without conditions. As far as Rory was concerned, his support of the mayor's campaign was a calculated business risk that had paid off. He had bought access and influence and did not hesitate to use it.

What Holcomb was up in arms about was what he thought was the effect of the unsolved murder of Bonz Bagley on business in the alley. Holcomb depended on rent from the buildings he owned there for the majority of his working capital. Most of the club owners who rented the spaces were operating on a very slim margin and most of the leases were short term. So, Holcomb's source of working capital was vulnerable to even short term fluctuations in the clubs' business.

There had been a notable downturn in alley activity since Bagley's murder there. Rory thought that if the murder was solved, presuming that the killer was taken out of circulation and so could not possibly be a threat any longer, the tide would turn and alley business would be back to its usual less than robust but acceptably profitable level.

So he leaned heavily on the mayor, told him to get his ass, and whatever other asses that were necessary, in gear and arrest somebody for God's sake. How hard could it be to solve a murder done with a totally unique weapon in broad daylight in the middle of the city the safety and security of which was the mayor's primary responsibility? Do your goddam job! Rory told him and slammed down the phone.

As soon as he finished with the call from Holcomb, the mayor called the chief of police. Without revealing what had prompted the call, the mayor essentially repeated Rory's tirade with some fewer obscenities, but not many. The chief assured him that they were making rapid progress on the investigation and that he was confident they would arrest the prime suspect very soon.

The mayor responded to the effect that such an eventuality should happen sooner rather than later and that the security of the chief's current position could well be related to the outcome of this case and the timing of its solution. That is essentially what he said although he didn't use those words exactly.

Consistent with the often observed effects of the earth's gravitational field on human excrement, the chief once again summoned Hardy Seltzer to his office. The chief had worked with Seltzer for a long time and knew that the detective did not respond well to being yelled at. He wouldn't yell at his star detective, but he would make it clear to him that the time had come to act. The chief was focused on results more than process, focused at that moment with laser like intensity on arresting someone for the Bagley murder who was at least a plausible perpetrator of the crime. It appeared to him that the only choice they had was Jody Dakota.

Seltzer was waiting for the elevator to take him from the subbasement of police headquarters up to his office when his cell phone rang. The screen indicated that the call was from the chief's office, so he answered it.

"Seltzer."

"Detective Seltzer," the familiar voice of Myra,

225

the chief's long time secretary said, "the chief wants to see you in his office immediately. He says it's urgent."

"Yes ma'am," Seltzer answered, "tell him I'm on my way."

Seltzer had gone down to the ballistics lab as soon as he saw the yellow note stuck to the screen of his computer informing him that Peter Harvey had called and would like to talk with him. Hardy had descended to the domain of Pistol Pete where he had endured a very long and detailed lecture on the elegance of the science of ballistics analysis — a careful description of the strengths and limitations of the process — before the eminent forensic scientist finally told him the results of the tests comparing the markings on the bullets test fired from Jody Dakota's gun with the markings on the bullets recovered from Bonz Bagley's cranial cavity at autopsy.

Seltzer had intended to return to his office to assemble all of the evidence in the case before taking it to the chief. But his boss was forcing the issue. No doubt political pressures were at work to which the detective was not privy. It was always politics that precipitated this kind of urgency. Hardy Seltzer was a methodical investigator and didn't like having his hand forced prematurely. That was particularly troubling when the forces were those of politics rather than justice. But he didn't have the final say. He would tell the chief everything he knew, put all the cards on the table, and see how things played out.

"We've got to move on the Bagley case, Hardy," the chief said.

The chief's secretary had ushered Seltzer into the office immediately without waiting to announce his arrival to her boss. The chief was pacing back and forth behind his desk. He didn't greet Seltzer, just waved toward the guest chair opposite the desk and launched into the subject at hand as Hardy sat down.

The chief continued, "I think we need to bring Jody Dakota in and charge him. You said yourself that we had a case, motive, opportunity and a murder weapon. Tell me why we should wait any longer."

"That's obviously up to you and the DA," Hardy responded.

"But, you're the detective, Hardy," the chief said and after a short pause continued. "The ballistics. Do we have those results yet? Harvey should have done the tests by now."

"I just reviewed the findings with him and was about to bring them to you when I got your call," Hardy replied.

"So?" the chief's impatience was becoming obvious in spite of his efforts to show respect for the detective's well-known deliberate approach to the analysis of the evidence in a case. "What about the ballistics?"

"I'll spare you the details of Mr. Harvey's lengthy explanation," Seltzer said. "The bottom line is that the results are a maybe; neither yes nor no. Mr. Harvey explained that in about ten percent of cases nationwide the ballistics results are equivocal. Harvey says his results are better than that; he can make positive conclusions in all but about five percent of cases. But this is one of the five percent."

"Damn! The chief responded, pounding his fist on the desk. "Damn!"

"Harvey offered a further opinion," Seltzer said. "He thought that since this is such an unusual gun — he says no more than thirty of this particular model were ever produced and probably many fewer than that still in existence and in working order — that the probability of two of them being owned by residents of a town the size of Nashville must be extremely low."

"So, we have a case," the chief said. "We have

motive, opportunity and very strong evidence that we have the murder weapon. Let me get the DA on the phone and let's move on this."

The DA had also received a call from the mayor, the content if not the tone of which was similar to that of the mayor's earlier conversation with the police chief. The DA had just hung up from that call when his secretary rang the police chief through to him. The DA was in a foul mood and was fully prepared to make the chief aware of that fact.

Foregoing any preliminary niceties, the DA answered, "What the hell do you want? Unless you're going to tell me that we can arrest someone for the Bagley murder we don't have anything to talk about."

"That's exactly what I'm going to tell you," the chief responded.

"So, talk to me," the DA responded, his tone softening only slightly.

"We have the ballistics."

"So?"

"That's the good news. The bad news is that it's not conclusive."

"What do you mean not conclusive? Ballistics don't lie."

The chief explained to the DA that the results of the ballistics were equivocal but that the fact that the gun was so rare still made it entirely possible, even likely, that Jody Dakota's gun was the murder weapon and Dakota was the murderer.

"Bring the little bastard in and charge him with murder one," was the DA's immediate and unequivocal response.

"We'll do that," the chief answered. "And I suggest that the two of us hold a joint press conference later today to announce the arrest. We need to get ahead of the media on this. I don't want the headline in the morning paper to be the first the public hears about it."

"Capital idea," the DA answered and ended the call.

The chief had put the call on speaker phone so that Hardy Seltzer had heard the entire conversation.

"You heard the man, detective," the chief said. "Do it."

"You're the boss," Seltzer replied.

Seltzer made no move to get up from his chair and they sat for a few minutes looking at each other.

Finally the chief said, "You don't seem entirely comfortable with this, Hardy. What's bothering you?"

"Well," Hardy said, "I did as you suggested and discussed the case with Shane Hadley."

"What does Sherlock Shane think about it?"

"Shane is convinced that Jody Dakota isn't the killer."

"Does he have a better idea?"

"He thinks he does, but I'm not convinced."

Hardy proceeded to give the chief what details he had about the mysterious Elizabeth Reid who had allegedly test fired a gun like Dakota's at a Brentwood firing range and Shane's efforts to find her through a connection to a dead Texas lawyer who had willed a rare gun collection to a daughter with that name. Hardy made it clear that there remained a lot of unconnected dots. In fact Hardy thought that Shane's theory was pretty much a collection of dots without enough connections to make anything close to a coherent story.

Seltzer very much liked stories to make sense and he was always troubled by the data gathering phase of an investigation unless there was a clear direction. That is exactly where he thought Shane was with his mystery woman theory. It could pan out, but it was impossible to tell whether that would be the case. Hardy would be surprised if it did.

The chief listened intently to the story, looking directly at Seltzer and occasionally scratching his head as though assimilating the information required some effort.

When Seltzer had finished, the chief paused for a minute and then said, "Tell you what, Hardy. Let's bring in Jody Dakota and charge him as the DA instructed. Turn all of the evidence incriminating Dakota over to the DA. But I have disregarded what seemed like outlandish theories by Shane Hadley in the past with some undesirable consequences, situations that I would strongly prefer not to repeat. Do everything you can to follow Hadley's line of investigation, but do it quietly. The DA doesn't need to know about it. Let him think he's got the killer unless and until there are solid reasons to believe otherwise."

As Seltzer was leaving the chief's office, he passed the secretary who held a note in her hand and seemed in a particular hurry to deliver it to her boss. She rushed past Hardy into the office and handed the chief the note.

"This call came while you were meeting with detective Seltzer," she said. "Mr. Coniglio said to be sure that you understood that it was urgent that you return his call."

"Thanks Myra," the chief said.

The secretary left, closing the door behind her and the chief sat behind his desk looking at the note and dreading the call that he knew he would have to make. He had no idea why the attorney X Coniglio would need to talk with him so urgently but it would certainly not be for any reason that the chief would enjoy dealing with. They were generally on opposite sides of any issue that involved both of them and Coniglio was a formidable opponent. The chief placed the call.

The secretary who answered the phone put him through to Coniglio immediately and the attorney got right to the point.

"Chief," he said, "your department is in possession of some property of a client of mine and I want you to see that it is returned. Can you do that?"

"Well X," the chief responded feeling as always that addressing the lawyer using only the near terminal letter of the alphabet that the attorney insisted was his actual name, not an initial, was awkward, "perhaps you can give me some more details and I'll see what I can do."

"I'm talking about Jody Dakota's gun," X responded. "An officer under your command has taken possession of a rare firearm belonging to my client, Mr. Dakota, and we wish it returned to him immediately."

"You're representing Jody Dakota?" the chief asked.

"That is correct, sir," replied X. "He employed me in that capacity a few days ago and he is here in my office at this moment extremely upset about the unauthorized confiscation of his property and by his treatment at the hands of your detective, one Hardy Seltzer."

"Your information is incorrect, X," the chief said. "Mr. Dakota voluntarily relinquished his firearm to Detective Seltzer. It cannot be returned to him now because it is being held as evidence in a murder case."

"Evidence?" X queried. "I guess we'll see about that. The gun was taken by one of your officers operating beyond the boundaries of the territory where the Metropolitan Police Department has authority and outside the legal boundaries that protect the property rights of a law abiding citizen. My client maintains that your detective threatened him, coerced him into relinquishing said firearm. I

231

seriously doubt that such behavior will be looked on favorably by any criminal court judge in this city. That gun will never see the light of day as evidence in any criminal case, sir."

There was a bright side to this, the chief thought. At least Jody Dakota was in the city and so could be arrested by the metro police legitimately.

"I must tell you, Mr. Coniglio," the chief said, avoiding the awkward use of just X to address the attorney, "that we are about to arrest your client, Mr. Dakota, and charge him with the first degree murder of Bonz Bagley. It would be most convenient if you could keep him in your office until my people arrive."

"He didn't do it, chief," X answered. "You aren't going to come out of this looking very good when the truth is known. And the truth will be known. You can count on that. Of course my client will cooperate in every way with the police. You may come here to arrest him but rest assured that I will accompany him every step of the way."

I'm sure you will, the chief thought. X Coniglio defended his clients with the ferocity of a pit bull on steroids. The DA would have a stroke when he found out who was defending Dakota. Coniglio was the one defense lawyer in town who had several notches in his gun handle as a result of duels with this DA. The chief of police always enjoyed seeing the two of them go at it. But the odds that Jody Dakota would walk were markedly improved by his selection of a lawyer. And if Bonz Bagley's murderer walked, it would reflect on the whole system, especially the police department.

Hardy Seltzer speed-dialed Shane Hadley's

home number on his cell phone as he was making his way back to his office.

"Hadley, here (*hee-ah*)," Shane answered on the fourth ring.

Shane had been on the deck enjoying the late morning sun and biding his time until he could rationalize having his first glass of sherry for the day. There was little action in the alley. It was too early for the clubs and there seemed to be fewer people in the alley most of the time of late. He looked across at the dead façade of what had been *Bonz's Booze and Music*, the sign now gone and the place looking as lifeless as its former owner.

"Shane," Hardy replied, "this is Hardy."

"Hi-ho my man," Shane responded. "You've no doubt called to tell me that you have suddenly located our mystery woman and are about to arrest her. Am I correct?"

"Not exactly," Hardy replied. "We are about to make an arrest in the Bagley case, but you're mistaken about the gender of the arrestee."

"So," Shane said, "the results of the ballistics tests were equivocal."

"Why do you think that?" Hardy said.

Hardy thought that the most logical guess about the results of the ballistics would be that they identified Dakota's gun as the murder weapon since they were obviously proceeding to charge him with the murder.

Shane answered, "It is the only possibility, my man. Since that gun is not the murder weapon the results could not possibly have proven that it was. And if the tests had ruled the gun out as the weapon of interest, you would not be proceeding to arrest and charge the owner of the gun with a murder which he did not commit. The only possible conclusion is that the tests were inconclusive, an unusual but not unheard of result of such tests. I suspect the DA, whose powers of reasoning are considerably less than optimal—he is, in fact, an idiot—reasoned that since it is such a rare gun and the ballistics left open the possibility that it was the murder weapon, that, in the context of the other evidence that has even you convinced of Dakota's guilt, a case, the DA would say a *prosecutable case,* could be made."

"Yeah, that's about how it went, Shane. Even though I still think Jody did it, I thought the chief and the DA were too anxious to make an arrest in the case, moving too fast. Sounds like pressure from above to me."

"Ah, yes," Shane said, "the ever recurring futile attempts to blend the immiscible elixirs of justice and politics."

Hardy concurred wholeheartedly with the fact that justice and politics didn't mix well but would have chosen different words to make the point.

"I fear you've acted prematurely, my man," Shane continued. "I warned you about that."

"I hope not, but it's out of my hands."

"If you're going after Jody Dakota," Shane said, "you're going to have to go through X Coniglio, you know. I saw the little fellow entering X's office the other day."

"That's the DA's problem."

"When the wee one walks, it will be your problem, my man, and the chief's," Shane responded.

"I guess we'll see," Hardy said, then added. "You may want to watch the news later today. There'll be a press conference. If nothing else it will be one of the rare occasions when the DA and the chief of police try to create the illusion that they actually like each other."

"Will do. Will do," Shane responded. "Always an interesting performance."

"When can we get together?" Hardy asked. "I'll have some more time once we turn the Dakota case over to the DA. We should stay after your mystery woman theory for the time being, see where it goes."

"Hardy, my man, do I detect a hint of actual interest in what you call my mystery woman theory? To what do we owe this change of heart?" Shane said.

"Actually, the chief suggested it although he would like the fact that we're working together on an alternative solution to the Bagley murder kept quiet for now."

"The chief actually told you to work with me? Amazing! When I knew the old warhorse, he didn't seem especially fond of how I approached things. We locked horns more than once."

"Not surprised," Hardy responded, "but he tells me that he's dismissed a cockamamie theory or two of yours in the past and wound up holding the short end of the stick. He doesn't want that to happen again."

"True, true," Shane said, "surprising how passing time can change one's point of view. Nonetheless, this is a wonderful development. Come by tomorrow whenever it's convenient and let's set about finding the real killer."

"See you tomorrow, Shane," Hardy said, smiling to himself. "It'll probably be afternoon. I'll call in advance."

It was still early in the day, but Hardy didn't feel like sitting around in his stifling office all afternoon. He wasn't going to attend the press conference, although the chief would have been perfectly OK with that. Hardy decided that he wasn't even going to watch the conference on TV. He didn't need to be reminded of how the criminal justice system worked. He was too well aware of that. He had his role to play and he played it as best he could. What happened upstream to his efforts often displeased him, but he wasn't responsible for the actions of the people who occupied the spaces nearer the headwaters of law enforcement.

After spending a while catching up on some long neglected paper work, Hardy decided to leave. He put on his jacket, lowered his window and left his office, heading for the elevator to the parking lot. He wandered around the underground garage trying to remember where he had parked the department's black Crown Vic, the aging behemoth use of which was one of the few dubious perks of his job. Having located the car, he decided to go to the Dew Drop Inn for a beer. He was also thinking that if it was Marge Bland's day to work the early shift, he just might ask her to go to dinner with him.

Hardy Seltzer was a solitary man. He had even been a solitary boy, an only child left pretty much to fend for himself on the mean streets of North Nashville. He learned how to do that early and those skills had done well by him over time. He was OK with that. Although he had been alone for a long time he had rarely felt lonely. It had been a while since he had felt any strong need for human company. But he was feeling lonely today, maybe had been feeling that more of late.

He was enjoying the fortuitous connection with Shane Hadley, the Sherlock Shane of departmental myth reincarnated as a quirky wheel chair bound ex-detective holed up in his Printers Alley flat. And then there was also Hardy's accidental rediscovery of Marge Bland. She seemed to be taking up some room in his head of late. Just as well see if he could figure out what that was about.

Hardy cranked up the car and headed out of the garage, lumbering down toward Broadway and up the First Avenue hill toward an anticipated rendezvous with his old high school classmate. As he passed the trendy Italian restaurant just at the crest of the hill, he was struck with the name of the place, *Sole Mio*. Maybe an especially appropriate spot for his dinner with Marge Bland, he thought.

21

Beth Bartalak hadn't gone to work at all. She would have preferred to stay in bed the whole day, but managed to rouse herself, make coffee and toast for Cy's breakfast and see him off. Cy didn't ask why she wasn't dressed for work. He probably didn't even notice, she thought. He seemed to notice her less and less recently. He was so preoccupied with doing a big deal with this drug thing that he didn't seem to notice much of anything else. And maybe she was neglecting herself some. Except for her daily long run through the park, Beth didn't do much lately. Most of what occupied her mind was that bitch Katya Karpov. She still had to go. Now more than ever. Cy seemed to have inordinate difficulty recognizing that fact.

Beth had recognized the documents from the folder that Katya had given Cy as the original data from the six month studies on subject number one in the drug study, the now dead Mr. Bagley. Beth had told Cy that it appeared to her that Katya had contrived some fake data sheets on subject number one, since the information in the file was not consistent with the data in the official file that Beth had diligently maintained and protected.

Those were the data that Cy had seen and presented to both the investors and the DSMB. On the strength of those data, the DSMB had agreed to break the code and if, as Cy suspected, the subjects who showed dramatic improvement were the ones taking the active drug, to stop the study for reasons of apparent efficacy. That would open the way for planning phase III definitive studies and guarantee a lucrative deal with big pharma. From there it was a straight shot to FDA approval and to the holy grail of the drug development business, a marketed drug.

After Cy left for work, Beth decided to go back to

bed and sleep until afternoon when she would get up and go for a run. She didn't feel bad particularly, just out of sorts, disconnected. The feeling was akin to that she remembered from being given morphine when she had broken her leg as a teenager.

At fifteen she had fallen from the high perch in a large live oak tree in the back yard where she often sat, daydreaming and imagining a life different than her real one. She sustained a severe compound fracture of her right femur in the fall. It was the prolonged rehabilitation from that injury that led her to discover the pleasure of distance running, a pleasure that had stayed with her ever since. She recalled that the morphine that she was given for the excruciating pain after the injury brought on a feeling of detachment. She had often thought that morphine didn't really relieve pain, it just caused you not to perceive it as yours, to view the pain from a distance. It felt like that was how she was viewing everything lately, from a distance, as though she were living in a separate space, apart from that other space where reality was happening.

Beth had slept for several hours when she was awakened by the sound of the TV set that she had left playing when she went back to bed. She wasn't sure why the sound suddenly awakened her. What she saw on the screen was a news conference that had interrupted the regular afternoon programming. The chief of police and the district attorney had called the news conference to announce the arrest of the alleged murderer of Bonz Bagley. Beth had never heard of Jody Dakota but she didn't care who he was. The news raised her spirits. She felt a lot better than she had for a while. She smiled to herself as she entered the bathroom to shower and dress for her run. Good, she thought. That little matter is over and done with.

Emerging from the shower, Beth paused in front

of the full length mirror mounted on the bathroom door. She still looked good she thought. Her long tan legs could still attract attention. She was sure that Rory Holcomb had noticed them. She donned her blue running shorts and an orange tank top and looked again at herself in the mirror. Cy ought to pay her more attention, she thought. She needed to work on that.

On her way to the door, she stopped by her study and took the hammer model Colt pistol from the desk drawer where she had placed it earlier. No need to hide it any longer. She held the gun for a few moments, relishing the heft, the substance of it and then placed it carefully in its rightful spot at the center of the rare gun collection in the glass display case. No need to hide it any longer.

Shane and KiKi did not own a television set. That was KiKi's idea and it was fine with Shane. He thought that watching TV was an activity that was usually an attempt to isolate oneself from reality. While he was not averse to blurring the lines between fantasy and reality in his mind, he didn't need the inanity of the telly to accomplish that. On the rare occasions when there was something being aired that he felt compelled to watch, he viewed it on his laptop computer, courtesy of their wireless connection to the Internet.

Shane poured a glass of sherry, picked up his laptop and wheeled himself out onto the deck. The alley was quiet. The afternoon sun painted a broad brushstroke of brilliant white across the private space that was his viewing stand for the parade of human activity in the small world below.

He turned on the computer and began a search

for the TV station that would broadcast the news conference. He located the site but the glare of the bright sunlight on the screen obscured the picture. He wheeled himself back through the French doors inside, continued down the long corridor to the bedroom and parked next to the windows overlooking Third Avenue.

Shane hadn't seen either the police chief or the DA in a long time and he was surprised at how changed they both were. Not surprisingly, they were grayer and thicker in the middle than he remembered them, but there was also something different about their faces that appeared to be more than the consequences of passing years. It bothered Shane that he couldn't define the changes more precisely.

But, they were the same guys, still capable of staging an accomplished public performance. Obviously in their element, the chief and the DA took turns speaking their well-rehearsed lines. To the uninitiated, it would appear that the two components of the criminal justice system which the men represented were parts of a well-oiled efficient and effective law enforcement machine that functioned smoothly in the relentless pursuit of any misanthrope who dared to threaten the safety of the *citizens of our fair city.*

Of course, Shane and anyone familiar with the reality of the situation knew that successes in capturing the city's criminals were largely the work of a few dedicated cops who did their job in spite of a seriously dysfunctional hierarchy. Shane supposed that the officials served a purpose. Someone had to stage the performances that were necessary to keep the larger audience at bay, defend the territories where the dedicated cops did their work from overzealous scrutiny by people who didn't understand the process.

As he watched the performance, Shane reviewed the Bagley murder investigation in his mind. It seemed patently obvious to him that Jody Dakota could not be the murderer. There was the matter of the gun. No matter how limited the ex-music star's mental capacity was he would not have voluntarily relinquished his gun if he knew that it was the murder weapon. Impossible.

Shane was surprised that Hardy Seltzer didn't grasp that critical fact. A single critical fact that cannot be made to fit the story negates the entire theory, collapses the house of cards. *Rule out all of the obvious possibilities and see what's left*, the great detective would have said. Well, to Shane's mind, Jody Dakota had ruled himself out when he gave up his gun to Hardy without putting up a fight.

Shane still thought of this as the *Case of the Devil's foot*. The unusual running gait that was vaguely familiar to him was a key. If only he could link the gait to a specific person Shane believed that the pieces of the puzzle would fall into place. He wondered if there was any way to get more information about Elizabeth Reid, daughter of the Texas lawyer and heir to the rare gun collection.

Was she an athlete? Did she have an old injury of some sort that altered her running gait? Was Elizabeth Anne Reid, formerly of Greensward, Texas, marked with Shane's imagined *Curse of the Devil's Foot* that would be her undoing? Was there any way to connect this mysterious woman to Nashville, any possible reason for her to pump four shots into poor Bonz Bagley's brain? The fact that there were four shots still puzzled Shane.

Shane really was surprised that the police chief had encouraged Hardy to work with him and for the two of them to pursue Shane's theory about the murder. He was pleased about that. Hardy's fully functioning legs as well as his investigative experience and his access to information would be major assets. And Shane was growing fond of the detective.

Shane thought that Seltzer had some things to learn yet about how to solve a murder, that his thinking was too conventional, but he was good at his job and he was entertaining company. Hardy took himself a trifle too seriously, but Shane was starting to loosen the old boy up a bit. If only Shane could convince Hardy of the benefits of a slowly consumed excellent sherry, he might possibly metamorphose into a real human being. That would also make him a better detective. Hardy Seltzer needed to learn how to enjoy himself.

When Shane turned his attention back to the computer screen, the police chief and the DA had been replaced by the familiar imposing persona of the attorney, X Coniglio. Apparently Coniglio had arranged his own press conference in an effort to counteract the public impression that the law enforcement officials had tried to create around the arrest of Jody Dakota.

Coniglio was a local personality who carefully cultivated an idiosyncratic public image. He was tall and thin with a mass of unruly shoulder length white hair. He usually wore a black waistcoat with a brilliant red ascot at his throat, and, on occasion, he either wore or carried in his hands, a tall black top hat with which he liked to gesture in an exaggerated way to emphasize a point.

Coniglio had created for himself a lucrative professional niche as the defender of highly visible personalities from the city's thriving music world, an activity at which he was remarkably effective. And the extracurricular activities of the music crowd were a constant and reliable source of business.

Some years earlier, X, a notorious activist for

liberal political causes, had run an ill-fated campaign for governor in the democratic primary. He attributed his ignominious loss of the contest to his odd single character first name, which he steadfastly refused to explain, and to a public bias against his obviously Italian surname rather than to political ineptitude.

Coniglio was in high dudgeon, railing at the blatant disregard of legal rights and human dignity by the police department — specifically naming detective Hardy Seltzer as one of the offenders — in their treatment of his client, an upstanding citizen who had been a significant contributor to the city's noble history, its legendary reputation as a bastion of country music.

Waving his top hat in the air, he exclaimed, "Little Jody Dakota is an innocent man who was living a quiet and peaceful life until this city's law enforcement machine descended upon him with outrageous charges of a crime of which Mr. Dakota knows nothing. Apparently our *city's finest*," he emphasized the words for sarcastic effect, "care less for the welfare of our law abiding citizens than for finding a scapegoat to obscure their abysmal failure to hunt down the actual perpetrator of a heinous murder committed in broad daylight on a Lord's Day morning in the very center of our city. Mark my words, people," he waved his hat in the air again, "the sword of true justice will rise to smite the misguided and illegal efforts of this city's law enforcement establishment and, mark my words, good people," he thundered," heads will roll!"

"Wow," Shane said aloud.

He closed the laptop and started back down the hall toward the front of the flat.

"Shane," KiKi's greeting rang out, echoing down the corridor, "I'm home."

"I'm on my way up there," Shane responded.

They met just as Shane was entering the living room. KiKi rushed to him, hugging him around the shoulders and pulling him close to her where she held him for a few moments. She finally released him and leaned down and kissed him full and warm on the mouth.

"Wow! Shane said, "Just, wow!"

KiKi did not appear particularly happy when she separated from him and walked over toward the fireplace. She stood there looking at him without speaking.

"So, my love," Shane said, "should I inquire as to what I owe this exhilarating display of affection or just relax and enjoy it?"

"It's just that when I occasionally get a glimpse of the forest of my life unobscured by the trees, I realize how fortunate I am."

"I wouldn't have thought that I would be considered a very reliable source of good fortune, my love."

"You are the luckiest thing that ever happened to me."

"I prefer to believe that this was destined by *The Fates* or whomever is in charge of human destinies," Shane replied.

"Well, whatever the reason, I still consider myself, us, fortunate."

"Can't argue with that," Shane answered.

Shane wheeled himself to the bar to refill his glass of sherry.

"Maybe I'll join you," KiKi said.

Unusual, Shane thought, but he didn't say so. He just opened the case that contained the Oxford sherry glasses, removed one, held it up to the light and then placed it on the bar and filled it with a generous portion of his Lincoln College Sherry.

He rolled himself over to KiKi, handed her the

glass and said, "So, tell me about your day."

She paused to drink deeply from her glass of wine.

"This is really very good wine," she said. "I can see why you're so fond of it."

"Tell me about your day, KiKi," Shane repeated.

"Yes, well," she said, walking over to sit on the sofa opposite him, "it appears according to Cy that the DSMB "

"Sorry, my love, DSMB?" he queried.

"That's the data safety monitoring board that oversees the studies of the drug."

"I see," Shane said.

He didn't understand what such a board would do but didn't want to change the course of the conversation and so didn't ask.

"The DSMB," KiKi continued, "has broken the code for the study at Cy's request and it turns out that the subjects who were taking the active drug were indeed the ones who showed marked improvement."

"And?"

"And, the results show such dramatic improvements in the subjects on the drug that, even though the numbers are very small, the board has agreed with Cy's request that the study be stopped for the reason of apparent efficacy."

Shane thought for a moment and then said, "At least that means that no one will continue to take the drug. Right? Isn't that what you wanted?"

"You mean the right thing done for the wrong reason," she said. "I suppose that's true. But what that means is that Cy will forge ahead with design of the larger definitive phase III studies that the FDA will require before approving the drug for marketing. He's probably scheming with some big pharmaceutical company at this moment, convincing them to buy out his little company at some exorbitant price. I'm

246

convinced that this drug is a potential killer, Shane. This can't be allowed to happen."

"I understand, my love," Shane answered. "I understand, but won't this at least buy time for your scientific misconduct complaint to force the issue?"

"I guess so," she said. "I guess it gives me time to get all my ducks in a row. This is going to be a dogfight and it'll be even more ferocious now. I'll need all the ammunition I can muster. Speaking of ammunition, did you get a copy of Bonz's autopsy report?"

"Not yet," Shane answered, "but Hardy Seltzer is coming over tomorrow and I'll see if he can bring a copy.

"Fine, fine," KiKi said, "I'll need your help with this, Shane. If I'm dealing with crooks"

Shane interrupted her, "We," he said, "not I."

"OK," She continued, "if *we* are dealing with crooks here as I suspect, we need to put together the best case possible before I take it to the dean. This is your area, not mine."

"I do have some experience in putting together cases, my love, "he responded. "I'm delighted to help."

Shane was in fact delighted that he might be of professional help to his brilliant scientist wife. It had always seemed to him that her profession and his former one required a very different view of things and different skills. He thought that those differences had sometimes threatened to put more space between them than he liked. It could be immensely interesting if the chasm he imagined separating the two endeavors were not as broad as he had thought.

As KiKi was getting up and starting for the kitchen, she turned suddenly toward Shane and asked, "Do you know a lawyer in the city named Mitchell Rook?"

"Doesn't ring a bell," Shane said. "What kind of a lawyer is he?"

"Not sure, maybe business law?"

"Why do you ask?"

"I had an odd email from him. Said he was doing some 'due diligence'," she drew the quotation marks in the air with her fingers, "that might have something to do with the company that Cy formed to develop his drug. Said he would like to talk with me."

"Hmm," Shane responded, "let me see what I can find out about him. Why don't you give me some time to do that before you respond?"

"Makes sense to me," she said.

22

Hardy Seltzer maneuvered the Crown Vic into a vacant parking spot in front of the long, low building with a corrugated steel façade displaying a sign that read *Williamson County Shooters Club* in large black letters.

When Hardy called Shane Hadley to arrange a time for them to meet, Shane assigned Hardy two tasks. Task number one was completed. On his way out of town, he had gone by the coroner's office and obtained a copy of the report of the Bagley autopsy. He didn't see why Shane wanted it. There was no doubt about the cause of death and, according to Dr. Jensen, there were no other findings that had any relevance to the murder. But, Hardy, charged now by his chief to follow up on Shane's ill-defined theory, did as Shane instructed.

Task number two proved to be something of a challenge. Although Shane had given Hardy the address of the shooting club, locating it wasn't easy. As always on the rare occasions when Hardy was called on to travel south of town, he had taken Franklin Road, US highway 31, the old road that exited the city toward the south and continued through Brentwood and Franklin, meandering through the low hills on to Pulaski, Ardmore on the Alabama border and then to Birmingham and points south. The interstate would have been quicker, but Hardy favored the views from the old highway.

Hardy drove out of town past the turnoff onto Curtiswood Lane that circled around through a leafy neighborhood of pretentious homes including the governor's mansion and next door, the place where the civic minded matron, Sarah Cannon, lived with her husband and her alter ego, the Grand Ole Opry comedienne Minnie Pearl. A little further out he passed the surprisingly modest bungalow where Hank and Audrey Williams had once lived when Hank wasn't on the road drinking himself to death. It may have been in that house where the lyrical genius translated his firsthand experience with the pain of addiction and a stormy relationship into poetry, the resonating homage to the pathos of *cold and cheatin hearts*, that was the richest and most durable part of the country music canon.

Hardy had then worked his way through the growing traffic of Brentwood, the once quaint village that was in the process of exploding into a sprawling haven of the *nouveau riche*. Hinckley Hollow Road turned off US31 between Brentwood and Franklin. Hardy had seen the road sign and made the left turn onto the two lane blacktop. However, the shooters club was located on a dead end road named, inexplicably, Carpenter's Run, that was supposed to be a right turn off Hinckley Hollow Road.

There were several roads that branched to the right and none of them were marked with road signs so that Hardy had made several false excursions into the depths of Williamson County before he hit by a sheer process of elimination on what was apparently Carpenter's Run, an uninviting one-lane gravel road that ended at the front of the Williamson County Shooters Club.

Hardy got out of the car and entered the building to confront a small wiry man with a large grape colored birthmark that started near the center of his forehead and spread amoeba-like to occupy a significant portion of his completely bald head. He wore army fatigues of the outdated olive green variety, and stood ramrod straight behind a low counter immediately opposite the entrance.

"I'm Clem Horsely," the man said, leaning across the counter. "How can I help you?"

"Yes, Mr. Horsely," Seltzer responded. "My name is Hardy Seltzer and I'm a detective with the Metro Nashville Police."

Horsely smiled broadly and said, "What have I done that brings our little operation to your attention, detective? You say Nashville police? I didn't think you city cops did business in Williamson County."

"No, no," Hardy responded, "my interest has nothing to do with your operation. But you had a customer I am told who interests us in a murder investigation, an Elizabeth Reid. Do you remember her?"

"Woman seems to be attracting a lot of attention for such a quiet sort," Horsely answered. "Some guy called just the other day asking about her."

"Yes, that would be my associate Shane Hadley. We're working together on the case. So you remember this Elizabeth Reid?"

"Oh, yes. Couldn't forget that fancy pistol she brought in to test fire. Like I told the other guy, Hensley was it? Like I told him, it was a really rare gun. First one I ever saw in the flesh so to speak. She came in a couple of times and fired a few rounds. Excellent shot. Quiet though. Didn't want to talk about the gun or anything else as best I could tell."

"What did she look like?"

"Small woman, but muscular. Looked like an athlete of some sort, maybe a runner, slim like runners get, but solid. At least that's how she looked to me. Dark hair. Good looking, but not pretty if you know what I mean. I'd bet she's a tough cookie but she didn't look like a killer to me. Too distracted. A sort of vacant look about her, now that I think about it."

"My associate said that she signed into a log of some kind."

"Yep. I make them all sign in. She paid cash so all I got was her name in the log book."

"Would it be possible for me to get a copy of her signature in the book?"

"Sure, bud," Horsely replied, "I've got a little Xerox back in the office."

Horsely took a large ledger-like book from behind the desk and started thumbing through the pages.

"Here it is," he said. "It'll just take a minute. I'll just copy the page where she signed."

Horsely disappeared toward the back of the building.

At long last, Hardy had completed task number two. He took the photocopy of the page from the log book and after looking to be certain it contained the signature of Elizabeth Reid, folded the sheet lengthwise, placed it in his inside jacket pocket, thanked Clem Horsely and bid him goodbye.

"No problem," Horsely said, "anytime."

Hardy left the Williamson County Shooters Club, cranked up the Crown Vic and headed back toward town for his rendezvous with Shane at his Printers Alley flat.

As he drove north back toward the city, Hardy thought about the previous day.

Although he still believed that Jody Dakota was probably the guilty party in this case, he didn't feel the sense of satisfaction that he usually felt when he was happy with the solution to a murder case. Turning over an airtight case to the DA for prosecution always caused him to feel a complex blend of satisfaction and relief with maybe some other sensations that he couldn't define very well. But, he wasn't feeling any of those things.

Regardless of what he thought was the truth, the case against Jody Dakota was certainly not airtight. Hardy liked doing his job successfully and worked hard at it. But he thought the chief and the DA had moved too quickly.

It had happened before when a murder got excessive publicity. No detective really liked to get that assignment, the high profile murder. Too many people looking over your shoulder, second guessing everything, speculating. But, Hardy was at least satisfied that he had done his job until the Bagley case was taken out of his hands. He had done what he could do.

After leaving work early the previous day, Hardy had driven up to the Dew Drop Inn where he had sat at the bar talking with Marge Bland and nursing his way through a couple of Bud Lights, stretching out the time. He sat there making idle conversation and ignoring the press conference featuring the police chief and the DA that was showing on the TV over the bar. Marge glanced up occasionally at the TV but the sound was turned down and she seemed more interested in talking to Hardy anyway. At least that was what he thought.

However, when the familiar figure of X Coniglio appeared on the screen, Marge turned up the sound.

"Old X always puts on a show," she said. "Let's see what he has to say."

What X had to say, the parts that stuck in Hardy's mind, were that detective Hardy Seltzer, whom he mentioned by name, was a particularly offensive member of the police force, and then the attorney's final bombast, "heads will roll." The possible connection between himself and a rolling head was not a pleasant thought for Hardy.

The only possibly positive result of X's tirade was that the inference that Hardy might be in mortal danger seemed to soften Marge Bland's attitude toward him. She seemed, in fact, genuinely concerned. And when Hardy, having established that she was working the early shift and would get off work about six, suggested that the two of them have an early dinner together at *Sole Mio* just down the street, she immediately agreed.

Nothing earth shaking had occurred at dinner but it was a very pleasant interlude for Hardy in what had been, of late, a less than completely pleasant period in his life. On parting, they agreed, without specifying a time and place, to repeat the experience. Hardy felt surprisingly good about that.

Hardy parked the car in the garage below the police headquarters, removed the copy of the page from the shooters club log from his jacket pocket, put it in the folder that contained the autopsy report and got out of the car. He decided that he would walk directly over to the alley without going back to his office since it was very close to the time that he had told Shane he would be there.

The warm day was overcast and the air had the humid feel that often comes before a thunderstorm. There was a soft breeze and Hardy was aware of the pleasant sensation of the warm wet breeze caressing his face.

Hardy wondered what Shane had in store for this little project. No doubt he would have a specific idea of how to go about things. That was fine with Hardy. He was authorized to go along with wherever the reactivated ex-detective was headed and also Hardy would be interested in how Sherlock Shane, given his head, would proceed. It would be an interesting ride regardless of the final destination. And, if Shane's theory was right and could be proven, it would be a truly satisfying and hugely informative experience.

Hardy felt that at this point it was a no lose situation. That is, unless X Coniglio's well-known and considerable political clout was sufficient to make good on his now very public threat. Hardy refused to think about that. He had no idea what he would do if he could no longer do this job.

"Hi-ho, my man," Shane called from the balcony as Hardy approached. "You look remarkably chipper today given the threat of X Coniglio's guillotine poised above your neck. Come on up."

"Thanks for reminding me, Shane," Hardy answered, recalling for some reason Edgar Allen Poe's *The Pit and the Pendulum* short story that he must have last read when he was classmates with Marge Bland at North High.

To his surprise, when Hardy exited the elevator into Shane's living room, Shane greeted him without a glass of sherry in his hand. Hardy occasionally wondered if Shane had a serious drinking problem. It didn't seem that way. Even though Shane was almost never without the glass of sherry, he never appeared the least bit intoxicated. Maybe the glass of sherry was a prop, like some men — in Hardy's experience mainly traffic cops, small town sheriff's, and the grimy bail bondsmen who hung around the courthouse — always held a cigar in their mouths that was never lit. Maybe Shane didn't actually drink that much, although Hardy would not have been surprised to discover that Shane drank excessively given his disability. Had he shared Shane's fate, Hardy suspected that he may well have chosen to drown himself in a bottle of Jack Daniels.

"Have a seat, my man," Shane said, gesturing toward the sofa that fronted the fireplace. "We have work to do."

"Here's the material you asked me to get for you," Hardy said, handing the manila folder to Shane.

"Very good, Hardy. Did you encounter the character at the shooters club?"

"Yes," Hardy answered, but didn't elaborate.

Shane paused expecting the detective to say

255

more.

After a lengthy pause, Hardy continued, "Let's have at it, Shane."

Hardy took a seat opposite where Shane had parked himself in front of the couch.

Shane said, "I would repeat my habitually refused offer of a glass of sherry, but unfortunately my supply of the golden elixir is exhausted at the moment, a situation that is obviously of considerably more concern to me than to you. Ah well, the situation will be remedied shortly."

"Thanks anyway," Hardy replied.

"So," Shane got down to the business at hand, "I have concluded that we must, as a matter of utmost urgency, find out everything possible about Elizabeth Anne Reid, sole heir of the deceased Archibald Stewart Reid of Greensward, Texas. Are you free to travel, Hardy? Could you make a trip to Texas if that were deemed important?"

"As far as I know I'm free to travel," Hardy responded, "but Texas wouldn't be high on my list of possible destinations."

"I agree, my man," Shane replied, "but then an investigation often leads one into places that left to one's own devices, one would not choose to go."

"You can say that again," Hardy replied, hoping that Shane would not take him literally which he didn't.

"I have started the inquiry," Shane said, "by attempting to identify potential sources of information. And, with the invaluable assistance of the information cloud, I've made some progress there. Greensward, Texas is located in Pinellas County and the sheriff of that county is one Barret, known locally — I suppose inevitably given the region's proclivity for assigning unimaginative nicknames — as Bubba Teasdale. He has been the sheriff there for several decades and, thus, may be familiar with the lawyer Archibald Reid and perhaps even remembers the man's daughter. If you do not think it improper for me to identify myself as a legitimate agent of the metropolitan police, I will place a call to him and see what I can find out."

"I don't see a problem with that," Hardy answered, awaiting his own assignment which was bound to be imminent.

"Then, we need information from Elizabeth Reid's sojourn in Houston," Shane continued. "Do you have any connections there that might be of use?"

"Not really," Hardy replied, "but I can contact the police there and possibly find somebody who's sympathetic to a murder investigation in another city. As you no doubt know, even big city police, maybe especially them, are sometimes sympathetic with the plight of their professional brothers in other cities."

"Excellent, excellent, my man," Shane replied. "This is where we'll start, but if we encounter obstructions, you should be prepared, I recognize against your preference, to make a trip there."

Hardy didn't respond but he seriously doubted that the chief would approve the expenses for such a trip unless they had more reason for it than Hardy was aware of at the moment.

"One more thing," Shane said.

He opened the folder that Hardy had given him and retrieved the copy of the page from the shooters club log. He ran a finger down the list of names, stopping at the name of Elizabeth Reid inscribed in meticulously neat script.

"It occurs to me," he continued, "that if the person who signed this log was really planning a murder at the time of her visits to the shooters club, she might not have used her real name. However, it strains credulity to accept this as coincidence. We know from the copy of Archibald Reid's will that you so kindly obtained earlier ..."

Hardy remembered the difficulty he had had convincing the police in Texas to go to the trouble of getting a copy of the will and FAXing it to him. But they had done it and much more quickly that he had expected.

"... that there is, somewhere, an Elizabeth Reid who inherited a gun of the very rare type that killed Mr. Bagley. And we know with reasonable certainty that a woman who signed that name in the Williamson County Shooters Club log possessed such a gun. The rarity of the gun makes it highly unlikely that there are two women by the same name who own identical such weapons. And, if there were two female owners of such a gun with different names, it seems even more unlikely that the woman who test fired the gun at the shooters club would have randomly chosen to sign the name of the Texas woman who just happened to own an identical gun. I conclude that they are the same woman. But, if so, why can't we locate her in Nashville? There is a possibility that she has somehow evaded having her name and personal information captured in any of the available data bases, but I doubt it.

"Perhaps there is another explanation," he continued. "Suppose that Elizabeth Reid of Greensward, Texas married while living in Houston and subsequently moved to Nashville. And further, if she did not wish to sign her actual married name in the shooters club log, perhaps she signed her maiden name which she may have thought, and correctly so it turns out, to be difficult to connect with her in our city."

"So," Hardy responded, "an interesting theory but mainly conjecture, don't you think?"

"Right," Shane said, "it is conjecture at this point.

But you, Detective Seltzer, are going to obtain the information that will make it at least plausible conjecture. From your Houston contacts, assuming you can persuade them to cooperate, you need to find out everything possible about Elizabeth Anne Reid from Greensward, Texas during her sojourn there — what she did, where she worked, any associates who knew her and especially whether and if so when she moved from there to Nashville. But, you will also persuade your contacts to search the marriage records there to find whether anyone by that name was married during the appropriate time frame and if so the name or names of the groom, or grooms, since it is quite possible that there will be more than one such marriage. The name is not that uncommon and Houston is a large city."

"OK," Hardy replied, "I'll do what I can. But don't get your hopes up."

"Ah, detective," Shane responded, "my hopes are forever up. You should try that approach to life, you know. It works reasonably well, even without the wine."

23

"So, Mitchell," Dom Petrillo said. "Here's what I've been able to find out about the neurologist Katya Karpov."

Rook had called Petrillo the previous day and given him Dr. Karpov's name and Petrillo had set about using his considerable resources to research the woman. The two men now sat in Rook's unique corner office in the Batman Building. Each of them having finished a cup of espresso that Rook prepared with careful attention to the ritual that he believed added to the pleasure of the drink, Petrillo opened the conversation.

"Yes," Rook said, "Please go on."

"Dr. Karpov is an associate professor of psychiatry at the university, as you told me, the department headed by Cyrus Bartalak. She received her medical degree from Green College, Oxford where she completed her residency and fellowship in neurology. Shortly after completing her training there, she was recruited to the university here by the previous chairman of the department of psychiatry, apparently a distinguished member of the faculty for many years.

"When Bartalak became chair, he replaced most of the faculty whom he inherited, except for Dr. Karpov. Dr. Karpov is married to one, Shane Hadley, a former Rhodes Scholar, whom she met when they were both students at Oxford. When the couple moved to Nashville, Mr. Hadley joined the Metropolitan Police Force as a detective and over the next few years achieved a considerable local reputation for his work on several murder cases. He is something of a mythical figure still among members of the police force, where he is sometimes remembered as Sherlock Shane."

"I think I remember reading about him in the newspaper some time ago," Rook said. "Wasn't there an accident of some kind?"

"Correct. Several years ago, Mr. Hadley sustained a gunshot injury to his spine that left him paralyzed from the waist down. He took a disability retirement from the police force at that time. He has been confined to a wheelchair since then. The couple lives in a big apartment in one of the renovated warehouses that sit between Printers Alley and Third Avenue. Mr. Hadley is only rarely seen in public."

"They live in Printers Alley?" Rook queried. "That's unusual. And potentially interesting. Wonder if they had any contact with Bonz Bagley. The alley is a pretty small world. But go on. What about Dr. Karpov's professional activities?"

"She works in Bartalak's lab with the professor's wife, Beth. Both of them are involved in the clinical testing of this new drug. It doesn't appear that Dr. Karpov has any connection with the business side of the drug's development. Bartalak seems to play those cards very close to his vest. However, Karpov is responsible for much of the clinical part of the drug study. Beth Bartalak apparently handles the data. She's a biostatistician."

"Yes," Rook said, "I knew that much. Any gossip about the Bartalak lab? Academic types are usually inveterate gossipers and my friend Syd Shelling said there was what he discreetly described as *tension* between Karpov and the Bartalaks. Did you find out any more about that?"

"Not really," Petrillo answered, "as you say, the fact that Karpov and Bartalak's wife are not fond of each other is common knowledge among the university faculty, but the speculated reasons for that run the gamut from jealously of the chairman's attention to what some believe to be differences in how they approach their work."

"Differences?" Rook asked. "What differences?"

"Well, apparently Dr. Karpov is a meticulous investigator for whom scientific integrity is paramount. There's a vague notion of some faculty that the Bartalak's are much more concerned about appearances. The chairman is a consummate salesman and old school academics are always suspicious of people like him."

"Hubris, I think I called it," Rook replied.

"None of my sources used that word, but some certainly implied it."

Rook got up from his chair, walked to the window and peered for a moment through the telescope aimed at the cityscape to the northeast.

Without turning around, he said, "So, Dom, it seems unlikely that Dr. Karpov would know anything about Bartalak's business operation, but she might know something about the drug study that would help us. We need some kind of inside information that threatens the value of Bartalak's startup company before we can spring the trap, don't you think?"

"Yeah, Mitchell, that's right. Why don't you follow through on trying to meet with Dr. Karpov, feel her out, so to speak?"

"Judging from her picture on the university web site, feeling her out might not be an unpleasant task," Rook said.

"Try to stay focused on the job at hand, Mitchell," Petrillo smiled.

"Oh, I'll do that alright," Rook answered. "I'll contact her again and try to set up a meeting."

"Great," Petrillo answered, "I've written down her work and home phone numbers and her home address in the alley for you. I walked by there, incidentally. It's an interesting spot, a balcony on the second floor trimmed with New Orleans style wrought iron. It's almost directly opposite where *Bonz's Booze and Music* used to be."

Rook hadn't been in Printers Alley in many years, but he vaguely recalled some less than memorable forays there as an undergraduate at the university when he and his friends were in a slumming mood. Rook would not have wanted to live there and was surprised that it would appeal to a high powered academic type like this Karpov woman. Interesting.

It was just past noon when Shane was surprised by the sound of the garage door below rumbling open. He wondered why Katya had come home so early. After a few minutes, the elevator opened and Katya entered the room. Her Gucci briefcase was slung over her shoulder and she was lugging an obviously heavy cardboard box with the words *medical supplies, handle with care* stamped on it in large red letters. She set the box on the bar, dropped her briefcase and walked over to kiss Shane.

"Ah," Shane said, "the provisions have arrived."

His ration of Lincoln College sherry was delivered at regular intervals to Katya's lab at the university disguised as medical supplies, the reasons for which Shane did not know and had not asked about. He assumed it had something to do with the logistics of importing spirits from a foreign country. KiKi was indeed a resourceful woman, a quality from which Shane benefitted in many ways.

"To what do I owe the pleasure of such an early arrival home?" Shane asked.

"Two reasons," KiKi replied, "or maybe three. The wine was delivered and I thought it best to get it home promptly. And I wanted to spend the afternoon enlisting your help in writing my letter to the dean."

"The fateful scientific misconduct letter, I assume," Shane said, then asked, "And reason number three?"

"A very strong desire to spend the afternoon with my gorgeous husband," she answered smiling broadly and walking over to kiss him again.

"I prefer to assume that you haven't given the reasons in order of their priority, my love," Shane said.

"A reasonable assumption," she answered.

He wheeled himself over to the bar and began opening the box containing his cherished sherry.

"Let me uncrate the wine," he said, "and perhaps sample a bit of it to make sure this lot is of its usual quality, and then I'll tell you what I've been able to learn about the lawyer, Mitchell Rook."

"Great," she replied, "I've been wondering about that."

KiKi sat on the sofa and watched Shane remove the bottles from the carton and place them lovingly in the rack beside the bar. He put the empty box on the floor and reached for the leather case, removing one of his prized Oxford glasses. He held the glass up to the light and studied it admiringly.

"Will you join me?" he asked, as he always did, expecting that his near teetotaling wife would graciously decline the offer.

To his surprise, KiKi answered, "Yes, I believe I will."

Shane removed another of the glasses from its red satin nest in the leather case, opened one of the newly-arrived bottles and poured some into each of the glasses. He held both glasses in one hand, grasping them carefully by their bases a maneuver that he had mastered in order to leave a hand free for maneuvering the wheelchair rolled over to KiKi and handed her a glass.

"To truth and the certain fate of the bad guys," Shane said, holding his glass out to clink against hers.

They both sipped at the wine and then looked at each other for a moment. She reached for his hand and held it, an especially tender gesture that she knew Shane valued.

"Mitchell Rook," he finally began, "is the majority partner in the law firm of Rook, Lipchitz and Associates. He attended the university here as an undergraduate, obtained his law degree from Yale and worked for a short time with the justice department in Washington. He then came back to Nashville and joined with an old friend, Marvin Lipchitz, who was a blue blood Nashvillian with connections in the business community, to found the firm which bears their names. Their firm is now the major group dealing in business law in the city with offices occupying two floors in what is commonly referred to as the Batman Building just down the way."

"What about Rook himself?"

"Yes, well, Mitchell Rook is apparently a brilliant, if somewhat idiosyncratic, attorney whose services are valued by the city's highest rollers in the business world. And, from what I'm able to determine from the Internet, he is especially valued for his integrity, honesty and fairness. He's received multiple awards and commendations from the legal and business communities. He is even a recipient of the Governor's Award for Integrity in Business, an apparently rarely granted and highly coveted citation."

"Jesus," KiKi responded, "sounds like the guy walks on water."

"Quite likely, my love, from the information I have. But I was unable to verify that specific fact."

She smiled. She deeply admired whatever there was in her husband's makeup that caused him to maintain a sense of humor in his approach to life, no matter how serious or challenging the situation. He was an extraordinary man. Her need for Shane was not because she wasn't fully capable of caring for herself. It was that he brought a different dimension to her life, expanded the boundaries.

"So, my love," Shane continued, "my advice would be to talk to the gentleman and see what he's up to. I don't see how it could hurt and it might even be interesting."

Their conversation was interrupted by the ringing telephone. They often ignored the phone, but for some reason, KiKi got up, walked over to the bar where the phone sat and lifted the receiver.

"Hello," she said.

"Hello," a male voice that she didn't recognize responded, "I'm trying to reach a Dr. Katya Karpov."

Although the man who called the Bartalak lab and asked for Dr. Karpov had not identified himself, Beth thought that she recognized the voice of the lawyer, Mitchell Rook. Rook spoke with the barest hint of a southern accent and his voice had an unusual low rasping quality that Beth had noticed in the meetings of the *Renaptix* investors; she was certain that it was he who had called. When she told the caller that Dr. Karpov was not there, he just thanked her and hung up. Beth wondered what possible reason there could be for Rook to want to contact Katya and she was troubled by that.

Beth had decided to go in to the medical center for a specific reason that was unrelated to her work in the lab. She hadn't intended to go to the lab at all, but rather to go directly over to the Institute of the Neurological Sciences. However, distracted by her thoughts about the task she had set for herself, Beth had taken her habitual route from the parking garage to the fifth floor lab.

Upon entering the lab, she discovered to her relief that Katya was not there and when the phone rang, she answered it. She had accidentally discovered the troubling fact that Mitchell Rook was trying to contact Katya.

Beth left the lab and ventured over to the Institute for the Neurological Sciences. Her goal was to find the schedule for the Sunday morning meetings of the group who called themselves, Beth thought pretentiously, the *Brain Trust*. She knew that the group of neuroscientists met periodically, allegedly to discuss research in the field, and that Katya regularly attended the meetings.

The fact that Katya had continued meeting with the group after Cy took over the chair of the psychiatry department had been a matter of some friction between Cy and Katya. Katya was the only member of the psychiatry department who was invited to attend the meetings. Cy felt that institutes which crossed departmental lines were organizational anomalies that threatened the traditional university power structure and he also disliked the institute director for reasons that went beyond his professional position.

Cy especially disliked the neurological institute because he saw it as in direct competition with his own department. The friction over this matter between him and Katya was exaggerated by the fact that she was a neurologist, not a psychiatrist, and it was well-known that neurologists and other practitioners of the harder sciences generally considered most psychiatric research lacking in adequate scientific rigor. Although Katya did not necessarily share that view, Cy didn't like her fraternizing with those people.

The so-called *Brain Trust* met in the neurological institute's large cherry-paneled conference room located at the geographic and intellectual epicenter of the institute beside the director's office in a newly renovated north wing of the sprawling maze of buildings that housed the medical center.

Beth found her way there and scanned the meeting schedule that was posted on the conference room door. She noted the next date for the meeting of the *Brain Trust* at eight AM on a Sunday. She took a note pad and pen from her pocket and wrote down the date and time in large dark block letters underlined twice and followed by three exclamation points.

Beth thought about going by Cy's office just to say hi, but decided against it and made her way back to the parking garage. She felt good as she drove out of the garage and headed south on West End Avenue toward her refuge in Belle Meade, the verdant and insular enclave of the well to do.

The pathologist, Sydney Shelling, had successfully avoided getting involved in university politics throughout his long career, although accomplishing that had become increasingly difficult as the institution had evolved in recent years. Shelling was closing in on sixty. He had spent his entire professional life at the medical center, as a student, pathology resident and then as a faculty member for the last couple of decades. Even at this stage of his career, he was still an associate professor, but he was OK with that. Promotion to the rank of professor had come to require the kind of political maneuvering that didn't interest him. He enjoyed his work and just wanted to be left alone to do his job.

So, Shelling was genuinely troubled by the ethical dilemma in which he found himself. He had always valued honesty and integrity in his work. Those qualities made him realize that he had to do something with the information that he had come by in the course of doing his job that could be important to the welfare of innocent people. However, revealing the results of the Bagley autopsy to Cy Bartalak, the Principal Investigator of the study of the drug that may well have damaged Mr. Bagley's brain, would, Shelling feared, precipitate events that would drag him into a political morass that would almost certainly turn out badly for everyone involved. And, Shelling reasoned, although the coroner had provided him with a copy of the final autopsy report, that was technically confidential information; sharing it with anyone would be a breach of confidence.

Shelling tried to rationalize the situation by telling himself that Bartalak would almost surely get a copy of the report on his own; the PI of a clinical study would usually obtain such information on any subject who died during the course of a clinical study regardless of the apparent cause of death. But, Shelling also felt that Bartalak should have the information immediately. If the drug was toxic, innocent people could be harmed by any delay in recognizing that; Shelling felt an ethical imperative to do something.

After agonizing over his situation for some time, the pathologist decided on a compromise. He would deliver a copy of the autopsy report to Cy Bartalak anonymously. He would take the report to Bartalak's office during lunch time when he knew that Cy would be attending a regular administrative meeting with the dean and when Bartalak's secretary was likely to be away from her desk.

Shelling tucked the folder containing the report under his arm and made his way to the suite of offices belonging to the psychiatry department chairman. He scanned the office through the glass door, confirming that it was vacant. He then entered, slid the folder under the closed door to Bartalak's office, and immediately returned to the comfort and familiarity of his laboratory, convinced that he had done the best that he could do without risking his own job security and peace of mind. But he still didn't feel good about it.

Had Beth yielded to the urge to drop by Cy's office as she was leaving the medical center, she would have discovered her husband puzzling over the coroner's report of the autopsy performed on the body of Bonz Bagley that he found in an unmarked folder on the floor inside his office door upon returning from his regular noon meeting with the dean. He wondered who might have left the report there and why it was left so mysteriously without any clue as to who had left it. His attention was fixed especially on the part of the report that read, "... *some vacuolization and unusual cellular inclusions in the right hippocampus, likely the result of exposure to a chemical toxin ...*"

24

As Mitchell Rook walked from the Batman Building up Third Avenue toward Printers Alley, he reflected on his brief conversation with Katya Karpov. It was he who suggested that he come to Dr. Karpov's Printers Alley home at the end of his workday. The reason he gave her was that his office was nearby and he didn't want to inconvenience her in any way.

The real reason for wanting to meet at her apartment was that in his experience people were likely to be more forthcoming with information in a setting where they felt comfortable, and so he wanted to have a conversation with Dr. Karpov on her own turf. Somewhat to his surprise, she had readily agreed. She had informed him that her husband would also be present, Rook thought possibly to make it clear to him that they would not be alone. It would not be surprising if the lovely doctor was accustomed to establishing the rules of engagement with strange men who seemed to be a little too curious.

Rook also reflected on the contents of the conference call that Cy Bartalak had hastily arranged with the three *Renaptix* investors that afternoon. Bartalak had arranged the call to inform them of the decision of the DSMB to terminate the phase I-II studies based on the exciting preliminary results that indicated possible efficacy of the drug in the treatment of Alzheimer's disease. Bartalak would proceed immediately to identify either a venture capital firm which would provide round two financing of *Renaptix* enabling them to proceed with phase III definitive studies or a big pharma partner or both. Successful completion of either of those deals would dramatically increase the value of the three original investments.

"Gentlemen," Cy had intoned, "you may be

participating in a major pharmaceutical discovery that will give hope to millions of people for whom hope had been abandoned."

Rook also contemplated the meaning of the word *hubris*.

Entering the alley from Church Street, Mitchell Rook walked under the big arch emblazoned with the words Printers Alley in brilliant red neon and into the carnival montage of sound and light that was just taking shape in hopes of luring in clientele for the clubs as the evening wore on. Rook thought it a gaudy and tasteless scene, but then maybe that was the point of the alley; perhaps gaud and tastelessness were its *raison d'etre*. But who'd want to live there?

It was easy to locate the address he was looking for. The building was on the right just past the middle of the block-long alley and it was the only building with a balcony. Following the instructions that Dr. Karpov had given him on the phone, he went to the door that opened from the ground level and pressed the button beneath the words Karpov/Hadley in bold black letters in some unusual font that Rook couldn't identify.

There was a loud buzz that signaled release of the door and Rook entered. The elevator door that occupied half the wall of the small foyer promptly opened and he got on. After the short ride to floor 2, the door opened and he exited directly into the center of a large living room tastefully furnished in expensive modern furniture and into the presence of a beautiful blond woman and a thin handsome man sitting in a wheelchair and fondling a glass of wine.

Katya walked over to Rook and extended her hand.

"Mr. Rook," she said, "I'm Katya Karpov."

"Yes, Dr. Karpov" Rook replied, "I recognize you from your picture on the university web site. But do call me Mitchell."

"An awful picture and I'm Katya, please," she said. Gesturing toward Shane she continued, "This is my husband, Shane Hadley."

Shane wheeled himself over to the visitor and they shook hands.

"I'm very pleased to meet you Mr. Rook ... er ... Mitchell," Shane said. "Please have a seat. May I offer you a sherry? It's a special wine from my old Oxford College and it's quite a pleasant beverage."

"That would be very nice," Mitchell replied.

As Shane went to the bar, poured a glass of wine for their visitor and refreshed his own glass, Katya showed Mitchell to the sofa and took a seat opposite him in a comfortable leather chair that she liked. Shane delivered the wine to Rook and parked himself just beyond the margin of the space separating Katya and Mitchell. Katya and Shane had discussed this earlier, and agreed that this was to be Katya's conversation and Shane would be only an observer, a role with which he was entirely comfortable.

Shane's observations of their visitor to that point were focused on his accent and his shoes. The accent was that of a southerner who had spent time elsewhere and had consciously attempted to shed the unmistakable vocal evidence of his origins. That effort was almost never completely successful. A few tenacious residua of a person's original way of speaking invariably persisted and were obvious at least to the practiced and attentive ear. And the shoes. Rook was a slim, fit middle-aged man wearing an obviously expensive sport coat and trousers, an elegant pale blue shirt, probably silk, open at the throat and then the incongruent shoes — black clunky numbers that resembled orthopedic appliances of some kind more than shoes that would have been appropriate for the rest of the attorney's outfit.

Shane was forever intrigued by incongruities. He thought that incongruities were unconscious attempts to convey the message that things might not be exactly what they appear to be to the casual observer. Shane suspected that there was a great deal more to Mitchell Rook than he wished them to perceive.

Rook sipped from his glass and said, "Very nice, Shane, a very nice sherry," he gestured toward Shane with his glass, and turned his attention to Katya. "I'm sure that this may seem an odd disturbance of your evening, Katya, but I appreciate you taking the time for us to talk."

"That's true, Mitchell," she replied, "but I'm happy to help if I can."

She felt a little uncomfortable calling the stranger by his given name. It seemed to imply a level of intimacy that she didn't feel.

Mitchell said simply, "Thank you," and drank another swallow of the wine.

"Before I answer whatever questions you have," Katya began, "can you tell me how you identified me as someone who might be able to help you?"

"Of course," he replied. "As I said on the phone I'm working with a client who has a business relationship with the company, *Renaptix, Inc.*, a startup company out of the university that was founded by Professor Cyrus Bartalak who is, I believe, the chairman of the department where you work."

"That's correct."

"I'm responsible for doing what we lawyers call *due diligence* on the company."

"I'm not likely to be much help to you," Katya said. "I'm a physician and a scientist. I have nothing to do with Dr. Bartalak's business ventures and know nothing about them."

Rook answered, "I'm aware of that which is the reason I wanted to talk with you specifically. The company's sole asset is the new drug for Alzheimer's disease that's in clinical trials and I understand that you're one of the investigators doing the trials. Is that correct?"

"Yes," Katya answered, "I'm responsible for the clinical examinations that are part of the study of the drug. The laboratory testing is not my responsibility."

"I understand," Mitchell paused for another sip of sherry.

Katya felt a little uncomfortable with the conversation. She and Shane had spent the afternoon composing the scientific misconduct letter which she intended to deliver to the dean and so her concerns about the drug study were fresh in her mind. She wanted to be certain that she didn't reveal anything inappropriate to this stranger. She had also, uncharacteristically, consumed several glasses of sherry over the afternoon and so would have to pay close attention to be sure that it was she and not the wine that was doing the talking.

"According to my client," Rook continued, "Dr. Bartalak is extremely excited about the preliminary results of the drug studies. Is that your impression?"

He paused a moment and when she did not respond, continued, "Oh, but I didn't answer your question about how I came to seek you out, did I? Well, a member of the medical faculty and I were undergraduate classmates at the university many years ago and we still stay in occasional contact. I asked him about who was involved in the study of Dr. Bartalak's drug, and he mentioned you as a possibility."

"Who is your friend?" Katya asked.

"Syd Shelling," he answered. "I think he's a pathologist or something. Not sure exactly what he does."

Katya didn't respond but she wondered how

much Syd had told his old classmate. Katya was pretty sure that Syd wouldn't share anything she had told him in confidence. Syd just wouldn't do that. But, she wondered what else he might have told Rook.

"So," Rook continued, "no real mystery there. And the preliminary results? Do you share Dr. Bartalak's enthusiasm?"

"Some of the preliminary results are quite interesting," Katya replied. "But they are preliminary."

"Of course, of course," Mitchell said, "but apparently
Dr. Bartalak is very excited about them. I sense that you don't share that excitement. Is that correct?"

"I'm a scientist, Mitchell. We scientists tend to be excessively skeptical, I suppose."

"Are you implying that Dr. Bartalak isn't a scientist?"

"No, of course not," Katya answered. "He has a distinguished scientific reputation. But Cy has other skills that I don't share. Not many academicians are Cy's equal as communicators."

"I understand that. My client has made the same observation. And Dr. Bartalak's wife," Mitchell continued, "I understand that she is also part of the investigative team?"

Rook noticed a distinct twitch of the right side of Katya's face.

"Yes, Beth is the biostatistician on the study," Katya replied.

When Rook paused as though thinking of what to ask next, Katya rose from her chair and said, "It's getting rather late, Mitchell, and my husband and I haven't eaten dinner yet. I don't think there is anything more that I can help you with."

"Of course, of course," Rook said, rising and walking over to shake her hand. "I really do

276

appreciate you permitting the intrusion. This has been very helpful. Let me leave you my business card," he took a small leather case from his pocket, extracted one of the beige cards and handed it to her. "If you think of anything else that might be of interest, please do contact me."

"Thank you," she replied as she ushered him to the elevator and pressed the call button.

"Good to meet you, Mitchell," Shane called to their visitor, waving at him from across the room; those were the only words that he had spoken since Rook and Katya began their conversation.

As Rook made his way back down the hill to the Batman Building garage to retrieve his car, he reflected on the conversation with Dr. Karpov. She had been deliberately evasive, he thought. Dr. Bartalak "has a distinguished scientific reputation," rather than he is a distinguished scientist. And retreating behind a cliché, the excessively skeptical scientist, instead of saying whether she agreed with her boss about the interpretation of the preliminary data. And his mention of Bartalak's wife that caused Dr. Karpov to abruptly conclude the interview, had clearly struck a nerve.

It was obvious from his conversation with Syd Shelling and this conversation with Katya Karpov that both of them knew something that was too important to reveal to him. That's the information he needed. Rook resolved to have another go at his old classmate. That seemed to be his best chance. Rook had a special feeling of antipathy for crooked businessmen. He wouldn't allow an academic conspiracy of silence to protect this Bartalak guy if he was a crook.

Cy Bartalak was feeling a complex mixture of

exhilaration and concern as he drove home from the medical center. He had managed to convince the DSMB to take the action that he wanted. He had made certain that his investors understood the significance of what was happening. He had called Susanna Gomez, his contact at Global Pharmaceuticals, Inc. and opened the conversation, he thought effectively; that just might culminate in a deal. He sensed that his GPI contact was trying to restrain her enthusiasm when he told her about the preliminary results with the drug, but he could sense that she had taken the bait. He would get at least a verbal deal done quickly. He would bet on that.

Bartalak also thought about the autopsy report on his drive out West End to his home in Belle Meade. Belle Meade. He had done his homework before moving to Nashville and had concluded that he needed a presence in the old area whose residents comprised an echelon of Nashville society entry into which could not be bought. No problem. Cy had no particular need to break into the social scene. He needed access to the city's money and putting a foot on the ground in that part of the city was a potential entrée into old money.

New money was another issue, but area of residence and lifestyle were less important to accessing the assets of the *nouveau riche*. Cy had some experience in how to go about charming the new rich who often believed their good fortune was a result of their superior intellect. Cy's experience had taught him otherwise. He had found that people who got rich on their own were by and large the fortunate recipients of the largesse of the Fates rather than because of any exceptional personal qualities. Those guys were an easy sell for the most part.

But the autopsy report haunted Cy for several reasons. He was still concerned about the mysterious way that the report had arrived in his office. Who might have left it? And why should they be concerned about revealing themselves? And then there was the content of the report. The fact that some pathologist had made some vague comments about findings in what remained of Bagley's brain probably didn't really mean anything.

Even if it did, there would be no more information obtained from the unfortunate Mr. Bagley, so the cause of the nebulous autopsy findings would never be known. But, if those autopsy results became common knowledge and if someone linked the unfortunate Mr. Bagley to the clinical study of RX-01, the value of the drug and, therefore, the startup company, perhaps even any possible deal with Global Pharmaceuticals, might be compromised. Timing was critical.

He headed the black Mercedes up Jackson Boulevard, turned left through the black iron gates and maneuvered the car up the winding driveway. He pressed the button signaling the garage door to open and parked the car inside.

Upon entering the house, he was surprised that Beth didn't greet him. She was always alert to his arrival and often waited for him at the door.

He dropped his battered briefcase by the door and called out, "Beth, Beth. I'm home."

When there was no answer, he went to the den, again expecting that his wife would be there preparing, as usual, the dry martini that he favored at the end of the day. But, the door to the bar was closed and the room was dark.

He switched on the lights and looked around the room. He almost didn't notice that a high backed chair had been repositioned with its back toward the room, facing the French doors that looked out on the formal garden. He walked over to the chair.

Beth sat there staring out at the garden. She wore a pair of cherry red running shorts and a cropped sky blue tee shirt, both of which appeared fresh; although dressed for it she didn't appear to have been running. She held a piece of paper in her hand.

"Beth?" he said.

She turned and looked up at him.

"Oh, Cy," she said, slipping the piece of paper under the waistband of her shorts, "I didn't hear you come in."

Although he had been aware of some changes in his wife's behavior of late, this was the first time that it registered with him that something clearly wasn't right.

"Are you OK Beth?" he asked.

"I'm fine," she said, "I'm fine. Maybe I'm coming down with a virus or something."

But Cy didn't think that she was alright. And he didn't think it was a virus. There was something troubling about the vacant and unfocused way she looked at him. He thought about her recent behavior — less time spent at work, less concern about her appearance.

Cy's professional experience made him wonder about drugs. But Beth was practically obsessive about her diet and her exercise routine was a matter of pride. She was careful about her body. He just didn't think that Beth was the type to get involved with recreational drugs.

"Are you sure you're OK?" he repeated. "You haven't been quite yourself for a while now. Maybe it's time you got a thorough checkup."

"I'll do that, if it's what you want me to do," Beth said absently.

"Good, good," he replied, "I'll call Oscar Orbitz tomorrow. I'm sure he'll arrange to see you. If he's in town, he'll probably even carve out some time to see you tomorrow."

Oscar Orbitz, known as *The Double-O* among the characteristically irreverent medical students, was chairman of the department of medicine. He was a world-famous endocrinologist who had achieved fame by discovering a minor hormone produced by the adrenal glands, a rare deficiency of which caused a clinical syndrome that bore his name. No doubt he had a grueling schedule, but if Cy insisted, Orbitz would make time to see Beth.

"That's fine, Cy," Beth said. "That's fine."

She turned back around and stared out at the garden.

25

Shane placed the call immediately after he saw Katya off to work. Katya had not slept well and her restlessness kept Shane awake much of the night. Neither of them said much as Katya showered, dressed for work and sat with Shane for coffee and a bowl of instant oatmeal that he prepared for their breakfast. The events of the previous day, the ordeal of preparing the letter and the odd visit from Mitchell Rook, weighed on both of them.

As Katya placed the brown envelope containing the letter to the dean in her briefcase, she hesitated for a moment and then snapped the case closed, slung it over her shoulder, kissed Shane and set off to do the deed that she felt compelled to do, but the consequences of which she feared. It seemed likely that she was embarking on a course of action that would change their lives. She didn't want her life changed. She liked it the way it was.

Shane had obtained the number of the Pinellas county sheriff's office in Greensward, Texas from a real live information operator, one of many anachronisms in that area of Texas. His call was answered by a female voice with the distinctly nasal character of a rural Texas drawl.

When he identified himself, stating his association with the Nashville metro police in the investigation of a crime and requesting to speak to the sheriff, the voice said something that sounded like "S-h-o-r-e-I-l-l-r-i-n-g-B-u-d-d-y-f-o-r-y-a," the words stretched out to the limits of their tensile strength but run together with no distinct spaces between them. There was a rather long pause and then the call went through and the sheriff answered after a couple of rings.

"This here's Shurf Tisdel," the sheriff answered.

"Yes, Sheriff Teasdale," Shane responded, deliberately pronouncing the man's name with care, feeling the need to emphasize the contrast between his and the sheriff's speech pattern. "Thank you for taking my call."

"Jes say what you got to say, boy," Teasdale answered. "I'll help if I can but cain't take all day with it. Got my own stuff to worry about."

Shane supposed that the secretary had identified him to the sheriff before putting the call through since *Shurf Tisdel* didn't seem to need an explanation from Shane.

"I need some information about a previous resident of Greensward."

"Who?" Teasdale interrupted. "If it's anybody who's lived in Greensurd in the past thirty years, it's likely I knowd 'em."

"The person's name is Elizabeth Anne Reid."

"Archie's kid," the sheriff answered immediately. "Archie raised her here, but she got out soon as she could manage."

Shane continued, "Can you tell me anything about her before she left?"

"Not too much to tell. Archie and her moved here from somewhere back east when she was a tyke. Just her and him. Archie never talked about the kid's mother, at least if he did I didn't hear about it. Archie was a lawyer, a dee-fense lawyer. He set up shop here and did pretty well for himself for a lot of years gettin' crooks off light. Did'n give a good goddam if they did it or not. Just aimed at getting' 'em off as light as he could. He was good at it."

"Did you know him well?

"Well enough. We was on different sides of most things, me bein' law enforcement and him seein' the law as somethin' to be worked around instead of obeyed. We both did our jobs but they was different

283

jobs and came up against one another most of the time."

"And Elizabeth, his daughter?"

"Elizabeth was a cute kid. Good student. Kept to herself a lot. That was 'specially true after the accident."

"Accident?"

"It was sad, but I guess turned out OK. She fell out of a tree when she was about fifteen I'd guess. Broke her leg. The big bone in her thigh. Nasty break. Right leg I recall. Had to go to Houston for some surgeries and she was laid up for quite a while. Archie paid to have one of them physical therapists to come down from Houston and live in town for a few months to help the poor girl get over it. She was a trooper, though. Seemed determined to get straightened out. Did too."

"Turned out OK?"

"Well better'n that I guess. After she got her leg workin' again, she took up runnin'. Ran all over the place. I'd see her ever mornin' on my way in. And when she went off to TCU to college, she ran cross country races. Word was she won some trophies and stuff for the horny toads."

Shane smiled. He was aware that the TCU athletic teams were known as the *horned frogs* which was amusing enough but *horny toads* conjured up something different and perhaps more appropriate for teams of adolescents with surging hormones.

Teasdale continued, "I don't think she was ever perfect after the accident though. When you'd see her runnin' around here, she still had a little hitch in her gitalong even after a lot of years went by."

"What about after college? Did she return to Greensward?" Shane asked.

"Not really," the sheriff answered. "Even when she was in college she was pretty scarce around here.

Her and her daddy never did seem close. Oh, he taught her to shoot and he'd take her huntin'. He loved guns, collected some goddam expensive ones that he'd take out to the woods and show his daughter how to shoot. Seemed to me like he wanted her to be a boy and she tried to do it but couldn't ever be the kid he really seemed to want. So seemed to me that once she went off to college she left this town pretty much for good. And after that, she moved off to Houston I think to get some kinda advanced degree. Never came back. But by then old Archie was fading fast and maybe she just did'n want to be around to see it. Cain't say as how I blame her for that. Twern't a pretty site."

"So you never saw her again after she moved to Houston?"

"Yep, that's pretty much right. Well, 'cept when Archie kicked the bucket which was way past due when it happened. Archie's timing never was any good. Elizabeth showed up then, claimed his stuff and got him buried."

"His stuff?"

"Not a hell of a lot considerin'. The house in town got sold to pay for Archie's stay in the nursin' home. He was there for a few years, just rottin' away. It cost a pretty penny to stay in them kinda places. But he had to be somewhere, I guess. She got his guns, but sold'em off to the locals 'cept for the antique pistols. They seemed to mean somethin' to her and she packed 'em up and took 'em off to Houston with her. Prob'ly 'bout the only thing she kept of his. It was pretty sad, the whole thing. I wad'n no great fan of Archie Reid but his dyin' was sadder than dyin' oughtta be."

"Just one other question, sheriff," Shane said, "Do you have any idea where she is now?"

"Not really," Teasdale answered, then paused.

"Guess she's still in Houston. Word was, and there weren't much news that I heard anyway. Word was that she got a degree in somethin' that got her a job at the university. And a few years ago when Sadie Griswold had her stroke and Alford took her up to the stroke center in Houston, Sadie came back sayin' she heard that Elizabeth Reid was workin' there. Seems, now I remember, that some nurse or technician or somebody told Sadie that the Reid woman from Sadie's hometown had stirred up some gossip there. Somethin' bout takin up with a married man. Big city gossip oughtta be better'n that, dontcha think? Hell, nothin' like that's surprisin' anymore, even in a town no bigger'n Greensurd, y'know?"

"That's certainly true, Mr. Teasdale," Shane said, then, "Thank you very much for talking with me sheriff, you've been a great help."

"Yer welcome, son," Sheriff Bubba Teasdale responded, "Hensley, was it?"

But Shane had already hung up. He had taken notes during the conversation and was looking them over and jotting in additional items that he had missed getting down as they spoke.

Hardy Seltzer was due In Printers Alley shortly and Shane wanted to have his notes organized so that he could share the information with Hardy. Shane was also very anxious to discover what Hardy had been able to learn about Elizabeth Reid's life in Houston and wherever she currently resided.

Hardy Seltzer would arrive in Printers Alley, but he would not be there at the agreed upon time. That was indirectly the fault of three people: the lawyer X Coniglio; the DA; and a freelance news reporter who occasionally wrote stories for the morning paper.

Hardy's delay was more directly the fault of the chief of police who had summoned Hardy to his office on a moment's notice and grilled him at some length about where he and Shane Hadley were with their investigation of the mystery woman whom Shane thought was Bonz Bagley's real killer.

When Hardy entered the chief's office, his boss confronted him with a copy of the morning newspaper. It was a headline on the front page of the paper below the fold. The story under the headline, Metro Detective Botched Bagley Murder Case, didn't really deliver on the headline's claim, but it did accuse Hardy Seltzer by name of wrongful procurement of a gun that the DA claimed was the murder weapon and of illegally interrogating the accused murderer, Jody Dakota, well outside the geographic boundaries of Davidson County and thus outside the force's legal jurisdiction. The chief held up a copy of the paper to Hardy immediately on Hardy's entering the office. He hadn't seen it before.

"Apparently," the chief said, "X Coniglio is determined to dismantle the DA's case against Dakota and do it in view of the widest public audience that he can possibly attract."

"Why do you think it's X's doing?" Hardy asked.

"Look at the source," the chief responded. "The article says it's based on exclusive information from, 'a source very highly placed in the Bagley case investigation'. Assuming that wasn't you or the DA himself, neither of whom I take to be masochistic, it has to be X. X has been determined from the outset to try this case in the media and to make it a trial of the Metro police department as well. My guess is that this is the first salvo with a lot more to follow. This could get a lot worse, Hardy. Apparently X has the ear of whoever this reporter is and X is off and running. Of course if the DA's case starts to fall apart, that sonofabitch would be delighted to shift the blame to the police department. And X is stalling, doing everything he can to delay the trial. The DA isn't going to get Jody Dakota before a jury of his peers for a lot longer time than the DA had hoped."

The chief then asked Hardy for all of the information he had on the investigation that he and Shane Hadley were pursuing and he told the chief everything he knew. But there wasn't much more than interesting nodes of facts without enough hard connections between the nodes to support a complete story. Still a lot of speculation involved. However, Hardy outlined the direction they were taking and made a sincere effort to sound more optimistic than he actually felt.

When Hardy was finished, the chief said, "I must tell you, Hardy, that I'm getting some pressure from higher up. If this personal attack on you in the media persists, I may be forced to put you on leave until it gets sorted out. I don't want to do that, but it could be necessary. If so, I hope you'll understand. In the meantime go after the mystery woman with everything you've got. In the unlikely event that you can develop evidence that unequivocally incriminates someone other than Jody Dakota as Bonz's killer, the department could still come out of this smelling pretty good. In that case we'll just have to hope like hell that the real killer doesn't hire that grandstanding sonofabitch, X Coniglio."

So by the time Hardy Seltzer was greeted from the Printers Alley balcony by Shane's habitual, "Hi-ho, Hardy my man," the detective was in less than a positive mood. What he had been able to discover about Elizabeth Reid in Houston did little to combat the effects of the morning's meeting with the chief. Hardy wasn't especially anxious to reveal the disappointing results of his effort to Shane.

"Just let me in, Shane," was Hardy's curt response.

Shane did not answer but disappeared through the French doors into the flat. Hardy went through the routine, the buzz of the electronic door latch, the unmanned elevator door opening suddenly before him (*Open Sesame!*) and then ejecting him on the second floor into Shane's apartment.

"Allow me to suggest, Hardy my man," Shane said, gesturing the detective to sit on the sofa that fronted the fireplace, "a remedy for your obviously dark mood that I can guarantee from personal experience over many years, will dispel your demons of darkness."

"I don't want any sherry, Shane," Hardy replied.

"I have found, my man," Shane responded, "that forming opinions about a thing without experiencing it is a course that is bound to deprive one of many of life's pleasures. Do you not think that a reasonable conclusion?"

"Just give me a glass of the goddam wine," Hardy replied.

He was in no mood to encourage Shane's banter. He just wanted to get on with the work at hand and decide where to go next. He'd drink a glass of Shane's goddam sherry if that would shut his friend up about it.

Shane sensed that it was apparently not a good time to try to engage his friend in a light conversation and so just wheeled himself over to the bar, poured Seltzer a glass of sherry in one of the Riedel glasses, not one of his cherished Oxford sherry glasses, and delivered it to Hardy who sat forward on the sofa with his elbows resting on his knees.

"You're a bit later than the time we set, my man," Shane said, "and I deem from your mood that you didn't spend the time engaged in joyful pursuits."

"Have you seen the morning paper, Shane?" Hardy asked.

"Only briefly," Shane replied, "but long enough to learn of your developing notoriety. Does that concern you?"

"Damn right, it concerns me," Hardy answered; he took a gulp of the wine most of which he apparently aspirated since he went into a coughing fit for a few minutes before continuing. "The chief may put me on suspension if this public thing goes much further."

"I sense the workings of our devious friend X Coniglio in the matter, don't you think? Perhaps he's enlisting the power of the press to assist him in honing his guillotine. Well, your head is still intact at least. It just means that we need to move more quickly. We're on the trail of the real killer, Hardy. I am certain of that. We just have to locate her. Which brings us to the matter at hand. Tell me what you've been able to find out about Elizabeth Reid of Houston."

"Yeah," Hardy answered, "I'm sure X has a bee in his bonnet, but you're right. We need to move on."

Hardy took another drink of the sherry, but sipped this time and thought the wine tasted pretty good. He didn't tell Shane that.

"Here's what I've got," Hardy said. "I was able to get connected with a hotshot computer kid in Houston police department. Said he could find out anything about anybody and I'm sure did his best."

"And?"

"Elizabeth Anne Reid of Greensward, Texas did indeed live in Houston for several years."

"Not to step on your lines," Shane said, "but are

290

you going to tell me where she lived next?"

"The short answer is no," Hardy replied, "but let me finish. She received a degree in biostatistics from the university there. She stayed on the faculty for several years after receiving her degree and disappeared."

"Disappeared?"

"Well, that's what my computer whiz says. He can't find any record of her after she resigned her post at the university. She disappeared."

"Did he check death certificate records?"

"Yep. She didn't die. Just disappeared, like Bonz's murderer disappeared somewhere between Printer's Alley and Fourth Avenue. I don't like people disappearing, Shane. When it looks that way, it means we're being fooled, like a magic act."

"I certainly agree, my man," Hardy said. "People do not disappear although they may appear to do so. Appearances and reality, critical to understand the difference even if you choose to ignore it. So what about the marriage records?"

"Nothing there either, I'm afraid," Hardy said, sipping again from his glass of sherry. "The marriage records during the time from when she moved to Houston until she resigned her faculty position at the university and disappeared lists some Elizabeth Reids, but none of them checked out to be our girl. Dead end!"

"Bloody hell," Shane exclaimed.

Shane then refilled his glass at the bar and proceeded to recount to Hardy his conversation with the Pinellas County sheriff, reviewing the information that encouraged Shane to believe that this Reid woman was the murderer they sought. But Hardy was right. They were at a dead end and Shane couldn't think of where to go next. They agreed to spend the night digesting the information they had and to meet the next day to try to decide what to do. The answer wasn't obvious to either of them.

26

Susanna Gomez did not rise rapidly through the ranks to her present position as Vice President in charge of neurological therapeutics at Global Pharmaceuticals, Inc. (known by insiders as GPI or just Global) by being indecisive. It was her prescient recognition of the potential of an antidepressant several years earlier, a drug discovered in the laboratory of a little known investigator at a second tier medical school, that jump started her career. She found out about the drug before it had undergone any clinical testing and was so impressed with the preclinical data that she convinced the powers that be to license the agent.

Although she was in a very junior position at the time, she was put in charge of designing and managing the clinical trials and shepherding the drug through FDA approval and on to market. The drug became a blockbuster and proceeds from its worldwide sales were a major source of income for the company for the past several years. That experience propelled Dr. Gomez into the top echelon of the company's management and also imbued her with considerable confidence in her gut feeling about a new opportunity.

But, the patent on the antidepressant was due to expire in a couple of years and the company didn't have a successor in the pipeline. In fact, GPIs pipeline had pretty much run dry. Dr. Gomez was under a lot of pressure to remedy that problem. So when Cyrus Bartalak called and relayed his excitement about his drug for Alzheimer's, she was more than a little intrigued.

She convinced Bartalak to take a flight the next morning to Newark and spend the day in an airport meeting room with her and a handpicked group of her people summarizing all of the preclinical data and the data from the preliminary clinical studies. Bartalak had given a masterful PowerPoint presentation for an hour and a half. He had expertly fielded questions from Gomez and her group over the three hours following his presentation and she had seen him off on a late afternoon flight back to BNA.

On her drive from the airport out to the Global campus, a hundred-acre complex in rural New Jersey, she pondered the situation. Bartalak made a very convincing case. Her only previous contact with the highly reputed academician had been when she had tapped him as an *ad hoc* consultant on a couple of occasions. She had thought him knowledgeable, articulate and perceptive in that role. He was highly regarded in academic circles and chaired an important department at a major university. While she was less than enamored of the man personally, and he was incredibly ugly, he was otherwise credible.

There was work to do, but if things panned out as the good doctor had led them to believe they would, she wanted to do this deal. And the sooner the better. At this early stage, it was likely that they could get exclusive rights to the drug at a reasonable price. There couldn't be more than ten or fifteen million dollars invested in the startup company, *Renaptix*.

GPI would be happy to pay several times that to acquire an exclusive license for the drug and control of the further clinical testing, regulatory approval, manufacture and eventual marketing. Those were things that GPI was expert at doing. If the efficacy was as dramatic as it appeared, the phase three trials might not have to be that big. And they could be expedited since there was no currently effective therapeutic for the target disease.

An effective drug for a devastating major disease with no competing products! Gomez could barely imagine the value of such a product for her career and for the company. The antidepressant drug she had developed had become a blockbuster, but it had to compete with several other effective products. To be the only game in town for a target disease that was hopeless and already claimed millions of victims could put Global in a position to name their price. And the increasing incidence of Alzheimer's as the American population aged could guarantee the company's financial situation for years to come. This might be the last deal Susanna Gomez would ever have to do, the crowning glory of her successful career.

Gomez drove into the garage under the administration building that housed the offices of the senior Global executives and parked in the space marked, *Reserved, Dr. Gomez.* She took the elevator to the sixth floor and joined her colleagues in the executive conference room. She had arranged the debriefing ahead of time and her people from legal, regulatory and clinical trials who had attended the airport meeting had assembled awaiting her arrival.

"Gentlemen," Gomez said, taking her place at the head of the long conference table, "and lady," she added, nodding to Carol Handschuler, head of the regulatory division who was the only other female member of the group. "Please take your seats."

For two hours, they reviewed the meeting with Bartalak, each in turn commenting on the matter from their special perspective. The consensus of the group after the discussion was that they should pursue the deal. There were several positives. The preclinical work had been done and had been sufficient to get FDA approval for the initial clinical testing. It shouldn't be necessary to do any more animal and laboratory work.

They would need to review the material that

Bartalak's group had submitted in the Investigational New Drug application that resulted in FDA approval for the phase I-II studies, but the fact that FDA had approved the IND application was encouraging. None of the discussants, least of all Dr. Gomez, bought Bartalak's argument that it would be possible to move directly to phase III definitive studies, there was just too little clinical data to justify that no matter how dramatic the results.

But, even if they needed to do a larger phase II trial first, the drug was still well along the path toward full approval. And it seemed likely that if they moved quickly to consummate the deal that they could do it at reasonable cost, maybe even at a bargain basement price, given the potential.

As the meeting concluded, Gomez charged the group with obtaining all of the data from Bartalak's team for careful scrutiny and to begin discussions with *Renaptix's* legal people. They should move as rapidly as possible. In the meantime, Gomez would present the matter to Global's executive group for their approval, but she was confident enough that she felt they didn't need to wait for that to get moving.

It was obvious that Gomez was excited. Those members of the group who had worked with her for a while were especially glad to sense again the fire in her belly that they knew was there but had been latent for a while.

The Nashville City Club occupied the top floor of a bank building at the corner of Church Street and Fourth Avenue. That location had been the site of the venerable Maxwell House Hotel that had lent its name to a brand of coffee advertised as *good to the last drop*. As it turned out, the coffee, still marketed under the Maxwell House brand, had outlived the institution for which it was named. The hotel burned several years earlier, and was replaced by the tall building just opposite the L&C Tower, the city's first skyscraper, with a local bank as the anchor tenant.

Mitchell Rook had convinced Syd Shelling to join him for lunch at the City Club and Rook was making his way up the hill from Commerce Street. He had chosen to walk up Second Avenue to Church Street and then turn left on Church up the two blocks to the Fourth Avenue corner. As he passed by the arched entrance to Printers Alley on his right, he recalled his conversation with Katya Karpov and, struck with how desolate the alley looked in the middle of the day, wondered again why anyone would want to live there.

When Rook exited the elevator on the top floor of the bank building, Syd Shelling was waiting for him, sitting on a leather sofa and thumbing through a magazine. He had been surprised by the invitation to lunch coming so close on the heels of the first conversation that he'd had with his old classmate in it must have been almost a year.

Shelling was also still a little out of sorts over the thing with the autopsy report, not totally convinced that he'd done the right thing. He wished that the whole mess would just go away. But he knew in his heart of hearts that wasn't likely. The most he could hope for was that he could keep his distance from the affair. He was determined to do everything he could to be sure of that.

"Hi, Syd," Rook said, "Sorry to keep you waiting."

Shelling got up, dropped the magazine on the sofa and walked over to shake his friend's hand.

"No problem, Mitchell," Shelling said, "just catching up on the local news."

Shelling had been reading a locally published monthly magazine that dealt almost exclusively with the doings of prominent Nashvillians. Among the numerous pictures of well-dressed people who all seemed either to be drinking something that appeared to be alcoholic or standing in front of a church, or both, there was no one whom Shelling recognized. That didn't surprise him. He had little interest in the lives of prominent people. He preferred to be as anonymous as possible and so kept pretty much to himself, avoiding any possibility of being caught unexpectedly in the reflected glare of the glitterati.

Rook had reserved a table by a window with a view out over the city. The *maître d'* seated them and left menus. They each ordered sparkling water with lime from the unattractive, but pleasant waitress, and began perusing the menus. Shelling waited for Rook to open the conversation. After all, Mitchell had created the occasion. But, if he had done it for a specific purpose, he didn't seem in any hurry to reveal that.

After a few minutes, Rook put down his menu and looked out the window.

"Syd," Rook finally said without taking his eyes from the view of the city, "tell me something."

"Sure, Mitchell," Shelling responded.

"I haven't been around the academic scene for a long time, so maybe I'm naive about how the system works now. But I thought you went that route because of the integrity of it, the *disinterested search for truth*," he emphasized the familiar phrase, "and all that. Am I wrong?"

Shelling wanted to be honest with his old friend, but it was hard to answer the question honestly without saying more than he wished to.

Shelling paused for a few moments and then said, measuring his words, "Well, Mitchell, that's true.

As corny as it may sound to you, that is why I chose the career that I did. And it was a good choice for me for the most part."

"And the other part?" Rook looked directly at his friend.

"I guess things change over time. It seems to me that medical institutions in the last several years have become driven by different motives than when I started out."

Mitchell sighed and said, "You mean money? Well, medical institutions don't have a corner on that market. Money has come to drive a lot of things that used to be driven by more noble motives. Even business. Seems like a lot of people think making money is the only goal for business and, unfortunately, that any means are justified by that end."

"Yeah. I thought we were doing medicine because we wanted to do something positive for the human race. Now I'm told that yes, that's true, but you can't do good without money and the more money you can amass, the more good you can do. The problem is, I don't buy that when what I see is more time and energy being spent trying to make money than trying to do good."

"So, how do you do it, Syd? How do you stay true to yourself and deal with the apparently, shall we say, *evolving mores*," stressing the words, "of the institution that employs you?"

"You know, Mitchell," Syd responded, "basically I hunker down. I'm just a good pathologist with a job to do and I do it as best I can. I do everything I can to stay as far away from the politics and the large issues that the institution faces as possible. I do my committee work on the Animal Care Committee or sometimes the IRB. I decline any invitation to sit on committees that deal with big institutional issues.

Well, at least that's what I try to do, but it doesn't always work."

"Yeah, I know," Rook said. "Sometimes you get dragged into something you would rather avoid specifically because people know you don't have a personal agenda. It's happened to me. Quite a lot, in fact. I've lost clients that way. But in the long run I think the firm has gained more than it's lost by trying to keep true to its basic principles."

"That's true. Sometimes you come by information that you don't want and that forces your hand. Understand?" Syd said, but immediately wished that he hadn't said that.

The waitress reappeared to take their orders. They each scanned the menu again. Shelling ordered a Cobb salad and Rook ordered a grilled salmon pannino with watercress pesto and microgreens, confirming that the fish had not been frozen and specifying that it should be cooked medium rare.

"I think I do understand," Rook resumed the conversation, "and actually that's the reason I wanted to talk with you."

"I thought our lunch invitation was a little sudden. And a little too close to the conversation we had about Cy Bartalak."

"And Dr. Karpov."

"Yes, Katya Karpov. too."

"I met with her."

"And?"

"My sense was that she didn't tell me the same things you didn't tell me."

"So, Mitchell," Shelling said, "why are you so interested in this? I don't see that it has anything to do with your business client. This is a university matter and it could get really complicated. Do you understand?"

"No, Syd," Mitchell replied, "I don't understand

at all. Perhaps you could enlighten me."

"Well," Syd said, "it's like we were saying. When money drives the system, the people bringing in the money hold the power."

"I understand that very well, Syd. I deal with people every day who believe that their sole mission in life and their worth as human beings depends on how much money they can make."

"Well, yeah, but in an academic setting it may be more complicated than that. There are still some of us who have different motives. The money guys can't ignore that entirely."

"But," Rook replied, a note of indignation in his voice, "you, even you who claim to be driven by more noble motives, still protect your own, circle the wagons when a threat looms."

"Maybe that's true. But that's because we still believe that universities are the only hope for perpetuating more noble motives. And, I might add, convincing the next generation to change the direction of things from where our generation appears to be taking them. We, or at least I, don't want to undermine the stature of the university."

Rook was ready to move directly to address the reason he had arranged the meeting. At this point he thought that he had laid enough groundwork.

"Syd," Rook said, laying down the fork he had been fondling, resting his elbows on the table and leaning aggressively toward his friend, "I'm going to give it to you straight. If that doesn't cause you to tell me what you know about the Bartalak situation, then God help you."

"Whoa," Shelling replied, leaning back in his chair, "that sounds like a threat, Mitchell."

"It is a threat, Syd," Rook said, "but just hear me out. And I wouldn't do this except for the fact that I trust you to do the right thing. I always knew you to care about what was right, maybe even more than I did back when we were classmates."

Shelling didn't respond in any obvious way. He sipped at his water. The waitress arrived with their food. Shelling started to eat, avoiding his friend's eyes.

"I trust that what I'm about to tell you," Rook started, "will be held in confidence."

Shit, Shelling thought. The last thing he needed was more confidential information.

"Wait a minute, Mitchell," Shelling said. "Do you really need to do this? I don't want any confidential information from you or anyone else!"

Rook smiled, "I'm not going to give you a choice, my friend. I'm going to give you confidential information and trust you to do with it what you believe to be right."

Shit, Shelling thought.

"So, here is the story," Rook began.

He told Shelling of the suspicion that Cy Bartalak was a crook, had probably dealt illegally in a drug development fiasco in Houston, and was strongly suspected by the federal authorities to be scheming to make an additional killing by committing securities fraud yet again. It was suspected that after inflating the value of his startup company by doing some kind of deal with VC or big pharma, and knowing that the odds of the drug succeeding were much less than he had claimed when doing the deal, he would unload his interest in the startup company at the inflated price on the pretense that the university viewed his further involvement with the startup company and the drug as a conflict of interest for him and for the institution. Rook did not tell his friend of the planned sting operation in which Rook was to play the starring role.

When Rook had finished, Shelling said, "OK,

Mitchell. I'll tell you what I know if you will promise not to reveal your source. I know that may sound cowardly to you, but understand that if I were identified as the source of what I'm about to tell you, it is very likely that I would lose my job and maybe my professional credibility. I'm just not willing to go there."

Rook accepted the conditions and Shelling, at long last, unburdened himself. He told his friend of his meeting with Katya Karpov and her claim to have documentation proving that some of the data from the clinical studies of Cy Bartalak's drug had been falsified. He told Rook of Katya's plan to file a formal charge of scientific misconduct against Beth Bartalak.

"And what did you advise her about that?" Rook asked.

"I gave her the same advice I'd give to anyone who asked. Play by the rules. There's a process for investigating scientific misconduct and the proper way to deal with such a suspicion is to play by the rules. File a formal complaint with the dean. He'll appoint a committee to investigate the charges and report back to him and a decision will be made."

"Will she do that?"

"I'm quite confident that she will. Katya Karpov is not only uncommonly bright, she is also still driven by the motives that I think you and I admire. She would be taking a big risk to level such charges against Cy Bartalak's wife, but I don't think Katya will be deterred by the possible personal consequences of her actions. She'll do what she thinks is right."

"And her documentation? Is there any way I can get a hold of that?"

"Not likely. She apparently pirated it from Beth Bartalak's computer. I haven't seen it."

They were both quiet for a while. Shelling pretended to be admiring the view out the window, but actually he was considering whether or not to tell Rook about Bonz Bagley's involvement in the drug study and the results of his autopsy. Shelling finally decided that he had told Mitchell Rook quite enough and so didn't say any more.

As soon as Mitchell Rook arrived back at his office in the Batman Building, he placed a call to Dom Petrillo. Rook was told by a secretary that Mr. Petrillo was out of the office and Rook left a message for the attorney to call him ASAP.

27

When Katya Karpov arrived at work that morning she went directly into her office and closed the door. She removed the envelope containing her letter to the dean from her briefcase and placed it on her desk. She then sat down at the desk and stared at the envelope for a while, screwing up her courage. She knew she had to do this and she would do it. But it was probably the most difficult thing she had ever had to do during a career that had for the most part brought her pleasure and satisfaction.

There was nothing either pleasurable or satisfying about leveling a charge of professional misconduct against a colleague, regardless of how disagreeable the colleague happened to be. And leveling such a charge against the wife of her chairman, who may even be involved in the deception, might very well be, as she had told Shane earlier, professional suicide.

Finally, Katya picked up the phone and rang the office of the dean. She told his secretary that she needed to meet with the dean about an urgent matter as soon as possible.

"Well, Dr. Karpov," the secretary replied, "I'm looking at his schedule and it may be at least a day or two before I can work you in. He has a board meeting this morning and some important standing meetings during the afternoon. How about tomorrow at five?"

"It really can't wait, Lynda," Katya responded. "I must see him today."

Everyone who had any business with the dean knew his long time secretary and knew that she controlled his calendar with a vengeance.

"I'm really sorry," Lynda responded, "but I can't schedule you today. Tell you what. If this is really that urgent, let me check with him and see if he wants to rearrange things in order to work you in."

"I would greatly appreciate that, Lynda," Katya said.

"Good. Let me check with him as soon as he returns from the board meeting and I'll call you. Will you be in your office?"

"Yes, I'll be here," Katya said and hung up the phone.

She removed the letter and the two accompanying documents from the envelope and spent the next couple of hours going over everything again, carefully studying each document. She tried as hard as she could to come up with an explanation for the information that would justify a conclusion different from the obvious one. But, for the life of her, she couldn't imagine any other explanation.

She replaced the material into the envelope and sat staring out the window. She thought about her career at the university. It had been an excellent situation for her, at least while Larry Walker was department chair. But even when Cy took over, things were still OK for the most part. This drug study had not been a positive for her. It had taken most of her time away from her own research that was at a critical stage. But she had done what Cy wanted her to, tried to be a good citizen, a team player. She couldn't do that any longer, not with the information in the envelope on her desk.

The phone rang, and she answered it immediately, "This is Katya Karpov."

"Oh, Dr. Karpov," the dean's secretary responded, "I'm glad to catch you. I was afraid you'd be at lunch. Dean Corbett can give you a half hour at one if that's alright. He'll just delay attending his scheduled one o'clock. Can you be here then?"

Katya answered, "I'll be there, Lynda, thank you."

It was a quarter to one. Katya picked up the envelope and held it, staring at the digital clock on her desk for the next ten minutes and then left her office, took the stairs to the sixth floor and made her way to the office of the dean.

Harmon Corbitt had been medical dean at the university for twenty years. At the time he accepted the position he thought it was exactly the job he wanted. That had turned out to be true. He had played a major role in increasing the size and the academic quality of the school faculty. He had spearheaded a major expansion of the physical facilities for both the clinical and research components of the enterprise. Research funding for the school had quintupled since he took over. He had developed exceptional skills as a fundraiser and had even come to enjoy that role. He had generally good relationships with both the university board of trust and his faculty.

Corbitt had to admit, though, to himself if not to others, that there had been a major shift in the direction of medical institutions in recent years. There was an emerging new breed of leaders who appeared to be setting the course for the future. These people were different than the old school academicians whom the dean had always admired. This new breed marched to a different drummer.

As he awaited the arrival of Katya Karpov for her urgently requested appointment, he thought specifically of his department of psychiatry. The transition of leadership of that department had been difficult for Dean Corbitt, but he was satisfied that the right thing had been done. While he had great respect and affection for Larry Walker, the world of academic psychiatry had passed him by. Cy Bartalak was of the

307

new generation of bright, articulate, effective academic entrepreneurs who were the future not just of this institution but of academic medicine in general. It was that conviction that led Corbitt to recruit Bartalak and his group from Houston and that had turned out to be a stellar move.

Bartalak had not only had a major impact on the institution's research funding from federal and foundation sources, but had, in just a few short years, come up with this unique drug that may just prove to be the major pharmacological advance for chronic neurodegenerative diseases to happen in the last century. There was the potential for enormous institutional credit for such a major advance in therapy and they also stood to reap substantial monetary rewards. Corbitt knew of course that there was a ways to go before discovering whether those things would turn out to be true. Bartalak knew that, too. But the potential was there.

Granted, Corbitt thought, Bartalak was aggressive. His push to ascend to the chairmanship was ahead of the schedule that both the dean and Bartalak had agreed on when the psychiatrist was originally recruited. But it was true that Larry Walker was riding the downslope of the academic hill. And Bartalak didn't resist the dean's insistence that he keep Katya Karpov on the faculty, even though it was common knowledge that she was a special favorite of Walker's. Corbitt insisted on keeping her on the faculty because she was a rising star and there were far too few of those around.

Corbitt got up from behind his desk and walked around to greet Katya when the secretary showed her in. They shook hands and he motioned her to a sofa in the corner of his large office where he met with visitors. He took a seat in an upholstered chair opposite her.

"Can I have Lynda bring some coffee?" Corbitt asked.

"No, thank you," Katya replied.

Corbitt met with Katya only occasionally and it had been a while since they last spoke. He had forgotten what a striking woman she was. It wasn't just her physical appearance, but that she seemed to radiate an air of modest self-confidence, maybe self-assuredness was a better word for it. Someone had described her to him once as *pleasantly aggressive*, a description that he thought oxymoronic at the time, but there was truth to it.

"What can I do for you, Katya? Why the urgency?" Corbitt had only half an hour to spare and wanted to get whatever this matter was dealt with expeditiously.

"Thank you for making time to see me, Harmon. I realize how busy you must be," Katya said, aware that the dean insisted that the faculty address him by his given name.

"Of course, of course," he responded, "never too busy to deal with urgent matters of my faculty. So what is it?"

"I've come to do a very unpleasant task," she began, "unpleasant for me, in fact the most difficult thing I've ever done. And it will be unpleasant for you as well and for a lot of others."

"What could possibly be so ominous, Katya?" Corbitt said, leaning forward and looking directly into her green eyes.

Katya laid the envelope she had in her hand on the coffee table between them and continued, "This envelope contains a confidential letter to you leveling a charge of scientific misconduct against Beth Bartalak."

"My God, Katya," the dean interrupted her, "you can't be serious. I mean I know the two of you have

309

had your differences. Cy has told me about that. But scientific misconduct? Come now, Katya."

"I realize the gravity of this, Harmon, and it is not done without a lot of agonizing. However, as you'll see from the other documents, I have what I believe to be incontrovertible proof that Beth has falsified data related to the study of this Alzheimer's drug of Cy's that makes the results of the study appear more favorable than they actually are."

"How could you possibly have such information? Where did it come from?"

"I'm hesitant to tell you only because it reflects negatively on me. But I obtained it from Beth Bartalak's laboratory computer without her permission. I recognize that is an ethical violation and accept responsibility for it. At the time I did it I thought it was justified."

"Jesus H. Christ," Corbitt exploded. "I can't believe this, Katya, any of it. I can't believe that you of all people would compromise your ethics. And I certainly can't believe that this charge has any merit. There has to be an explanation. Have you discussed this with Cy?"

"Yes, I have. I told him of my suspicion and gave him most of the documentation that is included in this envelope. As far as I know he's taken no action. That's why I've come to you. I don't think I have a choice at this point. And there is another thing."

"Please don't tell me anything can be worse than what you've already said."

"Possibly so. The initial subject in the clinical trial of the drug was the elderly gentleman who was murdered in Printers Alley recently."

"Old Bonz Bagley?" the dean asked.

"Yes. He is, was, the only subject to have completed the six month study. He had completed the laboratory tests and was scheduled to come in the day after his murder for the final clinical examination."

"Too bad on all counts," Corbitt responded, "but how is that relevant?"

"It may be relevant because of the coroner's autopsy findings. Although Mr. Bagley was shot several times in the head so that much of his brain was destroyed, parts of what remained showed what was interpreted as possible exposure to a neurotoxic chemical."

"Who knows what the old guy was exposed to? What's your point?"

"We know that he was exposed to the experimental drug over six months. And the data from the lab tests that I retrieved from Beth's computer are entirely consistent with some severe injury to critical areas of his brain."

Forty-five minutes had elapsed since Katya entered the dean's office. The secretary knocked on the door and cracked it to remind the dean that he was way overdue for a meeting.

"Look Katya," Corbitt said, summoning his most deanly tone of voice, "let me review what you've brought here. I will keep it in confidence until I've had time to decide what to do. I will, of course, go through with the investigation of whatever charge you wish to bring. You are aware that there is a process for doing that. I will do everything I can to protect the integrity of this institution. Rest assured of that. But I must say that I find this difficult to believe. I also must tell you that I hope to God you're wrong."

"Thank you, Harmon. That's all anyone could expect. And, for the record, I also hope to God that I'm wrong."

They left the office together without speaking further. They parted in the corridor. The dean scurried off to his important meeting. Katya took the stairs down a flight and returned to her office. The deed was done.

Dom Petrillo exited the Kefauver Building and walked the short block south on Broadway past what had been the grand old central city post office building now reincarnated as an art museum. He entered the Union Station Hotel just beyond, also a reincarnation, a hotel instead of the main train station that it had been for years until the passenger rail business dried up. He entered the bar directly from the side entrance that faced Broadway, ordered a Manhattan and sat down at a small table in the corner of the room to await Mitchell Rook's arrival.

By the time Petrillo had returned Rook's call it was almost six and Rook suggested that they meet for a drink at the bar in the hotel that was close to Petrillo's office and also on Rook's route home. Rook said they needed to talk and he preferred that they do it in person.

Petrillo was anxious to discover what information his old colleague had been able to garner. Petrillo thought that they were making some progress on the Bartalak case. He was anxious to pull the trigger on the planned sting as soon as they had enough information to support that decision. They didn't have that yet and Petrillo thought that Rook had the best chance of getting it. Maybe he had done that.

"So, tell me what you've got," Petrillo said just as Rook was joining him at the small table.

"Let me order a drink and I'll fill you in," Rook replied. "I think we may be close."

The room had filled up and Rook was unable to attract the attention of a waitress. He got up, went over to the bar and ordered an extra dry Plymouth gin martini, stirred, up with a single olive. As with most of what he did, Mitchell Rook gave very precise instructions for preparing the drink. He felt strongly about the importance of controlling with precision the things in his life that affected him directly.

"Sure," the bartender sighed, "I'll have the girl bring it to you. You're in the corner with the fed guy, right?"

"Right," Mitchell smiled.

Seated back at the table, he said, "Well, Dom, it looks like some fecal matter is about to encounter the wind currents."

Petrillo smiled and said, "Go on. But first can you tell me how you came by this information? Is it credible?"

"No and yes," Rook replied.

"What do you mean?"

"I can't tell you my source; I vowed I wouldn't reveal it. But it is credible. I'm sure of that."

"OK, shoot."

"It seems," Mitchell began, "that our Dr. Karpov believes that she has information indicating that Bartalak's wife, Beth, the biostatistician, fudged some of the data from the subjects in the drug study."

"How solid is the information? Does she have documents? Does Cy Bartalak know about this?"

"My source, whom I trust and who knows Dr. Karpov well, says that she does have documentation but that she obtained it at least unethically and maybe even illegally. My source hasn't seen the documents but is certain that Karpov has them. He also says that Karpov went directly to her boss, gave him copies of her documentation and told him about her suspicions, but that he hasn't done anything about it."

"Any way we can get our hands on the documents?"

"From my brief encounter with Dr. Karpov, I

seriously doubt that. She was very guarded with me. And she's married to that ex-detective so he's likely advising her as well."

"So what do we do?"

"There's more information," Rook said.

An attractive young woman wearing a short black skirt and a black tee shirt with the words *Jolly Roger* scrawled beneath a large skull and crossbones on its front approached their table, placed Rook's martini in front of him without speaking and walked off swaying her hips and dangling the drink tray at her side.

"Yes?" Petrillo queried. "What more information?"

Rook sipped from his drink and said, "It seems that Dr. Karpov is going to lodge a formal complaint of scientific misconduct against Beth Bartalak with the dean of the medical school. That will precipitate an internal investigation. And "

"Sure," Petrillo interrupted, "but they'll claim it's not true. Those investigations are done by faculty committees and we know how rare it is for those guys to hang one of their own. Medical faculties are no different from faculties of law or anything else."

Rook responded, "That may well be, but here's the other development. Bartalak has stopped the drug study because of the marked positive effect it appears to have had on the few subjects studied. He thinks he has enough to do a deal, probably with big pharma, that would greatly increase the value of the startup company. And if there was this charge of scientific misconduct hanging over the thing that alone might be enough to queer the pharma deal regardless of the eventual outcome of the investigation."

"Hmmm," Petrillo said, "so timing. Timing is critical. We need to spring the trap before there is common knowledge of the scientific misconduct charge but after Bartalak is close enough to finalizing a deal to make it credible to unload his interest in the startup at an inflated price."

"My thinking exactly," Rook said.

"When is Karpov going to file the charge?"

"My source didn't know that but suspected that she would do it sooner rather than later. Could have done it already. But the way these things work, apparently it will take the dean a little time to review the charge, appoint a committee, all that stuff. So it won't be common knowledge for a little while."

"What about the other piece? Where is Bartalak in the dealing process?"

"I don't know that either, but he'll move fast. He'll move especially fast if he knows something that he's not telling. He'll want to get everything nailed down. At any rate," Rook continued, "given the fact that I'm one of Cy's angels, I should know as soon as he has anything solid to say."

"Never really thought of you as an angel, Mitchell," Petrillo said. "Good guy, but angel?"

"Well, I suppose technically in this case I'm borrowing that identity. It's your money."

"And," Petrillo added, "I trust it will have been well spent."

Rook finished his martini and said, "I guess we'll see."

28

Cy Bartalak arrived home late after his day in New Jersey. Beth was asleep and he didn't wake her. He hoped that she had seen Oscar Orbitz. Cy had arranged that and was interested to know what the examination showed. He was concerned about Beth.

Cy was surprised when he got up early the next morning, showered, shaved, dressed for work and went to the kitchen to find that Beth wasn't there. No coffee, nothing for breakfast. He went to her bedroom, cracked the door and looked in. She appeared to be sleeping and so he left her there and headed for work. Although he couldn't remember Beth ever having failed to prepare his morning coffee and habitual light breakfast and see him off to work, he had other things on his mind and so didn't dwell on whatever was his wife's problem.

He stopped by a Starbucks on the way in and bought a grande Sumatra which was all he really needed to get started with his day.

When he arrived at his office, Cy's secretary was not at her desk. There were three pink message slips on his desk left there the previous day. Each message, one from Mitchell Rook, one from Oscar Orbitz and one from Susanna Gomez at GPI, requested a return call as soon as possible. He was especially interested in the call from Gomez. He felt really good about the previous day's meeting. If he read the situation right, GPI was going to want to move quickly toward a deal for the drug which is exactly what he had hoped would be the case.

He arranged the three message slips in order of their priority — Gomez, followed by Rook, followed by Orbitz. He switched on his computer and entered his password. He clicked on the Outlook icon and then on contacts, scrolled down to Gomez and dialed the number.

He was surprised that the call was answered after the third ring by Susanna Gomez herself.

"This is Sue Gomez," she said.

"Oh, hi, Sue," he responded after a short pause. "This is Cy Bartalak and I'm returning your call from last evening. I'm surprised that you answered the phone. Don't vice presidents get a secretary to do that for them?"

"Thanks for calling, Cy," Gomez said. "I often answer my own phone, actually. It can be interesting to catch callers off guard sometimes. You should try it."

"Perhaps," he responded, thinking that he wouldn't do that, didn't like the impression it would leave, "but thanks again for setting up the meeting yesterday. I enjoyed meeting your folks. Are we going to be able to work together?"

"That's why I called," she said. "I think that's a real possibility. I've asked my people to get with you and whoever else is relevant there to review everything, do the due diligence. But if it all checks out as you led us to expect, I'm ready to move forward with this."

"Great news, great news, Sue," he replied. "Just have your people let me know what they need. We'll have to get the confidentiality agreements signed and whatever other preliminaries are necessary, but this sounds exciting.

"I agree, Cy. Look forward to it. My people will be in touch shortly."

Cy hung up the phone and sat staring at it for a few minutes, reviewing the conversation with Gomez and pondering the next steps when there was a knock on his office door. The door opened without waiting for him to respond.

"Cy," Oscar Orbitz, said, walking into the room

and taking a seat opposite Cy's desk, "got a minute? I was up here for another reason and thought I'd drop by and give you a follow up on Beth."

The medicine chairman was a no-nonsense, straightforward professional who was more than a match for the chair of psychiatry if for no other reason because he was older and had more equity in the university system. Cy knew that Orbitz was an outstanding clinician and respected him professionally even though he viewed him as a competitor.

"Oh, thanks Oscar," Cy answered. "Sorry that I had to be out of town yesterday, but thanks so much for seeing her. What do you think?"

"I'll get to that, but I wondered if you could answer a couple of questions."

"Of course."

"I'll put this as delicately as I can, Cy. I'm concerned about some kind of drug abuse. Is there any possibility of that?"

"I entertained that thought briefly myself, but I don't think so. Beth just isn't the type for one thing."

"Yeah. And the tox screen was negative so there's no concrete reason to suspect it. It's just that the clinical picture looks a lot like that. But, let me tell you what I think. Something is going on with Beth and I'm afraid it could be something serious. She has some neurological signs that don't fit a pattern but are troublesome. What I recommend is that she see a neurologist, get an MRI and an EEG and whatever else the neurologist recommends. See if we can identify anything. I gather she has been slipping for a few months. Is that right?"

"I guess," Cy answered. "It's been subtle. I don't think I really noticed anything until more recently than that.

"Here's what I suggest, Cy," Orbitz continued.

318

"Let's bring her into the hospital for a few days. She can be in one of the executive suites up on eight south."

Cy knew that eight south consisted of six suites virtually indistinguishable from deluxe suites in a five star hotel. The wing had its own gourmet kitchen and *chef d 'cuisine* with meals prepared to the patients' orders. Spa services—manicures, pedicures, facials, massages—could be scheduled. In addition to the patient bedroom, there was a sitting room, a work area with FAX machine and computer with internet connections. There was a sofa bed for a family member to stay overnight if they wished.

The cost of these suites was exorbitant and only a fraction of it was covered by even the most lavish medical insurance. But, for the well to do who thought the privacy, convenience, and amenities worth the price, it was a very nice way to spend time in a hospital if that became necessary. Cy had toured the area and had seen a VIP patient or two there as a psychiatric consultant. If Beth needed to spend a few days in the hospital, that's where she should be alright.

"Of course, of course," Cy answered. "If you think that best, then that's what we should do."

"Good," Orbitz replied, "I can arrange her admission under my name. I'll get the tests ordered and organize at least a neurology consult. I'd recommend Sol Feltzer and I'm happy to arrange that. If we need other consultants it will be easy enough to get those done while she's in. Could you bring her in tomorrow assuming I can get a bed?"

"Well, I suppose if that's what you think I should do," Cy answered. "But is it really that urgent?"

"Cy," Orbitz placed his hand on Cy's desk and leaned toward him, "I think we should get to the bottom of this as quickly as possible. I don't know if it's urgent, but it could be."

Cy was a little rattled. He had a number of pressing things to do. He had to talk with the *Renaptix* investors, give them the good news about Global Pharmaceuticals. And there was this message to call the lawyer, Mitchell Rook, that concerned Cy. He had been a little worried about Rook from the outset and couldn't imagine any felicitous reason why the lawyer would want to talk with him privately.

Beth had always been a source of unquestioning support for Cy. And she didn't need a lot of attention. That had been a major source of pleasure for him, a big reason why he valued their relationship. He was not accustomed to organizing his life around her needs. He wasn't anxious to do that, especially now. He needed to concentrate on finalizing this deal with GPI. But he really had no choice.

"OK, Oscar," Cy responded, "and thank you for seeing Beth and making these arrangements. I really do appreciate that."

"Glad to help," Orbitz replied. "If there's any problem with getting a bed for tomorrow, I'll let you know. Otherwise just bring Beth in at your convenience."

"So, let's begin, Hardy, my man, by reviewing the facts. Always a good place to begin, don't you think?" Shane said.

"Sounds good to me," Seltzer replied.

Hardy had arrived in Printers Alley later than they had agreed on. He had again been called into the chief's office. This time the chief was less guarded about the likelihood that Seltzer might be suspended. The chief had had Seltzer review the status of his work with Shane. When Hardy had done that, the chief asked him whether he thought that Hadley's mystery woman was the real murderer and Hardy responded that it appeared to him to be a real possibility.

The chief answered, "Detective Seltzer, possibilities aren't going to save your neck, I fear. X Coniglio is on a real tear and he's got the mayor and the DA breathing down my neck now. X is going to move to dismiss the charges against Jody Dakota and, from what the DA says, that might just happen. Apparently X has a credible witness who will swear that Jody was in the city but nowhere near Printers Alley when Bonz was killed. If the charges against Dakota are dismissed we're back to square one with shit on our faces and with you squarely in the crosshairs of a lot of powerful people. We may have a day or two, but not much longer."

The chief's tirade still reverberated in Seltzer's head as he sat in the Hadley living room, trying to concentrate on what Shane was saying.

"First," Shane said, "we can rule out Jody Dakota as the killer. Are you ready to accept that?"

"Maybe," Hardy replied. "The chief says X might even get the charges dismissed. A situation that doesn't please either the chief or the DA and may allow X to go through with his threat."

"The rolling of your head, I presume you mean," Shane said. "Well, we can't allow that to happen, can we? But let me continue.

"We have identified the killer, Hardy. The woman originally known as Elizabeth Reid possesses what I am convinced is the murder weapon. She has test fired the weapon in the environs of our city. And this is the crucial piece of information, she had a childhood injury to her right leg that caused her to have a persistent oddity to her running gait. As Sheriff Teasdale so colorfully put it *a hitch in her gitalong."*

Hardy listened intently to Shane. It would amaze the detective if Shane's original observation of how the fleeing murderer ran would turn out to be the critical clue that eventually led them to the killer. But, it was starting to look like that was a possibility.

"Well we have a problem don't we?" Hardy said. "While we know someone signing her name as Elizabeth Reid test fired a gun like the murder weapon at that Williamson County place, we've drawn a complete blank in either locating her in Nashville or tracking her here from Houston."

"So far, Hardy my man. So far," Shane responded and after a pause continued, "I believe that the hour is sufficiently advanced for a glass of sherry, now Hardy. Would you join me?"

Shane wheeled himself over to the bar, retrieved one of his prized glasses and poured a generous amount into it. He gestured toward Hardy with the bottle questioningly.

"Sure," Hardy sighed, "I'll have some."

Shane removed another of the Oxford glasses from the case and, after holding it up to the light, filled it with wine. He rolled over to Hardy and handed him the glass.

"There is a story to these glasses, Hardy, that perhaps one day I will relate to you. I think they add to the pleasure of the wine. See if you agree."

"OK," Hardy answered.

Hardy raised the glass carefully to his lips and took a sip. The wine really did taste quite good. He didn't say anything but nodded to Shane who raised his glass and returned the nod.

"So," Hardy said, "what do we do now?"

"Yes, yes," Shane responded, "I have a suggestion. After considering the possibilities, excluding the impossibility that our mystery woman has actually disappeared from the planet, I propose the following."

Shane took a swallow of the wine and sighed.

"Suppose," he continued, "that our woman did indeed change her name immediately upon arriving in our fair city, prior to establishing a residence or transacting any business that would have placed her original name in any of the databases. And suppose that was several years ago so that she felt that signing Elizabeth Reid in the shooter's club log did not risk revealing her true identity."

"You mean legally had her name changed? You think she came here with the plan of eventually killing Bagley and so covered her tracks in advance and then waited several years to do it? Isn't that farfetched? What about motive?"

"Very astute of you, my man," Shane responded. "I am certain that we have the killer, but motive? I am still puzzled there. The four shots to the head are surely telling us something but I'm unsure what as of yet. Did Bagley have any connections with Texas?"

"Not that we uncovered. He'd been in Nashville forever."

"No country music connections? Did any of Bagley's mentees in the business have Texas roots?"

"Probably," Hardy responded. "A lot of the business goes on between here and Texas. But we don't know anything specific about that in this case."

Shane paused, sipping from his sherry, then continued, "Well, my man, we'll continue to ponder motive. However, I have a suggestion for action in the meantime."

"What's that?"

"I suggest a foray to the local marriage license bureau, the written signature of our Elizabeth Reid in hand. I have a personal experience with that office. When one obtains a marriage license in this city, there is a quaint procedure that involves each of the parties signing their names in a massive ledger, volumes of which line the walls of the small office in the basement of one of the buildings at the place known as the Old Howard School."

Hardy knew the place. There was a complex of buildings that had been acquired by the metropolitan government when Howard High School moved elsewhere and the complex was still known as the Old Howard School. It may even have been officially named that for all Hardy knew. Several local government offices were housed there. It was on Third Avenue a few blocks south of Lower Broad.

Shane continued, "The task may be a bit arduous, but if our Elizabeth Reid changed her name in our city by way of matrimony, the most likely device for achieving that end, there will be a signature in one of those ledgers at around the time that Ms. Reid disappeared from Houston that exactly matches the signature from the shooting club log. And further, the adjacent signature of the man whom she was to marry will provide us with our murderer's current identity."

Hardy had almost finished his glass of sherry and wondered whether the fact that Shane's reasoning seemed brilliant was an effect of the wine. But even if not brilliant, it was something to do.

"Are you up to the task?" Shane asked.

"I'll have a go at it. Shouldn't be too difficult," Hardy responded. "Maybe not very exciting, but not too difficult."

"I suspect that there will be excitement," Shane responded. "I suspect, Hardy my man, that there will be excitement enough to spare."

"The alley's changed since Bonz's murder,"

Katya made the comment offhandedly.

She and Shane sat on their balcony. They had eaten sushi at the little place just at the Church Street end of the alley. They were both fond of sushi and that place was close and the food was good enough to compensate for the surly attitude of the middle-aged Japanese man who ran the place; they referred to him privately as *The Sushi Nazi.*

Shane had a glass of sherry and Katya was drinking sparkling water from a wine glass. A clear glass cylinder still half full of the Voss water that she favored sat on the small table between them. It was just turning dusk. The alley was uncharacteristically quiet. But it was early yet.

"I agree, my love," Shane responded. "Something more than Bonz may have died. He embodied the spirit, if that's not too strong a word, of the place. Seems as though the life of the alley itself suffered a serious blow, possibly a mortal one."

They sat for a while without speaking, enjoying the cool evening breeze.

"Ironic," Katya said.

"What," Shane responded, "The alley? I suppose that's one apt descriptor of the place."

"No, Shane, I didn't mean that. I was thinking about Bonz. He was scheduled to come in to see me for the clinical exam on the day after he was killed. He'd come in for the lab tests earlier, and the final clinical exam that the protocol required was to happen on that Monday, the next day. I'd even scheduled him for some more lab tests that wouldn't have been part of the drug study because I thought he was getting worse just from seeing him in the alley. Those tests would have been part of his regular medical record and wouldn't have been sequestered behind Beth's firewall where she hid the study data. If he had lived one more day, I'd have come by the proof of Beth's treachery without having to compromise myself."

"Would've saved a lot of trouble if someone hadn't killed the old guy," Shane, feeling the effects of the sherry more than usual, replied, "and the irony?"

"The irony, my love, is the collateral damage of an apparently random event."

"I've rarely found murders of this sort to be random events."

"Well," Katya said, "maybe not random, but surely unrelated to the effects it had on me, potentially on us."

"Certainly appears that way," Shane replied. "I think it probably qualifies as irony. I'll grant you that. But I must add that true irony in my experience, while a useful literary device, rarely happens in real life."

29

Cy Bartalak was driving out West End toward home and thinking over the last couple of days. He decided not to stay at the hospital with Beth. He had gotten her checked in early that morning and Orbitz had scheduled a bunch of tests as well as the neurological consultant; that all happened over the day. Cy had gone by to see Beth before starting home. She was sleeping and he didn't wake her. He thought briefly about staying with her in the suite that night, but didn't like the thought of sleeping on a sofa bed in a strange place that, while perfectly nice, lacked the comfort of his own bed.

Cy thought that he had things moving in the right direction. On the previous afternoon, he had organized a conference call with his three investors and brought them up to speed on the GPI deal. He was confident that the deal would happen and the potential of this drug was so enormous that GPI would pay a premium to get control of it at an early stage. He told his investors, and he believed it was true, that at the signing of the GPI deal, the value of *Renaptix, Inc.* would immediately increase from probably six million or so to at least fifty million dollars and probably more. And with subsequent milestone payments and royalties if the drug was eventually successful, the value of their little startup company could well exceed a billion dollars. Even if the drug didn't pan out for some reason, they still stood to make millions. This was really heady stuff.

Cy wended his way up his driveway and parked the Mercedes in the garage. He dropped his briefcase in the foyer, went to the den and turned on the lights. The house felt cold and empty without Beth there. He opened the bar and made himself a martini. He sat down and thought about his relationship with Beth.

The days shortly before they left Houston were when the passion ran hot, like nothing Cy had experienced before. And Beth was so devoted to him. She'd insisted on assuming his name even before his divorce was final and was anxious to tie the knot as soon as the papers came through shortly after they arrived in Nashville. Beth was a perfectly competent woman on her own, but she wanted him, seemed to need him.

That was what attracted him, a lovely woman who needed him because of who he was rather than because he made up for some deficiency of hers. Even after the passion cooled, Beth had been loyal, committed, a reliable and useful companion. Maybe there was more to it than that, he thought. The house did feel her absence. Maybe he felt that some, too.

He sat sipping his martini for a while. The conversation with Mitchell Rook had seemed strange. Rook had asked Cy to return a call and then suggested that Rook just stay on the line with him after the conference call concluded and the others had rung off. But Rook only wanted to ask whether Cy was aware of any other early stage investment opportunities in the medical field. Apparently the lawyer had some more money to invest and felt so positive about the *Renaptix* experience that he was looking for other similar deals.

Bartalak had told Rook the truth. He was not involved in any other ventures at the moment, but he promised to keep his ear to the ground and let Rook know if he heard of anything. Cy liked the fact that the big time business lawyer was asking him for investment advice. He liked that a lot. Could open up some opportunities later. He filed away the episode in his mind for future reference.

Cy put his empty martini glass on the bar and wandered about the house. He went into Beth's study.

He stood for a moment looking into the display case with the collection of rare pistols. He knew nothing about guns, but according to Beth these were valuable collector's items. She certainly valued them, no doubt about that. Beth had rarely spoken of her father to Cy, but he knew that she had inherited the guns from her father and that seemed to explain their sentimental value. If she had any other mementoes of her father he was unaware of them.

He sat down at his wife's desk. He had rarely been in that room. There had been no reason for it and Beth seemed more than a little territorial about that space. That was fine with him. He had no problem giving his wife as much space as she needed.

He opened the center drawer of the desk and looked though its contents. Pencils, paper clips, a Swingline stapler. A familiar looking folder lay to one side of the wide drawer. He picked up the folder and recognized it as the one Katya Karpov had given him that supposedly contained evidence that Beth had falsified some of the drug study data. He hadn't looked at the contents before and Beth had assured him, without much explanation, that the material was irrelevant. He'd assumed that Beth had destroyed the material but obviously she hadn't.

He was interrupted by the sound of the telephone ringing. He walked into the den to answer the call.

"This is Cy Bartalak," he intoned into the mouthpiece.

"Cy, glad I caught you," Oscar Orbitz responded.

Cy thought that Orbitz sounded somber, but then he pretty much always sounded somber. Oscar Orbitz was a somber person.

"Yes, Oscar," Cy said. "Do you have some information about Beth?"

"Yes, Cy, that's why I called. I dropped by your

office and when I didn't find you there, assumed that you had gone home," Orbitz answered. "We don't really have an answer, Cy, but Beth is clearly suffering from some kind of disease or condition of the central nervous system that is affecting many of her higher integrative functions."

"That certainly seemed to be the case to me recently," Cy said, thinking how neurological examinations usually just confirmed what was obvious to any careful observer of behavior.

"There are also some troubling test data, Cy," Orbitz continued. "Both the EEG and the MRI are abnormal. The abnormalities are diffuse, throughout the cerebral hemispheres, frontal lobes as well as elsewhere. The patterns are not specific for anything known but they are very real and not subtle. Although we've done an extensive tox screen that's negative, I'm still worried about some kind of drug reaction. You don't have any more information or thoughts about that do you?"

"None whatsoever," Cy responded. "Like I told you earlier, I just don't think Beth is the drug abuser type. What do you suggest at this point?"

"Two things," Orbitz replied. "I suggest that we keep her in the hospital for a week or so. If she's been using some drug that we can't identify and if the effects are reversible, we should see some improvement in her symptoms in a setting where she can't possibly have access to the drug."

"That sounds reasonable," Cy said. "What else?"

"I've talked at length with the neurologist, Cy, and we both think that if her symptoms don't improve pretty quickly that she should have a brain biopsy. The pathology might provide some definitive answers that we can't get otherwise."

"A brain biopsy?" Cy was incredulous.

"It's not a decision that has to be made tonight,

but think about it. As you know, the procedure isn't dangerous. And your wife has something that may be very serious. If it's not reversible, well, you know the long term implications. Chronic neurodegenerative diseases present many difficult challenges."

"You don't have to tell me that, Oscar," Cy said. "But thank you for calling. Let's just hope that this is something
transient even if we never understand it."

"Yes, Cy," Orbitz said, "let's hope for that."

When he had hung up the phone, Cy laid the folder he had retrieved from Beth's desk drawer on the table beside the chair in the den where he was sitting. He got up and went to Beth's private bathroom just off the large bedroom where he had occasionally spent a pleasant night; not frequently of late, he thought. He opened the medicine cabinet above the sink and surveyed its contents.

There were several bottles of pills, all of which appeared to be over the counter supplements. A multivitamin, fish oil, vitamin D, chondroitin, something called SAM-e (from the label he saw that this was s-adenosyl methionine, a naturally occurring chemical that he knew to be an antioxidant). When he had removed these bottles from the cabinet shelf, he noticed an amber plastic container at the back that looked like the containers pharmacists use for prescription drugs. He retrieved the bottle and looked at the label.

Cy stared at the label for a long minute, his mind scrolling back through the past to a specific conversation that he had had with Beth probably six or seven months ago when they were reviewing the studies of his drug in mice. He had been ecstatic about the results of those animal studies. It appeared that the drug not only had a dramatic effect on the mice with experimentally induced Alzheimer's, but even the normal control mice got smarter. The normal mice receiving the drug learned how to negotiate the complicated mazes several times faster than normal mice that didn't get the drug. Cy had told Beth that he thought this meant that the drug enhanced the function of even normal brains. He was wildly enthusiastic about its potential.

He read the label on the amber bottle — *Cy's Wonder Drug* — in Beth's unmistakable handwriting. He removed the cap and poured one of the pills into his palm. These were the brown oval pills, the drug formulation they had made for the laboratory tests. They didn't look like the round white pills used in the formal human drug study; those pills were designed so that an identical appearing placebo could be easily made. But, except for some differences in the filler that had been used, the pills were identical. The active ingredient of the differently appearing pills was the same drug.

Cy's Wonder Drug, he thought. So Beth had taken his speculation that the drug improved normal brain function to heart. She was always looking for a supplement that would improve the function of her body. She must have squirrelled away a ration of the pills from the lab experiments. And she must have been taking them, a brain supplement to go along with her catalogue of body supplements, a complete regimen for the health conscious consumer.

He replaced the other bottles into the cabinet, but carried the amber container of *Cy's Wonder Drug* with him back into the den. He retrieved the folder he had left there, went into his study and laid the folder on the desk. He sat the bottle of pills on the desk beside the folder.

He opened the folder, removed the document and began to study it. The document was labeled with a subject study number and it contained tables of laboratory results with columns labeled baseline, 1month, 2, months, 3, months, and 6 months and rows with labels indicating the tests that were done.

He focused on two kinds of test results: measurements of cognitive function and blood levels of the protein that he believed indicated disease activity. The tests showed marked improvement from baseline in the first three columns, but in the last column, the six month data, the measurements showed marked deterioration to levels that were even worse than at entry into the study.

Cy replaced the document into the folder, closed it and sat the bottle of pills on top of it. He stared at the information that he was now forced to try to assimilate. Stupid, he thought. How stupid could she be to take a drug that had never been given to humans? Everybody knows that there are gazillions of drugs that have looked promising in animal studies that didn't prove effective or were even toxic in humans. Beth was too smart to ignore that.

Well, apparently not. Apparently her unquestioning confidence in him had blinded her to any possibility other than that, like the maze-solving mice, she would get smarter by taking this drug. There was no other explanation. Stupid. Really stupid.

And, he had to accept the fact that the data in the folder before him were most likely the true data from subject number one and that the data Beth had given him were false. He had his problems with Katya Karpov, but she would not have manufactured the material in that folder. She just wouldn't have done that. The first three month data would have been enough to do a deal with big pharma. If the six-month data didn't look so good, just don't reveal it. Or destroy it and stop the study. It was true that the six-month data were icing on the cake, but they had the cake even without it. Stupid! Stupid! Stupid!

He went back to the bar in the den and made himself another dry martini. He needed a plan of action. The fact that Beth had been taking the drug need not be revealed to anyone, least of all to Oscar Orbitz. If the drug had long term brain toxicity, if that is what the information from Bagley, subject number one, including the autopsy data, indicated, it was still not known whether those effects were reversible. Perhaps Beth's response would clarify that. Her unfortunate stupidity in taking the drug might still provide some useful results. And, if Beth did not appear to improve with time, there would certainly be no brain biopsy. He would see to that.

Beth's second act of stupidity might prove to be a more difficult problem. As far as Cy knew, the only other person to have a copy of these six-month data was Katya Karpov. He didn't believe that she would pursue this issue beyond informing him for several reasons. Her only recourse would be a charge of scientific misconduct against Beth and that would be a foolish move by a woman who was anything but foolish. Foolish because taking such an action is extremely serious and not infrequently the one making the complaint winds up the victim, labeled a *trouble maker*, a *difficult person*, dramatically reducing their value in the academic marketplace. Katya knew that. Everybody knew that.

Then, and Katya had surely thought about this as well, it could be claimed that her supposed evidence was the false document rather than the material in Beth's official database. He and Beth could claim that and it would be a classical he said/she said situation where his word would surely carry the day. Everybody knew that Katya and Beth didn't get along and it would not be difficult to convince people that Katya had it in for Beth and that this was a desperate attempt to discredit her.

Even Katya's self-incriminating claim that she retrieved the information from Beth's computer was open to serious question. Most people would think it unlikely that Beth would have left her computer accessible to anyone else if it contained such important information, certainly not if she intended to alter the data before entering it into the official record. It was just not a credible scenario.

And finally, Cy just didn't think the dean or anybody else in the university hierarchy had the *cajones* to take him on. He was too important to both the academic stature and the finances of the place. They just wouldn't do it. He would have that two bit sorry excuse for a dean, Harmon Corbitt, for lunch if the wimp even thought about it. And Corbitt knew that! Cy had made it clear to the dean where the power was on more than one occasion.

So Cy didn't fear the academic consequences of the evening's discoveries. However, he did fear the potential financial consequences. The remote possibility that Katya would lodge a complaint of scientific misconduct, even though it would be foolish and a battle that she would lose, the very fact that there was such an investigation in progress could delay the GPI deal and might also sensitize them to their job of due diligence. Timing was critical here. He had to sew up this GPI deal promptly. He thought that should be possible, but there were several potential hitches.

The hitch he feared most was the consequence of Global Pharmaceutical's scientists reviewing the results of the clinical studies. They would obviously have to be given access to the files that Beth had kept under lock and key. There was no reason to suspect that there was anything fishy about any of the data except the six-month studies from subject number one. But, how clever had Beth been with her little ruse? Wouldn't a perceptive expert find something to suspect—a cleverly photo-shopped electrophoretic gel (that's how Cy's biomarker protein was measured) was hard to detect but not impossible. There might be other clues if one was looking for them. Cy would need to spend some time with those files before turning them over. But even he wasn't as skilled with the analytical procedures as the GPI folks would be. This could be a problem.

He picked up the bottle labeled *Cy's Wonder Drug* and the folder. He returned the folder to Beth's desk drawer where he had found it and replaced the bottle of pills on the shelf in Beth's medicine cabinet. He then decided to go to bed. He realized that he had eaten no dinner, but he didn't feel hungry.

The house missed Beth, Cy thought as he made his way to his bedroom. He undressed and lay down hoping for a good night's sleep. Tomorrow was going to be an interesting day.

30

The next day turned out to be more interesting for Cyrus Bartalak than he could have imagined. When he arrived at his office there was a message informing him that the dean wished to see him as soon as possible. The message sounded as close to a summons as he could remember receiving from the dean and Cy was not happy about that. He considered ignoring the message but thought better of it.

He went to the dean's office but he did not arrive there in a good mood. He strode past the secretary, ignoring her attempt to detain him, and entered Corbitt's office without knocking. Surprised by the unannounced intrusion, Corbitt looked up from the material that he had been studying on his desk.

"Come in, Cy," Corbitt said, making no attempt to hide his annoyance. "Do sit down." He motioned to a straight chair in front of his desk instead of to the sofa and coffee table arrangement in the corner where he normally met with visitors.

"What do you want with me, Harmon?" Cy said. "And why the urgency?"

"Yes, well, professor," Corbitt replied, "we have a problem that I thought it best to make you aware of before proceeding to the next step."

"Problem?" Cy queried. "What problem?"

The dean removed two documents from the folder that was open on his desk and slid them across the desk toward Bartalak.

"Katya Karpov has lodged a complaint of scientific misconduct against Beth," Corbitt said.

"Surely not," Cy responded. "Katya's had some difficulties with Beth, but charging her with scientific misconduct? I can't believe Katya would do that."

"That was my response as well. That is until I had the chance to review these documents that she provided with her letter to me."

Bartalak looked at the documents and immediately recognized the table of data that Katya had given him earlier and the Bagley autopsy report that had appeared mysteriously under his office door. He spent several minutes looking the documents over in an effort to appear that he hadn't seen them before.

"Do these documents look familiar to you, Cy?" Corbitt asked, looking directly into Bartalak's eyes.

"I've never seen them before," Bartalak replied.

"Dr. Karpov tells me that she gave at least one of the documents to you earlier and told you that she thought it was evidence that Beth had altered some of the data from your drug study. Is that not true?"

Bartalak laid the sheets of paper back on the desk. He got up and began to pace back and forth in front of the dean. He sighed and ran his hand through his hair. Corbitt was struck with how ugly Cy Bartalak was; he was a really ugly man. Odd, Corbitt thought, that he hadn't been so aware of that before.

After a long pause, Cy walked back and stood directly in front of the dean. He stood there for a few moments, neither of the men speaking.

Finally Cy said, "Harmon, Katya did give me a file that may have contained this material and she did express concern about Beth's handling of the drug study data. But, Katya has had a problem with Beth ever since we arrived here. I really didn't think there was anything substantive to her complaint. And, in retrospect unadvisedly, I gave the file to Beth and asked her to review it and let me know if there was anything of concern. She did that and told me there was nothing to be concerned about. I basically forgot about it."

"What?" Corbitt interrupted. "It was Beth's behavior that Katya was questioning. You were relying on Beth's judgment about the validity of the complaint against her? Come on, now, Cy, that makes no sense at all."

"Harmon, I trust Beth. She's honest. I agree that in retrospect it wasn't the best decision, but, as I said, Katya has it in for Beth, has for a long time. I really thought that this would go away."

"Not good," Corbitt said. "Not good at all."

Bartalak paused, rubbing his temples with both hands and then said, "You're probably unaware of this, but I admitted Beth to the hospital yesterday. Oscar Orbitz is taking care of her. She's developed some kind of neurological disorder that no one seems able to diagnose. But Oscar thinks it may be serious. I'm pretty distracted by that right now. You can appreciate that I'm sure."

"My God, Cy," Corbitt responded, "did this come on suddenly? Why didn't you tell me?"

"I've noticed some changes in Beth's behavior for a little while but I didn't think it anything to worry about until recently. I'm really very concerned about her. I can only hope that, whatever it is, it's reversible."

"I'm so sorry, Cy," Corbitt said. "Is there anything I can do?"

"Thanks, Harmon," Bartalak replied. "Well, maybe you can delay proceeding with this scientific misconduct thing until Beth's condition is clearer. Neither she nor I need to deal with that right now."

Corbitt paused a moment, thinking, and said, "Cy, I'm going to have to go forward with this. Of course it will take a few days to put a committee together. I may be able to stall a bit, but there will have to be a thorough investigation of the charge, review of the evidence, etcetera. You understand."

"I understand the technicality. You do understand that this is a technicality. I don't know what Katya Karpov is up to, but if you go ahead with the committee, complete investigation, that sort of thing, she's going to be the one who's hurt. And maybe you as well. It won't do the university any good either, once the media get wind of it, which of course they will. I don't envy you, Harmon."

"Cy, I'll do what I have to do," Corbitt said, rising from his chair. "Please give my best to Beth and keep me informed of her progress. I am really sorry about her illness."

Corbitt was obviously ending the meeting. Cy locked eyes with the dean for a second and then turned, walked to the door and left the office without saying anything more.

Back in his office, Bartalak felt that things were becoming clearer. He clicked on the contacts icon on his computer, scrolled down to Mitchell Rook's number, lifted the receiver on the desk phone and punched in the number. He would arrange a meeting with Rook, following up on the odd conversation they had had the previous day. The chances that the GPI deal might crash and burn seemed to be increasing. Cy needed to be proactive if he was to realize any of the reward he had been expecting from *Renaptix*. He had been counting on that money. He needed it.

When the call came through, the US attorney, Dom Petrillo, was sitting in Rook's office. Professor Bartalak had been the topic of their conversation for the past hour or so. They had been reviewing their strategy for giving Bartalak the opportunity to show his true colors in a way that provided admissible evidence that he had committed a crime. This was not as easy as both of the men thought it should be. They had agreed earlier that Rook should let Bartalak know that he was looking for additional investments in the medical area. Rook had done that. If, as they suspected, Bartalak had what he thought was private knowledge of something that when it became generally known would deflate the value of *Renaptix*, he might be tempted to offer part or all of his share of the startup company to Rook at a price that did not take that private knowledge into account. If Bartalak did that, and they could prove it, they had a prosecutable crime.

That is assuming Dr. Karpov would testify that Bartalak had received the incriminating information. Their direct informant, Rook's pathologist friend, would be useless in court since his testimony would be hearsay and therefore disallowed. Rook needed to make sure that Katya Karpov would do it. He would have to contact her again when he could be more forthcoming about what they needed from her and why. If she was as honest as Syd Shelling seemed to imply, she shouldn't be a problem, but that needed to be confirmed.

Since *Renaptix* was not a publicly traded company, the common, *fraud on the market* charge couldn't be made. But, it was still a crime to knowingly withhold information that would affect a stock's value in order to sell the stock at a higher price than the seller knew it was worth. The tricky part was that Rook had to dangle the bait in front of Bartalak, make it irresistible, without it being so obvious that Bartalak would smell a rat.

Rook was less worried than Petrillo about scaring Bartalak off. Hubris was often the Achilles heel of people who were less smart than they believed themselves to be; Bartalak certainly fit that description.

The two lawyers had enjoyed the long discussion of the nuances of law. That's what had attracted them to the profession in the first place.

Mitchell Rook was surprised when his secretary rang him and said that Dr. Bartalak was on the line. Mitchell took the call and after some idle banter, Bartalak asked him if they could meet later in the day, just the two of them, to talk. Of course, Rook readily agreed and suggested that Bartalak come to Rook's office downtown at around three. After a brief hesitation, Cy agreed and they ended the conversation.

Hardy Seltzer felt that he was having more difficulty than he should be having accomplishing the simple task of going through the marriage license records. Had he believed in Providence, he would have been tempted to invoke Providential Hindrance as an explanation.

He had gone to the license office the previous day – driven out Third Avenue, located a parking place with some difficulty and then wandered around the Old Howard School complex for a while until he found an office with a sign painted on the door that read "Marriage License Bureau." Good, he found the place. However, there had been another sign that was hand written on a blank sheet of letter size paper that read simply, "Closed for the day." Just that. No explanation. It was not a holiday. How can they just close for the day for no apparent reason, without any justification? Hardy thought.

He was angry as he often was when confronted with irresponsible behavior of metro employees. Assuming he ever found the Marriage License Bureau office open, he would have a word with the person in charge. Hardy was a city employee and took his work seriously. If his fellow employees didn't do the same, they should be replaced. It was that simple. Justice!

Dammit! Justice!

Hardy had intended to go back to the Marriage License Bureau first thing that morning, but he was summoned again to the chief's office. Hardy had stopped reading the morning newspaper since the series of articles berating the police department, often singling out detective Seltzer as a prime example of the department's incompetence, started appearing under the byline of a freelance journalist he had never heard of. Hardy feared that the morning paper featured yet another headline on the topic and that that was why he had been summoned by the chief.

The chief's office door was open and, after rapping lightly on the door facing and being invited in, Hardy entered. The chief sat with his feet propped up on his desk staring out the window. Seltzer thought that the chief had aged visibly in the past couple of weeks. The furrows in his broad brow had deepened into ravines and his eyes were puffy and sad.

The chief slid the morning paper across the desk toward Seltzer and said, "Have you seen this?"

The headline below the fold on page one read:

Bagley Murder Case: Dakota Charges Dropped, Police Clueless

Seltzer had no desire to read the article, but stared at the headline for a few minutes without speaking.

"So, detective," the chief finally spoke, "clueless, are we?"

"So X got Jody off without a trial? How'd he do that?" Seltzer said.

"The case fell apart," the chief answered. "Or more accurately, X dismantled it. Found a witness who'd put Dakota elsewhere at the time of the murder. Got the gun ruled out as evidence claiming you took it under duress and illegally, not that the gun was much help anyway. And Rory Holcomb, the Printers Alley real estate guy who told you of Dakota's old grudge against Bonz, refused to testify to anything. So no opportunity, no motive, no weapon. Ergo no case! And, of course as you'll see if you read the article, the DA is more than happy to put the blame on us."

Hardy had thought a case against Jody Dakota had been building, but it had not matured. If the chief and the DA hadn't been in such a hurry, this probably wouldn't have happened.

"So, answer my question, detective," the chief continued. "Are we clueless?"

Seltzer had kept the chief pretty much up to date on the progress he and Shane were making on the investigation of Shane's mystery woman theory. What Seltzer had not done was convey to his boss the fact that Seltzer had gradually become convinced that Shane Hadley was in fact correct, that Elizabeth Anne Reid was Bonz Bagley's murderer. But, Seltzer was still troubled by their failure to come up with a motive and by the nature of the murder, the four shots to the head. And, of course, they hadn't found her yet. They were relying heavily on the marriage license log to give them a name.

The chief continued when Hardy still didn't respond, "What about Hadley's mystery woman? Have you found her yet?"

"I think we're very close, chief," Seltzer responded. "And Shane has me convinced that he's right about this. It's a convoluted story, but it's starting to make sense. More than that, it's starting to look like the only possibility."

The chief put his feet on the floor and leaned across his desk toward Seltzer.

"Like I told you earlier, Seltzer, a possibility isn't going to save your ass. Or mine! So how close are you? When can you give me something concrete? I want Bonz Bagley's murderer delivered accompanied by an air tight case!"

"I think, chief," Seltzer replied, "that there is a good chance we'll identify the killer today, that is, have a name. If so, we should be able to wind the whole thing up in a day or two."

"Two days, then, detective," the chief said. "I'll give you two days and if you don't have this thing solved once and for all by then you're suspended without pay until further notice. I hate ultimatums, Hardy, but I really have no alternative."

"I understand," Seltzer replied.

He did understand, but he thought he was being made the fall guy in a situation for which maybe he shared some of the blame, but he didn't deserve it all. There was plenty of blame to go around.

Hardy went back to his office and decided to call the Marriage License Bureau before making another trip out there. The phone was answered by a female voice that Hardy thought sounded like it belonged to an older woman who assured him that the office would be open until three PM today. When he asked her what the usual hours of operation were each day, she replied that the office had no usual hours of operation. Due to reductions in staff resulting from budget cuts, she was the only employee there and she was part time. She opened the office when her other responsibilities permitted which was for a few hours most weekdays. She did not specify what her other responsibilities were.

With considerable effort, Hardy restrained himself from responding, hung up the phone and left his office for the parking garage.

By the time Hardy had located the Crown Vic, driven out to Old Howard School, located a parking place and walked to the Marriage License Bureau, his righteous indignation had subsided and he was concentrating on the task at hand.

The elderly lady who greeted him from behind a small desk wore a name tag which read *Myrtle Cathcart* and under that *How may I help you?* Ms. Cathcart, apparently feeling that the information expressed on the tag that she wore was a sufficient greeting, did not speak when confronted by detective Seltzer, but rather looked up from something she was reading on the desk and made a noise that sounded like something between a grunt and a sigh. She looked her visitor over briefly and looked back down at whatever was on her desk.

Just do what you came here to do, Seltzer thought to himself.

"Ms. Cathcart," Seltzer said, "if I'm not interrupting, I would "

"Actually, you are interrupting," Myrtle replied, "as you can plainly see, Mister ... to whom am I speaking?"

Seltzer brandished his badge and replied in his most authoritative voice, "Detective Hardy Seltzer, Metro police."

Myrtle glanced at the badge, clearly unimpressed and said, "What do you want detective?"

Seltzer asked if he could look through the marriage license ledger, the book signed by the applicants, for a specific year, naming for her the year in which the record of Elizabeth Anne Reid's existence in Houston ended.

Myrtle Cathcart, with a grand show of how much this request inconvenienced her and sighing deeply, rose from her chair, located a step stool and removed a thick black ledger from a high shelf behind her desk. She dropped the book on her desk and told Hardy that he could sit at a carrel across the room to look at it. He did not thank her but took the book and sat down at the carrel.

Hardy lay the book down and removed the sheet of paper with the copy of Elizabeth Reid's handwritten signature from the shooting range log on it from his inside jacket pocket. He smoothed the sheet out on the desk, opened the book and started going through the pages of names carefully, line by line.

Since the names had been entered in chronological order, and he had only the year with no specific date, there was no shortcut to the name he was looking for. It was not a difficult task, but it required prolonged concentration and tenacity. Hardy was pretty good at those things; they were skills that he had learned early in life and they had often come in handy in the practice of his chosen profession.

The entire process took more than two hours, including a cigarette break that Seltzer could not resist taking as a brief respite from the boring and tedious task. It was the first smoke he'd had in two days and it tasted uncommonly good. About three quarters of the way through the thick book, the name Elizabeth Anne Reid appeared two thirds of the way down the right hand page.

Hardy spread the copy of the signature from the shooting club out beside the signature in the book. He was not a handwriting expert, but the small carefully formed backwardly slanted letters in the two signatures looked identical to him. He took out his cell phone and snapped several close-up photographs of the page, making certain to get both the Reid signature and the signature of the groom-to-be in the pictures. He took a pen from his jacket pocket and copied the name of the groom, paying careful attention to the spelling, on the sheet of paper bearing the copy of Elizabeth Reid's signature. Hardy didn't recognize the man's name.

31

Dom Petrillo and Mitchell Rook would have preferred to wait a couple of days for the meeting with Cy Bartalak. There were still some i's to dot and t's to cross. But Bartalak had forced their hand and they needed to be fully prepared for whatever the meeting revealed. If he took the bait and proposed to sell some or all of his stake in *Renaptix* to Rook, they needed that documented. The fact that Bartalak had agreed to meet in Mark's office was a plus.

So, after Bartalak and Rook talked, Petrillo put in a call to his people and arranged for a listening device to be installed in Rook's office. It was a rush job, since there were only a couple of hours before the meeting and Petrillo met some resistance at first. However, shortly after he spoke about the matter with his superior, the technicians arrived on the fifteenth floor of the Batman Building and went about their work.

The device was installed so that the overheard conversation would be recorded. In addition, Petrillo was set up in an adjacent office where he could listen to the conversation in real time. By two thirty, the device was installed, all the arrangements made and the technicians, except for the one who was stationed with Petrillo in the adjacent office in case there was a need for technical help, were gone.

Caroline, the Rook and Lipchitz receptionist on the fourteenth floor, had been alerted to expect Dr. Bartalak. She greeted him when he arrived and directed him to the elevators to the fifteenth floor. Caroline rang Rook's secretary and told her that Dr. Bartalak was on his way. The secretary met Bartalak at the elevator and escorted him down the hall to Rook's corner suite. She knocked lightly on Rook's office door and the lawyer opened it, greeted his expected guest, and ushered him into the office.

Bartalak stopped suddenly on entering the space and stood, not speaking for a few moments. This was not the right place for this meeting, he thought. He should have insisted that it be on neutral ground somewhere, or even better, on his turf.

Bartalak hated the décor of the office. A bunch of kitsch attempting to masquerade as serious art. Exactly what was that bunch of colored tubes mounted on the wall supposed to mean? And the steel and wood furniture? Where were the rich dark tones of polished cherry and the earthy smell of expensive leather that one had the right to expect in a successful lawyer's office? Bartalak had been a little leery of Rook from the start and this office only reinforced that feeling.

Rook allowed Bartalak to stand and survey the office for a few minutes and then said, "Please have a seat, Cy, and thank you for coming downtown."

Rook gestured toward one of the bright aluminum chairs that sat in front of the steel and wood desk. Bartalak didn't like the looks of the chair, but he took a seat anyway, shifting around in an effort to make himself as comfortable as the hard chair permitted.

"Yes," Bartalak replied, "of course. It's true that I rarely get down here. No real reason to ordinarily. Most of my work is at the university and points south."

"I realize that," Rook said, "but I appreciate you making this exception. May I offer you an espresso?"

"Espresso would be very nice," Bartalak replied.

Cy was starting to relax some, recovering from the shock of the truly unexpected appearance of the space where Rook worked. He looked around as his host got up and went to a sideboard where sat a very interesting, and no doubt very expensive, espresso machine. Bartalak noticed the telescope over by the window and wondered what it was doing there. But then, he didn't understand anything about this office.

Rook returned with two China cups of steaming espresso resting on matching saucers and sitting on a small tray that also held a container of sugar and one of milk. Rook sat the tray on his desk and sat one of the cups directly in front of his guest. Bartalak picked up the small tongs and deposited two brown cubes of raw sugar into this cup, stirring it with the silver spoon that lay on the saucer.

"How civilized," Bartalak said. "We pay too little attention to life's niceties in our usual rush, I'm afraid."

Bartalak was warming up his act, Rook thought.

"True, Cy, true," Rook replied, sipping at his coffee.

Rook was content to bide his time. He would let Bartalak carry the conversation in whatever direction he wished.

After a few minutes, Bartalak sat his cup and saucer back onto the tray and said, "So what do you think about this *Renaptix* thing, Mitchell? Pretty exciting, huh?"

"It is exciting, Cy," Rook responded, "quite exciting. I admit to being more than a little surprised by the scope of what appears to be happening."

"Scope is right. As I told the group, this GPI deal is on the move. *Renaptix* is about to be worth orders of magnitude more than we've invested in it. And down the line, who knows?"

"Not often one gets a chance to reap that kind of return on an investment," Rook said.

"Uh, Mitchell," Bartalak started.

He stood up and walked over toward the window. Mitchell wasn't sure if the listening device would pick up Bartalak's voice from there and so he stayed seated behind his desk hoping that Bartalak would return to his seat.

"Mitchell," Bartalak continued, turning toward Rook, "You inquired about other investments in the medical field. There may be a possibility. How much are you talking about?"

"Substantial," Rook replied.

To his relief, Bartalak returned back to the seat that he had vacated and looked directly at Rook.

"This is a bit of a delicate matter, Mitchell. I trust this conversation is in strictest confidence."

"Of course."

"Suppose you had the chance to buy additional stock in *Renaptix* … now."

"How would that be possible?"

"This is the sensitive part, Mitchell, but I'll be honest with you. You may have noticed that my lifestyle is considerably more, shall we say lavish, than one might expect on a university professor's salary."

"That's certainly true. But I thought you'd made a considerable amount of money from the deal you did in Houston before you came here. And, you're on a couple of advisory boards that must pay something."

Rook had done some homework.

"Bah," Bartalak spat, "a pittance. Companies take advantage of academics all the time by paying us a fraction of what we're worth to sit on their boards. I wouldn't do it except for the fact that it extends my network. You're correct about the other deal, though. I made a tidy sum from the Houston deal, but that was a onetime thing and has, quite honestly, dwindled faster than I had planned for. The truth is, I've been counting on the money from *Renaptix*'s success. And as it turns out, I have a pressing need to cash in on that sooner rather than later."

"But you'd obviously cash in at a higher price if

351

you waited a bit, until the GPI deal is written in stone and maybe after a milestone or two is made."

Bartalak stood up again, but this time just stood in front of Rook's desk.

He leaned toward Rook, placing his palms on the desk and said, "I can't wait, Mitchell. I know I'll have to sell at less than I could demand later, but I can't wait. I need the money. And there is another potential complication looming as well. I met with our dean this morning and I got the distinct impression that he and a number of the faculty are extremely uncomfortable with me holding an interest in *Renaptix*, especially since it will involve so much money. Academics are like that, you know, can't stand to see a colleague succeed, especially if there's money involved.

"At any rate, I strongly suspect that I'm going to be required to divest myself of any financial interest in the company. And, they'll want me to do that before the full value of *Renaptix* is realized. If I do it proactively, I'll be viewed more favorably in the eyes of my academic colleagues. I do need to pay attention to my academic reputation, you know."

"Yes," Rook said, 'yes, I'm sure that you do."

"So here is my proposal," Bartalak said, grimacing slightly as he sat back down in the metal chair. "I will sell you my entire fifty percent share of *Renaptix* immediately, before the GPI deal is finalized."

"Wait, Cy," Rook said, "until that deal is finalized, *Renaptix* isn't worth any more than we have in it. Are you going to sell at the company's earlier valuation?"

"Come now, Mitchell," Cy responded, smiling broadly, "you surely don't think me that simple. The GPI deal is essentially done. The fact that there are technicalities to take care of to make that official may make the current value of the company slightly less than it will be when that deal is actually signed, but only slightly. The Global deal is a sure thing, Mitchell."

"So what sort of valuation are we talking about?"

"Fifty million. My half share for twenty-five."

"You aren't discounting the value much pending the actual signing of the GPI deal."

"I'm telling you, Mitchell, that deal is done. And, when it's signed, the value will take another jump, at least another ten million. You'll make money immediately and downstream you could well make a killing!"

"You know of absolutely no reason why the GPI deal might not be done and no reason to doubt at this point that the drug will prove to be effective?"

Bartalak stood again, leaned across the desk and looked directly into Rook's eyes.

"Absolutely none," Bartalak said.

"OK," Rook replied. "OK. I'll do it for twenty mil."

"You drive a hard bargain, Mitchell," Bartalak responded. "But I'm at something of a disadvantage here. I'll have my legal people draw up the papers."

Hubris, Rook thought.

32

As Hardy Seltzer walked down Second Avenue from the Metro Police Department headquarters, turned right up the Church Street hill and then turned right into Printers Alley, he checked his pocket to make sure that he had his cell phone and the sheet of paper both of which contained the information that Shane had asked him to get. It was almost three thirty, half an hour past the time he had agreed to be there. He expected to find Shane on the balcony that overlooked the alley half way between Church and Union Streets, crystal glass of sherry in hand who would call out to him the now familiar greeting, *Hi-ho Hardy my man*.

But, the balcony was vacant. Hardy went to the door and pressed the button labeled Hadley/Karpov. The door buzzed. Hardy opened the door and entered the small foyer. As though anticipating his arrival, the doors to the elevator opened. He entered the car which promptly rose to the second floor and stopped. On entering the now familiar living room Hardy was surprised to encounter not only Shane, but a truly gorgeous woman with flowing blond hair and deep green eyes whose smile as he entered seemed to illuminate the room.

"Ah, Hardy, my man," Shane said, wheeling over to shake his hand, "and only a bit late. I want you to meet KiKi ... er ... Katya, or perhaps more to the present point, Dr. Katya Karpov. She has many identities, I fear. You've heard me speak of her, but I think you haven't met her before. I have the extreme privilege then of introducing you to my lovely wife who alas wears other hats as well. I asked her to arrive home a bit early today since the substance of our meeting will be of interest to her and she may have some knowledge that will help us complete the story."

Katya walked over to Hardy and offered her hand which he took. He was more than a little discombobulated by the presence of this extraordinary woman. By her remarkable persona and also by the fact that Shane had wanted her present at their meeting. He didn't see the connection.

"I'm very pleased to meet you, detective," Katya said. "I understand that you and Shane have solved the Bonz Bagley murder. Congratulations."

Seltzer was not aware that they had solved the case and so was surprised at her statement. What had Shane told her?

"I'm not so sure," Hardy responded. "Did Shane tell you that?"

"Yes," Katya answered, "but he hasn't explained anything more. I sense that you are wondering why I'm here. I'm wondering that too. Shane does on occasion tend toward the dramatic."

"Ah, Hardy, my man, you are much too modest," Shane said. "But of course we've found the murderer. In fact you have on your person, if I am not mistaken, the name of the culprit, a name, I might add that will be more familiar to KiKi than it is to you. But let me pour you a sherry and let's relish this moment."

Without waiting for a response, Shane rolled over to the bar, refreshed his glass, took one of the Oxford glasses from its case and poured in a generous portion of the wine.

Shane raised the bottle questioningly toward his wife and said, "And you, KiKi, will you join us?"

"Sure," Katya replied.

Shane retrieved another glass and filled it. Leaving his own glass on the bar, he delivered the others to Hardy and KiKi and the returned to claim his own.

"Let's sit here in the living room," Shane said.

Katya and Hardy sat on the sofa that faced the fireplace. Shane parked himself in front of them.

After they had sampled the wine, Shane said, "Let me explain the situation for you, Hardy. I'm sure you didn't expect KiKi to be here."

"I was surprised, but delighted to meet her at last," Hardy replied.

"Actually, I asked her to be here for our meeting because she will be especially interested in what takes place here and she has some additional information that will interest you as well. KiKi just arrived, so I haven't been able to ask her some questions that may be important. If it is alright with you, KiKi," Shane turned his attention to his wife, "may I raise those questions with you now?"

"Shane," Katya said, "you told me that you had identified the killer. What questions could there be?"

"Indulge me, my dear," Shane said. "I think it is important to complete the story."

"Well, alright, what questions do you have?"

"They are questions about your nemesis, Beth."

"Who is Beth?" Hardy interrupted.

"Ah, yes," Shane responded, "I have neglected to inform you about another investigation that KiKi has been pursuing in parallel with our pursuit of Bonz's murderer. I assure you that was not deliberate; it's just that I saw no connection between the two efforts until today. Beth is, shall we say, a colleague of KiKi's. They are both involved in a clinical study of a drug and KiKi has evidence indicating that Beth falsified data from the study in order to make the results appear more positive than they were. And," Shane gestured emphatically toward the alley with his free hand, "the unfortunate Mr. Bagley was a subject in the drug study. There is more but let me clarify a few things with KiKi."

"OK," Hardy answered, "but I still fail to see the

connection."

"Patience, my man, patience," Shane responded and turned to his wife. "KiKi, was Beth married to the professor when they arrived in Nashville?"

"Yes," Katya responded, "at least I think so. They've lived together since arriving, she has used his surname and they have certainly behaved as though they were married. I understand that there was a divorce back in Houston, but all that seemed to be over when they arrived here as far as I know."

"Have you ever noticed anything odd about Beth Bartalak's gait, how she runs?"

"Well, I haven't seen her run, although I know she is a runner. I do notice gaits though, part of my neurological training. Let me see."

Shane said, "Recall an elaborate party at the Bartalak manse a while back. Beth was playing tennis."

"Yes, yes," Katya said, "I do remember that and yes, she slightly favored her right leg as she ran about the court although she was very nimble in spite of that."

"The two of you may be amused to discover that I have thought of this case, given my wont to associate real cases with detective Holmes's imaginary ones, as the *Case of the Devil's Foot* because of the odd gait of the murderer as I saw her fleeing the alley. Of course Mr. Holmes's case had nothing to do with an actual human foot, but sometimes I find it necessary to take some, shall we say *investigatorial license*. Even when they are strained, I find these associations amusing and sometimes useful."

"Shane," Hardy interrupted, his impatience clearly showing, "I still don't get it. Of course I know how much stock you put in an oddity of the fleeing killer's gait, and I appreciate how that has led us to where we are, but how does that implicate this colleague of Dr. Karpov's at the university? A lot of people must run funny if you look closely enough. And motive, what about a motive?"

Katya was speechless. Was Shane saying that Beth Bartalak was Bonz's murderer? Surely not! Beth was a thoroughly disagreeable and likely dishonest person, but a murderer? Not likely.

"Ah yes, motive has perplexed us all along hasn't it?" Shane said. "Consider the facts. Bonz was killed a day before KiKi would have discovered Beth's deception with the study data; he was scheduled to come in for a physical exam and some tests on that Monday. And the four shots to the head. Those, too, have troubled us all along. Perhaps a vendetta we thought. But, perhaps not. Suppose Beth had falsified some of Bonz's data from the drug study and knew that she was about to be found out. Killing Bonz would solve that problem. But it is common knowledge that there is always an autopsy on anyone who is murdered. She knew that his tests of brain function had deteriorated while on the drug and must have feared that there would be postmortem evidence of drug injury to his brain. So, she did everything she could to destroy his brain and almost succeeded.

"And there's more," Shane looked at KiKi now, registering the shocked expression on her face. "Unless I am seriously mistaken, Hardy, my man, you have in your possession evidence that Elizabeth Anne Reid originally of Greensward, Texas, was married to Cyrus Bartalak in this city shortly after they arrived here. Elizabeth Reid inherited a rare gun collection from her lawyer father and she test fired a very rare gun identical to the one that was the Bagley murder weapon at the Williamson County Shooters Club shortly before the murder. Hardy, can you show us what you have?"

"Shane, Shane," Katya interrupted, "this isn't

possible. Beth is desperately flawed, but I can't believe that she's a murderer."

"I am only going where the facts in the case lead me, KiKi," Shane replied. "On their surface, murderers commonly appear ill-suited to the role."

Hardy was amazed at how Shane had assembled the case working from what would surely have been considered a trivial observation by anyone else if noticed at all and chasing after that other gun when there was no reason to. And keeping at it with remarkable tenacity until what appeared to be widely disparate and unrelated pieces of information fell together into a coherent story. How did he know which facts were important and which weren't before there was a story to fit them into?

Hardy removed the piece of paper from his jacket and handed it to Shane.

"Detective Seltzer has reviewed the records of the local marriage license bureau and retrieved the names of couples who were married in the relevant year," Shane continued. "He has discovered there the signature of one Elizabeth Anne Reid and of the person to whom she was to be wed," he looked carefully at the paper, "one Cyrus Demetrio Bartalak. Elizabeth Anne Reid is the murderer and Elizabeth Anne Reid is Beth Bartalak."

"Who's Cyrus Bartalak?" Hardy asked.

"Professor Bartalak," Shane answered, "is chairman of the department of psychiatry at the university. He is KiKi's immediate superior and the inventor and developer of the drug the study of which appears to have cost Mr. Bagley his life. And he is married to Beth Bartalak, nee Elizabeth Anne Reid."

Katya was stunned. She could see no flaw in the story Shane had assembled. The facts that he had dug up with Seltzer's help when coupled with the information Katya had uncovered made the conclusion that Beth was the likely killer impossible to deny.

"You should know," Katya said, "that Beth is in the hospital. She was admitted yesterday. According to the fellow on the clinical service, she had symptoms of some kind of central nervous system disorder. I looked up her lab tests on the computer, and she's had an abnormal EEG and brain MRI. Apparently the consulting neurologist is unsure of the cause but fears that the condition is severe."

"That's interesting," Shane responded, "is this something new?"

"Well," Katya said, "she had been behaving oddly, maybe over the last couple of months. She's been coming to work only sporadically which was a distinct change from the workaholic she was known to be. But as far as I know she hadn't sought medical attention until now."

"And," Shane said, "your professional opinion about her condition?"

"I don't have one. From the tests I was able to see, it doesn't look like a brain tumor which might have been my first guess. Her tox screen is negative which doesn't totally rule out some kind of drug abuse, but moves that down the list. If I were taking care of her, I'd suggest a brain biopsy."

"So, Shane," Hardy said, trying to understand the situation, "do we arrest the wife of a university professor while she's in the hospital with a severe neurological condition? I hate to think what would be in the morning paper."

"It seems to me that we arrest the killer," Shane responded. "We cannot help her current condition or location. Besides, I should have thought, Hardy my man, that you'd have given up reading the morning paper some time ago. There's been little good news there for you lately."

"Shane," Katya said, "are you sure of this? I mean, this is going to be a major scandal at the university. Are you sure?"

"I know, KiKi," Shane said. "I understand the implications, and I am absolutely sure. However, the unequivocal proof will be the ballistics. If Beth Bartalak possesses a gun of the rare type that killed Bonz Bagley and we can retrieve it, ballistics testing should prove that it was the murder weapon. If so, it seems to me that the case is air tight."

"We need a search warrant," Hardy interjected, "and the sooner the better. I'd better see the chief first and be sure that he approves. This is going to be a major kerfuffle given the people involved. But we need to get a search warrant for the Bartalak house and get a team there. We don't need to give these people time to do anything that would complicate things."

Before Shane could respond, they were interrupted by the chime of the doorbell.

33

Mitchell Rook and Dom Petrillo had conferred after Bartalak's departure from the Batman Building. They agreed that they had concrete evidence of Bartalak's offer to sell his share of *Renaptix* at an inflated price. They also had concrete evidence that he claimed to have no knowledge of anything that would be likely to affect the value of the company or would raise any doubt about the efficacy of the drug. However, the only evidence they had that Bartalak was lying was hearsay, the pathologist Shelling's recounting of his conversation with Dr. Karpov. Karpov would have to testify that she had personally given Bartalak the information. Before charging the professor, they needed to make damn sure that Dr. Karpov had the information that would seal Bartalak's fate and that she would be a cooperative witness. Rook agreed to take on that task.

When Rook called Dr. Karpov's laboratory, the plaintive voice that answered had the sound of a lonely graduate student who had been assigned a duty that was interfering with other more attractive plans. The voice informed him that Dr. Karpov had left work early saying that she was going home. With that information, Rook decided that he would walk up to the Printers Alley residence of the good doctor, thinking that a surprise visit might actually serve his purpose better that a forewarned one. He walked to the entrance and pressed the button under Hadley/Karpov.

"Yes, who is it?" Katya's voice came through the small speaker by the door, distorted, but clear enough.

"It's Mitchell Rook," he replied. "I apologize for appearing unannounced, but I need to speak with you about a matter of some urgency."

"Very well," Katya replied, shrugging her

shoulders in Shane's direction.

She pressed the button to release the door and walked over to the elevator so that she would know when their visitor entered the car and could call it to the second floor.

Hardy Seltzer was, once again, completely confused.

"Who is Mitchell Rook?" he asked, having overheard the brief conversation over the intercom.

"Mr. Rook," Shane answered, "is a business lawyer who is apparently involved with the startup company that Professor Bartalak formed to develop his drug. He contacted Katya earlier, but it wasn't clear exactly what he was looking for. I suspect that we're about to be enlightened."

Rook exited the elevator into the living room. He didn't recognize the third person in the room, but was quite sure that he was with law enforcement. The persona of the breed was unmistakable even if the person pretended otherwise and this was an officer of the law who was without pretense.

"Mr. Rook … er … Mitchell," Katya greeted the visitor, recalling his insistence on first names, a level of intimacy that she still felt unwarranted; she gestured toward person number three and continued, "you may not know Detective Hardy Seltzer. He's with the Metro Police Department."

Rook walked over to shake the detective's hand and said, measuring his words, "Oh yes, Detective Seltzer, I believe I've seen your name in the papers recently."

"I'm afraid so, Mr. Rook "

"Please," Rook interrupted, "Mitchell."

"OK, Mitchell," Hardy said. "Not publicity that I've asked for, obviously."

"Yes, unfortunate," Rook said. "Unfortunate."

Rook was trying to imagine why the detective

was there and why the three of them seemed so seriously cautious with him. It seemed as though he had interrupted something important. Maybe Seltzer and Shane Hadley had been compatriots when Shane was on the force. But if this was a social call it seemed a particularly chilly one.

"Are the two of you old friends from the days of Sherlock Shane?" Rook asked, recalling the moniker that the press had invented some years back.

"Actually," Hardy replied, "we never worked together when Shane was on the force."

Katya interjected, anxious to find out the reason for the unexpected visit, "So, Mitchell, what can we do for you?"

"I had hoped to speak with you privately, Katya," Rook said.

"Whatever you have to say is perfectly fine for Shane and Hardy to hear," Katya said.

"If you say so," Rook replied, obviously not entirely comfortable with the arrangement. "But some of what I have to say is strictly confidential for now and very sensitive information."

"We can handle it," Shane said, a bit impatiently.

Rook was still not sure how much to reveal. He paused for a few moments, obviously thinking. The four of them were still standing in front of the elevator. Finally, Rook decided to play it straight. That would have to happen sooner or later if Katya was to be a witness.

"Katya, I was not completely forthcoming on my previous visit here, I'm afraid," Rook began. "There was good reason for that as you will see. But the information you implied, if not actually stated, on that visit was very helpful."

"I didn't realize that I had given you much information," Katya said.

"You didn't, that is not explicitly. But there was a

great deal of information in what you did not say. However, let me come clean at this point. I have been cooperating with the US attorney's office in an investigation of Cyrus Bartalak, your chairman. The investigation was instigated at the highest level of the Department of Justice and was based on the suspicion that Dr. Bartalak was guilty of a crime in an earlier transaction in Texas which had so far been difficult to prove. That suspicion was sufficient to lead the US attorneys to surmise that fraudulent business transactions were a pattern of behavior for Dr. Bartalak. When they got wind of this new venture, *Renaptix, Inc.*, set up to develop the new drug, the similarity to the Texas situation was so striking that they enlisted me to pose as an investor in the company while actually acting as an informant. I agreed to participate as the front man in a sting operation that was intended to provide evidence of Dr. Bartalak's criminal activity if such there was."

The three members of Rook's audience were spellbound.

"And?" Shane spoke up.

"And, to cut to the chase, as they say, there certainly was criminal activity. We have documentation of Dr. Bartalak's intent to sell his share of the startup company at an inflated price based on a pending big pharma deal and on his contention that the drug showed near miraculous results in the preliminary clinical studies. We have information that he has knowledge that casts doubt on both of those factors, knowledge that would negatively impact the value of the company. He explicitly denied having any such information and did not even hint at such a possibility in attempting the sale of his share of the company. That is a crime."

"Interesting," Katya said, "but what do you need from me? I had absolutely no involvement in or knowledge of Cy's business dealings."

"The information we have that Bartalak had knowledge that would negatively impact the value of the company is, unfortunately, hearsay, and therefore not admissible in court. It comes from a source that I am sworn not to identify but whom I believe is impeccable. And the information is that you personally gave Dr. Bartalak documents that raise questions about the value of the drug, the only asset of value that the startup company has. Is that correct?"

Katya was torn. She was surprised that Cy would get caught doing something criminal. Surely he was smarter than that. And this would be a scandal of major proportions that would reverberate throughout the academic community, well beyond the local university. If she got involved, there was a real possibility that her own stature in the larger community, her *value in the academic marketplace*, would suffer. But she had to live with herself. Honesty was, to her, the essential core of her profession. She must not betray that.

"As I said," Katya finally answered, "I know nothing of Cy's startup company. I have no idea what assets that company has and don't really care."

"Very well," Rook continued, "let me be more direct. Are you willing to testify that you personally gave documents to Dr. Bartalak, the contents of which raise questions about the efficacy and safety of the drug in question, and that you expressed to him concerns that Beth Bartalak, the statistician on the study and Professor Bartalak's wife, had falsified some of the clinical data. That is the evidence we need."

"If required to, I will testify to the truth. What you stated is the truth. However, it may not be without personal consequences, you know."

Rook replied, "I appreciate that. And very much appreciate your willingness to cooperate."

"You may also want to speak with the medical dean at the university," Katya added.

"Why is that?"

"I have filed a formal complaint of scientific misconduct against Beth Bartalak with the dean and have given him the same documentation that I gave Cy. I would be very surprised if the dean hasn't shared that with Cy. If so he could also provide relevant testimony, it seems to me."

"An excellent suggestion, Katya, thank you," Rook said. "I will do that. One other thing, can you provide the US attorney with copies of the documents that you gave to Bartalak and to the dean?"

"I'm not sure," Katya responded. "Those are confidential documents."

"I understand, but if subpoenaed, I presume that you would surrender them?"

"Yes."

"I very much appreciate this, Katya. The US attorney, his name is Dom Petrillo, will be in touch with you. He's an old friend of mine and I think you'll find him amiable enough to work with. But feel free to contact me if at any point you have questions."

"Now," Rook continued, "my curiosity gets the better of me. I must ask, why detective Seltzer is here if it is not a social call and why the pall of sobriety hanging over this little gathering? Something is obviously going on. Anything you can share with a curious observer?"

Shane said, "May I offer you a glass of sherry, Mitchell? And why don't the three of you have a seat and make yourselves comfortable?"

"A sherry would be nice," Rook replied. "Is this your Oxford sherry that I enjoyed earlier?"

"The same," Shane said.

He rolled himself over to the bar and went about the familiar ritual that always resurrected for a moment the pleasant sensations that he associated with the place from which the sherry, no doubt illicitly, found its way to its unlikely destination in Printers Alley.

Shane delivered the glass to Rook, returned to the bar, refreshed his glass and then took the bottle and made the rounds, refilling the others' glasses as well.

When he had replaced the bottle on the bar, he turned to face the group, now seated on the sofa, and raised his glass, "To the inevitable fate of the bad guys," he said. "May they always lose in the long run."

Each of them raised his glass.

Rook was heard to say somewhat timidly, "Here, here."

The toast stated a fundamental principle that had driven Shane Hadley's life. He smiled. It was good to feel once again the satisfaction of justice done.

Shane thought to himself, *and to the abiding inspiration of the adventures of Mr. Holmes*. He raised his glass again unobtrusively and took a long warm sip of Lincoln College's best, relishing the taste and the memory of it.

34

As predicted, the late afternoon search of the Jackson Boulevard home of Cyrus and Beth Bartalak yielded the Colt Hammer model handgun that ballistics later proved to be the weapon that fired the four bullets into Bonz Bagley's brain. The search produced two other items that Hardy Seltzer, who had led the search team, discussed with Shane Hadley and Katya Karpov.

The strange bottle of pills with the handwritten label, *Cy's Wonder Drug*, were identified by Katya as the laboratory formulation of the experimental drug that was the subject of the clinical study. Katya recalled Cy Bartalak's enthusiastic speculation that the drug might improve the function of the normal brain based on the animal studies. Katya guessed that Beth who, judging from the collection of other pills that the search discovered, would take almost any kind of supplement that she thought had any chance of improving her health, must have taken the drug based on Cy's excitement about it.

Later, when questioned during one of her increasingly rare lucid moments, Beth admitted to that. She had started taking the drug about the same time that the clinical studies were initiated. She stopped taking it when she saw the results of the six month follow up tests from subject number one.

The other item recovered in the search that attracted Seltzer's attention for some reason that he didn't understand was a slip of paper found in Beth Bartalak's desk with a date and time written on it in dark, deliberate block letters that were underlined and followed by exclamation points. Katya immediately recognized the date as that of the upcoming Sunday morning meeting of the *Brain Trust*. Neither she nor Shane would speculate any further about the possible significance of this item and Hardy didn't press them. It is likely that all three of them suspected that the note had a meaning that was too frightening to speak of and in view of Beth Bartalak's decreased ability to function, no longer a concern.

Beth Bartalak was charged with the first degree murder of Bonz Bagley. She was arrested and put under guard in the hospital immediately. The nature of her mental condition was never determined and Cy refused to permit a brain biopsy as recommended by the doctors caring for her. The case was turned over to the DA who announced that he would seek the death penalty. When her neurological condition continued to deteriorate, Beth was confined by court order to a chronic care facility.

Her husband hired Herbert Sandlin, a nationally prominent defense attorney who worked out of Nashville, to represent both himself and his wife. The attorney convinced them that Beth should plead that she was mentally incompetent to stand trial, which she did. She would spend the rest of her shortened life in a mental hospital. Her husband would be rarely seen there.

A series of articles appeared in the local newspaper beginning on the morning after the search of the Bartalak house. The articles detailed the series of events that led up to the solution of the Bagley murder case, praising the creativity and tenacity of the Metro police department, especially their lead investigator Hardy Seltzer. Detective Seltzer had persisted with his pursuit of the real killer in the face of rampant public criticism of him and his department. His investigation leading to the identification of the guilty party was an example of truly exceptional police work. The city was fortunate to have a department and people of this quality responsible for the security of its citizens.

The series of articles, under the byline of Harvey Green, a long time police reporter for the paper, frequently contained quotes from Hardy Seltzer and from the chief of metro police. The name of X Coniglio quickly disappeared from the news. The byline of the freelance reporter who had authored the earlier newspaper articles that were critical of the metro police department's handling of the case was never seen again in the local paper.

Shane Hadley's name appeared in only one of the newspaper articles. He had acquiesced to a single interview with Harvey Green, the substance of which was Shane's elaborate complements of the work of Hardy Seltzer on the case.

When asked directly whether he missed being a part of the force, Shane brandished his glass of sherry and replied, "There is satisfaction enough, my man, in seeing justice done, however that comes about."

Cyrus Bartalak was formally charged and released on a bail of a million dollars. His attorney, Herbert Sandlin, embarked on a series of legal maneuvers that would delay trial of the case at least for several years and maybe forever. The case made national and international news off and on for several months. The National Institutes of Health launched an in depth investigation of all of the research supported by their grants in which Bartalak was involved. The NIH team uncovered several instances of misuse of funds as well as strongly suggestive evidence of scientific dishonesty in much of Bartalak's work. The NIH withdrew support of all grants on which Cyrus Bartalak served as Principal Investigator resulting in a several million dollar loss to the institution. Further, he was banned from receiving any government research support at least until his legal troubles were resolved and perhaps longer.

The university investigation of the charge of

scientific misconduct against Beth Bartalak was never completed. The Global Pharmaceutical scientists who reviewed the information from the drug studies raised serious questions about the integrity of the data and Global terminated their interest in *Renaptix* and Cy Bartalak's drug. An FDA audit of the data raised similar questions and the FDA approval of the IND was withdrawn. The dean concluded that the charge that Beth Bartalak had falsified data was almost certainly true and that because of her severely deteriorating cerebral function, an investigation was both impossible and pointless. Bartalak steadfastly denied any knowledge of Beth's manipulation of the data and the dean did not pursue the question of whether Cy was a co-conspirator.

At the dean's urging, Cyrus Bartalak elected to take a year's sabbatical without compensation. Although he retained his faculty appointment, he was relieved of his role as department chair and was placed on probation pending resolution of his legal problems. Katya Karpov was named interim chair of the department of psychiatry, a position which she accepted on the condition that the university bear full financial responsibility for the lifetime medical care of all of the subjects who had been entered into the clinical trial of the drug, RX-01; the dean gladly accepted that condition.

A committee was appointed to conduct a national search for the pathology chair. The pathologist, Sydney Shelling, was named to chair the committee. It was widely speculated among the medical faculty that the committee was appointed only as a formality and that Dr. Karpov would be named the permanent occupant of the chair.

Renaptix, Inc. ceased to do business. Rory Holcomb and Will Hadley both lost the million dollars that they had invested. That especially disappointed Dr. Hadley because he had intended his investment in the company to be a gift to his son and daughter-in-law, a way for them to profit from Katya's work on the drug beyond the compensation the university paid to her. Will Hadley was unaware of his daughter-in-law's specific role in the drug study but believed what Cy Bartalak told his investors and assumed that Katya concurred or she would have objected.

Dr. Hadley failed to understand that Katya's objection was registered appropriately. She felt duty bound to protect the integrity of scientific research. But neither she nor the university felt responsible for protecting gullible investors. Had Katya known of her father-in-law's intent, she would have behaved no differently.

Texas Senator Warren Hedgepath insisted on speaking directly with the US attorney responsible for nailing *that crafty sonofabitch Cy Bartalak*. It was the first conversation that Dom Petrillo had ever had with a sitting US senator and probably the last. The senator was very pleased with the work of the justice department in this case and would see to it that the department, and specifically the attorneys involved, would be appropriately rewarded. Mitchell Rook received a citation recognizing his extraordinary commitment to integrity in business from the Attorney General of the United States. He stored the gilt framed plaque in a small basement room of his Belle Meade house where he kept the several other such citations that he had received.

"Shane," Katya said.

They sat on their Printers Alley balcony. The sun had disappeared to the west and the soft twilight seemed to smooth the sharp edges off the bustle of human activity in the alley below. Shane nursed a glass of sherry. Katya drank from a wine glass periodically refilled from the cylinder of Voss sparkling water that sat on the table between them. They were enjoying the time before the dinner that they had arranged at *Mere Bulle*.

"Yes, my love?" Shane responded.

"One thing, well maybe more than one, but especially one still puzzles me."

"And what is that?"

"Well," Katya said, "You solved the case. Why does Hardy Seltzer get all the credit?"

"Yes," Shane answered, "Well, it wasn't easy to accomplish that. Hardy refused to allow it at first. I insisted that the public perception of how the case was solved must not involve me. Hardy vehemently refused to accept that until his chief weighed in. The chief, to his credit, recognized that my insistence on being a silent partner in the process was wise. The department, especially Hardy, was in serious need of a major success if they were to regain some favor with the public. Solving this case was exactly what they needed. If it were known that the department had relied on help from a retired paraplegic detective, long since absent the force, rather than on their best and brightest, X Coniglio and his toadie freelance reporter would have had a field day."

"So," Katya said, "you are party to a deception."

"Deception, my dear," Shane responded, "can be a useful device if judiciously employed. Shall we go to dinner?"

When they arrived at *Mere Bulle*, Hardy Seltzer and his guest were already seated at the table overlooking the river. Shane had requested that specific table when he made the reservation. Hardy introduced Shane and Katya to his old friend, Marge

Bland. Shane was surprised that Hardy asked if he could bring a guest when Shane suggested the dinner. He had been completely unaware of Hardy's social life which, Shane strongly suspected, was not that interesting. Perhaps the tide was turning. To Shane's surprise, Hardy was drinking what looked for all the world like a glass of sherry. An apparently untouched glass of white wine sat before his guest.

When they were all seated and drinks were ordered, Hardy opened the conversation.

"Shane," Hardy said, "there is one point in the investigation that I confess completely baffles me."

"Baffled?" Shane mused. "Not a bad emotion generally. Can spark a creative impulse at times."

"Well, whatever," Hardy continued. "But it's the gun. When the Texas dealer told you that he had sold a gun similar to the one that wound up in Jody Dakota's hands to someone else? That seems to me completely irrelevant information. Why did you pursue it?"

"I believe, my man," Shane responded, "that I may have mentioned to you at some point the *principle of the other gun*. The explanation of the principle being that there is more to be learned from the gun you don't see, the other gun, than the one you see. And, I'm quite sure I said this to you before, *there is always another gun*."

"Yes, Shane," Hardy responded, "I know. I remember that. But in this case, there was absolutely no reason to think that the gun sold to a Texas lawyer had anything to do with the case we were investigating."

"Quite right, Hardy my man," Shane replied. "That is what made it so interesting. They were very rare guns. Coincidences of very rare events are to be studied carefully. I found the information absolutely irresistible. It simply had to be pursued."

"If you say so," Hardy answered, thinking how drastically his own approach to criminal investigation differed from Shane's.

They ordered dinner and spent the meal in idle chatter, getting to know Hardy's friend a bit and reinforcing the bonds that had developed over the course of the past few weeks.

Lingering over coffee and desert, Hardy asked Katya, "So what is the situation with Beth Bartalak?"

"Sad," Katya answered. "Her mental condition continues to deteriorate. I'm convinced that Cy's drug is the cause although he refused to allow a brain biopsy that might answer the question conclusively."

"The DA was going for the death penalty," Hardy said.

"That's what I read in the paper," Katya said. "But she was in no condition to stand trial for murder."

Shane interjected, "So Beth may be the only person whose life will ever be saved by Cy's drug."

"Maybe," Katya replied, "but I think the drug was also responsible for the act that threatened to cost her her life. I was impressed from the tests I saw that the drug affected the brain's frontal lobes. That's where we control our behaviors, parse out right and wrong. When I said that I couldn't believe that Beth was a killer, I believe that I was right. She would never have done what she did without the effect of the drug. It caused her to commit the crime that could have sentenced her to death and then protected her from that fate, at least for a while."

"Ah, ironies," Shane mused. "How uninteresting life would be without them."

About Ken Brigham

Ken Brigham is Emory University emeritus professor of medicine. His medical degree is from Vanderbilt. He completed his medical residency at Johns Hopkins and had additional training at the University of California San Francisco. He has edited three science books and has published over 400 original works in the scientific literature. Most recently, he was associate vice president for Health Affairs at Emory, a position from which he retired in 2012. Ken has coauthored two novels with Neil Shulman (Spotless and The Asolo Accords), published a short account of his personal experience with cancer (Hard Bargain) and, most recently, coauthored a non-fiction book (Predictive Health) with Mike Johns. He lives with his wife, Arlene Stecenko, in midtown Atlanta. www.kenbrigham.com

Keep up to date with Ken's work at: http://kellanpublishing.com/authors/
Feel free to leave a review at: http://kellanpublishing.3dcartstores.com/Death-in-Printers-Alley_p_36.html

CPSIA information can be obtained at www.ICGtesting.com
Printed in the USA
LVOW10s2121021015

456788LV00008B/27/P